ALISON LURIE

"A natural writer . . . . a very sure and unusual gift of characterization, plus delightful irony."

Louisville Times

"Her career will bear watching. LOVE AND FRIENDSHIP is vivid . . . intense . . . provocative."

Chicago Tribune

"One of the more gifted novelists around today."

Meyer Levin

LOVE AND FRIENDSHIP

ALISON LURIE

AVON
PUBLISHERS OF
DISCUS • CAMELOT • BARD

FOR JONATHAN

AVON BOOKS
A division of
The Hearst Corporation
959 Eighth Avenue
New York, New York 10019

Copyright © 1962 by Alison Bishop.
Published by arrangement with The Macmillan Company.
Library of Congress Catalog Card Number: 62-7996.

The quotation from "The Lover's Ghost" is
reprinted from A DREAM OF GOVERNORS, copyright
1957, by Louis Simpson, by permission of
Wesleyan University Press.

First Avon Printing, March, 1970

AVON TRADEMARK REG. U.S. PAT. OFF. AND
FOREIGN COUNTRIES, REGISTERED TRADEMARK—
MARCA REGISTRADA, HECHO EN CHICAGO, U.S.A.

Printed in the U.S.A.

"Alas! (exclaimed I) How am I to avoid those evils I shall never be exposed to?"
                    —*Love and Friendship*

PART ONE

CHAPTER

1

THE DAY ON WHICH EMILY STOCKWELL TURNER FELL OUT of love with her husband began much like other days. As usual, Emmy lay in bed twenty minutes later than she should have done, with her son Freddy playing cars over her legs, and when she finally got up it seemed as if things would never be sorted out. But somehow breakfast was made; Freddy was fed and dressed and sent off to nursery school in the car pool, and at length Emmy stood outside the house watching her husband leave for work on time.

"Looks like snow," said Holman Turner, an instructor in the Languages and Literature Division at Convers College, as he stood beside her on the frozen lawn in his overcoat. It was a chilly, dark morning early in November, and Emmy wore only an old cashmere sweater and slacks, but she was the kind that never feels the cold.

"Oh, good; do you think so? But it's only the first week in November. I'm afraid it's much too soon."

"It probably snows early here," Holman said, and climbed into his car and shut the door. Through the glass he could see Emmy look round at the clouds, smiling. What a magnificent creature she is, he thought, as he frequently did. She was a big girl, tall, tanned like a gypsy, and with a high color. Her heavy, bright brown hair had not yet been done up for the day; it hung down over one shoulder in a thick braid. She was twenty-seven, and still had, as on the day he married her, the look of a carefully bred and beautifully groomed animal, kept permanently at the peak of its condition for some high use which has not yet arrived and possibly never will arrive. Holman had seen it often on boys and girls of Emmy's class, though seldom to such a degree or accompanied by so much beauty.

Emmy continued to stand beside the car, waiting for her husband to roll the window down, so he rolled it down.

9

"Goodbye darling," she said, stooping to kiss him.

"So long, baby," Holman replied. He rolled the window up again and drove away down the drive.

Emmy stood on the lawn, smiling, and watched his car, a little gray Volkswagen, turn into the road and grow smaller as it went away from her along the highway, between low hills covered with scrub pines and birches. It disappeared around the corner, and Holman would not be back until five-thirty—for though he was a teacher he kept businessmen's hours—but Emmy did not go in. She liked this particular spot in the yard because from here she could see, to the north beyond the road and the trees, the top spires and towers of Convers College. In all directions the view was closed in a few miles away, for Convers, and Convers College, lay in a narrow valley. The cross-state highway passed fourteen miles to the south, behind a range of mountains; the nearest passenger railroad station was ten miles to the west, beyond hills and a river. No one came to Convers except to go to school. The local farmers took their onions and tobacco and corn over to Hampton, and bought their clothes and furniture there. They could not afford and did not want the button-down shirts and imported ski sweaters which were sold in the two local men's shops, or the hand-rubbed chairs displayed by the Convers antique dealers.

After the noise of the car had died away everything was under a heavy, oyster-colored sky. Emmy held out her arms. "Snow!" she said aloud, in the tone of voice she might have used to a waiter. She laughed to and at herself, and repeated: "Snow, please! I want to see what it looks like."

Although all her living male relatives (and many of her dead ones) had spent four winters of their youth here, Emmy had never seen Convers under the white icing with which it was usually photographed and painted. She had visited the town often, but her visits had been made either before the real life of the college started or after it was over. She had been there early in the fall when her brothers were driven up to school—standing waiting under high canopies of elm while sets of leather luggage were unloaded from the Cadillac in front of the Stockwell fraternity house. And she had been there at graduations in June when the grounds were strung with flags and lights and awnings, beneath which her father's face, in a red-

and-white cardboard hat marked with his class year, always formed the center of a group of cardboard hats.

Emmy thought it unfair, really, that she had seen so little of Convers. For Convers belonged to the Stockwells, the Stockwells felt, though they would have said (and did say at alumni dinners) that if anything the Stockwells belonged to Convers. Though they had never lived there, they thought of it as their spiritual home, which the expensive New Jersey suburb where they had resided for forty years was not. Not physically New Englanders, they had the tradition of being spiritually so. They believed that in their four years at Convers the sons of the family breathed in the air of a higher spiritual state, so deeply that it left a deposit in their lungs for the rest of lives which would, inevitably, be spent among more practical men in a warmer and more material world.

The Stockwells felt closer to Convers (and far more responsible for it) than their friends who were graduates of great catch-all colleges like Harvard and Yale could ever be to their alma maters. For most of the past fifty years there had been a Stockwell on the Board of Trustees and on the Alumni Fund-Raising Committee. Emmy's family was also represented at Convers in a more substantial way by a dining hall, four squash courts, and a large library fund for the purchase of books on geology and geography (the Stockwell money was primarily derived from the manufacture of mining machinery). Emmy had often regretted that girls could not attend Convers College. She saw both of her brothers go off, noisy children interested only in cars and boats and tennis; she saw them come back important men, still cheerful on the surface, but quieter, heavier, more serious. They or their friends said in graduation speeches that they had found themselves at Convers, but it seemed to her that they had found someone better than that.

It began to snow. "It's starting," Emmy said to herself, and smiling with pleasure she turned back toward the house. The flakes fell very finely; it would take a long while for them to whiten the ground.

In the kitchen the dishes still stood in the sink and various objects lay about on the floor: paper napkins, plastic parts of toys, a broken comb, and a crust of toast with jam on it. They were all relatively clean and had only been on the floor for an hour or so, but the sight of them

11

filled Emmy with irritation. Brought up in a house where someone always came around to pick up anything that fell, she could not get used to domestic disorder. She did not grow especially tired either of or from housework, but she could not do it casually and she saw by now that she would therefore never do it very well. She could wash out a whole room as thoroughly as if she were giving herself a bath, but she lacked the ability to tidy up without thinking about it as she went along.

Thinking about it, therefore, she picked up the comb, the napkins, the toast, and the toys. Most of them belonged to, and had been thrown down by, her four-year-old child, Frederick Stockwell Turner, who was now at nursery school. He had only been going for a month, and Emmy still found the house strangely vacant without him; impersonal, like a hotel suite. She was so used to Freddy's company that after the housework was finished she hardly knew what to do with herself. The pleasure of going on errands alone had quickly worn off; and besides, Freddy was always furious when he discovered—and somehow he usually did discover—that his mother had been to the store without him. At home, this would have been the useful kind of morning on which one has one's hair washed and set, visits a museum, helps with publicity for a charity party, or investigates the cost of having some prints framed so as to match some other prints. The Stockwell children were never encouraged to lie slack around the house, whatever their friends did. But Convers was too far out in the country for any of these activities; it was, for example, two hours' drive to the nearest place where Emmy would have thought it possible to have her hair washed.

She went into the downstairs bathroom. Standing before the mirror, but not really looking into it, she did up her braid again and coiled it into a figure eight with hairpins. Then she turned on the water in the kitchen sink and began to do the dishes. But she stopped almost at once, for she had remembered that this was the day on which the new cleaning woman was coming.

Turning to the stove, Emmy poured herself a cup of cold coffee (she preferred it so, partly out of laziness). She broke open a new box of coconut cookies which she had bought the day before when Freddy was not looking and hidden behind the cans of soup on the top shelf. She

12

took yesterday's *New York Times* and went to sit by the window in the front room where she could see the cleaning woman coming.

Emmy sighed with pleasure as she sipped her coffee, and even more as she ate the cookies. She loved to eat, and now that she was relatively thin she could do it with a clear conscience. She knew she would never be fat again; Holman, unfortunately, was not convinced of it. Whenever he saw her bring in a dish of mashed potatoes with butter on top, or help herself to a second piece of pie, a nervous warning look came on his face. It was as if he saw the ghost of the fat girl he had first met.

She shook out the paper. When it came she usually turned first to the society page, where she always found something to amuse, instruct, or shock; and then to the advertisements of the large stores and theaters, although it made her cross now to read descriptions of plays and concerts she was not going to and dresses she could not try on. But she had done all this the day before. Now she folded the paper back to page 1, for Holman liked her to be well informed, and he was right. RUSSIAN ENVOY PROTESTS NOTE; FARM PRICES INFLATED, SAYS EXPERT.

Ten minutes passed. Then Emmy, looking up, saw the mail truck come over the hill through the fine haze of falling snow and begin its slow progress down from box to box. At last it stopped at the Turners', and a woman of indeterminate age and size got out. She started up Emmy's drive in a pair of men's black galoshes with flapping tops which left wet prints in the snow. She was also wearing a pink plaid coat and a flowered scarf tied under her chin, showing that she was a member of the nonacademic classes of Convers, and probably the Turners' new cleaning woman. Emmy met her at the door.

"How do you do?" she said. "Mrs. Rabbage?"

"Mrs. Rabbage," replied the visitor, scraping her galoshes on the scraper. "I come to do for you."

"Good morning! Come right in, please."

Mrs. Rabbage came in. She was now seen to be a strong-looking bony woman between thirty and forty with a long face and reddish hair done up in metal curlers under her scarf. "Bad morning if you're asking me," said Mrs. Rabbage. "I couldn't hardly bring myself to put my feet out of my bed this morning, the house was that cold," she continued as she followed Emmy down the hall to the kitchen. "Here's your mail." She pulled it out of her coat pocket, bent and damp. "My cousin that's staying with me while her husband is in the hospital over to Hamp left the window open in her room all night, is why. But I told myself Mrs. R. you've got to get out of bed you don't want to let Mrs. Lumkin down that told the party you would be there on time. Dishes first, huh? Where do you keep your scouring powder? ... Oke. I don't know what got into her to leave the window open all night to the bad air I mean my cousin, not that she ever had much sense but if I told her once I told her a million times the effect a draft always has on me I always feel it here in my back terrible and where I had my last operation it kinda aches all around here with a kinda dull ache." Mrs. Rabbage pointed to the spot with the dishrag; Emmy made a sympathetic noise. "Well I said to myself Mrs. Lumkin told the party, I mean you, that she could count on you, I mean me. And I don't like to let anyone down if my health doesn't prevent. I always try to keep my word as you'll find and particularly with a lady like Mrs. Lumkin I don't like to let her down. You want me to dry these or just let them drain?"

Emmy answered and left the kitchen rapidly. She put the bills from stores in New York and New Jersey which had come in the mail on the mantel to dry out, and sat down again with her coffee and the *Times*. Section 2. LIBRARY SHOWS RARE MAPS. DUCK FREED FROM MANHOLE.

"Where do you keep your cleaning rags?" asked Mrs. Rabbage from the door. Emmy followed her back into the kitchen to look. "Well I guess I can make out with that for today if I have to. Move to a new place you throw away a lot of things and afterwards you wish you hadn't. My sister moved up to North Greensbury last year threw away all the medicines the doctor gave her husband for his piles and the next thing you know the next year her oldest boy caught them the one that just got out of the Service. Well he was dead, that's why she threw them out. Her husband I mean." Mrs. Rabbage stooped down to wipe under the sink, which gave Emmy an opportunity to leave.

She returned to the front room, but this time instead of sitting down she stood looking out of the window. Mrs. Rabbage was the third cleaning woman she had tried since they had moved to Convers; she had been recommended

14

to Emmy by the wife of a Dean. In the Stockwell family it was considered a black mark against you if you could not keep servants. Probably you were terribly mean about money or there was something weird about your private family life. But Emmy knew that she was not at fault. It was just that her first woman had turned out to be absolutely dirty and incompetent, and the second one had gone and had a baby after two weeks, although she had promised not to have it for three months. Emmy knew that it was not her fault, but all the same she was afraid that somehow it might be. Her mother's last letter had said: "I trust you've found a good woman to clean for you by now; do let me hear about this." And if she did not let her mother hear, Emmy knew that these same words would appear in the next letter, and the next.

She wanted another cup of coffee, and so she had to go back into the kitchen, where Mrs. Rabbage had finished the dishes in a surprisingly short time and was scrubbing the floor vigorously around the stove that heated the Turners' hot water. "You oughta get a board or some kind of thing put up here in front of this stove door," she began at once. "These kinda old iron stoves aren't safe when you got children around you can wallop them a million times and they still got no sense my youngest that's working up to Shem's now when he was three he got a burn on his arm off one of these kinda stoves we had then that he had to stay in the hospital over to Hamp five days all burnt it was, kinda charred looking." She had worked round now and was scrubbing in front of the kitchen door so that Emmy could not leave without stepping over her back, which she could not quite bring herself to do.

"Excuse me," she said.

"You can still see the place on his arm," Mrs. Rabbage went on, not moving, "if you look for it if you happen to stop into Shem's of course I had walloped him a million times already for it but he didn't pay me no mind. And the crying and carrying on. You only got the one child?"

Emmy said yes.

"You gotta watch out for these things. Even if he didn't get hurt he coulda started a fire playing around with that door there." Mrs. Rabbage poked at the latch of the stove door with her scrubbing brush. "Well Mrs. Bliss got it on good and tight for you anyhow," she admitted. (Mrs. Bliss was the landlady.) "Not like the one they got down to

15

that college house where the three kids are living I said to their mother last week when I went in to do for her she better get ahold of Mr. Lumkin up at the college and get it fixed or she's going to be sorry one of these days one of her kids is going to put his hand in just for fun and get it grilled like a skewer of barbecue but she never paid me no mind they're all of them batty anyhow."

"Really! Dean Lumkin is a friend of my father's," Emmy said rapidly, with an unfriendly little laugh.

"I didn't say anything about Lumkin," Mrs. Rabbage retorted. "I'm talking about the tenants he's got in that house off the Greensbury Road, I got nothing against Lumkin." She fell silent, or rather speechless, and noisily one, two, three, moved her brush, her bucket, and herself out of Emmy's way.

"You needn't bother to wash the pantry floor, Mrs. Rabbage," Emmy offered in a conciliatory tone as she left. "Just sweep it."

"Might as well scrub," Mrs. Rabbage replied. "It's not as bad as the kitchen but it looks like it could use it." She sloshed water out.

Feeling rebuked, Emmy removed herself. This time she went upstairs and began to straighten out Freddy's closet. All I have to do to keep Mrs. Rabbage quiet is to insult her now and then, Emmy thought to herself, and she gave the kind of cheerful laugh that might be supposed to go with this kind of cheer, but she did not care for it. She was chagrined to think that she had spoken rudely to a servant.

From below, as she worked, Emmy could already hear the vacuum beginning in the dining room. Soon it moved into the front room; Mrs. Rabbage seemed to work very fast. Emmy went to Freddy's window and looked out past the curtains printed brightly with planets and spaceships which Freddy had chosen himself. He was a very modern little boy. He knew all about Mars and Venus and guided missiles, although he had never heard of Australia. She looked out at fields, farmhouses, and barns, decayed cornstalks and old farm machinery quietly rusting away. The Turners were the farthest faculty people out in this direction. Almost everyone else lived in town, in houses belonging to the college which were classified according to rank and rented out to the faculty at a standard fee. Assistant professors, for example, lived in assistant professor rank

16

houses, and when they were promoted to associate professor they moved. First-year instructors like Holman Turner had to live in the leftover army barracks called The Huts down by the heating plant, unless they could afford to buy or rent a private house somewhere near-by, which was not cheap, and could find one, which was not easy. Already Emmy had often wished that she lived in town like everyone else, but she had never wished that she lived in The Huts.

Emmy leaned her elbows on the sill and her face against the windowpane, so that she could almost feel the flakes brushing against her cheek as they landed and melted on the glass. Something ought to happen now, she thought. Brought up in a large household where everything was done in groups, in bright heated rooms or brilliant sunlight, the very silence and chill of Convers seemed promising to her. It suggested revelations in deserts and forests, Thoreau and Descartes. She fell into a vague reverie of shapes and voices, and did not hear the noise of the vacuum cleaner sucking its way up the stair carpeting toward her until it reached its mouth into the room, followed by Mrs. Rabbage.

"Sallie Hutchins was working over to your place for a while wasn't she?" Mrs. Rabbage began again, shouting over the vacuum. "Just afore she had her last baby."

"Yes," said Emmy.

"Had an awful time with this one too she certainly had. Well she brought it on herself if you ask me the doctor told her. . . ."

At twelve-thirty Freddy came home from nursery school. Mrs. Rabbage went on talking. At one-thirty Emmy shut herself into the bathroom and took a long bath, a thing she had not done at this hour for many years. Afterward she sat down at the desk and tried to write some letters. Mrs. Rabbage came in and continued the conversation. At four-thirty that afternoon, just as the sun was setting, Mrs. Rabbage left. At five-thirty Holman came home. The snow had stopped, and lay luminous over everything in the dark.

It was the Turners' habit to make a daily ceremony of the cocktail hour. Holman went upstairs and changed from the good suit that he had been wearing all day into

17

an old sweater and slacks. Emmy had already changed from the old sweater and slacks that she had been wearing all day into a dress. It was a family tradition with her to do this, and Holman had stopped remarking on it a long time back. It was all right with him if she wanted to dress for dinner; he didn't have to do the laundry. He even rather liked it. At the same time, it was a family tradition with him not to dress for dinner. His Uncle Ben always came to the table in his shirt sleeves, and when it was hot, the way it gets hot in Chicago in the summer, he came to the table in his undershirt. Holman's mother would not have stood for this, but Holman's Aunt Peggy did not seem to care one way or the other. Anyway Aunt Peggy and Uncle Ben were both dead now. They had died before Holman's wedding so that Emmy and her family had never had to meet them, which was just as well.

Holman made himself a drink in the kitchen, and a weaker one for Emmy. The television was turned on for Freddy, and they left him to it and went into the front room to tell each other the events of the day.

"Julian Fenn asked us to dinner," Holman began.

"Oh? When?"

"Saturday. I said I thought we could come but I would check with you and let him know."

"Let's go. I'd like to see what their house is like. I wonder if it's as weird as they are? Tell him we can come if we can find a sitter. What time?"

"Eight." Holman drank, reflecting that this invitation continued the series of dinner invitations from members of the English Department which he was beginning to suspect was a rule here. Was it then a rule to return them, and if so, when? He decided to ask about this before he mentioned it to Emmy, for she had rather too generous and elaborate ideas about entertainment for an instructor's wife.

"That's fine; I can put Freddy down before we leave. Eight is absolutely perfect!" said Emmy in what was not so much a finishing-school accent as a finishing-school voice. Holman was still taken aback by this voice when he heard it at certain times. He admired the natural, unself-conscious way in which Emmy could crush bores or boors at a party just by pronouncing the words "Oh, no, thanks," in a certain manner. But sometimes, say some time when she was in the bathroom and would call to him to ask if he would mind simply dreadfully fetching her a new roll of paper, it came to him to say: "All right, honey, you don't have to keep it up with me." He would never say it, because he knew by now that she was not keeping it up—it stayed up by itself.

When they were first married, Holman had taught Emmy to delete some words from her vocabulary, so that now she did not swear "Jiminy Crackers!" or exclaim after they had made love: "Oh, how utterly scrumptious!" But though he could edit the words, he could do nothing about the tone.

"The new cleaning woman came this morning," said Emmy.

"I thought the house looked different. How was she?"

"Oh, as a cleaning woman, terribly good I think. But darling, if she's going to come again—and I suppose I must have her, she got through absolutely everything— I've simply got to get out of the house somehow, because she talks *all* the time. And it's all the four forbidden topics. Nothing *but* domestics, descendants, disease, and death."

"What other topics are there?" said Holman who felt depressed from an academic meeting which had lasted two hours that afternoon, full of tensions and references he had not understood.

"Oh, but all about her relatives who have awful accidents and illnesses; hives, and get caught in fertilizer-spreaders and dreadful childbirths and piles and rheumatism. The people she knows seem to have the most old-fashioned diseases. What's piles?" Holman told her. "And a growth. Her sister-in-law had a growth. I suppose that means cancer." Emmy grew depressed at the sound of this word, and her face fell. Holman, on the other hand, was beginning to cheer up. The whisky was working inside him, and he looked at his wife, glowingly pretty in her red dress, and felt even better.

"Well, there would be other topics, the opposite ones," he said. It was his habit to argue both sides of a case. "Ancestors and health and birth. And instead of servants, well, noblemen. 'Good day, my lord, you are looking well. Let me congratulate you on the anniversary of your mother's birth.' "

"And there's always the weather."

"That was covered by the 'good day.' Oh, all right.

19

'Charming snow we're having, my lord.' That's elegant enough. Much better than, what. 'What a pity, the charwoman's nephew had died of the cramp.' "

Emmy began to laugh, and her laugh had no society accent; it was the kind of delighted, unaffected sound that an actress might have traded a year of her life for. "Did you have a good day today?" she finally said.

"All right," lied Holman. All through graduate school he had talked freely to Emmy about his work which he was not at all interested in, though she did what she could to show interest because she was interested in Holman. "Oh, marvelous," she would say with real feeling, and feel it too, when he described the thesis on Samuel Johnson's poetry he was writing, or when he recovered a notebook that had been lost in the stacks of the Princeton library. Now that she was interested in his work for its own sake, he would not talk about it. He sat tipping his glass back and forth, sliding the ice cubes about. He was thinking of another drink, but it was against his principles to have more than one drink before dinner.

"That's good," Emmy finally said. She knew, or suspected, that he was lying. She knew it without thinking, as she knew most things. But because of her education she kept correcting herself into distrust of this knowledge which was not founded on facts or propositions. During the first weeks of school, Holman had come home to announce that it was not all right, that he couldn't figure out who was running what and it was getting worse and worse. Now suddenly he had become silent, or talked to her about abstract theories of education. He did not report any more on the weekly staff meetings for the course called Humanities C, and the strange things that happened there, although this was what Emmy wanted to learn most of all.

The Humanities C course at Convers was famous. Academicians as far away in every sense as Los Angeles had heard of it, and alumni as unacademic as the Stockwells remembered it with respect. Hum C was often called the theoretical (or the actual) center of education at Convers. All incoming freshmen were compelled to take it; more than that, all incoming instructors in the Languages and Literature Division were compelled to teach it. In many ways their individual futures at Convers depended on how well they did so, how quickly they caught on.

The course was run, as it had been for twenty years, by its inventor, Professor Oswald McBane.

According to some articles which had once appeared, Hum C was really a course in semantics based on positivist and operationalist principles; it should be said at once, however, that the use of words like "positivist" and "principles" was absolutely taboo. No textbooks were used; instead the students were sent out with pencil and paper to draw a picture of the view from College Hall, or with a tape measure to measure the length of their feet and their friends' feet. Then they would come back and write papers describing what they had done. After this, they would be asked to write more papers defining what they meant by the important words they had used in their papers, words like "observation," and "average," and "really there."

Hum C was conducted by a kind of mean Socratic method; that is, the teachers would ask difficult questions and when a student gave the wrong answers the teacher would just mark a black mark on his paper and write more questions on it. "The meaning of this word (or line) depends on the other words (or lines) which surround it at the time I use it," was the basic answer to the current set of questions, but the students had to find this out for themselves, and nobody was allowed to tell them. For one thing, this statement or any similar one was too full of abstract words to be written on the blackboard. For another, it was believed that the students had to learn the truth themselves in terms of their own experience.

Though many new instructors flopped and gasped for months, Holman was intellectually sophisticated enough to have grasped by now this much of Hum C. He was well disposed to the theory of the course, and he enjoyed the practice of it. He had spent twenty of his twenty-eight years of life answering questions in schools, and he did not mind asking them for a change. But what really concerned him was to discover the inner power politics of both Hum C and the Languages and Literature Division, and in this area he felt he had accomplished nothing. He could not even make the ordinary starting assumptions based on the ranks of various professors and the size of various departments, the humanities program seemed to cut across subjects and ranks so. The individual departments apparently did not have much importance—or did they?

The other essential task at the moment was to finish his thesis, for if he did not get a Ph.D. degree very soon he would not be requested to stay at Convers and whatever discoveries he had made there would be quite useless.

"Did you bring me the new assignment?" Emmy asked.

"Yes." Holman reached for his brief case, took out the following, and handed it over.

Here is a photograph, an airview of Convers College.

a) Let us assume you are now somewhere in the middle of the area contained in the photograph and you recognize this as a photograph of the spot you are now on. What do you do to recognize this?

b) Define, in the context of a) "the spot you are now on."

c) What difference do you see between this spot and the one in the map in Assignment No. 10?

"I don't understand it," Emmy said after two minutes. "Is there some trick? This airplane photograph really is of Convers; well, I know it is, because, look, there is the spire of Baird Hall, with those funny Gothic windows. It couldn't be any place else. And the athletic field. Is that what I'm supposed to say?"

"Go on," said Holman, drinking. Since the beginning of the year Emmy had been pretending that she was taking Hum C along with her husband's classes.

"And so that white spot there must be the roof of Gibson house where your office is," she went on, but Holman stopped listening. He had spent two hours already that day discussing the assignment in class, and he was tired of it. He wished as he had wished before that Emmy would go away and write out the assignment if she had to answer it, and he thought as he had thought before that if he suggested this to her again she would think it unfriendly of him.

". . . the difference is, in the photograph you can tell much more about what it really looks like, and then you can see the trees and bushes too. The map has only two dimensions and the photograph has three, I suppose I should say."

"Both have two dimensions," Holman said.

"What?"

"How many dimensions has that photograph?"

Emmy looked again. "Three."

"No." Holman pulled the sheet of paper out of her hand and shook it back and forth so that it rattled. "Two."

"Well, but. Oh, I see. If you want to put it that way. Is that what I'm supposed to say? That the photograph is a kind of map?"

"What do you mean by a 'kind of map'?"

Emmy looked at her husband crossly. "I mean a sort of diagram of lines which shows the size and relationship in space of objects," she said, trying to recall the material of previous conversations. She did not want to believe or to remember, what she had once been told, that questions and answers such as these were the central material of Hum C. She did not want to believe it because it would have been too disappointing if there were no more of a mystery than this stupid word game at the heart of the mystery Convers. She felt that there must be some more important secret, if only from the gnomic behavior of her husband and the other Hum C instructors.

Silence. Holman had taken up the newspaper and was turning over the pages. The sport he loved best, football, was now in season. Emmy held the map of Convers and the aerial photograph, one in each hand, and studied them.

"Is there a trick?" she asked. "Is there some building or something in this picture that doesn't show on the map, or the other way around?"

"No," Holman said firmly. He was tired of the whole thing. It was pretty clear by now that his wife had little aptitude for abstract ideas. She was well educated: she knew a lot about art and a fair amount of literature and history. It was not necessary for her to learn semantics; it would also not be easy for her to do so, and once she had done so she would not be interested and so, although she had an excellent memory for things like her relatives' birthdays and the minor painters of the Renaissance, she would forget it very soon. He thought that it was ridiculous for this beautiful woman to want to pretend that she was a Convers freshman. Suppose he were to affect to be a freshman at Bryn Mawr.

"What happened in meeting today?" Emmy asked.

"Nothing much," her husband answered from among the newspaper. Emmy looked at him.

"You never tell me what you do at school any more," she said.

"You make me sound like a third-grader. 'I learned simple division, Mummy, and drew a picture of an Eskimo going into his igloo—' "

Emmy did not reply.

" '—and got sent to the principal's office for hitting another little boy.' "

Emmy did not reply. She said to herself that Holman did not realize or would not realize how serious she was about Convers. It struck her calmly, generally, for the first time, that how Emmy felt simply did not affect how Holman felt. He was on his own side, not on hers. She had thought this a few times before, but only fleetingly, in the midst of some lively but unimportant argument.

"Shall I say: 'What did you do at college today?' "

"I'm not in college any more. Thank God."

"Well, really, what shall I say? Shall I say: 'What did you do at the office?' "

Holman would in fact have preferred this version of the question, but he was honest enough to realize that he would have answered it in the same evasive way. He said: "No. Forget it." And breaking his rule: "Can I make you another drink?" He got up.

"No, thank you." As she spoke, Emmy looked at her husband again, and suddenly he looked unattractive to her, a heavy young man with a red face and blurred features, standing in the frame of the door, blocking her way out. Actually, most people found Holman good-looking, in an agreeably unobtrusive way. Even Emmy's family had had to admit that there was nothing in his appearance to suggest the weakness and over-refinement of the academic stereotype. Neither fair nor dark, he had broad shoulders and a compact, athletic build. His face was boyish in design but serious in expression; he could have been a junior executive in a big company which manufactured something of real industrial importance, such as mining machinery. And as a matter of fact, after meeting him, Emmy's mother—who had opposed the engagement more strongly than anyone—tried to persuade Emmy's father to go to Holman and offer him a job. "If he wants something from me let him come to me," replied

Frederick Stockwell, uttering one of the principles which had guided his life. Holman declined to do this, and so nothing ever came of it, although Mrs. Stockwell still mentioned to her daughter at regular intervals what an opportunity had been lost.

"I suppose you'd rather I didn't ask you any questions at all about Convers," Emmy said. "I suppose you'd rather I simply stayed home all day and did the housework."

"God damn, Emmy," Holman said, holding the *Times* aside. "Don't take on so! What's the trouble? I thought you said you had a cleaning woman in today. What's the matter, did something happen?"

"No, nothing happened!" Emmy exclaimed; she felt herself quivering with a rage which she could not express because she could see no reasonable object for it.

Holman laid the paper down and considered. "Are you having your period?" he asked.

"No, I am not." Emmy managed to control her voice this time, but her rage continued, increased by irritation at Holman for forgetting that she wasn't due for at least two weeks—thus showing his typical lack of interest in such matters. "I'm perfectly well."

"Well, all right then." He picked up the newspaper again.

Emmy clenched her fists on the cushion of her chair, and opened her mouth to speak but at this moment Freddy's television program ended and he came bounding in demanding his regular routine of noisy play with Daddy and Mummy. Emmy performed her part with outward energy and good humor but inwardly she remained furious and it was a relief to her when Freddy's collapse from laughter into hysteria showed that it was time for his bath. She did not stop to calm him into a state in which he could walk upstairs by himself, but carried him off kicking and shouting, all forty pounds.

Once in the tub among his boats and submarines, Freddy recovered and began to direct a naval battle. Emmy's anger had partly subsided too, and when she had finished washing him she sat back on the bath mat to consider. She tried out the statement: "Really, it is stupid of me to be so childish." This had no effect. So she called upon her love for Holman: it did not come. This had never happened before. What was the matter with her?

Freddy sank a canoe full of soap, sloshing water onto

his mother and the floor. "No, no, Freddy darling!" she said, and as a test she called upon her love for her child, a thing she had to do much more often. It came bubbling up as thick as ever—dear Freddy, my darling, my puppy, my big boy!—although her dress was quite soaked.

During the rest of the evening Emmy continued to brood, over supper and then over the novel she was supposed to be reading, in a manner most unlike her. Holman did not appear to notice either this or the frequent questioning stares she favored him with. Each time she looked, it was worse: her husband appeared more and more like a stranger, a stranger she did not especially like.

The day ended like other days. The doors were locked, the thermostat turned down, the alarm set, and the Turners got into bed, but Emmy knew that something unusual and terrible had happened. She was glad that Holman did not offer to make love, and this was unusual and awful in itself, since love was an event which to Emmy's mind took place too seldom, especially when her husband was working.

The lights were extinguished, and Holman was soon asleep, but Emmy lay awake. She felt almost calm now; her anger had gone, but so had all other feeling. She lay on her back, the covers drawn up under her arms, in a white cotton nightgown threaded with pink ribbon from Best's, the kind she had worn since she was a little girl. As her eyes grew adjusted to the dark, she could make out the window to her left, snow heaped against the panes. In the daytime and on moonlit nights some of the buildings of Convers College were visible from where she lay, and Emmy always left the blind partway up so that she could see this landscape when she woke. But now not a light or shape showed between their house and the mountains. The trees and roofs and towers had all sunk down into the dark, leaving no trace behind.

*   *   *

A letter from Allen Ingram to Francis Noyes

November 7
... I'm afraid I can't keep up my original enthusiasm for this place, now that its handsome autumn has withered

into a hideous old age, and my house turns out to have little or no insulation. The pleasure of being introduced to everyone as "the Novelist who is teaching here this year" is wearing more than thin, especially since I still seem to hear them all whispering behind their hands: "Remember what I told you about Him." And I know I am disappointing everyone by not speaking in an affected voice and wearing purple silk socks and a green carnation.

"Delusions of reference, again," I can hear you saying, but this time you are wrong. You can have no idea of how morally primitive it is here. For example, the students have to attend compulsory morning chapel twice a week. Not for religious reasons, for moral ones, it has been explained to me. They really believe that it is good for body and soul to get up at dawn and run half a mile in the rain or snow or what have you to sit in a cold auditorium and be shouted at for twenty minutes before breakfast. As good as a cold shower. On Monday and Wednesday mornings there is "Non-Religious Chapel" (wonderful oxymoron for your collection) so that the eighteen Jews, seven agnostics, and three Buddhists here can obey the rules without insult to their Beliefs. I didn't make up these figures, I got them from a pamphlet bursting with this kind of data which is sent round to all the faculty. God knows (or would He?) what happens at Non-Religious Chapel. I haven't the strength to get up that early.

The lecture course is going well enough. I have given up trying to be impossibly brilliant every time and merely chatter along about the novel they are supposed to be reading. When I want to wake them up I give out one of your or David's aphorisms. But the short-story writing course is worse and worse and worse than you predicted. I was so delighted at first to find two or three reasonably intelligent ones that I forgot what the rest were like. That hour after hour and week after week I would have to sit and talk to thirteen hopeless idiots who have already proved over and over again that they will never be able to construct a sentence let alone a story. It is like being condemned to go to the worst party you ever attended three times a week for months, and no chance to get off in a corner with the few possible people there. . . .

I don't really advise you to come up. The scenery is not worth the trip, whatever the guidebooks say, and if we appear in public together it will simply provide the local harpies with a real-life demonstration of the love that dare not speak its name. And the climate is *worse than Edinburgh*.

CHAPTER

2

"WHAT SHALL I WEAR TO THE FENNS'?" ASKED EMMY ON Saturday evening. She stood at the head of the stairs, wearing at the moment only a white slip; Freddy, in pajamas printed with cowboys, clung to one of her bare legs. Hearing these words he began to wail over and over:

"Mummy, don't go to a party! I don't want you to go out to a party. Don't get dressed up, Mummy. Mummy, don't go out now!"

"Don't get dressed up, Mummy-Mummy," Holman said from the hall below, "just go as you are."

"Go to hell," Emmy said cheerfully. Since her feelings about her husband had changed, she was most at ease with him when she could insult him in jest during some imitation domestic spat. The joke showed that she did not really mean the insult. Or vice versa. An uneasy equilibrium, but one that she now even sought to provoke. "Did you ask Julian Fenn how formal it was going to be?"

"No." Holman went on putting on his coat. His air was that of the man in cartoons whose wife is never ready on time. Emmy found this irritating, since she often was.

"But you said you would when you saw him at the meeting Tuesday; oh, really, you are simply impossible!" She laughed to take the edge off this. Freddy went on whining.

"He wasn't at the meeting."

"He wasn't? Freddy, be quiet. Why not?"

Missing the weekly Hum C meeting was a sin forgiven only grudgingly even in the case of illness. Instructors often earned merit by attending when they should have been home in bed with severe colds.

"His excuse was that he went on a bird-watching expedition and forgot the time," Holman said.

"Well, maybe he did." Emmy, unlike her husband, had been brought up to believe that this was a possible avocation of adult males. "That isn't so dreadful. Why shouldn't he go looking at birds if he feels like it?"

"Because he was supposed to be at the meeting, that's why."

"I don't see it." Emmy realized she was starting to pick a fight with Holman about nothing again, but she couldn't stop herself. "Was it really so dreadfully important, your meeting?"

"No. But it was important to go to it. It's the principle of the thing. Besides, McBane keeps a list."

"He'll get in trouble, you mean," Emmy said.

"He already is in trouble."

"Did they say anything when he didn't turn up?"

"Yes. McBane said: 'I see we are going to have to discuss this week's assignment without the help of Mr. Fenn's original criticisms' . . . I'm going to get the sitter now."

"All right."

Left to herself, Emmy dressed rapidly for the coming occasion in dark, formal, expensive clothes such as those her mother always wore. Clothes like these gave her no pleasure—she liked bright colors, orange and pink and lemon, bunches of flowers—but they were safe.

It was cold when they set out for the dinner party. The snow that had fallen earlier was still on the ground, though by now it had been blown away here and piled into heaps there by the strong wind. But their car had an excellent heater. It was a Ford station wagon, hardly six months old. The reason Holman and Emmy had two cars was that they were rich, comparatively, or rather they had recently become so; since Holman had been teaching at Convers they had had two incomes. While they were in Princeton Holman, like many graduate students, had lived on his wife's income, with the difference that his wife did not have to work for it. Then he had been only grateful; he liked coming home to a clean apartment and a good dinner. All the same, he had looked forward to making more than Emmy had, even the two hundred dollars more that his starting salary at Convers represented. But between the time when he accepted the position and the time school began, her income had risen almost four hundred dollars. Such was the business acumen of Mr. Stockwell that this was always its general tendency. Holman had never regretted it before; but he was beginning

30

to suspect, with an irritated fatality, that unless there were a severe depression his income would probably never catch up with Emmy's. However hard he worked, she would receive more money for doing nothing.

"What time is it?" Emmy asked as they turned into the street where the Fenns lived.

"Quarter past."

"We're late." Emmy was not naturally punctual, but she knew the rules; five or ten minutes past the arranged hour would have been right, but more was too much. She jumped out of the car as soon as it stopped and started up the unshoveled path. Holman followed her.

They stood on the porch and rang the bell, but nobody came.

"Do you suppose it's out of order?" Emmy said.

"Who knows?" Holman looked around him. The Fenns' front porch was very large, but it was in bad repair. The floor was warped, the paint scaling, and the railings broken in several places. Nothing could be seen through the windows, which were covered with cracked yellow shades. "We could knock."

He knocked, and so did Emmy, but without result. Instead, from the inside there was the noise of something heavy falling and crashing, and a man's voice shouted: "God damn it to bloody hell!"

Holman and Emmy looked at each other to determine that each had heard this. At this moment the door opened. A thin, peculiar-looking little boy about six years old, in a dirty bathrobe, stood there.

"How do you do?" he said.

"We've come to dinner," said Emmy. "Are your father and mother in?"

"Yes. Come in, please." He led them into a large empty hall, lit by one dim bulb in a dusty chandelier. Rooms opened off it, but nobody was visible in any of them. Somewhere above another child could be heard crying. "It would have been more polite if one of you had said how do you do back," the boy told them.

"Well, I can make up for that," Holman said. "How do you do?"

"Very well, thank you. Who are you? I'm Charles Stephen Zorro Fenn."

"Very pleased to meet you," Holman said. "I am Holman Turner and this is my wife Emily."

"How do you do?"

"How do you do?"

"How do you do?"

"Charles!" a woman's voice called from above. "Come here at once! You let Hecate in again, and now she's made a mess on Katie's bed! Charles, did you hear me?"

"Yes, Mommy. Mommy, Mr. Turner is here with his wife Emily."

There were confused noises. The crying continued. Then steps on the stairs, and Miranda Fenn ran down into the hall. She was wearing a long green velvet dress hung with ropes of jet, but no shoes or stockings. Under one arm and by the scruff of its neck she carried a large black and white cat which was squirming and scratching. "Oh, excuse me," Miranda said hurrying past the Turners to the front door. She opened it and threw the cat out. "I'm terribly sorry," she said, "our cat has been sick lately. Julian!" she screamed in quite a different voice. "Everything seems to be a little disorganized tonight," she went on. "But please come in."

Since the Turners were already in, they continued to stand in the hall, gazing at Miranda Fenn with embarrassed smiles. They saw a thin, pale woman about thirty, with pale red hair and pointed features. She had large, pretty gray eyes decorated with black mascara; imitation eyebrows had been drawn above them with black pencil. She had either not had time to put any lipstick on her small, pale mouth, or else she did not intend to.

"I think we met at the president's reception," Holman finally said helpfully.

"I never go to presidents' receptions," Miranda replied. "Oh, you mean the house-and-garden party. Yes. Oh dear, you know, Will Thomas couldn't come tonight. He said to tell you he was very sorry not to meet you."

"Will Thomas?" Holman asked.

"He's in the Music Department," Miranda said. "Didn't Julian tell you he was coming? That's just like him. Grrr. How provoking."

"But he isn't coming," Holman said.

"So it doesn't matter," Emmy added, laughing nervously.

"No," Miranda admitted. "But it's the principle of the thing."

32

They continued to stand in the hall. Charles pulled at his mother's skirt.

"I didn't let Hecate in, Mommy, it was Richard."

Miranda looked down and opened her mouth as if to answer Charles, but at the same time she appeared to notice that she was barefoot. She quickly looked away, perhaps so that Emmy and Holman should not notice too. "I'm sorry everything's so confused," she said. "Can I take your things?"

"That's quite all right," the Turners said in unison, beginning to remove their coats and scarves and galoshes and give them to Miranda.

A door to the left, which Emmy had taken to be that of a closet, opened, and Julian Fenn stepped up into the hall out of the cellar. In contrast to his wife, he was fully dressed and appeared quite calm.

"Nice to see you," he said to Holman. They shook hands.

"You know Emily," Holman said.

"Of course. How do you do?"

"We met at the president's reception," Emily said. "How do you do?"

They shook hands. The crying upstairs went on.

"Go on up to the bedroom," Miranda said to Charles. "Tell them I'll be up in a moment. What should I do with your fur coat?" she asked Emmy. "Is it best for it to hang it up?"

"Oh, anything, throw it absolutely anywhere," said Emmy. While they watched, Miranda carried their coats away down the hall and hung them carefully in a closet. She remained in the closet for some time; perhaps she was looking for some shoes, but if so she did not find them.

The howling upstairs became louder, and a little boy about a year younger than Charles appeared on the landing in torn pajamas. His face was half covered with a fringe of black hair, and when he paused for breath it could be seen that he was strikingly pretty, with great dark eyes. Charles stood behind him.

"Richard wants his pet flashlight, Mommy!" he interpreted.

"All right. Excuse me." Miranda went upstairs.

"Come into the parlor," Julian said to his guests in an unconcerned manner. "Would you like sherry? I think there still is some." He ran his hand through his hair,

33

which was as long and as dark as Richard's. He was tall and very thin, with an exaggerated, almost theatrical Black Irish face. He had thick charcoal eyebrows and high, hollow cheeks; he looked overexcited, as if he were about to die of consumption or lead a small raid for the Sinn Fein. On his jaw was an X-shaped dueling scar (the result of a bicycle accident at the age of eleven). Emmy noticed with disfavor that both his neck and his nails were dirty.

"Let me put on some light," Julian said.

The first two lamp switches he tried did not work, but at the third a long room full of shabby chairs and sofas became dimly visible. Green velvet drapes hung at the windows and dragged on the floor. Over the mantel was a black crayon rubbing of a tombstone, with skulls and wings. On the hearthrug below it a little girl about Freddy's age, dressed in cowboy costume, lay asleep, her fists clenched.

"Oh, there's Katie," Julian remarked. He opened a cupboard by the hearth and began to take out wineglasses. As he seemed to intend no other action, Emily said:

"But hadn't she better be in bed?"

"I suppose so," Julian said. Delicately, he poured out three glasses of sherry and handed them round. "Here's to, what?" he asked, holding his up.

"Convers College," Holman suggested.

"No. Confusion to Convers College!" He bumped their glasses with his glass and drank. Then he put the glass down, picked up Katie from the hearthrug and hung her over his shoulder. She did not wake.

"We weren't too late," Emmy said as soon as Julian had left the room. "We were too early. We should have come half an hour later."

"It wouldn't have made any difference," Holman said.

"Do you think it's always like this?"

"It wouldn't surprise me." Holman leaned back into a soft, lopsided Victorian armchair with a sense of relaxation he had not felt, outside of his own house, since they had come to Convers. Julian Fenn was obviously so mad and Miranda Fenn so mad and nervous that there was no reason to be on one's guard here. Any possible slip in his best Convers manners would scarcely be noticed, let alone used against him. "Good sherry," he remarked, a bit surprised, noticing the bottle. "I wonder how they afford it."

"Her dress is incredible," said Emmy, who felt something of the same relaxation. "Do you suppose she made it herself?"

"Out of the curtains," Holman suggested. Indeed, one of the windows was bare. They began to laugh.

Julian returned at once, but it was almost nine by the time his wife reappeared, and nearly an hour later before, dazed with sherry, they all sat down to dinner. Miranda had been dodging in and out of the kitchen for a long time. "Oh, Julian, don't talk about that now, I don't want to miss it!" she kept saying, darting round the swing door and then vanishing with a swish of her dress, now wrapped in a great dirty apron.

At the table they settled down to a discussion of Hum C. Holman began by praising the course; it was his rule always to begin with praise if he could, and in this case he hardly wanted to do anything else.

"Oh yes, I was very much taken with it at first too," Julian said in his lilting voice. "As a game, you know. The first year I was here they had a series of assignments on optical illusions. Now you see it and now you don't. It was quite fun."

"But then you lost interest?" Holman asked.

"Not that, exactly. You might say I became too interested. I had a run-in with the Administration about it last spring."

Holman opened his mouth to say: "Oh?" in a manner calculated to invite confidences, but Julian was going on without this encouragement. "You know in the second semester they always go over some of the material that's being assigned in the freshman courses. So they were doing *Walden*, and one of my students took it seriously and suggested that they ought to go and actually try living in the woods. I thought, why not? So a lot of us got sleeping bags and we went off up toward the reservoir one weekend. Dean Lumkin was all shaken up by it."

"Really, why?" Emmy asked. "Because you hadn't asked his permission?"

"That, too. Mostly because some of the boys missed freshman track practice that Saturday. The coach went around to Lumkin to complain. We hadn't told everyone we were going, so nobody knew where we were. Officially. We should have made a report in triplicate to McBane and Lumkin and President King. More meat?"

"What happened then?" asked Holman, too interested to answer.

"Oh, nothing. McBane called me in. He was funny about it. He said he was beginning to think he had been born to carry messages between the administrative officials of Convers and a troop of loony overgrown Boy Scouts of America." Julian laughed at this definition, so Holman laughed too, although he agreed with it. "Were you ever a Boy Scout?"

"For a while, yes," Holman said.

"I never was. They didn't have them in Yugoslavia. Anyway, only for Yugoslavians."

"What were you doing in Yugoslavia?"

"Oh, living there. My father was in the State Department."

"Sometimes he was in the State Department," Miranda said. "Among other things."

"Don't speak ill of the dead," Julian said, passing his plate down to his wife for more green peas. Holman looked from one to the other. Impossible to tell whether either was angry. He admired this: most people were too transparent. After all, eccentricity was as good a disguise of one's feelings as convention. However, it was more trouble.

"That's a generous maxim," he said.

"Superstition, really," Julian replied. "Pagan survival. The idea is that the dead will hear you and be revenged; they're floating around us in the air all the time."

"Listening," Miranda said with a smile.

"I'm safe," Emmy said. "Both my parents are alive."

"Well, take it easy," her husband told her. "My father isn't."

"Oh, I wouldn't say anything about him," Emmy giggled. "I never even met him." Holman noticed that she was rather drunk; he felt a little hazy himself. It was past ten by his watch (he looked at it under the table), and they hadn't even started dessert.

"What did your father do?" Miranda asked Holman. "Would he be likely to haunt you?"

"He worked in a bank," Holman said flatly; he disliked this kind of creepy cute talk, and disliked it even more if it were only a disguise for Miranda's trying to place him.

"Well; what about yours?" she asked Emmy. Obvious, Holman thought.

"My father? Oh, he's retired. . . . He used to work in a bank too."

"The same bank?"

"No," Holman said, before his wife could answer. It irritated him to think that whereas Emmy had belittled her father by this description, he had aggrandized his. The senior Mr. Turner had worked in a Chicago bank as a bank guard. Holman, who had been seven when he died, remembered him as a large man in a gray uniform with a gun hanging beside his stomach. Besides, almost everybody in Convers knew who Emmy's father was, and though Miranda Fenn apparently didn't she would soon learn, and then she would think— He checked himself in this tedious habitual calculus by a glance at Miranda's pale peculiar face, hung over with wisps of thin red hair. What she thought, after all, would not matter.

"I'll bring in dessert." Miranda finally stood up and began to collect plates. "Please, don't get up" (no one had made a move to do so), "just go on talking."

As usual, this caused everyone to fall silent. Julian took a piece of bread and began to wipe his plate with it dreamily until Miranda took the plate away. No doubt, Holman thought, he learned that in Yugoslavia.

"There's a lot of pre-Christian superstition still around," Holman finally said, returning to the most recent impersonal topic he could recall. And why do I have to take it upon myself to keep this conversation going? he asked himself. Everyone's too potted to care.

"Yes, I always get a funny feeling when I'm visiting somewhere and I see umbrellas opened to dry in the house, that's bad luck, you know," Emmy said.

"Oh, so do I, I'm just the same way," exclaimed Miranda, putting down a pile of coffee cups. "Or broken glass."

"That's nothing," said Holman, "why, right here in town they're running pagan rituals."

"Right where?"

"At the fraternities. At least if they're anything like mine was. We had animal worship ceremonies every year."

Somewhat confusedly, Holman began to describe the initiation rites he had taken part in at his state university, the more fully since Julian turned out to have had no

37

experience of fraternities and seemed to be interested. He told about Rush Week: the primitive suspicion and isolation, the division into tribes. Then he described Hell Week which followed pledging, telling how he and the other twenty-four freshman pledges lived during this week in a basement room at the fraternity called the Black Hole. This room was twenty feet square and next to the furnace; it was painted black throughout. It was hard to sleep at night in the Black Hole (on the floor) because of the heat and the noise from the furnace, so when the pledges were let out after breakfast to attend classes and study they would go and sleep in corners about the campus, in the library stacks or in empty classrooms, or (if it was warm enough) outdoors, wrapped in coats.

On the second day of Hell Week, the crowded state of the basement was increased. The pledges were sent out after supper to steal a dog, and forbidden to return without one. They spent all night crawling through shrubbery and running around corners away from whatever looked like policemen or police cars in the residential district, dividing into small search parties and then joining up again in clumsy mobs, for none of them could agree to let any of the others crawl off to get some sleep. The streets of the town were shut up tight for Hell Week, and the only dogs loose were watchdogs, bloodhounds, and Great Danes straining and barking on the ends of their chains. The pledges gathered finally, discouraged and exhausted, at the gate of the Humane Society at dawn. When the pound opened at eight they purchased a half-grown mongrel wire-haired terrier. The terrier was taken back in triumph to the frat house, announced as having been stolen, and christened James Dawg at a brief breakfast ceremony. He was then shut up in the Black Hole, where he passed the rest of Hell Week in the company of the twenty-four pledges, and proved to be affectionate, dirty, noisy, and incontinent.

Hell Week reached its climax on Friday and Saturday. On Friday night was held the ceremony of Inquisition. The twenty-four candidates were brought upstairs from the cellar one by one, dressed only in their underpants (the costume which they wore throughout Hell Week except when attending classes). Each one was taken into a dark room, placed before a battery of lights, and questioned minutely on their sex lives: "Are you a virgin? . . .

When did you become a man? ... Describe the incident in detail ... And then? ... And then? ... When did you last have sexual relations? ..." The rest of the pledges sat in the basement with James Dawg, waiting their turn. If you had no heterosexual stories to tell, they whispered among themselves, it was best to make some up, or else you would be questioned on still more embarrassing matters.

"Heavens," Miranda Fenn said. "How primitive."

"Not really," Julian said. "There are post-Christian elements. It's very modern, actually; almost Russian."

"Aaoh, aaooh!" Muffled sobbing from the hall; then Katie Fenn tottered into the dining room, her hair tangled over her eyes, her face streaked with tears, dressed in an old flannel nightgown. She ran to her mother and buried her face in Miranda's lap, howling loudly.

"There, there. It's all right, baby. There. What's the matter? There, there."

"There's a tyrannosaurus under my bed."

Holman, Emmy, and Julian burst out laughing; Miranda gave them a quelling look. "There, there, lovey." She gathered Katie up and sat her on her lap. "It was just a bad dream. You sit here for a while." Katie gave a final sob and settled herself against her mother's shoulder. "I told you so," Miranda said to Julian. "It was that book. You frightened her with that book you were reading to them."

"I did not," said her husband; "it was Charles. He was telling them both that the eggs you bought from the man today were dinosaur eggs and as soon as you took them out of the icebox all different kinds of dinosaurs would hatch out of them."

"Well," Miranda said. "There, there" (as Katie showed signs of crying again). "Charles was just trying to scare you. He was just being naughty. Now you curl up and go to sleep. All our eggs are just ordinary eggs. I'm sorry, Holman. Please finish your story."

Holman hesitated. The effect of the wine was wearing off. What am I telling this for, he thought, to prove I made a tough fraternity even if my old man was a bank guard? Nobody here gives a damn. As for Emmy, she thinks that everyone in the world was in a fraternity, but it's a shame if yours was at a state university. One of the prices he paid for having come so far, he had often thought, was that his past triumphs had all turned into disgraces, like the blue suit and tie he had knocked himself out to earn for his high school graduation. The tie had big silver fleurs-de-lis on it; he had thought them very sophisticated.

"Please, do go on," Miranda said, leaning forward over Katie, her artistic beads dangling on the table. Holman looked at her, and the intuition came to him that she would have recognized the suit he wore to graduation because she had once owned a dress like it, or not much better; she had made the same trip he had. It did not make him like her any better.

But he went on. Saturday, he told them, was the last and most important day of Hell Week. On Saturday morning one of the pledges (chosen by lot) was sent down to the basement with a loaded revolver to shoot Jim Dawg. (He had been glad that it was not he.) Then they were treated to a short lecture, the point of which was that they had come through Hell Week satisfactorily, and had but one more ordeal before them; however, that was the hardest.

That evening was held the great Dog-Eating Ceremony. No supper was served, but at eight o'clock the twenty-four pledges, in their underpants, marched in procession into the dining hall where Jim Dawg, now cold and stiff, was lying on his back on a platter. The first man was given a knife, with which he had to slit James Dawg open from neck to tail. The knife was then passed from man to man; each had to reach in, cut off a handful of the internal organs of Jim Dawg, and place them on a plate which was held out to him by one of the fraternity brothers. Next they filed out one by one into the kitchen, where they were blindfolded and branded with hot wax. (The mark usually lasted for a year or two.) Still blindfolded, they were led back into the dining hall; a voice commanded them to lie down on the floor on their backs. Holman did so, and unseen hands placed something which felt like a piece or raw calf's liver on his mouth. (It was, in fact, a piece of raw calf's liver.) He and the others lay there, silent, while the president of the fraternity read aloud the traditional *Tale of Wooglin*. It was not brief, but briefly the story described the famous hunter Wooglin and his march through the great desert with his faithful companion James Dawg. He had marched for many days; he is exhausted and starving; he feels he cannot go on. As Wooglin is about to fall, however, Dawg rolls over on his back and looks up at him touchingly, while a voice speaks out of the sky: "Rip Open the Dawg and Eat!" At this point all the frat brothers repeated in chorus: "Eat! Eat! Eat!" Blindfolded, lying on their backs, the twenty-four pledges opened their mouths and tried to swallow the raw liver.

All of them succeeded. "Candidates!" the president of the fraternity announced. "You have passed the ordeals of the order! You may rise and sing." Stiffly, the pledges sat up, pulled off their blindfolds, and got to their feet. In unison they sang the official fraternity song, which they had been practicing all week in the cellar. Beer and sandwiches were served, and there was general rejoicing.

"Incredible," Miranda said. She looked down at Katie, who was now asleep in her lap. "I'll take her up to bed. Don't say a word till I get back."

Obediently, they sat in silence until she reappeared. Then Julian said to Holman: "Oh, you're quite right. It's straight out of the Golden Bough. Puberty rites; death and rebirth; everything."

"But a late form of the ritual. Nobody really dies. The dog was our scapegoat."

"It must have been cannibalism originally," Julian said. "After all, that christening ceremony; the dog became the twenty-fifth pledge. You were actually eating a freshman."

"Or maybe the other way around," Miranda suggested. "Maybe they were all turning themselves into dogs. Living cooped up together in the cellar that way."

"At least it's the totemic animal," Julian said.

"In a way," Holman half agreed.

"Oh, definitely. I've read up on it. You get as close to it as you can; you wear its skin and you eat its heart, and then you acquire its qualities."

"Today I am a wire-haired terrier," Miranda said. Everyone laughed, but Holman laughed a little crossly. "It really fits very well for freshmen at your university, don't you think? Wire-haired terriers are so eager to please, but they're awfully noisy and demanding and jumping around all the time, and they're not really very intelligent."

You are wrong, wire-haired terriers are one of the most intelligent breeds of dogs, Holman thought, but he caught himself in time not to say this. Instead he asked Miranda if she had by any chance been at his university.

"Oh, no," Miranda said. "I went to a little college in Ohio nobody's ever heard the name of."

I bet they haven't, he thought; and apparently we aren't going to hear it either.

"I can't understand it," Miranda said. "Killing that poor animal out of the pound."

"Yes, we felt bad about that ourselves," Holman said flatly. Miranda looked at him scornfully. Yes, he thought, your house is falling apart and you let your kids sleep on the floor and meanwhile your heart is bleeding for a dog that died in 1947.

"What if you had refused to do any of those things?" she asked. "What would have happened? Would you have been thrown out of the fraternity?"

"I don't know," Holman said. "I suppose it would depend partly on who you were, how much the frat wanted to pledge you." He made a habit of answering questions which implied a personal criticism like this, flatly and fully, without showing his anger. "We did use to talk about it of course, especially about eating the liver; it had got round that that was going to happen but nobody knew for sure if we would get dog's liver or what. We used to talk about what diseases you could get from eating the liver of a sick dog out of the pound and whether Jim Dawg was sick. But then by that time we had been through so much it didn't seem worth taking the chance and refusing; and we knew that if we went through with it and got into the fraternity we would get our turn later."

"Your turn?"

"When the next year's candidates came up," Emily explained.

"It hardly seems worth it," Julian remarked.

"So for the next three years you got a chance to frighten freshmen with dead dogs," Miranda said; Holman's method had partly succeeded, for her tone had declined from righteousness into ridicule; "and burn them with hot wax, and sit behind a searchlight asking them embarrassing questions."

"I got to watch," Holman said. "It was the officers of the fraternity, the president and treasurer and so on, who asked the questions. The rest of us just looked on."

"While they told you all their guilty secrets," Miranda finished, and Holman heard in her voice the tone of one who likes the way secrets taste.

42

"We kept their guilty secrets," Holman said. "We had to swear an oath never to reveal anything that went on in initiation ceremonies. I'm breaking it now," he admitted, realizing this.

"We won't tell on you," Miranda promised. She smiled at Holman, but he did not smile back. His technique almost always worked: it disarmed the opponent and won him over; but it took a good deal of self-control and offered no outlet for Holman's own rage until the end, when he could in effect bite the hand held out to him.

"You won't have the opportunity," he said coldly. Now maybe you will be more careful next time, he thought, but looking at Miranda he doubted it.

"Please have some more coffee," she said.

"No thank you." Holman glanced over at Emmy, and they exchanged a signaling look. "We ought to be leaving," he said loudly and firmly.

Emmy came home from the Fenns' dinner party in a good mood. As she and Holman went over the high points of the evening she stated that the Fenns were crazy, peculiar, weird, and simply impossible, but rather nice. Still, think of having to live with either of them in that house! Emmy reflected as she took off her clothes that after all she would rather be married to Holman than to someone who constantly got into trouble with the authorities and never washed his neck.

"Imagine being married to someone who doesn't wash himself, like Julian Fenn," she said. "How does his wife ever stand it?" She took off her clean petticoat.

"Why should she notice? She's worse than he is," said Holman who was sitting on the side of the bed taking off his clean socks.

"Oh, Holman, she isn't. Miranda Fenn isn't dirty." Emmy took off her girdle.

"No, not dirty exactly. Just dusty and gritty gray, like something that's been left in a drawer for years and years."

"Oh, honey. How can you say that? That was just her weird dress. He's much, much worse." Emmy took off her bra and crossed the room to get her nightgown out of the closet, but as she passed Holman he stopped her with a hand on her stomach.

"It's sexual," he said. "You think he's worse because you can't stand the idea of sleeping with him, and I think she's worse because I can't stand the idea of sleeping with her." Holman put his other hand on his wife's behind. She made a move as if to go, but he got up, stood in her way, and embraced her.

Emmy held still, and rather stiff, though she put her arms around Holman's back as usual, feeling his flesh and the cloth of his undershorts against her stomach. She had no doubt that Holman intended to proceed with sexual intercourse, for he seldom touched her otherwise apart from the morning and evening smack. But I don't want to do this, I don't love you, she thought, and she dropped her arms and pulled away. Holman misinterpreted her move.

"O.K., go get ready, you beautiful thing," he said, releasing her and slapping her lightly on the bottom.

After Emmy was in the bathroom with the door closed, she realized that she had missed the opportunity to announce that she did not feel like it. And anyway, how did one announce that? In the five years of her marriage Emmy had never refused her husband his rights (his rights, she thought with a sinking feeling) except from a definite physical cause, but she could not open the bathroom door now and suddenly say that she was off or had the flu, which would be a lie besides. Physically she felt all right. Meanwhile she found herself automatically taking things off the top shelf of the cupboard and making ready. But she moved clumsily, though she was usually deft, and very slowly.

Holman was sitting on the edge of the bed waiting for her when she came in, with a box of Kleenex conveniently at hand. He turned out the light, and they assumed the usual position. I feel nothing, absolutely nothing, Emmy thought. I don't love you. I suppose prostitutes feel like this, she said to herself, meanwhile noticing that she was automatically gripping Holman's shoulders—how horrible. She let go, and it was worse, as if she were being assaulted like cases in the newspapers. I feel absolutely nothing, nothing. And he doesn't seem to notice. Well, in a moment it will be all over, she thought, recognizing the customary signal and raising her legs. But Holman, who had drunk nearly a whole bottle of wine, was lasting longer than usual. As he began to make his final effort Emmy felt a quiver of interest, but too late to enjoy it.

44

"More?" she said between her teeth as Holman, finished, fell a dead weight onto her chest.

"More?" he said. "The lady wants more," he exclaimed incredulously to the world, raising himself on one elbow and then dropping back with a thump.

Emmy said nothing; she did not even complain that he was squashing her lungs. She was overcome with shame; she felt a new and worse sensation than that of submitting to someone she did not love, the shame of asking someone she did not love for love.

"Oof," Holman said, lifting himself up at last. He fell back on his side of the bed and passed the box of Kleenex to Emmy.

*   *   *

Allen Ingram to Francis Noyes

November 14

... The most peculiar letter about royalties came today from the Enemy Agent. (I really must look round for another one.) As usual, he is working himself up into a state about nothings, but I suppose somebody ought to call him up and explain things to him Calmly. Could you possibly?

Here it's been very quiet. Now that everyone in town has had a good look at Wicked Allen, I sit up here on my hill and listen to them carousing down in the valley on football week-ends. The only people that keep on inviting me are Dean Lumkin and his wife. I don't know why. Perhaps she wants to start a *petit salon des artistes;* there was a cuckoo local spinster painter there too last time, a sort of Great-Aunt Moses, and a pianist from the Music Department, a sulky-charming young man who drank steadily and played Chopin on the Lumkin Grand when he was told to. We all had to shush up and watch Mrs. L. *feeling it.* I sat and wondered if she would dare ask me to recite from my Works next and picked out passages which would make her wish she hadn't. She didn't quite dare, but I know it's coming. She's got two of Great-Aunt's pictures already; one doesn't give *artistes* dinner for free.

Billy the Boy Dean Lumkin, on the other hand, probably asks me just out of Good Fellowship; he is the world's champion Good Fellow. About forty-five; he is the boyish type (but not my type of boy), all big sincere smile and straight-from-the-shoulder handshake. The worst of it is I don't think he's faking; he actually is good-natured, probably even fairly competent (he runs the college while President King is off on those long fund-raising trips—but he'll never be President himself, I'd be willing to bet: too much the ingenue). He is even intelligent, though at bottom, perhaps, puzzled that whatever he elects to do spontaneously it always turns out to be just right. Or do I only imagine he feels this? He has the students over for beer because he Likes Young People Around.

Mrs. L. is just the same and just the opposite. She holds all his opinions, but on her they sound like threats. "People who can't get along at Convers ought not to waste their time trying; they'd do much better to go somewhere else." When Billy the Boy throws this off frankly between frank gulps of whisky and soda, you want to burst into applause. But you ought to hear his wife (her name is Betsy, but among myself I call her Big Sister) say it. She is about forty and bitter about it, with brown curls and outdoor-girl hard-featured good looks, affects sporty plaids and horrid good-little-black dresses.

Give thanks: the weekend after this one is Thanksgiving. I am planning to cut my last class short on Wednesday and make the early train. Don't meet me, but buy a big turkey and ask Suzy and David and Jim and. . . .

CHAPTER

3

ON A COLD AFTERNOON IN DECEMBER, EMMY SAT IN Miranda Fenn's kitchen drinking coffee. This room, which she had not even seen on her first visit, had turned out to be the center of life at the Fenns'. They ate all their meals there, unless there was company; Miranda not only cooked and washed and ironed there, she mended and read and wrote letters and received visitors; and Julian corrected papers in the evening at the big kitchen table. The cat Hecate, the three Fenn children, and Freddy Turner, who had been sent out so that Miranda and Emmy could talk, kept coming back into the room to play and scavenge for food.

"That's the way he always is," said Miranda. "More coffee?" As usual, she was perched on a high stool beside the stove in a pixielike manner. Her costume today was pixie above the waist (a green and white sweater with a pointed collar), but below that it changed into demented charwoman (a bunchy gray flannel skirt, a dirty apron, and long black cotton stockings). The trouble was partly, Emmy thought, that none of the mirrors in Miranda's house was more than a foot square.

"Yes, please," she said.

Miranda tilted up the pot and poured coffee through the sunlight into Emmy's cup. Though a hard wind was blowing over frozen ground outside, the kitchen was warm. Two pans of freshly made coffee cake stood cooling on the stove, and the sink was piled with dirty dishes. On all the shelves and counters and window sills were open boxes of crackers, jars of jam and herbs, cans of grease, newspapers, novels from the library, withered apples and green tomatoes and spools of thread, an avocado seed sprouting in a glass, a pile of uncorrected papers, a bowl of water with a goldfish asleep in it. ... On the floor were wastebaskets, paper bags, toys, empty bottles, and saucers of milk and scraps for the cat.

47

"Oh, thank you," Emmy said, stirring her coffee and turning over the pages of the *Folk–Lore Quarterly*. During the last month she had fallen into the habit of coming to sit in Miranda's kitchen in the afternoon. Especially on Tuesdays and Fridays when Mrs. Rabbage came to her house to clean and talk, it was convenient to have somewhere to go with Freddy. Miranda lived halfway between Emmy's house and town, and, having no car, she almost never went out. She hated the cold weather; when it got really bad, as now, she stayed indoors for days at a time, even ordering groceries over the phone. She could usually be found sitting in her kitchen drinking coffee, the children playing near-by, and it seemed to make no difference to her whether her visitors talked to her or just read her old magazines.

"There's a good article about trolls in that one," she said after a pause. "At least I think it's that one. . . . Well, what it is," she went on with an earlier subject, "it's just fatal to let Julian get inside a store. Did I ever tell you about the time he bought the badminton set?"

"No," Emmy said, "tell me."

"It was when the vacuum cleaner broke down, last spring. They couldn't fix it here in town, so we tied it onto the bike—what a job that was—and Julian took it over to Hampton. I gave him fifteen dollars to pay for the repair. Well he didn't get back until about six that evening, and then he didn't have the vacuum. The first place he took it to said it couldn't be fixed, so he just left it there in an alley, just abandoned it. Then he started to walk around town and after a while he walked into the department store and bought a badminton set for sixteen dollars. I didn't know a badminton set could cost that much."

"But what did he want a badminton set for?"

"I asked him that. He said he saw it in the window and he thought it would be nice if we all learned to play badminton." Miranda cut a piece of warm coffee cake, handed it to Emmy, and licked the sugar off her fingers. "Here."

"Oh, yum. Thank you. And did you all learn to play badminton?"

"No," Miranda said regretfully. "I had to make him take it back. Luckily, they gave him the money again. They don't always."

"Badminton is a frightfully dreary game, anyway."

"That's what Will said. He told Julian it was a kind of chicken tennis for baby girls."

"Will?"

"Will Thomas. He's that friend of ours in the Music Department."

"Oh yes."

Miranda got up and began to wander around the kitchen. She put her finger into the soup which was simmering on the back of the stove, took it out, and tasted it. Then she found a bunch of dried herbs and an old carrot, which she cut up and threw into the pot. She put in her finger and licked it again, not attempting to conceal this insanitary mode of cooking, or seeming aware that Emmy might be shocked by it. And Emmy was no longer shocked; she took it for granted now along with Miranda's many other weird habits. One more or less hardly mattered, for Miranda was already completely unlike any friend Emmy had ever had. If it had not been for the awful isolation into which she had suddenly been plunged, she would not have dreamed of knowing her.

Before she came to Convers, Emmy had always found plenty of friends ready-made wherever she went, often ones already allied to her family by the consanguinity of birth or business. In college, where she had been fat and shy, most of her friends had been St. Kit's School alumnae like herself. They shared so many interests and assumptions that their conversations were quite meaningless to outsiders, especially when they met in large groups: a babble of special slang and shrieks of incredulous merriment. As to their private lives, the code was to say very little, even behind people's backs. Miranda, on the other hand, would and did say anything, and Emmy was beginning to feel that if she wanted she could say anything to her. It was doubly safe, because not only did nothing seem to surprise Miranda, but there would be no echo. Miranda was nobody's cousin or in-law, and she would not suddenly turn up in some other part of Emmy's life to betray her confidence. Talking to her was almost as safe as talking to the woman who did one's hair.

"I'm baffled, sometimes," Miranda said, giving the soup one last stir and sitting down again. "What would you do if you had a husband who went on the way Julian does?"

"Golly, I don't know," Emmy replied, startled.

"No. Why should you? Holman would never do anything like that badminton set in a million years. You know, I admire Holman very much. He is so—I don't know—so sound, without being at all stuffy about it. And he's very attractive too, of course."

"He likes you too," lied Emmy, after a pause.

"He does? I rather thought he didn't, you know. Well, that's nice. It must be pleasant to be married to someone you can depend on, I mean really depend on. And he always behaves so well to everybody. I was watching him at the Bakers' cocktail party."

"He doesn't always behave so well," Emmy objected, irritated by this praise. "You only see him in public." But her sense of justice protested. "Of course, heavens, I don't mean he behaves badly in private. But he doesn't keep up his company manners. He's always so preoccupied when he's at home, he doesn't seem to notice Freddy or me or anything." She laughed a little nervously, unused to expressing this idea.

"Perhaps it's just that he's got a new job and he's concerned about it."

"No. He's always taken his work seriously, but he never wanted to keep it to himself this way. When we were in New Haven he used to take me with him to lectures, whenever there was a good one. So, when he began to teach here, naturally I said I would like tremendously to go and hear one of *his* lectures; but he told me I absolutely couldn't come. Did you ever go to hear Julian?"

"Yes. I went last year when he was giving two lectures on the Ballad for Knight. But you know, after I'd been to the first one I found out that it isn't supposed to be proper for women to go to classes. Our landlady, Mrs. Lumkin, called on me especially to tell me. I think she did, anyhow; maybe it was just to snoop. Grr. I was cross as two sticks, because I was dying to hear the second lecture."

"Maybe that was it," Emmy said. "But then why didn't he tell me so? He simply never tells me anything lately. If he had only said that it was a rule here, of course I wouldn't go, any more than you did."

"But I did go," Miranda said.

"Not after you found out."

"But I did, you know." She took a dirty wet cloth out of the sink and began to wipe the table. "I disguised myself as a student and went."

"You did! How? Did anyone notice?"

"I don't think so. At least, nobody said anything to me. I'm not very noticeable, except that my hair is red, and I put it up under one of Charles's caps that's got earmuffs."

"Maybe I could do that," Emmy said, but only jokingly. "It would serve him right, really."

"I don't know," Miranda said. "I don't know as you could." She looked Emmy over. "You look awfully much like a woman, you know. You'd have to walk differently. And what would you do with all that hair? It certainly wouldn't go into Charles's cap. You'd have to cut it off."

"Certainly not." Emmy put up her hands to the heavy, glossy knot of hair.

"And then, the class I went to was a big lecture course. What you want to get into is a Hum C section meeting, where everybody probably knows each other. That'll be much harder."

"I wouldn't dream of it," Emmy said. She put her cup down. Miranda is really too weird, she thought; there's simply no point in coming here. But there was a point, after all. Emmy recognized the rule that if one wishes to keep one's friends, and even one's acquaintances, children can only be taken to visit regularly where there are already children of a like age. If she did not call on Miranda, the alternative was going down to The Huts, squeezing into rooms which were already much too small for their occupants, and spending the afternoon in great discomfort. The Huts had been carelessly built to start with, and by now all the windows leaked and the floors and ceilings had begun to sag at angles. They were stuffy and hot in the summer, and in the winter they were stuffy and cold. Worst of all, the Hut children and Freddy would be continually underfoot, shouting or whining according to their natures.

"Well, after all," Miranda said comfortingly, "it's not as if Hum C were interesting. They don't really discuss literature. And all that semantics and logic they keep going over and over is pretty pointless."

"Oh, I don't agree. I couldn't make much of it at first either, but now I'm beginning to. Those questions they ask may seem silly, but it's simply a way of finding out what you really feel."

"But it's not *about* anything," Miranda said. "And talk about pagan survivals; Hum C in a kind of Christian survival. Julian says it's just the last gasp of the silly lectures on ethics and theology they had when the college was founded."

Emmy had been taught theology at St. Kit's, and still thought of herself vaguely as a Christian. She changed the subject.

"Well, you see, Julian at least talks to you about the course," she said. "Holman won't even do that. He keeps telling me to stop trying to understand it. As if he thought I was less intelligent than any of the freshmen at Convers." This joke came out bitter. "He's never around to talk, anyhow," she went on, trying for a lighter tone. "At Princeton he used to do most of his studying at home, but now that he has an office I simply don't see him all day. He doesn't even come home for lunch."

"Yes, but you know where he is and what he's doing, and when it's suppertime I bet he always turns up, doesn't he?" Emmy admitted this. "The worst thing about Julian is that I never do know. I would be delighted if I could be sure he was working in his office, but most of the time I know he's just wandering around somewhere in the library stacks, or he decided to go birding, or have a drink, and he doesn't come back and he doesn't come back, and I just have to sit here and wait until McBane or the Registrar's Office or somebody calls up and says: Oh, Mrs. Fenn, do you happen to know where Mr. Fenn is, because he was supposed to have a conference with me today, or hand in his midterm grades, or something."

The door creaked open, and Charles Fenn put his head into the kitchen. "You and Mrs. Turner are eating coffee cake," he said accusingly, raising a black mask, "and we aren't having any."

"This coffee cake is bad for little boys," Miranda told him. "It stunts their growth. Here, have some raisin cookies instead."

"I don't believe you," Charles said, coming into the room and making a pass with his plastic sword at the stove.

"All right," Miranda said. "Don't say I didn't warn you." She held the pan out to him in one hand, and a plate of cookies in the other. "Go ahead, have some. Only don't come complaining to me when Richard and Katie get bigger and bigger and bigger than you."

Charles reached for the pan and then hesitated. "It's only coffee that stunts people's growth," he suggested.

"Not coffee cake." Miranda said nothing, and Emmy with difficulty, did the same. At last Charles took two raisin cookies. "Can I stay and listen to your conversations?" he asked.

"Not this time," Miranda said. "Go on now, Charles." He gave her a look, took up his sword, and left the room.

"Well I really ought not to talk that way about Julian," she resumed. "He's been so good ever since school started. The only thing he's done is to miss Hum C meeting that one time."

Those two times, Emmy thought, but did not say.

"But that's the trouble, whenever he's been good I get to worrying what he'll do next. If only he can manage not to do anything they can notice until vacation; that's when they're going to decide whether to make him an assistant professor."

"Oh, really? What do you think will happen?"

"Lord knows," Miranda said. "Both Knight and Baker hinted to him last spring that he would get it, but McBane hasn't said a word. Well, you know what he is like."

"Mr. McBane makes me uncomfortable," Emmy said. "I know he's brilliant, but he has such weird manners. The first time I met him, it was at the Hum Program party in October, I guess. We were introduced, and he didn't say anything at all, he just stared at me like—like an old owl, with those yellow-rimmed glasses and all that gray hair, in a zoo or something. It was so rude, really; and of course I couldn't be rude back. So I said: 'I'm awfully glad to meet you.' And he said: 'You are? Why?' So I sort of fell all over myself and I said, well, my husband had told me so much about him and of course both my brothers went to Convers and I'd heard about him and Hum C for simply years, or something; so he said: 'Who are your brothers?' So I told him. And then he laughed and said in this frightfully loud way, almost shouting: 'Oh, so you're Freddy Stockwell's daughter!' But I'm positive that he actually knew it all along."

"Yes, he was rather that way with me, too," Miranda said. "I'm sure you're right; he does it on purpose. But it's only the first time. After that he seems to forget about you. I don't think he likes women much except for Mrs. McBane, and nobody could possibly dislike her. Of course Julian admires him tremendously. And I must say he's been very nice to Julian; he's put up with an awful lot.

53

But it can't go on forever. The trouble is, Julian has no sense of proportion. He sees how stupid the rules are, so he breaks them. He doesn't plan to make things hard for anybody, but he does. The trouble is, it's like Will says—"

"Will Thomas." Emmy was getting a little tired of hearing this name, the owner of which she had never met. Not that she had any desire to meet Will Thomas; she imagined him as tediously sententious, since he was always being quoted; as messily Bohemian, since he was a friend of the Fenn's; and, since he was a musician, as long-haired, pale, and probably fat.

"Yes. Wait a moment, I have it right here." Miranda went to her kitchen bulletin board, which was cluttered with postcards and clippings and children's drawings and invitations and shopping lists pinned one over the other, some yellowed with age. "Here. 'The power of society is such that, no matter how much we despise it, our crimes are always against individuals.' "

The door creaked and then banged; Richard Fenn, with his black curls full of feathers, rushed into the kitchen, followed by Katie Fenn in a pink quilt and cowboy boots, and Freddy Turner with his head in a broken pleated lampshade. "Cookies, cookies!" Richard and Katie screamed. "You gave Charles cookies!"

"Come here, Freddy ducky," Emily said. "What are you doing in that lampshade?"

"Don't call me Freddy, Mummy. I'm a dinoseras."

"Well, all right. Come over here, dinoseras." Emmy lifted up the lampshade and kissed Freddy behind his ear, thinking as she did so how healthy and handsome and strong he looked in contrast to the thin, pale, peculiar Fenn children, who were never told to go outside to play, but instead permitted to hang around the house all winter, day after day, building caves under the dining-room table.

"I want a cookie too," Freddy said.

"Of course you can have a cookie," Miranda told him. "Here, have two."

"One, Freddy," Emily said, holding out her hand for the other. Freddy immediately crammed both cookies into his mouth. "Little pig!" she exclaimed, as the children banged their way out of the kitchen again, shedding crumbs. "I usually don't give him anything between meals," she explained to Miranda, and not for the first time.

"I know, but it seems so unfair, when the others have them." Miranda sighed, as if it were a law of nature. "I often wonder about the children," she went on. "Whether they're going to grow up to be like Julian, you know. Not Charles, of course he's so responsible. But Katie has such a strong will already, I don't think she'd let anyone stop her from doing whatever crazy thing she felt like. And Richard is so much like Julian already. He looks just like Julian's old photographs too, and you know that does mean something. It's not just a superstition."

"Mm," Emmy said. According to Miranda, Holman had once said in exasperation, no superstition was just itself. But Freddy, too, very much resembled his father; he had the same sturdy, snub-nosed good looks. Would he lose his serious, self-centered charm as he grew up, and become merely serious and self-centered? "But most boys look like their fathers," she said.

"Not like Richard does. And this anthropomorphism thing he has worries me. He really behaves as if he couldn't tell the difference between people and things; as if he thought everything in the house was alive. You know he has a pet flashlight named Dickie. After him. He sings songs to it that he makes up himself. And last night I heard him in the tub singing one to the bath sponge. It went: 'This spongey is a very nice spongey. He can do anything, including many things.' "

"But surely, that's harmless," Emmy said, laughing. "Heavens, even Freddy makes up friends, and he's not frightfully imaginative. He has a friend now who's a Martian and comes out of the television to visit him. Why, it's in Gesell, practically all children have imaginary friends."

"But they're not bath sponges. It makes me feel spooky to think of all these things being alive. Maybe he's right, you know." She smiled the fey, one-sided smile she reserved for the supernatural.

"What a horrid idea," Emmy said.

"Well, you never know." Miranda got up to taste the soup again. "More salt," she said to herself, and added salt. "It's not the imaginary friends I mind so much. It's the imaginary enemies. The most awful thing happened just before school started this year, Richard fell over a footstool in the living-room and hit his head. He wasn't really hurt, but he was awfully angry. He said the footstool had done it on purpose. You know people used to believe things like that. In the Middle Ages they used to try, oh, swords and pitchforks and furniture for attacking their owners, and even execute them. Of course Richard never heard of that, but the next day while we weren't looking he and Katie got the saw out of the tool drawer and tried to saw the footstool in half to punish it. It was completely ruined by the time I got there. The awful thing was, the footstool wasn't ours, it came with the house. I still haven't told Mrs. Lumkin about it. I keep hoping I'll be able to find one enough like it so she'll never know." Miranda sighed. "One crisis after another. I get so tired of it. If only things would stop happening, but they never do, don't you agree?"

"No," Emmy said. "Actually I keep wishing something would happen. I'm dreadfully bored."

"Really? I ought to cast a spell for you," Miranda said. She had played with magic for many years. She read the future in shreds of wet tea, listened for (and manufactured) spirit rappings around tables in darkened rooms, and set out saucers of salt and milk for goblins. Though unwilling to leave her house and act upon the real world to change it, she had occasionally designed considerable alterations. When events subsequently turned out according to her spells, she either took complete credit or laughed it off. She continually half-believed, and pretended to believe completely or not at all, according to her mood and her company.

"How would you cast a spell?" Emmy asked.

"Oh, I don't know. Wave my hands around and say something." Miranda passed her thin hand through the air in a circle over Emmy's hand as it lay on the table. "Abracadabra. Or something."

"Thank you," Emmy said, giggling. But without thinking about it, she brought her hand down into her lap and wiped it off on her skirt, as one does when a friend's conversation had sprayed one with spittle. "I'll probably be caught in a frightful snowstorm or something now, thanks to you," she said.

Soon Emmy put Freddy into his snowsuit and then into the car and started home. Though only five o'clock, it was already dark. The valley lay frozen around them, black and tones of black. Here and there a light showed in a house, or through the fogged windows of a barn. The wind had died; the only sound was the crackle of the snow tires on ice and cinders or the sucking sound they made when the road was clear.

Emmy drove slowly, thinking. It was depressing, one had to admit it; but after all, the heroes and philosophers of New England, all the founders of the Convers tradition, had lived through winters like this. Concord today was just a Boston suburb where cousins of hers lived, but in Emerson's time it must have been much the way Convers was now. Here one could still practice self-reliance; actually had to; one could listen through the long, cold, black evenings for the inner voice. She mustn't give up.

She put the station wagon into the barn and ran into the house with Freddy. Though much cleaner than Miranda's, her kitchen had the dreary, empty look of rooms where nothing has happened all day. The *Times* lay where she had put it that morning, on top of a pile of circulars. No interesting mail had come for days.

She hung up her coat and Freddy's snowsuit and continued with the evening routine. At five-thirty promptly Holman arrived. He changed his clothes, made drinks, threw the circulars into the wastebasket, announced that nothing of interest had taken place at the college that day, and sat down to read the *Times*.

"Golly, it was cold out today!" Emmy said. "How long is this going to go on?"

"This is nothing," her husband said. "Winter hasn't even started yet officially. Wait until February and March before you complain."

And it's only December, Emmy thought. She took a breath. "Freddy and I went over to the Fenns' again today," she reported.

"Oh?" Holman said without interest.

"I know you don't like Miranda but I do rather, and Freddy always has a good time with their children."

"That's nice," he said, reading.

"Miranda likes you, though. As a matter of fact, I think she has quite a pash on you."

"Oh?" Holman looked over the paper, but did not move it.

"Yes. She practically told me so. She thinks you're so-o-o attractive."

"She hasn't got a chance," Holman said. "Too skinny."

"She admires you because you're so-o-o serious and so-o-o hard-working."

"Oh, yeah."

"Yeah," Emmy said. "I can't see why, but she does."

Looking up, Holman confirmed his suspicion that Emmy was in a bad mood again; the same kind of bad mood she had been in most of the time for a month. There was nothing he could do about it, so he smiled at her and pretended not to notice.

Emmy, too, made an effort. "You know I was going over those last week's assignments of yours," she said, "and I think I see now what it's all about. They keep asking questions simply to clear away all the rubbish that everyone takes for granted and what's left is what you really believe; what you really see, I mean, the way *you* see it and nobody else. Like Emerson."

"Emerson?" Holman raised his head.

"Yes, like Self-Reliance. I was thinking about it this afternoon driving home. That Convers now probably looks a lot like Concord used to, and then when they were all thinking about the same things as in Hum C, it's really interesting."

"Mrm," Holman said. He was not bored; he too found Hum C more and more interesting as he saw principles in it which could be applied to the criticism of literature, but this was a technical matter which would not interest Emmy, and he despaired of trying to explain to her why the course was not a program of self-analysis, but completely the opposite. She would always want to see every idea from an emotional point of view, if possible as an emotion; the class of things that had no connection with feeling did not interest her. He did not mind—women should be that way.

Emmy looked at him. I am more isolated than anybody ever was in Concord, she thought. It may have been cold and old-fashioned and oil lamps there but they had friends to talk to. I bet Emerson talked to his wife.

"You never talk to me any more," she complained suddenly. "You never talk to me and you never play with Freddy, and absolutely all you ever do is work."

Holman pretended not to hear this, reading. It had not been said very loudly, and there was no point in their starting another argument. He hated arguments, and remembered too well the noisy, vulgar ones that had

58

punctuated his childhood before his father died. Nothing good ever came of them; they only led to embarrassment or sometimes to meaningless, embarrassing violence.

There was a long pause.

"It's so boring here, so boring!" Emmy burst out. "Nothing real ever happens!"

"Thank God," Holman said involuntarily. He had seen enough of the world in thirty years to know that when something "real" happened it was likely to be something bad; violent, irrational, destructive. He had escaped this kind of reality by the deliberate effort of climbing further and further up into the clear, bright realm of intellect. Convers, in its high valley, was the Everest of his journey. Every day he took great breaths of the pure, still mountain air. At the same time, he occasionally wondered at the innocence of the natives. They really believed that the outside world was decent, sane, and safe; that there, as here, ideals were upheld, promises kept, and arguments on abstract issues conducted with polite sincerity. They would talk about the latest horror or stupidity of international or national politics as if it had been invented by monkeys on another planet. When such and such a threat had been made, such and such a crime performed, they called it insane, incredible. Holman had no difficulty in crediting it, and as for sanity, wasn't that determined by majority rule? He had known plenty of people who would have been happy to smash the whole world into a cowpie if they had happened to have the opportunity.

But that was not what Emmy meant by "real." "I know what you mean," he said soothingly. What she meant was that he had plenty to do in Convers and she did not have enough. In addition to his course work and correcting papers he was advising students and attending meetings and trying to finish his thesis. It was boring for Emmy here because Freddy was growing up and she needed another baby. But Emmy knew as well as he did that they had agreed to wait until his appointment for next year was certain. He did not want to start this argument again, so he only said: "It'll be vacation soon, baby. Wait until we get to New Jersey and then you can go into town and go to all the parties and art museums and stores you can stand."

"That's not what I want to do," Emmy said.

"What do you want to do?"

As she hesitated, Holman smiled at her fondly and tolerantly.

"I know why you're smiling," Emmy said. "It's because you think I don't know what I want, you think I'm just a silly girl who doesn't understand Hum C or anything at all. But I do."

"I think you're a beautiful, brilliant girl, who doesn't understand Hum C."

"What don't I understand about it? Explain it to me."

"No, baby. Not again." Holman smiled, sat back, and took up the paper to read more about football.

Emmy stared at her husband. He's like Richard Fenn, she thought, he can't tell the difference between people and furniture. Only he thinks everything in the house is furniture. She had the impulse to throw her drink at him. She imagined his red, surprised face, and the ice cubes sliding down his shirt. From the adjoining room, long continued, came the sounds of cowboy television.

* * *

Allen Ingram to Francis Noyes

December 13

... Your description of your hectic evening on Macdougal Street and of coming home to find Tommy R. in a sodden hysterical lump on the doorstep, reminds me what a long way it is from here to Manhattan. I could walk through the center of Convers at midnight any weekday in drag, and meet not a soul except the grocery cats. Even the policeman on duty would be asleep with his head on his desk in the little neon office underneath the Town Hall. (This is a great masterpiece of Municipal Romanesque in red and orange brick knit. It is of course thought to be the local eyesore, and painted out of all the souvenir postcards of Convers Common—elms and routine Old New England Colonial church, inn, shops, parsonage, and New Old Colonial fraternity houses.) And whatever time I come home, I know I shall find nothing more (or should I say less?) symbolic on *my* threshold than a frozen puddle where the gutter has been dripping all day, or a dead leaf or two blown up the steps by the wind.

Lonely, naturally. But don't feel sorry: I have done

twenty-five pages more of the novel in the last ten days—a whirlwind of work for me. I now see the hopeless relationship between *J* and his father as working through. . . .

I can rest from these paper emotions by taking an interest in local gossip. Right now, the whole town is in an uproar over a one-alarm fire. I heard the siren while I was working yesterday afternoon and thought nothing of it, though there was a faint impulse to count the blasts and find out where it was by checking the Convers Fire Alarm Code (a printed guide for pyromaniacs which is sold at the fire station—every house I've yet been into has one posted). But I heard about it soon enough when I got down to school this morning. It turns out that the house where the fire was, like half the property in town, belongs to the college, which had it rented out to, *guess who* (I'm beginning to sound like Them), Julian Fenn and his wife Miranda, the Villagey types I told you about who had me to dinner and didn't feed me until ten P.M. The fire started in an old stove in their kitchen.

Nobody was hurt, and the house didn't burn down, but it's obviously going to be one of the events of the year. Mrs. Lumkin (Big Sister) was really ferocious about it when I met her in the market this morning. She was on her way to the Fenns' with a basket of foodies, looking just like the Wolf dressed up as Red Riding Hood. Billy Lumkin is in charge of faculty housing, and she definitely takes an interest, but she does her good works with bad grace. "I think someone ought to investigate the damage right away, before anything else happens," she told me. I wondered if I should call the Fenns up at once and warn them, she seemed so inflamed (pun). But I reconsidered. I'm not planning to get involved in this little story; and if I did, my support would hardly help.

CHAPTER

4

ABOUT TEN-THIRTY ON THE MORNING AFTER THE FIRE, Emmy drove up to the Fenns' house. The driveway and yard were cross-marked with the tracks of the fire engines' tires and the prints of boots; the bushes by the back porch had been broken and beaten down into the mud and snow.

Emmy crossed the ice and soot and climbed the back steps. The porch was smudged with black and three of the four panes in the window were smashed.

The door opened on a scene of desolate wreckage. The kitchen walls nearest to the stove, and the ceiling just above it, had been burned down to the lath and plaster, and everything was stained with water and smoke. The linoleum stood up in blisters; charred pieces of furniture and burned, sodden chunks of wallboard lay about. The icebox looked especially terrible, like toasted marshmallows. Much of what would not burn had been melted or broken, so that the shelves and floor were strewn with glass and odd-looking lumps which had once been plastic cups and plates.

"Miranda!" Emmy called. There was no answer.

She went through the soot-stained pantry and pushed open the door to the living room. It was almost undamaged, though very untidy. At first she thought it empty; then, with a start, she noticed a strange man lying at full length on the sofa.

"I was looking for Mrs. Fenn," she stuttered.

The man on the sofa had on a dark jacket over a black sweater, but no shirt, like a burglar. He also wore sneakers. Emmy's thought was that he looked dangerous. He stood up, turning out to be both large and tall.

"Awfully sorry, she's not here," he said in a voice which was low in both senses of the word. "They all went to the Christmas pageant at Charles's school."

"Oh." Emmy stood there, her back to the door.

62

"I told her I'd stay here and wait for Mrs. Lumkin or whoever comes."

"I'm not Mrs. Lumkin," Emmy protested.

"Thank God. I know you're not." He had a slight Southern accent. "You're Mrs. Turner. How do you do, Mrs. Turner?"

Emmy did not hold out her hand.

"My name is Will Thomas," he added as an afterthought.

"Oh, hello. Of course I've heard—" Emmy paused on the cliché.

"So much about me," Will finished, grinning. At second glance Emmy could see that if his clothes were those of a burglar, it was a burglar who shopped at Brooks Brothers. He had straight, very fair hair, a shade lighter than his skin but much the same color.

"I just came over to see if I could do anything for Miranda," Emmy said. "I brought a cake I made, because the stove. . . ." She put down her package.

"What an excellent idea."

"So if you could just give it to Miranda when she comes in, and tell her to let me know what we can do—I thought they might all like to come to supper at our house," Emmy added, wondering at the same time how Holman would take this. "Anyhow, if you could tell her to call me."

"You're not going."

"Yes, I really must," said Emmy, embarrassed—and therefore in her most society voice.

"No, you really mustn't," Will replied, but without imitating her tone.

Emmy began to giggle nervously. It was an old habit, not quite conquered, which had helped to make school proms an agony to her. Stop that absolutely stupid noise, she told herself.

"Miranda should be back soon," Will said. "Why don't you wait for her?" He leaned against the wall.

"I would like to see her. How soon?"

"Oh, very soon," he said dimly, looking out the window.

"Well, all right. I can stay a few minutes."

"Suppose you sit down? Then I can too."

"Oh, yes. I'm terribly sorry." Emmy sat with a plop onto the nearest chair and began to undo the clothespin-like fastening of her storm coat. She realized with irritation that her hair was still hanging down in last night's braid and that she had on no make-up. Will collapsed on the sofa again with a sigh, sliding down onto the end of his spine and extending his long legs out over the carpet. He smiled at Emmy and said nothing.

"It was tremendous luck that they put the fire out before it went any further, wasn't it?" Emmy said.

"Yes."

"You're in the Music Department, aren't you?"

"Yes."

This did not seem to be leading anywhere. Feeling warm, Emmy slid her shoulders and arms out of her coat and laid it over the back of the chair, while Will watched her. Underneath the coat she was wearing an old red sweater which as a matter of fact had shrunk somewhat since it came from Peck & Peck, but Emmy herself, as she was now conscious, had not shrunk. She crossed her arms over her chest and looked at a corner of the floor.

"It seems funny to be sitting in Miranda's house and not drinking coffee," she finally said, since Will Thomas still did not say anything.

"Would you like some coffee? I think there's a pot on the stove."

"Really?"

"There was one last night. If not, we can make some more. If the stove hasn't gone out. Let's go see."

Will got up again, groaning, and went into the kitchen, followed by Emmy. "No, it's as cold as hell," he said, feeling the stove. "Absolutely as cold as hell."

"Hell isn't cold," Emmy said.

"Oh, but it is. You wait and see."

"Really," she said, for this was after all an insult, and she tittered nervously again. Will either did not notice or pretended not to.

"I tell you what, let's have a drink instead," he suggested. "Miranda won't mind. . . . You don't think she'll mind, do you?" He held the scorched and blistered swing door for Emmy to pass by him.

"No. I don't know." Will opened the cupboard. "But it's so early," she protested.

"But this is a disaster area. Hm. Gin, Dubonnet, crème de menthe, ugh, Chianti, sherry. What would you like?"

"Oh, heavens. Sherry."

"Yes, let's. It's most respectable."

They drank.

"How did the fire start?" Emmy asked.

"Oh, the stove door wasn't fastened," Will said, "and a piece of coal fell out, or something."

"Oh."

"Officially, that is."

"What do you mean, officially?"

"You won't tell?"

"No. Tell whom?"

"Anybody."

"I promise I won't. On my word of honor," Emmy added, as Will seemed to hesitate.

"I believe you. Any girl who says 'whom' is bound to be a lady to the core. It was Richard, of course."

"Richard opened the stove door?"

"On purpose. The fire was restless; it wanted to get out and play, so he helped it."

Emmy began to laugh, and Will joined her. "I might have guessed," she said.

"Let's hope nobody else will." He sat up and began to unwrap the box Emmy had brought. "Hm, what have we here. . . . Fruit-cake! Could I have a piece, do you think?"

"You'll have to ask Miranda," Emmy said.

"Oh, come now. You haven't given it to her yet. Legally it's still yours. And I'm starving. Let's both have some," he added. Emmy did not protest again. "I'll get a knife."

Will went out into the wrecked kitchen, and Emmy could hear him swearing and pulling open drawers. He is perfectly crazy, she thought. At the same time she was more charmed than anything else. The half-destroyed house, the time of day, the oddity of the whole situation, somehow excused Will's behavior; it helped that he was very attractive.

"Can't find a thing," he said, returning. "Oh, well. If you don't mind this." He reached into his pocket and took out a large jackknife with "Boy Scouts of America" engraved on it.

"How convenient," Emmy said.

"Four different blades, bottle-opener, scissors, and screwdriver. Be prepared, you know." He cut the cake, handing a piece to Emmy. "And here, let's have some more sherry. . . . Oh, very good."

"Thank you. I made it."

"Did you! I always say— Oh, hell. Here comes somebody."

"Maybe it's Miranda," Emmy said, as the back door slammed to and steps crossed the kitchen. She felt absurdly exposed, sitting there with a piece of cake in one hand and a glass in the other. The new visitor could be heard walking back and forth in the other room, presumably inspecting the damage.

"Dammed sightseers," Will whispered.

The door swung open, and there stood Mrs. Dean William Wigglesworth Lumkin, in a red storm coat. Will leaped to his feet, first setting his glass of sherry down inconspicuously on the floor.

"Why, hello, Will!" she exclaimed. "What are you doing here? Isn't this the limit?"

"I'm waiting for you," Will began; but Mrs. Lumkin had caught sight of Emmy.

"Oh!" she said, or screamed. "Why hello there, Emily!"

"Hello, Betsy," Emmy said calmly. "Nice to see you." She had a great advantage over every other faculty wife at Convers in that she had known Betsy Lumkin since childhood. This local terror was for her only the wife of a minor acquaintance of her parents, and she had long ago absorbed their mildly patronizing attitude toward all Lumkins.

"Nice to see you," Mrs. Lumkin returned automatically in her harsh New England voice. "Well! What's happened to the Fenns?"

"They're not here," Will said. "I dropped over earlier and Miranda asked me to stay and wait for you. She forgot that this was the morning she had promised to take her children to the Christmas play at Charles's school."

"Oh, the children had to go to the play," Mrs. Lumkin said, not quite neutrally. "Well, she might have let me know. Lord God, what a wreck. I just can't take it in."

"Won't you sit down?" Will said.

"Thank you." Mrs. Lumkin sat on the arm of a chair and patted down her permanent curls, which had been turned inside out by the wind. "Euh," she sighed. "I had hoped it wouldn't be so bad, but the place is absolutely ruined. The walls, the ceiling, the linoleum, the refrigerator! You know that entire kitchen was painted scarcely a year or two ago. The soot! But soot at least can be painted over. But look at those walls, all wet and broken down, they'll have to be completely rebuilt. Really, I often think firemen do more damage than fires. Chopping down the walls and breaking the windows and pouring water into everything; so stupid and destructive. Why can't they leave things alone?" she rhetorically asked, but Emmy answered her.

"Golly, Betsy. If they'd let it alone, the whole house would have probably burned down."

"Well," Mrs. Lumkin said. "I suppose Julian Fenn isn't around either." Will shook his head. "My husband wants to talk to him about the insurance."

"I hope the college is insured," Will said.

"Naturally. Well, I'd better be going. You'll tell Miranda I stopped by, won't you, Will?"

"Delighted." He rose, smiling. "Shall I give her any message?"

"No. I'll call her later. Oh, and here are some things I brought along. Well, I'll just leave the basket. I can pick it up later."

"Things?"

"Oh, you know, food. I thought they might be short."

"What an excellent idea," Will said, taking the basket.

"Well, I just thought they might need something." Will looked at her admiringly. "When are you going to come and play for us again?" she inquired.

"Whenever you ask me." Will smiled at her as if she were fifteen years younger and prettier; she smiled back, with large teeth. This irritated Emmy.

"Some evening over the holidays? Will you be in town?"

"I think so. Until after Christmas, anyway."

"You must come to dinner, then. Bill has to go to some meetings in New York, so I can't plan anything now, but I'll call you."

"Don't forget."

"Don't be silly. Nice to see you again, Emily," she added flatly. "Give my best to your parents."

Mrs. Lumkin went out. Her steps could be heard walking about in the kitchen for a while, and then the back door shut.

Will whistled a theme from Wagner. "Fun and games," he said. "Wasn't she furious." He sank back onto the sofa and picked up his glass.

"But what was she doing here? I thought it was Bill Lumkin who was in charge of faculty housing."

"Yes, that's what it says in the catalogue."

"It's really her all along?"

"You surprise me. You mean Betsy didn't come to call on you the first Sunday you were settled in your little college house?"

"We're not living in a college house," Emmy said.

"Lucky you."

"Does she do it to everyone?"

"Oh, yes. Always unannounced, too. She likes to catch them *au naturel*. Of course she claims it's because she doesn't want them to go to any trouble. She comes all dressed up, too, in a hat and gloves, right from church sometimes. Poor Miranda hasn't got over it yet; well, you can imagine what it was like here the Fenns' first Sunday afternoon."

Emmy laughed, wondered whether Betsy had been to call on Will and where he lived, but did not ask. "She *was* in an absolute state," she said.

"Yes. I wonder why, you know. It's not her house."

"Still, if she's really in charge, she'll have to find the painters and carpenters and plumbers and heaven knows what and make all the arrangements, and that'll be a frightful bore."

"You don't know Betsy. She loves making arrangements and bossing workmen around."

"I do too. I've known her since I was ten."

"Oh? What was she like when you were ten?"

To tell the truth, Emmy could not remember. "She used to come on weekends to play golf with the men," she finally said. "She never paid much attention to us. I suppose she didn't like children."

"Let's hope so."

"Why let's hope so?"

"Because she's never had any."

"That's true," said Emmy, considering it for the first time. But she did not want to have to feel sorry for Betsy Lumkin. "Still, she could always have adopted some."

Will said nothing. Emmy said nothing, and began to feel nervous and embarrassed again. She started to reach for her coat to leave.

"That was nice, the way you took her up about the firemen," Will said. "So polite."

She laughed, pleased.

"More?" He held up the sherry.

"Oh, no. No thank you."

"Well then, perhaps I will."

"You didn't offer Betsy any sherry," Emmy remarked.

"I know. I did think of it, but it occurred to me that it might be the college's sherry." She looked blank. "The Fenns found a whole case stored down in the cellar when they moved in." He put his glass down and turned to Mrs. Lumkin's basket. "Let's see what's here. Very heavy. Baked beans. What's this other package? Oh, brown bread, of course. 'You've burned down my house, so I sentence you to live on bread and water and beans.' Well, look, knives and forks too, that's thoughtful." He raised the lid and thoughtfully began to eat. "It's not bad, you know. Have some?"

"I couldn't," Emmy said. "Really. I've got to be going. I don't believe Miranda will come. Heavens, it's nearly time to pick up Freddy. Please, don't get up."

Will got up. "Let me," he said, taking her coat from Emmy and holding it for her. "By the by," he added, as she put her arms in the sleeves, "what I told you about Richard's starting the fire, don't spread that around. It could do them a lot of harm."

"Of course not," Emmy said, looking round over her shoulder, for she felt uneasy with Will standing behind her holding onto her coat. "I won't tell a soul."

"Thank you." Will let go, turned aside, and slumped back against the wall.

"Well, goodbye," Emmy said. Will, looking out of the window, replied inaudibly. She went out.

The following day, which was Saturday, Holman stopped work about three in the afternoon. He had felt a cold coming on for days, and though he never gave in to his colds to the extent of going to bed, he thought he would go home early. Emmy and Freddy would be pleased to see him, and he would have a hot bath followed by a good stiff drink, something with lemons and whisky and hot water.

To make sure of being able to carry out this fantasy he drove first to the grocery where he bought two lemons, and then to the package store for a bottle of whisky. In spite of his headache, and a sore throat he felt starting, he enjoyed walking about, choosing what he wanted from the display on the shelves, speaking to the clerks. He admired the sun through the windows, the snow fresh on the common, the gangs of well-dressed children coming out of school.

In front of the package store he ran into Mrs. Rabbage, Emmy's cleaning woman. She was dressed as usual in odds and ends of old wool clothes, with a pink plaid scarf over her hair and black galoshes.

"Well, if it isn't Mr. Turner!" she exclaimed loudly. "How you been?"

"Fine," Holman said. "How've you been keeping yourself, Mrs. R.?"

"Oh, just fine. All this snow of course I've been feeling it some in my hip joints nights but the sun shining so strong most days I got to be thankful for it isn't too bad." She rested her bag of groceries on her hip as if in demonstration and Holman made an appropriate face. He got on well with Mrs. Rabbage, better than Emmy did in fact, and it was apparent that she approved of him. Since Holman had not grown up with the Turners' servants, it did not bother him that Mrs. Rabbage was unlike them. She was a lot like old Mrs. Mitchell who used to live across the alley back in Chicago. He fell easily into conversation with her, or rather listening to her. "Well and how you doing these days?" Mrs. Rabbage asked. "I didn't see you yesterday when I was out to the house."

"No, I had to work late."

"Eh you sure give them their money's worth up there at the college. I hope they know enough to be grateful for it that's all."

"So do I." Holman laughed.

"Well, it's not everybody will do that. I see plenty around this town strong as horses believe me the minute the boss's back is turned they go flop onto their rear ends they haven't got the strength to do a single thing, they do say brain work tires you out but you got to face it money's money and I would think shame to do the same if I was them. You going on home now?"

"I think so. I've got a little cold coming on. Better not stand too near me, Mrs. R."

"Aw, I'm not scared, Mr. Turner. There's germs flying round in the air all over the place this time of year, pneumonia and bronchitis and strep and every kind of thing, what I say is if they're going to get you they're going to get you. Say, you do look kinda peaked at that. Not real bad, just kinda wrung out."

"That's just how I feel," Holman agreed. He did not mind Mrs. Rabbage's comments on his and everybody's health, though Emmy did. Emmy was embarrassed to be told by Mrs. Rabbage that she looked "busting with health"; she resented even more being told that she looked poorly, as much as if it had been said of Freddy. In some ways she thought of her body as a favorite or only child.

"Well you take good care of yourself," Mrs. Rabbage said.

"Don't worry, Mrs. R., I will," Holman replied, glancing down and patting the bottle-shaped parcel.

"That's the way," she said, laughing loudly and, shifting her bag of groceries, started away. "Say," she added, turning back, "whaddayou think of that fire up to those friends of yours the other day, whaddyou think of that?"

"Yes, wasn't that something," Holman said a little impatiently. The wind up the street was cold, and he felt that he had exhausted his good will toward Mrs. Rabbage.

"It didn't surprise me none," she said. "Mrs. Lumkin should of known those people would do something like that some time. Crazy they are and always will be if you'll excuse my saying, I know Mrs. Turner's a friend of hers. But I been in there to clean for her and I know. Won't throw anything away, got closets full of junk you wouldn't believe, dirty old clothes, rugs, everything. Antiques. No good, the moths got into them long time ago. A regular firetrap the whole house. Oh, they're wild about it now up at the college I bet. Underinsured, that's what it was."

"Is that so."

"Well, it's always the way. Mean, those rich people are, think nothing ever going to happen to Them, think they can get away with something pinching the pennies that's what my nephew Ray says the one works over to the town hall and he gets a look at the records. He's not really my nephew only his mother married my husband's brother after his dad passed along."

Holman wanted to walk away; he made a face. Mrs. Rabbage misinterpreted it. "Yep. From T.B. it was, runs in the family they say but he hasn't shown any of the signs yet, my nephew I mean."

"Um," Holman said, "I—"

"So I'd better be getting along. You take good care of that cold like I said."

Convers College looked very well as Holman drove back past the campus. The sun stood low in the sky, giving the brick a golden tone. It had snowed lightly the day before, and the roofs and cornices were white against the most brilliant postcard blue. Behind the music building children in red caps and mittens were sledding down the hill. The whole scene was beautiful but unreal; it reminded Holman of expensive Christmas cards.

He remembered very well what Christmas had looked like near Garfield Park in Chicago where he had grown up; in the streets of rundown two- or four-family frame houses painted gray or buff to match the smut that hung in the air. The weather there did not cooperate with holidays: snow seldom fell until after the first of the year, and then it turned dirty immediately. Some of the houses on the street would have decorations in their front windows: electrical stars, red cardboard candles with flame-shaped bulbs, green plastic wreaths. The cleaners and the delicatessen would repeat these themes in more elaborate ways, and the druggist would put out his boxes of cards and ribbons and tinsel. At school, Holman would help his classmates paint snowdrifts on the windows with white poster paint, and A MERRY CHRISTMAS AND A HAPPY NEW YEAR TO ALL would be spelled out around the walls in embossed silver letters. On the last day of school he would take home the present he had made for his mother in shop class, stopping at the drugstore to buy the most elaborate wrapping-paper and card he could find. It was always a difficult choice: he stood a long time before the rack, staring at the bright idealized pictures of Santa Claus and angels and winter scenes.

Now, driving home along the Hampshire Road, chilled and a little dizzy with fever, Holman felt as if he had stood looking so long that he had been drawn bodily into one of these painted landscapes. The mountains to the south were topped with symmetrical evergreens, the road curved prettily between snow-covered hills, and he passed white farmhouses and cottages, each with a wreath on its door.

It made him uncomfortable. He had felt the same thing the other day on a walk with Emmy and Freddy. About a quarter of a mile down the road back of their house he had found a pine cone under a tree. His first thought had been triumphant: Eureka! and then: How accurate, after all, were the hundreds of imitations and representations of pine cones I have seen. He held the real thing carefully in his gloved hand; it was a unique treasure. "See, a pine cone!" he called out importantly to Emmy and Freddy. But they stood at the edge of a pine woods. When Holman looked up he saw ahead under the trees two, five, ten, hundreds of pine cones, and he was not pleased. It seemed imbecilic that there should be so many here and so few in Garfield Park. Freddy, however, was delighted, and Emmy gathered her pockets full. They ran ahead of him into the woods, under the branches where the cones were strewn so thick that they could not help stepping on some of them, cracking and smashing them underfoot.

Perhaps it was his cold that made him feel this way. He was not usually made uncomfortable by the contemplation of natural beauty and abundance, quite the reverse. The stone-walled orchards heavy with apples, the long rows of pumpkins in the fields that he passed every day on his way to work earlier in the fall, he had admired greatly. He even thought sometimes that he was the only one in Convers who knew how to value them because he would never take them for granted. Not that he condemned the natives for doing so. Their innocence was as natural as the scenery; as necessary, too, for Convers would have been spoiled if everyone were as conscious as he.

Under the term "native," Holman included not only the local farmers and townspeople, but the greater part of the permanent Convers faculty, and perhaps most of all Emmy. Born under a cornucopia, she took order and beauty and abundance for granted; it was her climate. Wherever she went, she would create around her, simply because she could not imagine any other way to live, order and comfort—comfort raised, by money, to its highest degree. Of all her gifts, Holman loved best perhaps this one which he never mentioned to her, partly for fear of breaking the spell.

He turned into his driveway. The house had formerly been a farm; the barn, now the garage, was still painted barn red. Emmy had hung a wreath of cones and evergreen tied with red satin ribbon on the front door.

Her station wagon was not in the garage. He parked

beside the empty space, and let himself into the empty house. The lights were on, so no doubt she would be back soon. As he put down his packages in the kitchen and picked up the *Times*, he thought he heard a noise somewhere. He forgot it, went upstairs, took off his clothes, put on his bathrobe, and walked down the hall to the bathroom. The door, for some reason, was shut, so he opened it. The room was cloudy with steam; the tub was full to the brim with green bubbles, which he recognized as Emmy's Elizabeth Arden bubble bath, and in it were two little boys whom he recognized, after a moment, as Richard and Charles Fenn.

"What are you doing here?" he asked them.

"We're washing," said the larger boy.

"Waiting for our mommy," said the smaller boy, whose hair was full of green foam.

Holman glared at them. "Well, you can get out now," he said. "I'm going to have a bath."

"It's not polite to come into bathrooms without knocking and look at undressed people," Charles informed him, not moving.

"All right," Holman said. "I'll be back."

He stood about in the upstairs hall for a while, walking about with his headache and his sore throat and looking out of the windows to see if Emmy and Miranda were coming. But when he opened the door again, Charles and Richard Fenn were still in the bathtub. Charles was making designs in foam on the shower curtain and Richard was playing with Holman's shaving brush, walking it along the edge of the tub.

"Good, nice, brave little brush," he said to it.

"Come on, get out of that tub," Holman told them.

"We can't," Charles said.

"Why not?"

"We haven't got any clothes to put on. Mommy took them all to the laundrymat, and she told us to stay here till she got back. Oh, were they dirty."

"Our hot-water heater is hurt," Richard volunteered. "It got hurt in the fire and the man can't come to fix it till yesterday, so we can't wash anythings."

"No, tomorrow," Charles corrected.

"Oh. Tomorrow." Richard put more foam into his hair.

Holman looked around the bathroom. There was water

all over the floor, and a heap of wet towels, but no clothes.

"Listen," he began, but heard a door slam below. He went out and started for the stairway, making up statements. Halfway there he stopped, turned around, and went back into the bedroom and put his pants on underneath his bathrobe for the sake of his dignity and Miranda's modesty. He thought that he would have a drink now, before his bath.

Miranda was not downstairs; nobody was there except Julian Fenn, who was sitting on the kitchen table reading Holman's fraternity alumni magazine. He looked pale and dirty. He was wearing a black chesterfield coat, torn cotton slacks that looked as if they ought to have gone to the laundromat with Miranda, and galoshes. A dark red wood scarf was wound several times round his neck.

"Oh, hello there," Julian said. "Have you seen my wife anywhere?"

"No," Holman said, "but two of your children are upstairs in my bathtub."

"Oh, really?" Julian murmured, reading on. Holman clenched his teeth and started to open the package which contained the bottle. But he hesitated, considering that if he made himself a drink he would have to offer Julian one and then Julian would probably hang around the house for some time dranking his whisky. He stood facing the window, trying to make up his mind. The sun was setting, and the snow-covered ground outside was pale red, crossed with long dim shadows.

"Funny thing," Julian remarked; "all the alumni in this magazine seem to be either raising hogs or selling insurance."

"Look," Holman said. "Would you mind getting your kids out of our tub? I want to take a bath. They say they haven't got any clothes to put on, but I'll find them something."

"All right," Julian agreed. "You want to take it now?"

"Yes, now."

They went upstairs. With some difficulty Charles and Richard Fenn were removed from the tub, dried, and dressed, one in Freddy's bathrobe and one in Emmy's Japanese kimono.

"It's very hard for a boy of my age to wear ladies' clothes," Charles protested.

75

"I'm cold," Richard said. "This bathrobe is too small. I want my mommy."

"You can go down and sit in the kitchen," Holman said. "I'll turn up the heat." They all went downstairs and he adjusted the thermostat. Julian had somehow got hold of Holman's *Times* and now he began to read it. Emmy and Miranda had still not arrived.

"Emmy and Miranda still haven't arrived," Holman said. "Do you have any idea when they're coming?"

Julian shook his head. "Nope," he said, reading.

"Say, your voice sounds funny today, doesn't it, Mr. Turner?" Charles remarked.

"It does, you know," Julian said. "Have you got a cold?"

"Yes, I have a cold," Holman said. He went upstairs and took off his pants and locked the bathroom door behind him and took off his bathrobe and turned on the taps and climbed into the tub. There was no hot water.

* * *

Allen Ingram to Francis Noyes

December 16

Convers is in the grip of Christmas—the old-fashioned kind with sleds and carols. Two main topics of conversation: 1) Where one is going for the holidays ("Oh, I'll be spending the Day with my family," I say cheerily, and they smile cheerily back, because they can't see Mother and Roy); 2) the fire I mentioned previously. Nothing happens here as a rule, so they make the most of what they have, and everyone's debating the great Question: should Julian Fenn be held morally, physically, financially, etc., responsible for his kitchen's burning down?

Each one considers it in his own style: I am even getting a new line on Oswald McBane, the head of the English Department and patent Great Old Man of Convers. Or Great Old Bear; he is far more bear than man. Think of him as that big gray grizzly up on his hind legs in the habitat group at the Natural History Museum, the one Jane liked so much. McBane has just that profuse, dead-looking gray fur, heavy paws hanging down, fiercely quizzical expression. The first time we met, as you recall, he did nothing at all but grunt.

Yet it is McB who counts in this department—the rest are nothing. The two other full professors, Knight and Baker, I have christened collectively Tweedledumdee. Trite, I admit, and if you could see them you would say it was inappropriate too. Knight is tall, lean, dark, with a thin, elegant, stupid wife; Baker is short, plump, fair, with a fat, dowdy, clever wife. But they weren't smart enough for Me. I soon found out that they are really twins in disguise. My first clue was that they have each other's centuries: Knight, so melancholy-metaphysical, specializes in the Victorian novel, while Baker, who looks like Thackery, is "in" the Elizabethan period.

This afternoon I was invited to sit in on a meeting of the big course that McBane runs, and what I discovered is that he absolutely detests Billy the Boy Dean; quite a feat, really. We were all sitting about before the meeting began and someone came out with the information that the college stood to lose money from the Fenn fire because Lumkin hadn't taken out enough insurance. "You don't say?" McBear grunted, and positively roared with laughter for three minutes. All the other members of the course, who are nothing but instructors, dutifully laughed too, except for Julian, who merely smiled, and a little man from Wisconsin who actually frowned. McBane saw him, stopped laughing, and growled: "Would you kindly get up and close the window, Mr. Green, and contribute something to this course?" "Yes, sir," said Mr. Green. The merest slap from McBear's forepaw can knock the little animals off their perches.

All this has set me to thinking—do I perhaps not practice enough economy of both cause and effect in my writing? If I were doing it, I probably would have taken care to burn the Fenns' house down completely—or more likely, I'm afraid, have one of my characters imagine the entire conflagration as he strikes a match on the stove. But comedy does not consist only of exaggeration; it can as well be an imbalance of ends and means. . . . Perhaps I should try a comic novel next.

I could do it here, if anywhere. Usually I feel myself dragged into life too suddenly and deeply (if only by my sympathies) either to giggle or gasp as I go under. I find it impossible to strike a comic attitude except toward persons and actions so simple and despicable that it would shame us both to mention them. The jokes one makes in washrooms, bassoon solos accompanied by the gurgle of polluted waters. But here in Convers, my tourist's position gives me, perhaps, the necessary interested detachment.

But writing comedy is a dangerous project. One extends oneself so much further, really, and lays oneself open to the fatal accusation of having no sense of humor, to which there is no comeback. The tragic position is much more impregnable; critics who are not moved by one's tragic works can always be called shallow; they have, obviously, no sense of compassion.

It's snowing again. How typical of it. I long for New York, for Friday. Expect me for supper.

CHAPTER

5

THE DAY BEFORE VACATION, EMMY AND FREDDY STOPPED by the Fenns' house to wish Miranda and the children a Merry Christmas. In the kitchen, most of the debris from the fire had been removed, but the walls were still streaked with soot and the icebox blistered; the broken glass in the back door had been covered with a blanket. The half-burned bulletin board was thick with Christmas cards. Miranda sat by the stove, her head in her hands, looking paler and plainer than Emmy had ever seen her; against her red hair, her skin was positively green. She looked up when Emmy came in and smiled wanly.

"We only dropped by for a moment," Emmy apologized.

"Oh no, do stay. Everything's so depressing here. Sit down; have some coffee."

"What's the matter?" Emmy sat and began to unzip Freddy's snowsuit.

"Oh, everything. Maybe if you could talk to me about Europe or the theater or something it would take my mind off it all."

Emmy was unable to speak at random on these topics. She opened her mouth a couple of times and shut it again. Freddy wriggled in her lap.

"What it is, is Julian had a fight with the Lumkins," Miranda finally said.

"A fight? Really? There you are, Freddy, run along and see if you can find Richard and Katie."

Freddy ran along; grown-up talk did not interest him. "Now tell me," Emmy said.

"It was awful. Mrs. Lumkin told Julian the fire was all our fault and we'll have to pay for it."

"No!"

"Yes. That's so ridiculous, it's just vindictive; how could we ever pay for a thing like that? We're in debt up to our hair as it is, it's going to be a very depressing Christmas.

But the awful thing is, too, Julian was so rude to them. I think it might have been all right if he had apologized for our making so much trouble, oh, and perhaps said he'd help with the repairs; but he was so rude. Cold and sarcastic, you don't know how he gets. I kept on trying to interrupt him but of course it wasn't any good. Oh, for instance he told her that if she knew anything about children she would have put a better stove in here in the first place and there would never have been a fire." Miranda's voice quavered with indignation and tears.

"Well, maybe he's right," Emmy said, getting up and looking for a coffee cup. People who got hysterical over minor catastrophes always made her impatient and nervous. She missed in the Fenns the half-joking, self-deprecatory tone in which her own friends and relatives described all but their worst troubles. Nor was this the deep, controlled emotion proper to a real misfortune. Miranda was whimpering and choking like a housemaid. Not knowing what else to do, Emmy turned round and took a cup and saucer out of the dish drainer. "Oh, Charles has bought another goldfish," she said to change the subject. "What a pretty one."

"Yes," Miranda said constrainedly. "Actually," she added after a pause, "it's mine. I know it was silly, but I couldn't bear to see the first one swimming around in there all alone. It seemed so restless."

"But they always do. Look at them now. Do they have names?" Tired of holding the cup and saucer, she put them on the table.

"Fish and Charles Fish," Miranda said. "Charles has no imagination. Oh heavens, let me pour you some coffee, I'm sorry. I don't mean to be inhospitable, I'm just so awfully distraught."

"But surely it's not that important. The Lumkins will get over being angry."

"I don't think so. They found out somehow it was Richard who started the fire. You know Richard started the fire on purpose, I suppose. It was a big secret, but everybody seems to know it."

Emmy said nothing. It couldn't be my fault, she thought. I didn't tell anybody except Holman, and he promised not to tell. He doesn't like Julian and he doesn't like Miranda; but he promised *me* not to tell.

"I haven't told you the worst thing," Miranda said,

although she had. "They sort of threatened us that they would make Julian leave Convers. Mrs. Lumkin said that he was persisting in an irresponsible attitude which didn't seem suitable for someone who was in a teaching position here, or something like that."

"What did Mr. Lumkin say?"

"He said he agreed with her."

"Oh, no. Bill Lumkin?"

"Yes. So I don't know, maybe we'll be leaving."

"Oh, Miranda, you don't really think they could fire Julian over a thing like this. It's simply incredible."

"They don't have to fire him. All they have to do is not promote him. It's usually up or out here after three years."

"But does Bill decide who's going to be promoted? I thought the English Department did that."

"Yes, but the president has to approve the appointment and if Mr. Lumkin tells him not to, maybe he won't, who knows?"

"I'm sure they would never do a thing like that, Miranda."

"Maybe. Julian's going to try to see McBane about it this afternoon. There is one good thing. Or maybe it's a bad thing: McBane hates Lumkin. And I suppose Lumkin must know it."

"It will probably all turn out all right."

"Possibly."

"Golly, I wish there were something I could do."

"Thank you. I'm going to make an image of Mrs. Lumkin and stick pins into it."

Emmy laughed, relieved at this lightening of tone. "You know, I'm sure the Lumkins won't really make you pay for the damages," she said. "How could they, anyway?"

"I don't know. She just started talking about how the college could sue us if they felt like it. It was awful. Julian says it was only a threat, of course; he won't take anything seriously."

"Could they really sue you? I mean, legally?"

"I don't know. Will said he'd try to find out for us. He knows some lawyer in town he was going to see. I'm hoping he'll come by soon."

Emmy liked the idea of seeing Will Thomas again; she congratulated herself that she had put on lipstick and done up her hair; he would see that she did not always go around looking like a Campfire Girl. "It's always convenient to know a lawyer," she said. This was one of her father's dicta.

"Oh, Will knows everybody in town. He should, he's always hanging around down there somewhere. It's too bad, really." She got up and began to look for something in the cupboards.

"Too bad?"

"It's such an awful waste of time, when he ought to be working." Climbing on her stool, Miranda investigated the top shelves.

"Oh." Emmy's voice was flat; she was already so opposed to overwork among college instructors that she could hardly disapprove much of the opposite fault.

From the stool, where she stood like a stork, her long scrawny legs in gray cotton stockings, Miranda looked around. "No, seriously," she said. "Will's hopeless. He hasn't done any work, I mean any work at all, for five years. All he does is go around town seducing girls. He hasn't written a word, I suppose I should say a note, in all that time." She climbed down. "It's a mistake for him to be in Convers at all, there's no musicians or concerts here. Not even any good students. He ought to be in some big city. It's a sort of refuge here, that's all. Mr. Oska got him the job out of admiration for his early work. People don't realize he's given up writing, they just remember that they heard somewhere someday that William Thomas was a promising young composer. But he doesn't do anything now except play the piano now and then, and talk."

"I never heard that he was a promising young composer," Emmy said. "What did he compose? I mean, was he really good?"

"I wouldn't know. Modern music all sounds the same to me. Hideous mechanical noises; like machines being tortured— Oh, heavens, what is it now?" she said to Richard, who had just come into the kitchen sobbing loudly. He was followed by Freddy and Katie, shouting:

"Katie bit me!"

"Mommy, Richard pushed me down!"

"They don't play fair shares in this house!"

Miranda and Emmy turned toward the disturbance, each remonstrating with her own children. "Really, if you can't be nice to your company, nobody will want to come

82

to your house," Miranda said, while Emmy remarked: "Freddy, if you can't play without fighting simply all the time, nobody will ask you to visit them." The argument settled and the children sent out, they turned back, to see Will standing in the kitchen door watching them.

"Speak of the devil," he said. "Hello, Emily."

"Hello there," Emmy pronounced self-consciously. She hated to be overheard speaking in the special voice modeled on that of her headmistress at St. Kit's which she used for disciplining Freddy.

"How do you know we were speaking of you?" Miranda asked.

"I hoped so." Will shut the door (the broken glass rattled in the frame) and came over to the table. "Good things, I hope."

"No, just facts."

"Ugh." He pretended to shudder. "Is there any coffee by any chance?"

"I'll heat it up." Miranda pulled the pot to the front of the stove.

"That's a nice shirt," Will said to Emmy.

"Oh, thank you. I found it in Bermuda."

Will looked over at Miranda and raised his eyebrows; she did not respond. He sighed and sat down.

"And so, all the time I was down in John Moore's office working my tongue to the bone for you and your family, you were sitting here slandering me to this innocent woman."

"Oh, you saw Mr. Moore," Miranda exclaimed. "What did he say?"

"You want to hear now?"

"Yes, yes. Go ahead, Emmy knows all about it; I just told her." Will looked at Emmy and half smiled, perhaps apologetically, she thought; perhaps suspiciously. She smiled nervously back.

"I'll spare you all the legal foolery he went through. And, by the way, don't let on to anyone that I consulted John for you. He's all worked up about the next primary elections, wants to be town dogcatcher or something. Before he would tell me anything he made me promise not to say where I got the advice."

"Yes, yes," Miranda said impatiently.

"So. The thing seems to be, starting a fire is a tort;

and parents aren't legally responsible for the torts of their minor children."

There were pleased exclamations from both Miranda and Emmy.

"But then, on the other hand, there's something called criminal negligence. When an adult lets a child have possession of a dangerous implement. If you gave Richard or Charles a loaded rifle to play with, for instance. Or if a child was known to have started other fires, he said, then its parents could be sued for criminal negligence."

"He hasn't started any other fires."

"Then that's all right," Emmy said. "I'm sure you're completely safe."

"Unless you wanted to call that stove a dangerous implement."

"Hateful thing," Miranda said, kicking the stove. "And do you know, when we first moved in here I was completely enchanted with it. Oh, lord." She snatched the coffee pot up just as it boiled over. "I'm so sorry. That just shows you. Do you still want some?"

"Please." Will held out his cup.

"If the stove is a dangerous implement, you could sue the college yourselves for letting children near it," Emmy suggested.

Will laughed. "Absolutely right," he said. "Why don't you? . . . Miranda, what in Christ's name are you doing?"

"Making a waxen image," Miranda replied. She held up a lump of candle wax, worked roughly into the shape of a body with head and arms, and then held it out over the stove.

"Going to roast your enemies over a slow flame? Which enemy is that?"

"Mrs. Lumkin, of course." Miranda began to pull out two legs from the main lump. "That is, it's going to be. I'll have to christen her."

"Golly, witchcraft." Emmy giggled. "What happens after it's finished, do you melt it and soften her heart so she won't want to sue you?"

"Mrs. Lumkin has no heart," Miranda said, "so that wouldn't work—I think I'll just stick pins into her. Not too many. I wouldn't want to kill her, but I'd like her to get sick enough to forget all about us." She bent up the ends of the legs to form feet. "There. Now what I need

84

is—" The phone rang. "Oh, bother it." She got up and flapped out of the room in her old slippers.

Left together in the kitchen, Will and Emmy looked at each other; both smiled.

"More coffee?" he said.

"No thank you. I'm just about to go, actually."

"You're always just about to go," he groaned, mock-tragic.

"Isn't it depressing, about the Lumkins," Emmy said.

"Very depressing." Will slid down in his chair again, his sheepskin-lined coat drooping onto the floor.

"I simply don't understand it. Why would the college want to sue them? Why don't they just collect the insurance?"

"That's what I thought at first too; but today I found out something. The house was underinsured. John Moore told me. Christ knows how he found out, one of his pals in the town hall I suppose. The insurance policy hadn't been changed since 1938. Lumkin's going to look damned silly if it comes out. They can't get half what they'll need."

"And that's why they want to make Julian and Miranda pay for it."

"It looks like it."

"What if they won't? Will the Lumkins have to pay?"

"I doubt it. They probably couldn't, anyway."

"Oh, of course they could. It won't cost much to fix this up."

"They're not as rich as they like to look." Scuff, scuff: Miranda reentered the kitchen. "They live pretty high." Miranda sat down in a chair and put first her hand, then her arms, flat out in front of her on the kitchen table. "Is everything all right?"

"No."

"What's happened?" Emmy asked.

"That was Julian. He just saw McBane."

"And?"

"And the Department recommended him for an assistant professorship, but the administration hasn't confirmed the appointment yet; and Lumkin told McBane they're probably not going to confirm it."

"Simply because of that fire?" Emmy asked.

"That's what he said."

"How utterly disgusting! I can't believe it."

"I can," Miranda replied. "After what the Lumkins

said, I expected it. McBane told Julian he'd do what he could for him, but not to expect too much. I suppose he means he'll speak to President King when he gets back from Washington next month. If that doesn't work the only thing he could do would be to appeal the case to the Faculty Council and make a big scandal."

"Hell, you don't want to stay in this God-forsaken village anyway," Will said.

"It's not that. But where'll we go? Who's going to want us?"

"Oh, come on. You know Julian won't have any trouble getting another job. He's got his degree and published articles and everything. It's not as if he were a bum like me."

"And, oh lord, the moving. You know, Emmy, we've moved six times in the last five years. And I don't get used to it, either; it's just worse every time. Oh, well."

There were noises of running and screaming, and Katie burst into the kitchen.

"Mommy, I want Freddy to go home!" she shouted, rushing at Miranda. "He won't play fair! He says he's going to rope me and brand me!"

Will laughed.

"Freddy," Emmy said to her son, who now stood by the door, red-faced and scowling, with a piece of clothesline in his hand. "You play nicely with Katie, Freddy," she said. "Will, please stop laughing. He'll think it's all a joke." Will did not.

"I don't like Katie, Mummy," Freddy said. "I don't like to play with little girls."

"I'm not a little girl," said Katie. "Don't you call me a little girl!"

"Little girl, little girl."

"That's not a nice way to talk, Freddy," Emmy said. "Katie's a nice, big girl."

"I am not!" Katie screamed. "I'm a cowgirl! Don't you know anything, you stupids?"

"I am not a stupid, you stupid bastard!" Freddy shouted, breaking out into the profanity that he had picked up from Holman.

"Katie!" "Freddy!" screamed the mothers, slapping their children.

Will laughed more than ever. Katie began to cry, and Miranda picked her up; Freddy hit back at Emmy, but since she was expecting this, she was able to ward off the blow. Charles and Richard, who had now arrived, stood watching the scene.

"Freddy wasn't going to hurt you," Charles told Katie. "He just wants you to pretend to be a cow for a little while and then it'll be your turn and he'll be the cow and you can rope him."

"Perfectly fair," Will put in. "I always do it that way myself."

"I want my turn first," Katie said, choking on a sob.

"No, I get the first turn," Freddy said. "I thought of it."

"We have to be going home, anyway," Emmy said.

"Oh, don't go yet," Will said.

"No, don't go yet," Miranda said. "You can give Freddy the first turn, Katie. After all, he's the company."

"I don't want to. Everybody's always the company. Why aren't I ever the company?"

"Because this is your house."

"It is not Katie's house," Richard said. "It's Mrs. Lumkin's mean old house. Mrs. Lumkin just lets us live in her mean old house because we pay her money."

"I really have to be going," Emmy said. "Golly, it's nearly four."

"Just time for a drink," Will said, getting up. "Miranda? It'll cheer you up—Emmy?"

"Oh no, no, I couldn't—Freddy, come on, love, here's your snowsuit. . . . Now the other leg. Come on. Miranda, I'm absolutely shocked by all that. I simply can't believe it. I'm sure there's something Julian can do, can't he write to the president or something?"

"What would he say? No—Oh, now what?" she exclaimed, as Katie began to howl again. She stooped down and put her arms around Katie, who sobbed and whispered into her ear. "Well, you told him to go home. (Now she's crying because Freddy's leaving, honestly.) No, he can't come tomorrow, he has to go away to the big city. . . . You should have thought of that before. There, there. Never mind, he'll be back again after Christmas. . . . I promise. Here, wipe your face, and then you tell him goodbye nicely."

"Goodbye," Katie sniffled.

"Goodbye, Katie," Emmy said. Freddy, already hanging on the doorknob, said nothing. "Goodbye, Miranda. Merry Christmas. Really, I'm sure things will turn out better than they look."

"Goodbye."

"I'll walk you to your car," Will said.

It was cold outside; the ground crackled with frost. The sun hung down in the trees, ready to set; it was the color and shape of a sticky red lollipop. Freddy ran ahead of them down the path.

"Honestly," Emmy said. "I think it's shocking about Julian's promotion. Do you really think he won't get it?"

"It looks that way."

"I wish I could do something," she said, stopping. "You know the Lumkins. Do you think it would do any good to speak to Betsy?"

"What would you say? It's a nice idea, but I can't see myself doing it."

"I can't either," Emmy sighed. "I know Betsy still thinks of me as an absolute child. She's polite to me because of Daddy, but— Oh."

"Oh?"

"I could speak to my father. He's a trustee here, you know."

"I know."

Excited by her idea, Emmy disregarded the ironic tone of this. "Really I think I will," she said. "Over vacation. Of course he could do something. I'll tell him the whole thing."

"That's very good of you," Will said, half seriously.

Emmy flushed. "Oh, it's nothing."

"Miranda won't think so."

"Oh, please don't say anything to her about it! Don't tell anyone. I don't want them to know until it's completely settled. Promise."

"All right." He gave her a smile which, nice as it was, was not quite one of complicity.

They walked on to the street. Parked next to Emmy's station wagon was a new red MG with one front fender bashed in. Freddy sat behind the wheel, pretending to drive.

"Come on out of there, Freddy," Emmy exclaimed. "That's not your car."

"That's all right," Will said. "He can't hurt it."

"Oh, is it yours?" Will nodded. "I didn't see it here the other day."

"It wasn't here. I only just got it out of the garage yesterday. Poor old thing." He stroked the hood.

"What happened?"

"It was in a crash."

"Were you in it?" Will nodded. "But didn't you get hurt?"

"Not to speak of. I never do, usually; I don't know why. It's a sort of fatality, I expect."

Feeling out of her depth, Emmy neglected to return the smile that went with this. She lifted Freddy out of the MG and opened the door of her car for him to climb in, which he did with protest. She didn't want to seem rude, so she turned back to Will and said:

"It doesn't look too bad. If you had that fender straightened, it would be quite all right, really."

"Ah, but it's the internal injuries." He put his hand on top of the door of Emmy's car, holding it open. Emmy got in. "Well, good luck with your mission." He shut the door, and put his elbows on the window sill, looking in. "Are you going to let me know what happens?"

"Certainly," she said uncertainly. "How shall I let you know?"

"I'll call you after vacation, shall I? What's a good time?"

"Oh, I don't know." Emmy felt flustered for some reason she could not identify. "Any morning."

"Okay. Well, so long, Mrs. Turner."

Will put his hand in through the window, and Emmy took it. A shiver ran up her arm. "Only not Tuesdays," she said. "Tuesdays I work at the Ladies' Exchange." She tried to give Will's hand a firm, friendly shake, but their relative positions made this difficult. So she smiled brightly and said: "Goodbye, Mr. Thomas! Merry Christmas!"

"Happy New Year," Will said. Leaning in, he kissed Emmy suddenly, quite hard, full on her mouth, which was still half open. For a moment she was too surprised to react; then, as he let go, she bounced away along the front seat. Smiling, quite undisturbed, Will stepped back. Emmy glanced around; in the back seat, Freddy sat looking at her with a solemn and inscrutable expression. Will waved; he was walking up toward the house. Since there was nothing else to do, she started the engine and drove home through the dusk.

Miranda was sitting in the same position when Will

returned. He shut the door, pulled up a chair, and sat down, sliding onto the end of his spine with his legs out toward the stove; she did not move.

"Don't take it so hard," he said. "Think of—"

"Yes, think of all the starving Algerians."

"I was going to say, think of me."

Will cocked his head up at Miranda in a way he had, but one she seldom saw. As a rule, Will did not treat her to the paraphernalia of charm he used on every other woman she had ever seen him with, including the elderly cashiers in Henry's Market and her own daughter Katie. The tone in which she now answered: "What shall I think of you?" showed that it was partly her doing that he did not.

"Well, I'll miss you. Who will I talk to if you leave?"

"Oh, you'll find somebody."

"*Whom* will I, I mean. I'm going to practice saying 'whom' now, like your friend does."

"*As* my friend does, you mean."

"Come on, one thing at a time. I'm just a poor southern hick, can't larn too fast."

Miranda laughed. "You do cheer me up," she said. She pushed back her hair, got up, opened the icebox and began to take out food. "You going to stay for supper?"

"If you'll have me."

"Oh, yes. It's only meat loaf."

"You need your friends around your meat loaf at a time like this. Besides, I've got to quit sponging on the Oskas for a while."

Will had an apartment in the house of Professor Georg Oska, the chairman (and only other member) of the Music Department. Professor Oska—he was the only member of the Convers faculty habitually addressed this way rather than as "Mr.," perhaps in deference to his European degrees, perhaps because his wife Mina always referred to him as The Professor—was a native of Austria. Some years ago, while a visiting lecturer at Harvard, he had heard some of Will's early compositions in the style of his dear friend Arnold Schoenberg. He had seldom met a more promising and agreeable young man, and he was sincerely upset when he heard that bad luck had entered Will's life, manifesting itself in marital troubles and peculiar ultramodernist scores. Luckily, the vacancy in the Music Department had occurred just at that time, and he was able to get Will away from the bad atmosphere of the city to recover at Convers. That had been four years ago, but it was still one of The Professor's dearest hopes that Will would begin composing again, in the style of Schoenberg. One must have patience; he had it, and also tact enough never to refer to these hopes. Meanwhile Mina continued to build up Will's strength with her good cooking, and Will taught the American games of baseball and football, according to the season, to their three fat little boys.

Miranda broke eggs into a bowl, poured cracker crumbs over them, and stopped to run her fingers up through her hair so that it stood out in all directions like pale-red straw. "Why oh why oh why did Fate ever send up a landlady like Mrs. Lumkin?" she asked. "Listen, Will, isn't she absolutely the most hateful woman who ever lived? . . . No, don't say anything, I know you can't agree, you like her dinners too much." It was a sore point with Miranda that Will not only ate the Lumkins' food, but praised it, and more often than he praised hers. If she had Mrs. Lumkin's money and Mrs. Lumkin's free time she felt she could do as well, if not better.

"And her piano."

"Her piano?"

"I just love her piano."

"She has a fancy piano? I suppose she would, she's so musical."

Will smiled to himself, but did not elaborate. It was one of his most private jokes. The Lumkins' piano was a good one, a Chickering grand. It was in fairly good tune, too, with one exception: C-sharp above high C was nearly half a tone flat. Will would not have mentioned this to Betsy for the world; it gave him great pleasure as it was. When he was invited for dinner or at a large party he especially like to play Chopin's C-sharp minor waltz. He performed it brilliantly, with what were almost drum-roll effects in the bass. That for you, Dean William Wigglesworth Lumkin, and your charming wife Mrs. William Wigglesworth Lumkin, he thought. At certain other times he would play only pieces which left the flaw unrevealed. Will had several private musical jokes of this sort. It sometimes amused him, sometimes appalled him, more often both, that he was almost the only person in Convers who would ever see (or rather, hear) them.

Buttering the pan for the meat loaf, Miranda said: "Do you think McBane will be able to do anything for Julian?"

"Christ knows," Will sighed. "Do you think he really wants to?"

"I suppose I do, rather. I've always had the feeling he likes Julian. Oh, nothing he's ever said, but you know one can sense these things. For instance, once we'd had the fire, I quite expected Mrs. Lumkin to behave this way. She's been against us ever since we moved in." Miranda fitted the meat loaf into the pan. "But one can't always tell. Dean Lumkin, now. That was a nasty one. I felt he would take our side, calm her down. But all he did was agree with her, he said just the same things. Of course he was much nicer about it."

"It's the same tune; don't let yourself be fooled by different performances," Will said, quoting himself.

"But the performance does make a difference. Heavens, a musician ought to think so."

"In art it does. In life, it's just decoration. 'Miranda Fenn, I am going to send you to the county poorhouse!' doesn't sound any better if it's set by Verdi and sung by Callas."

His rather good imitation of Callas was lost on Miranda, who only said: "I think she would like to send us to the county poorhouse. But I can't believe Dean Lumkin would. Why, even Julian thought he was his pal, until today."

"Everybody thinks he's their pal. Why shouldn't they? He thinks he's everybody's pal. He loves Convers and everyone in it so much he can't stay in his office, he has to go out and walk around the campus spreading joy. 'I'm in my heaven, all's right with your world.' "

Miranda put dishes in the sink and sat down. "Still, it's an achievement," she said, "with a wife like that, never to be unpleasant to anyone."

"He doesn't have to be unpleasant," Will said. "He makes her do it for him. Anyway, what's he got to be unpleasant about? He's got a good job, he's practically president of Convers College. He will be some day, I imagine, if he ever grows up. He's got lots of money and a big house and everybody loves him."

"Except you."

"Oh, well. One ex-musician."

Miranda did not take this up, though she knew Will

would have liked her to. She did say: "People who are all-round successful that way irritate me too, really. I don't mind the ones who've made their way with ambition or talent or hard work. I admire that. It's the ones who just float up to the top like great balloons, without even trying. I bet when Dean Lumkin was born his mother looked at him and said: 'Just what I've always wanted, a beautiful big baby boy,' and it's been that way ever since."

"That's what's the matter with me," Will said. "When I arrived my parents probably took one look and said: 'Well, here it is, and Christ, isn't it ugly.' If it hadn't been for me my mother could have gone on with her singing, and—" Will broke off, irritated, for Miranda had left the kitchen in the middle of his sentence. She had heard the story of his unfortunate childhood before, but still.

"I thought they were too quiet for this time of day," she said, coming back in. "They were cutting all the fur off Freddy Turner's bear that he left here. I hope he isn't especially fond of it. Heaven knows what I'll ever say to Emmy."

"She'll be nice about it, won't she?"

"Oh, I'm sure she will. She is so nice."

"She is. What's her husband like?"

"I like him too. He's very serious, you know, works hard."

"What's he look like?"

"Oh, big, good-looking sort of boyish face. Curly brown hair."

"That's how it always is," Will said. "Every time I meet a really attractive woman, it turns out she's married and utterly happy."

Miranda took up a grapefruit half and began to cut round it with a little curved knife. "I don't think Emmy's so utterly happy," she said.

"Oh? Has she told you so?"

"Not in so many words. But she complains about how Holman works all the time, that he's not home enough and when he is he doesn't talk to her."

"Neglects her, hmm. That's too bad. A girl like that ought not to be left sitting in the house all day, she needs attention, fresh air, exercise, entertainment."

"In fact, you."

"You really think she needs me?" Will glanced up at

Miranda, and she down at him; a peculiar look crossed her face, half a smile.

"I don't know," she said, shrugging her narrow shoulders.

Will stared at the stove, considering. "Do the Turners live in town?"

"No, out the Hampton Road. Way out, just before you turn off for the ski tow."

"What, in that big white house with the wagon wheels out front?"

"Um."

"Whew."

"Well, her father's a trustee. I expect they have money. Stop that!" Miranda shoved the grapefruit out of Will's way. "These are for supper."

"Maybe I'll go call on her." Will said this very, very casually; nevertheless Miranda looked up at once.

"Oh, you will? What does that mean?"

"Nothing."

"She's a bit out of your usual class," Miranda said. Though not even she knew of all the games he played, Will had quite a local reputation for his exploits among lively shopgirls and college secretaries. ("Opportunity is a great aphrodisiac," he was fond of saying; "especially for opportunists.")

Will's face changed, but not his voice. "I love big, beautiful, silly girls," he said to Miranda, who was none of these things. She cut round a grapefruit, put it on a plate, and took up another one. "You suggested it first, you know," he offered.

"I didn't." But Miranda smiled.

"You did."

"Besides, she's married. I thought you had a rule against married women."

"Well, not exactly a rule. I try to avoid them."

"By going out the Hampton Road and knocking on their front doors?" Will said nothing. "Emmy's so, I don't know, so innocent," she went on. "If you went out there a hundred times I don't think it would ever cross her mind that you'd come to seduce her."

"Then she'll be quite, quite safe," Will said. "You've forgotten my other rule: Women are not seduced; men are elected. I'm not going to attack her." He paused. "Maybe I won't even go."

"What about Avis in the bank?"

"Oh, that's all over. Her boy friend in the Marines is coming home for Christmas. They might even get married if he has enough leave. You know that was never anything."

"And I suppose you'll give Avis and her boy friend a silver-plated tea service for a wedding present."

"Electric blanket."

"What?"

"I suggested a silver-plated tea service, but Avis said she'd rather have an electric blanket. She likes to be warm in bed."

Miranda made a face, then laughed.

"How long until supper?"

"About half an hour. Julian should be home by then."

"I think I'll go out and do a little shopping. I thought I might get us some wine to celebrate Julian's promotion with."

"Thanks."

"It's nothing." Will got up, putting on his coat. He paused at the door. "Red?"

"I suppose."

Will shut the door behind him, and then opened it again. Putting his head in, he said: "Don't forget, whatever happens it was your idea."

"Don't be silly," Miranda said, but only to the door; Will was gone.

* * *

Allen Igram to Francis Noyes

December 25

Christmas afternoon in Palm Beach. We are all exhausted with smiling. Wastebaskets crushed full of wrapping paper and ribbon and foil, green, pink, mauve, off the packages we gave each other this morning. I suspect Roy, like me, would like to cram his presents in there too, expensive as they are. (Mother is simply planning how she will exchange hers.) I, for example, have a new lighter, too heavy, too silver, engraved with vulgarly tasteful abstract designs. I should blush to use it, even when quite alone. Of course it was well meant: "Poor Boy, lighting his cigarettes with those kitchen matches last time he was here; I know just what to get him for Christmas." And hard as I tried, she doesn't like my Gift either, two glass pigeons from Jensen that she was in raptures over last spring when she saw them in the *New Yorker*. Perhaps pigeons have gone out suddenly. But we all try so hard! We are so full of good intentions and good manners! Mother's oohs and ahhs as she undid my package, the moues of delight she felt she had to make, and all the time I could *see* it going through her tiny mind that Jensen's has no branch in Palm Beach so would it be too late to return them when she goes north in April, should she mail them back, would that be safe?

There is a pink plastic tree this year all done up in pink and mauve and silver balls—I am not exaggerating. When I remarked on it (*not* criticized) Mother told me they are all the rage in Palm Beach this year. A bit more expensive than the traditional kind, but *so* practical: they *never* shed, and when Christmas is over you simply dismantle them and store them in the plastic bag until next season. She didn't like it too well when I said why not go the whole hog and have a pink plastic palm. Oh, but, my dear Boy, it's the spirit of the thing. And all the time the weather hot, hot, hot, inside and out, with the heat of decomposition, the sea like consommé.

In the midst of all this, I find myself looking back on Convers with something like real affection. So cold there, so simple, so old-fashioned. Julian Fenn, the instructor whose house caught fire, has the rather attractive theory that it is a survival from the past, even the classical past: a little community supported by agriculture and education. With a transient population of slaves, I suggested; he wouldn't quite agree to that, but he did suggest that the place of the small harmless wars was taken by football and our other blood sports. This was at a hockey game, something I haven't seen for years. I came upon Fenn in the coldest, highest tier of the stands. Where I was too; hockey is quite beautiful if one sits far enough off to see only the ballet swoops and turns, and not the slime on the ice, the heavy red faces and bruised calves.

I asked Fenn if he shared my feelings, but he said no, he was afraid he was only sitting up there in the cold to avoid his colleagues. He thinks he is going to lose his job and is in the dismal position of having to wait until after vacation to find out. A pity, really; he is a very bright boy, though a bit twitchy. The cause of all his troubles (imagine) is that fire; it's become quite *célèbre*. The Lumkins especially are *enragé*—apparently he insulted them in some obscure way. It might not have mattered so much, but that Fenn was in trouble with the administration already over several administrative nothings. What they really can't stand is his being such a queer fish/duck (what's so queer about ducks and fishes, I ask you?) He has Dirty Nails and Wears His Hair Too Long and Doesn't Own a Car and Rides His Bicycle for Miles in the Rain and Snow for No Conceivable Reason. Big Sister actually listed these crimes to me. "You must admit that's unbalanced," she kept saying. Also: "His whole career here has been a failure." But what is success, after all, but the proof that one has come to terms with society?

For an eccentric, Fenn is quite sensitive to what goes on around him. "My colleagues are avoiding me, too," he pointed out. "Wait for half-time and you'll see." And true enough, when everyone filed out past us they gave Fenn embarrassed nods, or looked the other way as if by chance. "It's the uncertainty they can't take," he said. "They'll all be as nice as possible to me as soon as it's settled that I'm leaving. Even if it turns out that I can stay most of them will be nice to me." Meanwhile a student like a half-grown calf bounced up to Fenn and began to give him manuscripts and clumsy compliments on his last lecture. Obviously he hadn't heard. Utterly devoted: how is it I never inspire that kind of pure puppylike devotion in anyone? I flatter myself that I would have the strength not to abuse it. And don't say: "What about Larry?" Larry was never really a puppy, he just looked like one.

Merry New Year.

CHAPTER

6

It was nine in the morning of the day after Christmas. The winter sun shone brilliantly through the windows of the guest room, and over Holman as he lay in bed. On the other side of the night table, the monogrammed sheet was turned back over the monogrammed blanket; Emmy had risen earlier with Freddy. In a few moments he would get up, but now he lay back, admiring the signs of wealth and comfort everywhere around him: the genuine hooked rugs scattered over the wall-to-wall carpet, the shine of brass and mahogany, the whiteness and thickness of the towels visible through the half-open door of the bathroom.

There was nothing showy, nothing pretentious about the Stockwells' house; that he could not have stood, but of this solid luxury he could never have too much. Even on his first visit to Rabbit Hills, when Emmy's family had all been quite obviously hostile, he had enjoyed simply being there. He recalled coming in from his first tour of the grounds to wash for dinner, and half-luxuriously, half-viciously drying his hands on two lace and linen guest towels and then pushing them back wet and crumpled on the rack. One fell to the floor, and he let it lie there.

He yawned, stretched, and sat up. At the same moment his wife opened the door. She was wearing an old kimono; vermilion silk, wildly embroidered with pink, white, green, and bright blue flowers, which would have made most women seem pale and drab.

"You look gorgeous," Holman said. "Like a big Japanese doll."

Turning to the mirror, Emmy pulled up the corners of her eyes with her fingers and looked at herself. "Too much nose," she said.

"I don't think so."

"I meant, too much nose for a Japanese doll. Darling, guess what, Walter is taking Freddy down to town with

98

him when he goes to get a something or other for the snowplow, isn't that darling of him?" Walter was the Stockwells' gardener and handyman. "So we're utterly free. Until lunchtime. You needn't get up even unless you like." She turned away from the mirror and came to sit on the other twin bed, facing Holman. "And guess what Mummy said to me just now." For once, Emmy paused after a rhetorical question. Holman laughed. It was only when she was feeling childishly happy that she asked him to guess what. He indulged her.

"What?"

"She said: 'We are all very pleased with the way Holman's doing at Convers.' I told her you'd been asked to make up a set of assignments, you know. 'He's such a satisfactory son-in-law.' "

"She did?" Holman was naturally pleased, but he also thought, or heard Mrs. Stockwell's voice saying: "Such a satisfactory purchase, a satisfactory investment."

"Umhum." Emmy took off her kimono.

"And what did you say?"

"Oh, nothing. 'Thank you.' Of course, what I *really* wanted to say was: 'I told you so, I told you so.' But— Oh so sleepy." She stretched out on the bed. "Let's not get up, let's go back to sleep."

"Move over." She moved; Holman left his bed and got in beside her.

"Mmmm. Oh, do that again . . . again." This time Holman did not; he said instead:

"You still have it in?"

"Um hm. . . . You mean?"

"I think so."

Emmy lay back, pleased but somehow also irritated. It was a surprise and a treat to have her husband seriously interested in her two days in a row, but it was disappointing that he could only be interested in her seriously, that he would never come into her bed simply out of affection. I ought not to be cross, she thought, how would I feel if he had some frightful fault; suppose he drank, then I'd have something to complain of, or suppose he went around town seducing girls like Will Thomas. The picture of Will going around Convers seducing girls came vividly into her mind, as it had done several times since Miranda's revelation. She wondered whether, when he was with those girls, Will did the same things Holman always did

99

with her. Then, with a start, she realized that here she was with her husband, in the very act, imagining another man. She went stiff all over for a moment, but Holman seemed to take no notice. He went on with what was today a rather longwinded and monotonous performance, and at last brought it to a conclusion.

"I always get a funny feeling, doing it here," he at length said or explained.

"Imagining what if Mummy and Dad could see us." Emmy giggled. "I know."

"Not only that. It's even more the idea of all the years you spent in this room as a virgin. I feel like I was profaning something."

Emmy laughed. Holman did not.

"Oh, something else," she said, stretching sleepily. "Somebody's got to take Freddy over to the Kennicks' this afternoon, when he goes to ride the pony."

"And I'm somebody," Holman said. "Is that it?"

"Well, of course Mummy's going. But it would be a help if you were there. He hasn't been on a horse since last summer, and I don't think we should leave it all to Mummy."

"What help would I be, in God's name? I've never been on a horse." Hearing the irritation in his own voice, Holman thought: Am I being unreasonably jealous again? He had occasionally caught himself envying Freddy his advantages, though more often it pleased him to imagine how far his son could go with this kind of head start. In theory he was much in favor of the oligarchical system, as the most practical method of human progress, one that had proved itself in his own period, eighteenth-century England, if specific proof were needed. He looked over at Emmy and realized that she was making an effort not to tell him that it was his own fault if he could not ride, or that any time he wanted to learn, Mrs. Kennick would be glad to let him borrow Princess, who had never thrown anyone in her life and was as safe as a rocking chair. For five years false pride, which he recognized as such, had kept Holman from accepting this and similar offers. By now the very words "horse," "stables," etc., made him wince. He winced frequently, for although the Stockwells no longer kept horses, they all rode. It would be a good thing if he, too, knew how. As it was, every time the conversation turned upon horsy matters he felt how the

Stockwells were reminded that he came from outside their world. Still he could not face the ignominy of being seen to learn, jolting awkwardly about, falling off, in front of the Stockwells and their friends. A safe horse would be no help; the safer the horse the worse the ignominy. Before his marriage Holman had thought of horses, as of all animals, with indifference. Now he positively disliked them.

Emmy was still looking at him. "You know you liked Mrs. Kennick," she said.

"All right. I'll go. But you come too."

"Darling," Emmy said, falling over against him in the bed and kissing the side of his nose. "I would adore to, but I've been promising myself I would have a talk with Dads this afternoon."

"Oh?"

"Really, I must. I want to get him alone, darling, so I can ask him about the Fenns."

"The Fenns?" Holman echoed, as if she had said: "the Kangaroos."

"Yes. I've been thinking we ought to do something for them." She offered this tentatively, knowing Holman felt that they had already done quite enough for the Fenns by providing them with food, drink, baths, and clothing since the fire. ("Thank God we're getting out of town for a while," he had said only last week, "or the next thing you know they'd all be coming to live here." And he had added, when Emmy looked sheepish: "If you're thinking of lending them the house while we're gone, just picture to yourself what they'd do to it in two weeks, and don't." "Mrs. Rabbage could come in and clean up after them," Emmy had said, but she said no more.)

"You know, darling," she went on now, "the college hasn't done one thing about fixing up Miranda's kitchen. It's absolutely terrible." Holman laughed. "No, really, it's terrible." Still lying half on him, she raised her head and propped it on her hand. "Something's *got* to be done." Looking into her great eyes, now so serious, he reflected that Emmy always used intensifying adverbs to weaken her statements. "Absolutely terrible" was less terrible than "terrible." A becoming dress was "simply wonderful," but when, after months of rather agonizing suspense, he received the offer of a job from Convers College it was, simply, "wonderful."

A little frown appeared between her straight black brows. "Seriously, baby," Holman said, sitting up and resting his hand on her shoulder. "Your father is a trustee of Convers College, not a building-and-grounds superintendent. He's not going to know how Miranda can get her kitchen repainted."

"I'm not going to ask him that, stupid," Emmy said.

Holman stood up, yawning and adjusting his pajamas. "What are you going to ask him, then?"

Her head on her hand, Emmy looked up at him. The rubber band on her braid had snapped during their recent exertions; the thick plait hung loose. "I'm going to tell him the whole story. What McBane said about the attitude of the administration and the way Betsy Lumkin behaved and everything. It's all Betsy's fault, really. She's determined to see that Julian loses his job simply because he was rude to her, and I suppose Bill is letting her have her way because he's lazy. He doesn't want to fight about it, or maybe he's afraid of her. But it isn't right; it's got to stop. Julian actually hasn't done anything wrong. His thesis is supposed to be brilliant and everybody says he's a frightfully good teacher. I can't go and say all that to Bill Lumkin, of course, but Dad could do it."

Holman stared at his wife. "You're going to tell your father to stop Lumkin from firing Julian?"

"What's the matter with that?"

Holman looked up to the ceiling, as if calling on the God of Reason. "Oh, nothing," he said, heavily ironic. "I just don't like it, that's all."

Emmy hated irony. She rolled over and sat up in bed, naked and angry. Angrily she recalled that when she had told this same plan to Will he had been impressed and sympathetic.

"Have you mentioned this bright idea of yours to the Fenns?" Holman asked.

"No, I—"

"That's good."

"What's the matter with it? Go on, tell me."

"Well, in the first place, baby. The reason Julian's being let go isn't because he insulted Mrs. Lumkin."

"What is it, then?"

"There's no one reason. I don't know much about Convers yet, but I knew enough to realize that these things never work out that simply. There are a lot of factors.

Conditions in the Department, Julian's personality, McBane's personality, the budget, next year's enrollment—" He stopped, aware that Emmy was not listening, only staring sulkily aside. "Anyway, it's too late. Everyone knows Julian's going to be fired by now."

"What has that to do with it?"

"Everything." Emmy turned her head and regarded him incredulously. "These little power-behind-the-throne games have got to take place before the execution order is signed, honey," he said. Emmy said nothing. Holman, feeling that she was at least half convinced, went over to the chest of drawers and began to take out clean clothes. "It was a sweet thought," he said appreciatively. "But it's never a good idea for outsiders to mix in campus politics. It's not even fair, in the long run; not everybody who gets in trouble can have a wife who's the friend of a trustee's daughter. Your father will probably see it the same way. Besides—" he smiled at her, joking now, "you've got to save your influence to get me *my* assistant professorship." Clothes over his arm, he went toward the bathroom. Emmy was still sitting on the bed, her knees spread, her mouth set in a pout. He thought: She ought not to sit around like that with no clothes on; anyone might walk in. A wave of irritation crossed him, but he shook it off. "It's just the old Junior League spirit getting at you, baby," he said. "I know how you feel." He laid out his shaving things along the basin. "You've got to do someone some good, get up a party, ask for contributions. But the Fenns aren't Korean orphans, they're people. Even if you could help Julian in this behind-the-scenes way, he might resent it like hell. I know I would."

"So you're telling me not to," Emmy said suddenly.

"Yes."

"You want me to leave Convers alone, even if the Fenns' life is ruined, because it all belongs to you, and women and wives mustn't go near it, or know anything about it, they must just stay in their place outside and—"

"Emmy, good God—"

"Only I'm not going to." Crossing the room, Emmy slammed the bathroom door on Holman so hard that the towels fell off the pole. He stared at them for a moment; then swore under his breath, picked them up, turned on the hot water, and began to lather his face.

Half an hour later, shaved, washed, and dressed, he opened the door. The bedroom was empty. He made his way downstairs, where Helen, the maid, told him that Mr. and Mrs. Stockwell would not be back until lunch and that Miss Emily had gone out for a walk.

The elaborate order of the dining room, the sun glittering on the long frozen sweep of lawn outside, the covered silver dishes of toast and eggs and ham brought in and set down hot before him, somewhat restored Holman's spirits. He admired this luxury objectively; he was glad that Emmy's father was rich; only, for the first time, he wished that he was not a trustee of Convers College.

Some men, he knew, might have wished this long ago; they might even have avoided teaching at Convers because of the connection. Holman, however, knew that he deserved the job on his own merits, and he thought that there could not be too many connections. He had grown up in a disordered, transient world. Acquaintances, neighbors, schoolmates were continually appearing out of nowhere and then disappearing, never to return. At college, in the army, it had been the same; handfuls of people selected at random, whirled together for a while like odd pieces of laundry spinning in a washer, and flung apart.

How many times he had listened to sad little conversations of this form:

—You from Kalamazoo? Say, you don't happen to know a fellow named Rich Russell, do you?

—Can't remember anybody by that name. Sorry.

Or:

—What ever happened to that good-looking girl Kay Ford that used to hang around with the Young Democrats?

—Who?

One of the most striking of the striking discoveries he had made at Princeton was that a world existed where consistent relations were the rule. The Stockwells lived in such a world. Emmy had met almost no one in her life whose present whereabouts was not known to her. She knew, for example, what had become of each of the eighteen girls in her class at St. Catherine's; while of the two hundred and fifty who had graduated with him from high school he now knew nothing. The disorder of it appalled him, and the waste.

If he was cold now, slow to form friendships, it was

104

partly that he had learned the futility of it too well. His mother may have had friends once; after they moved to Garfield Park she had none. She kept herself apart from her neighbors and from the other teachers at Washington Junior High, and gave out somehow the idea that she was their superior. Superiority had been her forte for twenty years: she was superior to people, time, and circumstances. Bound in its iron knot, her hair did not turn. Even the suits she wore were made of incorruptible, eternal gabardine.

The front door banged, sending cold air down the hall and into the dining room. Noises of someone large stamping his large feet. Next, as Holman had expected, Robert Hoskins Stockwell, the younger of Emmy's two older brothers, crashed his way into the room. Red-faced, broad-shouldered, already going bald, he wore several wool shirts; snow clung to his leggings.

"Hiyah!" he greeted Holman. "Everybody gone out, huh? Having your breakfast?"

"As you see." It was Bobby Stockwell's habit to ask the obvious question; over the years Holman had fallen into the habit of giving a stereotyped professional pedantry to his replies, in spite of his distaste for this pose.

"Been out skiing," Bobby volunteered. The giving out of obvious information was his other conversational stock-in-trade. "Still a good lot of snow on the ground." Holman wished Bobby would sit down, or that he could stand up. On his feet he had an advantage of some inches over Bobby in height, though not in breadth.

"How was the surface?" As he used this word Holman wondered if it was the right one, and cursed himself for caring.

"Not bad. A bit crusty. Say, that coffee smells great. Think I'll get me some." Bobby rounded the table and banged through the pantry door, calling: "Mary!" Any of the other members of the family would have rung the bell, but this was not Bobby's part. "Oh, Mr. Bob!" Holman heard before the door swung shut. The whole household cooperated in making this middle-aged boob feel important. He had a job, which Holman suspected of being a sinecure, he had a penthouse apartment, a TR-3 sports car; he even had a wife from whom he was separated half the time, a baby-faced St. Kit's girl who drank too much. He weighed nearly two hundred pounds, and was thirty years old, but everybody treated him like a big baby.

Bobby came back and sat down opposite Holman with his coffee and a big plate of fried ham and rolls. "Say, that tastes great," he said. "Mary's still a great cook. Really warms me up. How's everything up in Convers?" he asked, eating on, apparently unaware that he had already asked this question on Holman's arrival.

"Just great," Holman said.

"It's a great place in the winter. Swell for skiing. I miss it like hell sometimes, y'know." He gave Holman a big ingenuous grin.

"They opened the new hockey rink this month," Holman said; he was quite ready to take an interest in any sport he knew something about. He had even played intramural hockey himself one year at college, a fact which he now considered working into the conversation.

"I heard about that. Say, I ought to go up sometime and take a look at it. Have you been to any of the games?"

"No, I didn't have the opportunity." Pedantry again. He should have said "chance."

"That's a shame."

"I'm going to go. I'd like to see that kid Russ Morrow they've got this year. He's supposed to be really good—I used to play hockey a bit myself, you know."

"Yeah? You did?"

"Oh, not seriously. I was on the freshman team at college."

"Say, that must have been great." He grinned at Holman, he had nothing against him—he had nothing against anybody. He liked Holman, unlike his older brother Clark, who had a deep polite contempt for him. Luckily, Clark was not in Rabbit Hills this vacation—he and his wife and three children had gone to Cleveland to visit her important family.

"You ought to come up some weekend when they're playing," Holman found himself saying. "Come up for the Amherst game, why don't you? We've got plenty of room."

"Say, that'd be great."

It would be dull, actually, but Holman was pleased to have given the invitation. Emmy would be pleased, and of

106

course Freddy loved Bobby. Besides, it was the sort of thing that ought to be done.

Bobby finished shoveling food into his mouth and went out again. Holman put down his napkin in a heap on the table (he had learned this by copying Emmy) and walked into the sitting room. Here the sunlight lay in blocks on the thick carpeting and the flowered chairs. Pots and tubs of real flowers, mostly poinsettias, stood about, and a seven-foot Christmas tree was in full bloom. The effect was that of a warm, windless summer day, kept up at considerable expense. It was not a fashionable room: some of the furniture was quite ugly. But everything was large, solid, and expensive. It had been recently vacuumed and dusted, and *Time, Fortune, Holiday, Town and Country,* and two morning papers lay in symmetrical rows on a coffee table. Every other horizontal surface above a certain level was crowded with Christmas cards.

As he walked down the room looking idly at them, he noticed, prominently placed, a card identical with one which his mother had sent to Freddy that year. Bright, cheap, sentimental in a Walt Disney style, it depicted a group of cherubs carrying packages. He picked it up. Inside was written, in his mother's clear schoolmistress hand: "With very best wishes from Vera Turner."

He was definitely, unpleasantly surprised. Not that he expected his mother to have perfect taste; but the bad taste of this card was so unlike her. That she could have sent it to Emmy's family was another proof of the strange alteration that had recently come over her.

It had started two years ago, when she reached the compulsory age of retirement from the public school system. Holman was not surprised to learn that she had decided to leave Garfield Park. Or rather, he was surprised, but corrected himself; it was an unattractive place, and after all she had no reason to stay there. He and Emmy had a bad few weeks planning what they would do if she proposed to move East and live with them or near them in Princeton. "We'll have to let her know absolutely the first thing that she can't criticize the way I handle Freddy in front of him," Emmy said, referring to several difficult incidents of Mrs. Turner's last visit. "Maybe she does know more about child development psychology than I do, but I don't want to hear about it when Freddy's listening. He's alive, after all." Holman was more concerned with whether his mother would expect financial help. If she did, he would have to give it, though nothing he could give would begin to pay her back for the sacrifices she had made to send him to college. True, she had a pension and some insurance; if he contributed something it would go to buy luxuries—but luxuries on a lower scale than, for example, his fraternity dues. His debt was irrevocable; but if the bill was not presented, was he morally bound to pay?

All their planned speeches were wasted; Mrs. Turner did not come East. Instead she moved in the other direction, to Los Angeles, where she knew no one. They had seen her twice since then, each time more changed. She did not bring her copies of the works of Emerson and Shakespeare when she came to stay, and her famous headaches were gone. She watched TV and complained intermittently of minor irritations. Only her voice at times still recalled the wind in February across cement playgrounds. Perhaps it was age. Her mind might even be affected, he realized. She seemed not to care very much about anything now; she was not especially interested in Emmy, not especially interested in Freddy. His own success, which she had worked for so long, did not especially interest her. Holman felt as if a wind which had been blowing at his back, blowing him forward for twenty-five years, had suddenly dropped.

Lacking this pressure he felt, he supposed, unsupported. A long time ago Holman had learned that if things got bad enough Mrs. Turner would take care of them. And she would make him pay for it afterward, so that it wasn't worth it to apply to her except in extremity. The time when he was eight, when he kicked the cement blocks off the shed roof into the man's greenhouse. And then he had been too stupid to run, or too terrified. He stood on the roof like glue, and soon there was the man standing among the broken glass and plants screaming: "You little bastard! I'm going to report you to the police!" Then he scrambled off the roof and ran up the alley, off the block, out of the neighborhood, up to the waste ground by the railroad tracks. He spent the rest of the afternoon there, among the heaps of tin cans and neglected garden plots and skeletons of automobiles. His mother had a rule that he had to be in the house by six, but he was afraid to go home. It got darker, it got colder, he got hungry, and finally about eight he gave up and went back, walking, then running. He stood panting on the porch and rang the doorbell and his mother opened the door. "Yes?" she said. He tried to go in, but she was blocking the way. "What do you want?" she said in a peculiar voice. "I want to come in and have my supper," he said. "And who are you?" she said. "Why, I'm me. I'm Holman Turner. I live here." "No boy by that name lives here," his mother said, and she shut the door in his face. He stood looking at it for a moment, dumfounded, and then he rang again. Later he kicked and knocked and pounded the door with his hands and ran around to the back and cried and shouted. But nothing happened, and the shades were drawn down over all the windows. It was much later—half an hour? an hour?—when he was lying exhausted on the front porch, that Mrs. Turner opened the door.

Holman had told this story to Emmy once, and she had not believed it. And it was true that it was impossible to believe of the woman Mrs. Turner had turned into. More completely than if she had died, his mother was entombed in this plump elderly woman who was photographed smiling under a beach hat and kept tropical fish.

Emmy was pleased with the change, insofar as she remembered that there had been one. "Oh, she's an absolute dear. She lives in California," he had heard her say of his mother. No doubt she, like her parents, found it more convenient this way. A dim elderly mother-in-law living on her income in the Far West was a presentable social fact. The farther away she got from her past the better.

Of course the same was true of him. Still, though the Stockwells would never have picked him out for Emmy, by now they more or less, more rather than less, put up with him. He was of the family, and his mother's Christmas card was placed in the front row. Who else was equally favored? Holman picked up the next card. "Holiday Greetings from the Arden Milk Company," it said. Beside it were: "Sincere good wishes—Newton's Coal and Oil, Inc." and "Best Wishes for the New Year from your County Savings and Loan Association." He noticed now that the desk on which these cards were placed was apart from the others, in a sort of limbo near the door. He did not look any further.

"Burned one of those old houses of Bill Lumkin's down

for him, did he? Ha, ha, ha." Mr. Stockwell laughed his loud, dominating laugh.

"He didn't burn it down, Dad; it was his little boy. Mr. Fenn wasn't even there, and anyway the house wasn't burned down," Emmy said. Her father paid no attention. He could always cheerfully not hear whatever he chose not to hear; he was especially good at not taking in the relevant details of a complaint.

"And a good thing, too. Those houses are all old wrecks. I bet the college was insured up to the neck. It wouldn't surprise me if Bill paid the fellow to put the match to it." It would have surprised him, of course; this was only his familiar brand of humor. Emmy giggled, but her face fell back directly into a frown.

"It wasn't insured hardly at all, Dads. That's absolutely the whole trouble. Mr. Lumkin forgot about it."

"Oh?" Mr. Stockwell's loose holiday face tightened, for a moment, into the solemnity of his photographs by Bachrach; he registered a meaningful fact.

At last, as so seldom, she had her father's whole attention. Emmy leaned forward and spoke clearly. "The house was insured about 1938, you see, and he simply hadn't done anything about it since, so it's still insured for whatever it was worth then."

"Ass." Mr. Stockwell stubbed out his cigar in an elaborate brass ash tray. He had always treated Bill Lumkin patronizingly because, though basically a fine fellow, he was comically bad at golf and made almost no money. For Betsy he had more esteem, for she was good at golf and had been a good-looking girl when for some unknown reason she had decided to marry Bill Lumkin.

He was no longer speaking to Emmy, but to himself, and Emmy knew it. Since she was a fat little girl she had been struggling for his attention, throwing herself in front of him with all her energy, while he good-naturedly put her aside. She was still the least important member of the household, the one whom no one took seriously, whom everyone could interrupt.

"You see, it's all his fault really, but he's trying to make the Fenns pay for part of it, even though they have absolutely no money, and if they won't Mr. Fenn's going to be fired. I thought that if you knew about it you'd be able to do something." Mr. Stockwell turned back and smiled calmly at his daughter; it was obvious that he had heard only her tone, not her words. "And I really think you ought to speak to Bill Lumkin about it," she finished.

"No, I couldn't do that," he said finally, smiling.

"Oh, Daddy. Can't you do anything? You know, it's really awful, firing somebody just to cover up a mistake like that. Suppose it got out and people heard about it, what would they ever think of Convers College?"

"Convers College can take care of itself," Mr. Stockwell said.

Emmy looked at her father, a heavy, handsome man in his sixties, quite bald, dressed in expensive "country" clothes. For the first time, it crossed her mind that maybe Convers meant less to him than he said. He always spoke of the institution with pride, even sentimental pride. At alumni meetings his strong, slightly off-key voice sometimes broke on the words of the song: "Still we'll yearn, To-ooh return—" but he did not return; even though he had practically retired he stayed right in Rabbit Hills.

"Can't you do anything?" she repeated. "If you don't want to speak to Bill about it, why couldn't you talk to President King? You see him all the time at those trustee meetings. He probably doesn't even realize what's happening." All through this, Mr. Stockwell went on shaking his head slowly, like a pendulum, smiling not at Emmy but past her.

"Can't do it," he said when she stopped, no more and no less put out than he would have been if she had asked for a car or a trip to Bermuda at the wrong time. "I let Charley King run his business and he lets me run mine. And his faculty is his business." He got heavily to his feet. Just as it would have been on Wall Street, this was a sign that the interview was at an end.

For a moment Emmy remained stubbornly and sulkily seated; then she got up. At the window, Mr. Stockwell said: "Nearly four o'clock. Patricia should be back soon." It was not merely a change of subject; Mr. Stockwell always liked to know where his wife was, to feel her moving all day through an orderly sequence of events. Through the years it had been her habit to relate in detail at breakfast what her schedule was going to be, just as at dinner her husband would describe what his had been. During her adolescence this had nearly driven Emmy crazy; now she sometimes regretted that Holman could not be persuaded to play the same game.

111

"She said they'd try to bring Freddy home by four." Emmy went to stand by her father; together they looked out across the long front lawn, now in shadow; the snow-covered slope the rhododendron bushes wrapped in burlap, the formal plowed drive. A truck went past.

"Newton's," Mr. Stockwell said. "Somebody's furnace must be out." The road was an isolated one, and in fancy part of his manor; at any rate, he took pride in knowing what went on there. He was a good neighbor. Mrs. Stockwell did not share this interest; she found it, perhaps, just a little vulgar. Outside of their own friends, such as the Kennicks, she confined her local interests to being a good employer.

Probably the Bellamys' furnace again, Emmy thought, but she was angry and would not say it. She said nothing. "Wonder how Freddy got on with his riding," her father said.

"I'm sure he loved it. He was wild to go. You know, he wanted to learn to canter today; but I told Mummy I thought he was too young."

"Little Clark can canter," her father remarked suddenly, after a pause.

Little Clark was Freddy's cousin. "Little Clark is seven," she said, quite crossly. "Freddy isn't even five yet." Her father said nothing; he did not even try to pretend that he had known it.

* * *

Allen Ingram to Francis Noyes

A POSTCARD FROM ICELAND

January 5

We are all frozen in together here, between the ice mountains. North road blocked by ten-foot glacier. West road impassable since Christmas. South road hazardous, unsanded, three cars wrecked trying to escape. No east road. My dear Renault died in the driveway this A.M. No sun. No mail. Forecast: cloudy and colder. Help help help help.

CHAPTER

7

FOR THE TENTH TIME THAT MORNING EMMY LOOKED AT
the phone. Why didn't it ring? She had been back in
Convers for four days, and Will still hadn't called.

Well, perhaps he had called early Monday morning
when she was out shopping. She had had to go, for there
was simply nothing to eat in the house; but she had got
through it as quickly as she could, raced her basket down
the aisles and fumed at the checkout stand. Helen, the
regular cashier, was a speed demon ("I'm a speed
demon," she often said), but she would not have dreamed
of letting anyone go by without a chat on a slow morning.

"Say, you're in a big hurry today, ain't you?" she said to
Emmy. "Got a date?"

"No; but I've just remembered I think I've left something cooking on the stove." Emmy giggled nervously and
thought: Imagine me lying to a woman like that.

It was ten-thirty when she got back on Monday, and all
the rest of the day Will did not call. Tuesday of course he
did not call, for she had told him she would be at the
Ladies' Exchange, but Wednesday also went by without a
word. It was provoking, for she had a great deal to tell
him. Not only what her father had refused to do for the
Fenns, but what she had done herself.

The idea had come to her on the long drive back from
New Jersey. Hour after hour the car purred north on its
new snow tires. Freddy was asleep behind the back seat,
and Holman seldom spoke when he was driving; he liked
to go fast, and believed that talking made accidents more
likely. Emmy sat looking at the snow-covered fields, hills,
fields, hills, thinking that she would have to tell Will
Thomas that she had failed, that she was not bringing
Miranda back the nice Christmas present that she had
planned; when she suddenly thought that she could give
the Fenns a Christmas present anyway, of money. What a
good idea! The sum occurred to her at once: two hundred

dollars. This was the amount of a check she had received on New Year's Day from her father. "Buy yourself some new clothes," he had said. "Something bright, hm?" She had thought at once of a marvelously becoming party dress she had tried on at Bendel's, taffeta printed with red and orange roses. But now she gave it up quite easily—for the same reasons she had not bought it in the first place: because Holman would think it too extreme, and because, in Convers, there was simply no occasion for such a dress.

The two hundred dollars was sorry-money anyhow. She knew perfectly well that Daddy intended it to make up for his stubborn behavior about the Fenns. Holman would probably have seen this too, which was one of the reasons she hadn't got round yet to telling him about the check. He might even think she ought to return it. The other reason was, simply, that she was furious with him for the way he had behaved about the whole thing. When he heard that Daddy wouldn't help, not only had he said I told you so, he had obviously been pleased.

Of course she would tell him eventually. Holman and Emmy had sensible, open arrangements about money. They had joint checking and savings accounts, proper life, fire, accident, and automobile insurance, and a large balanced budget which was discussed and revised regularly in an atmosphere of agreeable seriousness. For "windfalls" (which included not only presents from Emmy's relatives, but extra money Holman earned, say, reading papers) there was a standard arrangement. Half the sum was deposited in the savings account, and the other half went to the recipient, to be spent exactly as he liked. This would have worked out all right, for the dress at Bendel's was very reasonably priced, only seventy dollars.

Fields, hills went by. She could put one hundred dollars into the bank and give Miranda the other hundred dollars, and Holman could not stop her, but she knew what he would think of it, and he would say what he thought over and over. If she didn't tell him, she would have to appear to spend a hundred dollars on something else. Of course she could spend part of it and give Miranda, say, fifty dollars, but fifty dollars was not anything. One hundred dollars was all right, but two hundred dollars was better, for then they could pay for repairing the kitchen and still have something left over.

No. She wouldn't tell him at all. The Fenns really

deserved to have all the money, because if it hadn't been for them she would never have got it. It would be morally wrong, really, to put part of it into the Turners' savings account. She would give it all to the Fenns. She wouldn't tell anyone. No one— Except—perhaps—Will Thomas.

The telephone rang and Emmy leaped toward it, but checked herself as it gave out after two rings. One of the most annoying things about this house was that it was a party line. Half of the time Will couldn't have got through if he had called. She looked angrily at the instrument, and fancied that it returned her look. Miranda would have said that it did. It was an old-fashioned phone, with a long skinny neck and arms, like Mrs. Rabbage.

Eleven o'clock. Though it was still heavy and gray outside, the morning was nearly over. Tomorrow was Friday, and Mrs. Rabbage would be around all morning listening to all the telephone calls, if there were any telephone calls. Will had probably forgotten about it, just as he had probably forgotten having kissed her. The same train of thought that had chugged through Emmy's mind a hundred times in the past two weeks left the station again. Obviously the kiss had meant nothing to Will. It was simply a friendly gesture. After all, for somebody who habitually went around Convers seducing girls— Oh, not again. But the train chugged on relentlessly. Anyhow, she hadn't responded, so, thank heavens, he must have seen that she had no idea of— Oh, no, no, not again.

The telephone rang. Bzz, bzz, bzz; their signal. Emmy took it up suspiciously, and answered in her most formal voice. She was not going to be caught gasping eagerly at her acquaintances or at tradesmen, as she had on Monday and Wednesday.

"Hello? Mrs. Turner?"

"Yes."

"This is Will Thomas."

She knew it was. "Oh, hello there."

"Emmy. It didn't sound like you at all."

"I guess that's just my telephone voice." Emmy firmly choked down one of her giggles.

"How are you?"

"Oh, just fine." There was no response. "How are you?"

"Terrible. I have a terrible cold; can't you hear it?"

"Oh, I'm sorry." She forgave him for not having called before.

"I can't think why I have it. I've been very good lately."

"There's so many colds around now," Emmy said. "You probably caught it from one of your students."

"Oh, no. I never catch colds. All my illnesses are completely psychosomatic."

"Really?"

"Oh yes. Guilt, always.... Achoo!... You see. I have only to mention it. Achoo!"

"I'm so sorry."

"Thank you. I wonder if I'm having the guilt beforehand this time; do you think that could be it? Like the White Queen."

" 'Oh, oh, I'm going to prick my finger.' "

"Exactly." They both began to laugh. Emmy relaxed and leaned against the wall, idly winding the telephone cord around her arm.

"Achoo, achoo! Oh, Christ." His laugh had turned into a cough. "Excuse me. How was your vacation?"

"Oh nice . . . I don't know . . . disappointing, really."

"Oh? You must tell me about it."

"Oh, I will. I was planning to." Emmy picked up the base of the telephone in one hand.

"Good . . . Let's see; today." Will's voice died out. Emmy held onto the phone.

"I'm free this afternoon," she finally said, thinking how to arrange this.

There was a confused static noise: Will blowing his nose.

"Today," he said. "I'm afraid today is completely shot . . . You said mornings are best for you?"

"Yes, usually. Except for Tuesday morning, of course."

"Uh hm." There was an even longer pause. Emmy turned and leaned her face against the wall. "Well. How is tomorrow morning for you?"

"Tomorrow morning would be fine."

"I'll drop by then, shall I?"

"Here?"

"Um . . . That all right?"

"Uh, yes. Mrs. Rabbage will be here tomorrow. My cleaning woman, you know."

"Oh. That's not such a good idea, then."

"Well, she is rather tiresome. She talks so much, it's really terribly wearing. Mostly I try to go out somewhere the days she comes."

"Oh."

"And she talks about the most depressing subjects. I usually try to go shopping when she's here, or I go to the library or something. She simply goes on and on." Emmy heard her own voice going on and on. The palms of her hands were wet and warm on the telephone. Shut up, she told herself.

"If you're going to be in town tomorrow, we might have coffee together," Will finally suggested.

"Yes, that's an idea." Emmy was reassured by the normal tone of her own voice.

"About ten o'clock? Is that too early?"

"That would be fine."

"Hurrah! Now let's see, where shall we meet? Where are you going to be?"

"We could meet at the bank," Emmy said. "I have to go there anyway."

"No-o. Let's not meet there. I don't like banks; they remind me of all the money I haven't got. Besides, there's no place for me to sit down if you're late."

"I'm never late," Emmy said.

"Lucky you ... What about the library? The town library, I mean, next to the bank."

"That would be fine."

"Good. I'll see you there, then."

"All right."

"Goodbye."

"Goodbye."

Will hung up. Emmy put the receiver back on the base, which she still held, and leaned against the wall. A nervous giggle emerged from her. "Really," she said aloud. "Stop acting like a schoolgirl." It was only a phrase, for as a schoolgirl Emmy had weighed between 150 and 160 pounds and had had little opportunity to act like this.

Up to now Emmy had explained to herself that the reason she wanted to see Will was so that she could tell someone about what she had done for the Fenns. Now she admitted to herself that something more was going on. She was engaged in a flirtation; a harmless flirtation, naturally. It was something lots of married women did;

117

Emmy had seen them at parties. She had even made some not too successful attempts herself.

When they met, Will might possibly try to kiss her again. She would be ready for it, though, and she would draw back, putting him off with some friendly joke.

"Hurrah!" he had said. He was flirting too. Emmy had the definite feeling that he liked her, admired her. But there was nothing wrong with that. Every woman liked admiration, and most men liked their wives to be admired by other men. "He really goes for you," Holman had said to her more than once, of more than one of his acquaintances, and with good humor. It was utterly harmless. Smiling to herself, she put the phone slowly down, and found that she was so wound up in the telephone cord that she could not move away without taking the receiver off again and elaborately untangling herself.

The furniture in Professor Oswald McBane's office had a dark, moldy look: black horsehair, black wood. The office was in what had been the front parlor of Gibson House when that building had been a house belonging to a Mr. Gibson; it faced north and east. The wallpaper was dark brown, and a sepia photograph of Mr. Gibson hung over the blocked-up fireplace. Little light came in through the windows, against which branches of spruce were thickly pressed.

"I like you, Mr. Fenn, but I grow tired of standing between you and the administration," Professor McBane said. He stood behind his desk, resting one knobby fist upon it. It crossed Julian's mind that in Hum C terms McBane's statement was true; physically, if not symbolically, McBane was standing between him and the Administration Building. "Well?"

"I'm sorry."

"Why do these things keep happening, Mr. Fenn?" McBane asked.

"I don't know," Julian said quite openly and frankly.

"You don't know." It was the inflection which McBane used with students in whom he was disappointed. "What about that incident last spring?"

"You mean the overnight hike?"

"Yes, I mean the overnight hike." McBane fiddled with a pair of scissors. "That was rather an odd thing, was it not? Why did you do it?" McBane asked this question for perhaps the third time in nine months, now in a tone of simple curiosity.

"I don't know. I suppose it was because Tom Kimball suggested it. What would you do if a student came up to you and said he was going off to live in the woods because Thoreau told him to?" McBane made no answer, and the room was so dimly lit that Julian could not read his expression. "It seemed like a good idea," he went on. "After all, we were studying *Walden*."

"Propaganda." McBane looked at Julian owlishly through his glasses. "We are not concerned with propaganda in Hum C, but with style."

"Style *is* propaganda," Julian said in his own classroom manner, which was that of the eccentric iconoclast.

"But only for style."

In the dim room, the two faculty members looked at each other with some self-satisfaction at this interchange. "I can't agree; unless you want to say that everything is style," Julian concluded.

"I could say that. And I could say that it was quite possible to learn about Thoreau's style without spending the night in a sleeping bag."

"Maybe," Julian said. "Maybe for you, but not for Tom Kimball."

"Hm." McBane took off his glasses, wiped them with his handkerchief, and put them on again, while Julian waited for the renewed attack that always followed this maneuver.

"And you really maintain that his experience in the bag taught Mr. Kimball something about Thoreau?" Julian decided to say yes, but he did not have the courage soon enough. "On the same grounds, you would say, presumably, that inferior students of Melville should undertake a whaling voyage, and inferior students of Emily Dickinson should immure themselves in an attic."

"Why not?"

McBane gave a devastating sigh. "Really, Mr. Fenn. This intellectual confusion shocks me. After three years here, too. Don't you realize yet that it's not the part of a teacher to suggest actions to the students? We here at Convers deal exclusively in *ideas*." Julian looked up sharply; once or twice before he had heard McBane turn the edge of his irony inward like this. He did not know if

McBane met his look—he saw only the light glinting on the spectacles as he slightly turned his head.

"I am an old man," McBane resumed. He bent his head as if to illustrate this, and now the light glazed the bald, bony surface of his forehead. "I want to spend my last years here in peace. Not in explaining to the administration why members of my department burn down college houses and kidnap the track team and are put out of bars in Hampton for intoxication." Julian gave a start. "Oh yes, they know about that. This is a small old-fashioned New England community we have here."

"God!" Julian said, and began to laugh. McBane did not join in.

"I am glad you derive amusement from the situation," he said. Julian stopped laughing. McBane cleared his throat. "I hope I have made myself clear."

"Yes," Julian replied. "You don't want trouble. I'm sorry I've made you so much trouble."

"Not me; the administration. I have done what I could, believe me. But you know the ultimate decision in matters of this kind rests with President King."

McBane ended this statement on an up note, but Julian said nothing in reply. He did not believe McBane; he found it hard to imagine that President King, who was notoriously little concerned with departmental matters, would deny the appointment of anyone who was strongly supported by a powerful figure.

"I have always thought well of you, Julian," McBane went on, fumbling with a stack of bluebooks.

McBane never called even the youngest freshmen by their given name. "I have always thought well of you, too," Julian replied coldly; in his mind he added: "Oswald."

"You have made a real contribution to Hum C this past year." This past year, Julian thought, I've slaved for that course since I came.

"Thank you," he said; if McBane's remark was meant to be taken ironically, then his might too. "Thank you very much."

"You have a most unusual, original mind." The persistent sarcasm of McBane's tone had faded to shadow. "I wish sincerely that you could stay on at Convers permanently." He looked up and caught Julian with his mouth twisted, making such a face that it must have been obvious

120

he disbelieved the statement. Julian even hoped that it was obvious. Still, he said nothing, but resumed his customary face as quickly as possible—it seemed to take minutes.

McBane took off his glasses. Naked, his eyes looked red and blind. He held up his handkerchief, but did not really rub anything; instead he put the glasses on again. Then he turned and looked out the window into the close dark spines of evergreen. Julian recognized this as the signal for him to leave. McBane eschewed what he had called "the symbolic inanities of discourse." He was seldom heard to bid anyone hello or goodbye (his customary mode of greeting was to voice the name of the other person as if identifying some neutral object).

"Well," Julian said, to his mind inanely. He went toward the door. As he reached it, it occurred to him that perhaps McBane's last remarks had been sincere. "I wish I could stay too," he said to McBane's back.

The head of the department cleared his throat, but he said nothing, and he did not turn around. Julian remained by the door, waiting. For a full minute they both stood silent, facing in opposite directions. Then, furious, embarrassed, disappointed, Julian turned, snatched at the edge of the door, and went out, slamming the room behind him. Blam!

It seemed to shake all of Gibson House; upstairs, someone stopped typing to listen. Of course, he remembered, McBane never closed his door entirely when he was in, but left it about six inches ajar so that he could see whoever passed by. Since his office was next to the entrance, he was able to follow the movements of everyone who entered or left Gibson House. Julian looked at the door, and left it shut.

"It was very good of you, you know," Will said.

"Oh tremendously." Emmy giggled. It was early Friday morning, and they were sitting in a roadside lunchroom named Mae's Eats, on the highway north of Convers. Emmy had never been in a place like this in her life. She sat on the extreme edge of the seat, her hands in her lap. She could not bring herself to drink from the thick white cup cracked with brown lines, or to stir it with the greasy-looking aluminum spoon.

"Seriously. I admire you." Will drank. "I'd like to think

I would do something generous like that if I had the money, but I know I wouldn't. I'm too egotistic."

"Oh, no— You went and consulted a lawyer for the Fenns, after all."

"That didn't cost anything."

"Still, you did go—"

"Oh, I went. Maybe I'm a good guy after all. What do you think?"

Had she been either more or less sophisticated, Emmy would have answered this question. As it was, she said: "I don't know. I haven't decided yet."

Will stirred his coffee. "But you're working on it, I hope," he said.

"Oh, yes."

Will said nothing, and she couldn't make out his expression. The sun was bright on the snow outside, but in this back booth behind the rack of comic and scenic postcards it was dim. The woman who had brought them coffee had not put on any lights, and Will's head was dark against the glare. They were the only customers.

"Miranda thinks it was old Mr. Higginson," he suddenly remarked.

"I know."

"Oh?"

"She told me she thought so when I spoke to her this morning." A frown showed on Emmy's face. It was fun to be an anonymous Lady Bountiful, but part of the fun was definitely lost when one's gifts were ascribed to someone else. Mr. Higginson was a professor of biology, now emeritus, an eccentric bachelor given to kite-flying and keeping goats, frogs, and other unusual pets. He had been known to give financial aid, sometimes anonymously, to worthy students. Emmy had heard many anecdotes of him and his eccentricities from her father and brothers, and she had had to listen to more from Miranda. "Talking about that old Mr. Higginson wasn't you?" Mrs. Rabbage had said, propping the iron on end for a chat, when Emmy hung up. (One of the worst things about the Turners' telephone was that it was located in the front hall where everyone could hear everything said to it.) "Cuckoo, he is. Got his house full of bird dirt and what-all from one end to the other, Sallie Hutchins told me it made her sick to look at let alone try to clean it up when she was working over to his house and she's nothing particular for a housekeeper as

122

you know. There was parts of the mess he wouldn't even let Sallie touch, account of she might upset the birds, or that old blind cat of his he thinks the world of. I don't go for that; kind to animals, unkind to folks, I always say."

"You're frowning," Will said.

"Am I?" Emmy sat up. "I suppose I was thinking about the Fenns again." Under the table, she crossed her fingers against the lie. "It's so perfectly hateful to have to sit and wait for them to make up their minds. Do you really think they won't let Julian stay?"

Will shrugged.

"I'm so cross with my father," she went on, though she knew she was talking too much. "I really thought he would do something. He's always saying how much Convers means to him." Emmy became aware of a pressure against the top of her left ankle. "And so on," she finished lamely, taking a breath.

"Yes. My father was like that about the Congregational Church. Always shouting about what it had meant to him and how much he owed to its influence. When it came down to it, he didn't go to church any more than he could help, and he didn't practice any Christianity that I ever saw. He gave them a lot of money when he died, though, more than he left me."

"I suppose that shows something," Emmy commented, carefully not looking down and not moving her leg, against which the pressure continued. "After all, money is money."

"He didn't need money where he was going," Will said. In a lighter tone, he added: "What I really think is, they both got just what they wanted. My father would have thrown the minister out of the house if he'd come around suggesting that he might forgive a few of his enemies and stop increasing his substance by usury. And I guess the minister was just as glad not to have him meddling round in church affairs like most of the other parishioners."

"And your mother?" Emmy said, to say something.

"Oh, she's gone too. I killed her. Later on, that was, when I was in college. 'Willie, your behavior is breaking my heart,' she used to say. I didn't believe her, so she showed me by dying of a coronary. I'm just a poor orphan boy, thank God."

Emmy said nothing, and Will glanced up. "I'm sorry,"

123

he said. "I didn't mean to offend you. I forget that some people actually love their parents."

"Oh no, no, you haven't." Emmy said, distracted by the tingling that was running up her left leg. "I think you're probably right." About what? she wondered.

"You haven't drunk your coffee. Are you planning to? Or don't you want it?"

"Not really, I guess."

"Let's get out of here, shall we, then?"

"Yes, let's," Emmy agreed. Will stood up, but oddly enough the pressure on her leg continued. Getting up, she contrived to drop her scarf, and looked under the table, where there turned out to be a good deal of dirty chewing gum and a wooden crosspiece.

They came out into the glaring sunlight. Emmy took a breath that was nearly a sigh. Will held the door of the MG open and she got in, deliberately not looking back at the sordid little lunchroom.

"Would you like to drive around a little? There's some nice views up this way, if you like views."

"All right. I mean, I'd like it."

The car bounced and growled going up the country highway over ice and cinders. Loud gusts of wind came through gaps in the canvas. Packed into her bucket seat, Emmy felt as if she were sitting right on the road.

"Arra arra mm," Will said.

"What?" She could not hear him against the engine noise. He made no allowance for this, but spoke as low as ever.

"Arra reservoir over there." Keeping his hands on the wheel, he gestured with his head. His short, slightly beaked nose, the heavy curve of his mouth and chin, were outlined against the open window.

"Oh."

Will turned off onto a narrow hill road, unsanded. The car made noises as it climbed.

"Arra mm arra."

"What?"

"I said, I hope we make it."

"Oh." Emmy hoped so too. The idea of the car's skidding across the ice and down the steep drop on her side, to smash into the snow and rocks and trees, did not worry her as much as thinking how she would have to explain to

Holman and everyone after the accident what she had been doing there. She wished she had not come.

At the top of the hill Will pulled to the side and turned off the engine. "There you are," he said.

Through the windshield Emmy saw layers of interlocking snow-covered hills receding one after another out of a frozen white lake toward a glare of white sky. The lower parts were covered with bare gray trees in delicate fishbone patterns, the higher by stands of evergreen. Not a house or a road or a man showed.

"Well," Will said. He smiled at Emmy, but made no move. She tried to think of something to say, hunting nervously about in her mind, and managed:

"Breughel. It's like."

"Yes. Very."

"It's like 'The Hunters in the Snow,' with all the houses and people taken away."

Will made no comment. Finally he said: "Tell me about your parents. You like them, don't you?"

"Yes, I do, really," she heard herself answer.

"What are they like? Very old family and keeping-up-the-Stockwell-traditions?"

"Oh, no. You've got quite the wrong idea. The Stockwells aren't anything; really."

"Really? *Nouveau riche?*"

"I suppose so. Not frightfully *nouveau;* since about 1920. I don't mean to say that they weren't always respectable. Daddy's grandfather was a small-town lawyer in Ohio. Mummy's different, of course. She was an Evert."

"Oh? What's an Evert?"

Emmy giggled. "Well, it's a sort of important New Jersey family, but most of them lost their money and died."

Will laughed, and Emmy joined him, a little surprised to hear herself taking this tone about her relatives with a comparative stranger. She didn't feel normal today at all. She must, as they said at St. Kit's, get a grip on herself, on the situation. She sat up, her hand on the arm rest, and said:

"Tell me about *your* parents. What did your father do?"

"Terrible things." He groaned, mock-tragic, and put his hand on top of hers almost absently, then went on in a reasonable tone: "He worked for a box company in Tennessee. Business manager, and a little real estate on the side. Stuffy provincial upper-middle class ... Of course, in the South, everybody who wears shoes is Old Family. My mother most of all ... It used to get me down terribly. It was all she had, I suppose." He gave Emmy a sad, wry look, and took his hand away.

"Were you very poor?" Emmy asked this at random; she was not following very well. Her heart was thumping in her hand.

"Oh, for a year or so, in the depression. Not really poor. We had to let the colored girl go. But that was tragic." He laughed to himself. "Mother used to get up at five in the morning all that time to sweep the front porch and carry the trash out, so the neighbors wouldn't see her. You know a Southern lady isn't allowed to do manual labor. I was supposed to do it, but I always forgot; on purpose to humiliate her, she said." Will sat slumped down in the seat, staring out. "Ladies," he said. "I hate ladies."

I suppose I am a lady, Emmy thought, and said nothing.

"That was the whole trouble with Rosemary; she thought she was a lady. My wife," he added, looking at Emmy.

"Your wife! Do you have a wife?"

"Not any more." He laughed. "Don't get excited. It's been over for years. Five, to be exact. I'm surprised Miranda didn't tell you about it."

Not knowing what to say, Emmy said: "What was she like?"

Will considered. "She was beautiful and good," he finally said. "She was as good as she was beautiful, in fact. Just like in the fairy stories."

"Oh."

"Conventionally beautiful, conventionally good, of course. The men in the office where she worked voted her the girl they would most like to be cast away on a desert island with, because she looked good enough to eat. She was like a basket full of fresh, ripe fruit. Peaches and cream."

"Oh."

"She was also stubborn, ignorant, and conventional. Her favorite magazine was the *Ladies Home Journal*, the Magazine Women Believe In, and Rosemary definitely believed in it."

A silence.

126

"Wh—"

"Yes? Go ahead."

"It wasn't anything," Emmy said.

"Please. I want very much to know what you're thinking."

"Mm. I was going to say, why did you marry her?"

A closed expression came over Will's face, and Emmy wished she had not spoken.

"Why does anyone get married? I don't know. I suppose because I had to; the *Ladies Home Journal* had told Rosemary that she would lose her self-respect and I would lose my respect for her if she gave herself to me outside of matrimony. And then, she was so good and beautiful. And she sang so well ... I was in love with her, I suppose."

Another silence. "Did she have a good voice?" Emmy asked at last.

"She was a perfect Sunday-school soprano. God's dream of a Sunday-school soprano. She could have been much better trained but she really didn't want it. She agreed with the *Journal* that marriage and a family were more important to a woman than a career."

"But then she didn't get either," Emmy remarked.

"Don't feel sorry for Rosemary," Will said. "It was hard on her when we were breaking up, I admit; but now she has herself a successful doctor and three brats and a house with a circular drive in Orange County, everything she ever wanted, and I'm rotting away here. Don't feel sorry for her, feel sorry for me."

Emmy could not, quite, even as a joke. She felt sorry for herself, and embarrassed. She wanted to hear more about Will's marriage, and she wanted to hear less. Will had hardly looked at her since they left the lunchroom, and now he seemed to have forgotten that she was there at all, staring out over the cold hills. It certainly wasn't very polite. She had always liked the outdoors, but she couldn't see anything to look at in this colorless, motionless winter landscape.

"Will?" she said at last.

He turned and looked at her as if she had just arrived. Then, not smiling, he came closer. Emmy remembered that she had decided to move away if Will ever tried to kiss her again. But fitted into the bucket seat of the car as she was, there was no place to move. She let it happen.

127

It was a long, though gentle kiss; halfway through Emmy joined in. In the cold air Will's mouth was hot; his tongue hotter still. Emmy began to put her hands around his back; then, recollecting herself, she put them against his chest and pushed, pulling her mouth away. Will simply reached up and put his hand behind her head, forcing it back. For a moment she gave up, and then, renewing her efforts, shoved him off. She had to use a good deal of strength.

They came apart, both looking rather dazed.

"Really!" Emmy said.

"Really?" Will smiled.

"Well. Really. I mean, after all."

"What after all?"

"I mean, I don't do this. I don't simply go out in cars with men in the morning and simply start kissing them just like that."

"You don't?" Will was grinning.

"No."

"Like this, then?" Before she could stop him. Will gave her a quick peck on the cheek. "I don't see much fun in that," he said judiciously.

Emmy laughed. "I don't go out at all—" she began.

"More like this, maybe," he interrupted. Very gently he kissed the corner of her eye, her eyelid. "Um hm. That's more like it. . . . Salty," he remarked, licking the lashes. "Have you been crying?"

"No, of course not."

"Your eyes taste of tears."

How can I be letting this happen, Emmy thought. I must get it back onto another footing. Conversation, jokes. As far as it was possible, she moved back. Will let her go.

"You know, the first time I met you at Miranda's, you know, I thought you were a burglar." Will was listening politely. "I suppose it was that sweater. I mean, I walked in, and there you were, in that empty house that had just been practically burned down, and I thought maybe you were looking for something to take, like looters, you know."

"But I am a burglar," Will said. "Oh yes. A second-story man, a friend of mine once said. Climbing in at second-story windows, that is. That's why I wear sneakers."

It struck Emmy that he, too, was nervous. This gave her back some of her confidence, and she asked: "Are you good at climbing?"

"Oh, excellent."

"Socially too, I imagine."

"Well, not that so much. But I seem to be getting better at it lately. Don't you think?"

Emmy could think of no answer to this, so she only smiled. Will smiled too, and put his hand on hers where it lay between them on the arm rest. She thought he was going to try to kiss her again, and stiffened, but he only began to stroke the side of her hand slowly. "You're a funny girl," he said. "But I like you—I really do," he added, as if surprised.

"I like you, too," she returned cheerfully.

"I hear you have a nice house out on the Hampton Road."

"It is nice, I think. It's nice being out in the country."

"I'd like to see it." Will's hand had moved up—he was gently stroking her wrist, his forefinger under the cuff of her sweater.

"You should come to dinner. I was going to ask you to dinner with the Fenns."

"Oh? Why didn't you?"

"I don't know. It simply went out of my head. Would you like to come to dinner?"

Will pushed Emmy's sweater up her arm, inside the sleeve of her coat. "I always like dinner," he said, delicately running his nails down the soft flesh below her elbow. Again. "It'll give me a chance to meet your husband." And again. Emmy knew that she should take her arm away.

"You haven't met him?" she said instead.

"No."

"Of course, you should meet. It's ridiculous that you never have."

"Do you think we'll get on?" Will forced his hand farther up, and took hold of Emmy above the elbow. Involuntarily, she bent her arm tight.

"I hope so," she replied, hardly aware what she was saying. "He doesn't really care much for the Fenns. Oh, Julian, he doesn't mind, but he has absolutely no use for Miranda, he—"

"Shh." This time Will moved in so slowly and deliberately that she had plenty of time to turn away, but instead she found herself leaning forward, helping him on; she had her tongue in his mouth first. She didn't kiss Holman like this. With his free hand, Will began to stroke Emmy's face, then her neck. No, move away, stop that, she told herself firmly, but could not move an inch. Gently, pushing back her coat, Will weighed her right breast in his open hand.

"My," he said. He closed his hand and kissed her again, harder and more briefly. Emmy gave a big gasp as he let go.

"Jesus," Will said. "We're going to be so good together . . . Mm . . . Let's take off your coat."

In the cramped space, Emmy struggled dazedly out of the sleeve, while he helped. "There . . Just lay it back over the seat . . . Now the sweater."

"My sweater?" Emmy looked nervously around and out of the windows.

"Nobody'll see you. Come on."

"Don't you like my sweater?"

"I love it," Will replied, starting to pull the sweater loose from Emmy's skirt.

"But this is a public road! Besides, this is awful, anyway! What are we doing this for? Don't you know I'm married?"

"Mmm." For a moment, Will went on taking the sweater out on one side, while Emmy began to tuck it back in frantically at the other. Then, stopping, he held her hands.

"Oh, Emmy," he said. "No one's going to come by here at this time of year. Don't be so *nouveau riche*. You can put your coat around you afterward."

"All right," Emmy said in a small voice. Half passively, she let Will pull the sweater over her head. For a moment she was blinded by a fuzz of red wool. "This is terrible," she said from inside. "Why am I doing this?" Holding the sweater, the air cold on her bare brown skin, she stared at Will.

"I don't know. Because you want to, I suppose."

Emmy shivered, but instead of putting her sweater back on, she let herself fall forward toward Will, closing her eyes. As they kissed, Will reached past and drew the coat up over her shoulders.

Three minutes passed without a word. Then Will, strok-

130

ing Emmy's back, thrust his hand inside her skirt. On each stroke he reached further down, stretching the waistband tighter, until—

"No, no, no!" Emmy pulled back, hot and disarranged. Her eyes were big, her mouth smudged open. One breast hung free of the white cotton bra, its pale brown nipple puckered up to a point.

"What's the matter?"

"This is *awful*. I'm all disturbed."

"Emmy. Don't be disturbed. It's all right."

"No, it isn't at all. How can I be doing this? What time is it?"

"Eleven forty-five."

"Eleven forty-five! But I have to pick up Freddy at school at twelve! That's terrible. He'll be awful if I'm late." Emmy began to struggle into her sweater, her coat.

"We'll make it. We have plenty of time. Emmy. Don't get into a panic." He put his hand to her face.

"No. I must get back. Please. Start the car."

For a moment she thought Will was not going to; then he reached over and turned the key. She looked out of the window; the strips of shadows and sun, the hills, rotated one behind the other. Will steered the car around and started back down the road, saying nothing. He went rather fast, and drew up at the stop sign by the highway with a jolt.

"Freddy gets terribly upset if I'm the least bit late," Emmy said, giggling nervously. "He threw a tantrum once, and it wasn't even my fault, the car wouldn't start." Will shifted gears with a grinding noise. "You're angry," she said.

"No." But his face was averted behind the sheepskin collar. In the little mirror screwed to the dashboard between them his hands were reflected, white, freckled, the knuckles clenched heavily on the wheel.

"I'm sorry," she said. "Only, besides, all of a sudden I got the feeling that something frightfully dangerous was going to happen. I just got frightened."

"You are an innocent, aren't you?" he said, but gently.

"I suppose I am." They exchanged a timid smile.

"You needn't be frightened. Nobody ever did it in an MG. It's just not possible."

"Really." Emmy blushed, but laughed.

"Only the English would build a car that way, of course."

"I never did anything like this before," Emmy said. "I don't know how it happened. Of course, it was my fault as much as yours. I just let myself get carried away, I'm afraid. You know, these things probably happen all the time," she finished seriously.

"You really are funny," Will said after a pause. "Funny and lovely. You really are mixed up, though."

"I am not mixed up. I admit I did let myself get carried away, but it's not going to happen again."

"No?"

"No."

They drove for one mile. Will whistled occasionally through his teeth, but said nothing. Emmy felt terrible.

"It doesn't really matter, as long as nobody hears about it," she finally said. "You won't tell anyone, will you?"

"A gentleman never tells."

"Really. It would be so embarrassing and dreadful."

They drove into town silently, and Will let Emmy out by her car, which was parked around the corner from the library. Here in the center of Convers the winter was not so pretty; the side street was full of ashes, trash cans, and dirty churned snow.

"Goodbye," Emmy said. "Thank you for the coffee."

"But you didn't drink it."

"No, well, but thank you all the same."

"We'll try another place next time. I know somewhere you'd like. Hm. Are you free Monday morning?"

"Yes. But I already said I wasn't going to meet you again."

"Really? Not even as a friend?"

"Well, of course—"

"I tell you what, though, don't let's meet in the public library. It's too damned public. Even if there's no one there, those librarians are the biggest snoops in town. I know, why don't you come round to the back of the music building about ten? There's a place to park, and hardly anyone ever goes there. Please come. I want to see you again."

He waited for her answer, holding the door open. On the square a block away, the clock in the town hall began striking noon loudly in the cold air.

"All right," Emmy said weakly.

＊　＊　＊

Allen Igram to Francis Noyes

January 13

I have the car back at last, after you can't *imagine* what a struggle (never mind, I'll *tell* you). Having a sick Renault on one's hands in Convers is like a sick cow in the middle of Manhattan—it doesn't matter in the least that the ailment is minor, if no one for fifty miles around can cure it. The local garage tried to tie the car together with string, or something but what it really wanted was a little piece of engine made on the metric system, so we had to crawl for two hours through the ice and snow to a town the other side of the mountains where it was rumored to be. No, I can't tell you. The worst is, it is still not well. I can tell from its voice that something too terrible to relate happened to the poor dear in that garage beyond the mountains.

The *crise* had two good results: 1) Since I couldn't get out of the house half the time, I wrote one and one half chapters, and 2) as one always does in a *crise*, I found out a few things about the true character of my acquaintances. Julian Fenn, whom I like, was no help at all, since he has no car; he kept promising me that his friend Mr. Thomas from the Music Department would drive me there, or there, or just anywhere I wanted to go, but somehow Mr. Thomas never turned up. Fat Professor Baker and little Charley Green both took me to class and back a few times, but my real acquaintance-in-need was the other new instructor, Holman Turner, whom I don't like and who doesn't like me but who has a strong sense of social responsibility. Or maybe it's just the fellow feeling of his Volkswagen for my Renault; he would be equally helpless if the VW broke down, and I presumably would not be such an irresponsible cad as not to return the favor. As for the Lumkins, I must say that when Betsy finally did find out, she solved all my problems in a most regal way by lending me her very own Pontiac—along with a most shrewish lecture on the imbecility of anyone's trying to bring an old foreign car up here.

Speaking of the Lumkins, Julian Fenn has officially been fired—or rather, as they say here, *let go*. The euphemism is really more accurate. *Fired* suggests circuses and

133

cannons; you will get a much better picture of what's happened if you imagine a man hanging off a cliff on the end of a rope. With a shrug, the people at the other end *let go*. They are all quite willing to discuss the matter, when I ask in my polite innocent way. "He is not really the Convers type," said Bakerdum to me. "Not, perhaps, completely serious in his approach to teaching," Knightledee explained. And all of them, down to Green and Turner, repeating, so that finally it rang in the air like a gong, McBane's phrase: "He is a troublemaker"—as if it were a vocation, either by innate gift, like a rainmaker, or simply by profession, like a candlestickmaker—or both, which of course would be worst of all. Not one person has spoken for him, though some pretend to. Apparently he is being let go simply (or complexly) because of what happened to his house. Though in the legal sense innocent (he was not even at home when the fire started) Fenn is the victim of his own life style. God knows what will happen to him—he is of course utterly poor and has three small children—and nobody else cares, although they are all very *interested*.

"I thought you weren't going to get involved," I can hear you saying, Francis; you are still my conscience, if now only in artistic matters. But I'm not, I protest; or rather I am becoming involved only as an observer. And isn't that exactly what a novelist should be? In Convers I have a perfect microcosm to observe without the trouble of creation. Besides, everyone does it here. There is no movie in town, and unless the weather is just right, no television. As in ye olden times, people are reduced to watching their neighbors.

And, speaking of neighbors, something else has occurred which I really hesitate to confess to you. After all I've ever said against animals, and what I know you thought the very unreasonable way I behaved when Jimmy wanted to bring his cat to stay with us that time on the Island; well, as of today there is a hideous dog staying here. It's shut in the back pantry, though; it's not staying for long, and it's certainly not mine. Still, I admit, a moment of weakness. What happened was that early yesterday I got a telephone call. I mean Early. Barely eight. I was asleep of course, but I staggered to the instrument. "This Mr. Ingram? Lissen, Mr. Ingram, I can't keep that dog another day. I've had about all I can take from that dog and so has the mister." It was my neighbor down the hill, a local subsistence farmer and part-time house-painter named Hutchins; obviously in a State. What are you calling me for, I mumbled, what do you mean "dog"? I don't have any dog. "I mean this here dog that goes with that there house," (!) she said. It speedily turned out that all this time they have been keeping the Williamses' dog for them. "Listen to that there howling," she howled, apparently holding out the phone. It sounded awful; but what was more awful, I recognized it: it was the noise I had been hearing off and on from their house since I arrived, only louder. She and the mister could not take that howling another day, and if I didn't come and take that dog off of her hands she was going to fetch it over to the pound in Hamp. I tried to persuade her to get in touch with the Williamses—they are in Italy on sabbatical—I even offered to write the letter myself, since she sounded quite illiterate. Nothing was the least use, and I decided that I would have to keep the animal myself until I can hear from the Williamses. I've made inquiries; the vet in Hampton does board dogs, so I've written them suggesting this solution. I presume they want to preserve the animal; I can't think why. It is a great, greedy, ugly puppy, a sort of sheep dog I suppose, named Beowulf—the W's are nothing if not fey. (But they all are; even the Fenns have a cat named Hecate, pronounced "Here-Kitty." If I ever have a dog, it will be called Rover.) And how it howls.

CHAPTER

8

OUTSIDE THE WINDOWS OF THE FENNS' LIVING ROOM IT was cold, dark, and damp, a night of January thaw. It was cold, dark, and damp inside, too. Julian sat on the hearth rug, jabbing at the fire with a poker.

"It's wet, that's why it doesn't burn," Will said from the sofa where he was lying, drinking and reading the *Hudson Review*.

"Go to hell." Julian shoved the largest log over with a crash. A cloud of ashes blew out, and he backed away, sneezing miserably.

"Why don't you drink? Have some of my brandy. Drown your troubles."

"I can't drink if I don't feel well. The way I am now, with this flu, I'd only get sick and depressing."

"You're pretty depressing now." Will slid down farther, putting his long legs up on the far arm of the sofa. "Hanging around with that psychosomatic cold."

"I don't have psychosomatic colds," Julian said. "This is a somatic cold. I caught it from Richard." He sneezed.

"Maybe. If you got a job tomorrow morning, I bet you'd be well by tomorrow afternoon."

"A wager that is not likely to be run," said Julian, who had already heard from three English departments which had no opening on their staffs at the present time for a person with his qualifications.

"Oh, hell, you'll get something. You've got your degree and published articles and everything; you're not a failure like me."

"Let's say I'm a different kind of failure." (Will took a mouthful of brandy with a grimace; no one who calls himself names cares to be readily agreed with.) "I'm what you might call the 1929 type. I look all right for a while, even brilliant, but then comes the crash and everything goes wrong. When you come down to it, I suppose it's what you said once, the death-wish."

"You should be happy it takes that form. It's a damn sight more attractive than any kind of inefficient delayed professional suicide."

Julian laughed, blew his nose on a handkerchief, and stared into the fire.

"It's a shame failure isn't fashionable now," he said after a pause. "I think it never is in midcentury. Nothing will do then but complete success, from the cradle to the crematory. You have to be sane and well rounded, too. Webster, Marlowe, Keats, Gissing, Beddoes, of course, all that is out. No wonder I can't get my thesis printed." Julian's thesis: "Death's Jester: The Worlds of Thomas Lovell Beddoes," had been turned down by four scholarly presses. Two articles pieced together from it, however, had appeared in scholarly journals, and one in the *Yale Review*.

"At least they had their turn. In my field, failure is always passé. You can at least tell yourself you were born out of your time. Think what a hell of a success you'd have been in nineteenth century France, or seventeenth century England. Any less organized society. You'll probably do all right when everything comes apart after they drop the bomb on New York."

"Do you know, I've had that fantasy. Often. I think I would get on rather well— Raiding stores, you know. I'm not a bad shot—I think one might want to stay around here in that case, actually. All these farms, and there's a fair amount of game in the woods. It could be rather fun.

"For a time. Then it'd be a fucking bore—but then, what isn't?"

"But then, what isn't?" Julian agreed.

"Charles is asking for you, love," Miranda said, drifting into the room. She was wearing an old bathrobe that had once been brown velvet, with fringe. "He says you promised to tell him the next chapter of the story about the Boy Lion."

"Now?"

"Now. I want him to get to sleep."

"All right," Julian got up, blowing his nose, and went out.

Miranda drifted about the room, pushed at her hair ineffectually, and finally fell into a chair by the fire.

"I wish he could get over that cold," she said. "He's had it for two weeks now. He ought to stay home in bed, not

137

keep going to classes. It's not as if he owed them any-thing. . . . Don't you think he looks awful?"

"So-so. You don't look any too well yourself." This was an understatement. Miranda's sharp nose was red, her eyes circled in blue; she had the family cold herself and needed at least ten hours of sleep.

"I don't feel any too well."

"Have some brandy. Please do."

"No thank you. Oh, all right."

Will got up off the sofa, found a glass in the kitchen sink, washed it out, dried it, and poured Miranda a drink.

"Thank you. It's sweet of you." She took a sip and coughed.

"Good for colds."

"I hope so. It certainly tastes terrible."

Will turned to the fire. With some effort and newspa-per, he stirred it into a sullen blaze.

"Oh, that's lovely." Miranda held out her hands. "You are good to us."

"It's easy." Will sat down on the hearth rug and smiled at her. He liked the Fenns because they liked him and because their eccentricity kept them from judging him from the conventional point of view; he liked Miranda in particular for her wit and sympathy, though he felt sorry for her because of her physical appearance.

"It does warm me," Miranda said, drinking more bran-dy. "I think this is the first time I've been warm all day. The house is impossible this winter. I'm sure the furnace is bewitched. It keeps stopping and starting and it makes this clanging noise like a sinister warning. And we never get any heat."

"Complain."

"To the Lumkins? I don't intend to speak to them again as long as I live."

"I thought it was McBane you were at war with." He put on more newspaper.

"Him, too. Ahh." Miranda held out her hands again. In the firelight, with her red hair tangled, her bony white face set in a scowl, she looked like a minor witch from Jacobean drama.

"Christ, that's too hot for me." Will moved back to the sofa, picking up the magazine again. "What's the *Hudson Review* doing here?"

"It's Allen Ingram's. He wants Julian to send something to one of the editors who's a friend of his."

"Hm. Do they pay?"

"Not much, Allen said. But anything is better than those stupid magazines that don't pay at all and nobody reads."

Julian looked in. "I'm going to bed," he said in a stuffed-up voice. "I fell like hell. Good night, Will."

"I'll be up soon," Miranda said. "Take some aspirin."

"I have."

"Good night." Julian left. "Would you like me to go?"

"No. I'll never sleep now, it's only nine. I'd just keep him awake. Stay a little while and talk to me."

Will settled back and poured himself more brandy. "You ought to tell Julian to get his next job in a warmer climate," he said.

"If only— You know, I was so happy really when Minnesota said no. I couldn't stand for us to go any farther north. We would all just waste away and die. It isn't natural, this weather. It's like an evil spell. Half the people in town are sick this moment, I'm sure. . . . You ought to get away from here yourself, before it gets you too."

"Where would I go? I haven't got a profession any more. Besides, hell, it's too comfortable. Such a cozy little tomb, I mean womb. And I like the winters here. Maybe it's my Southern background, but I can't get over the feeling that the snow is a great treat arranged just for me."

"That's what Emmy said," Miranda remarked after a pause, in an unnaturally neutral tone. "She said that after every new snowfall the country looks so much like a beautiful birthday cake that she just wants to get out in it and walk and walk."

"She's very fond of nature."

"Maybe it's her Southern background," Miranda said. "She comes from New Jersey," she added. "In fact," Miranda said, "she came over here Monday afternoon to ask if she could borrow my snowboots to walk in the snow with."

"Did you lend them to her?"

Miranda gave Will a sharp look; she was almost certain that he already knew the answer to this question.

"Of course not. I don't have any snowboots, only my galoshes, and they'd be much too small for Emmy. I said she could borrow Julian's old galoshes if she liked, they'd about fit, but she didn't want to." Will laughed in spite of himself.

"Why doesn't she go buy herself some boots if she wants to commune with nature? She has enough money."

"I think she's going to," Will said.

"Oh?"

He looked half aside, not answering.

"So it's getting serious," she said almost at random.

"I don't know."

"I was thinking so; I was thinking, when Will was carrying on with Avis from the bank, or that girl who worked in the Registrar's Office, he used to come over during the day. But lately he's just here at night, so I decided you must be seeing someone who was only free in the daytime."

"Very ingenious," Will said. Miranda took this as a compliment, and smiled downward. "Has she said anything to you?"

"Not a word." Will smiled. "Only she talks about you incessantly."

"What does she say?"

"I don't know; nothing special. You're giving a certain course, or you have a certain kind of tweed jacket. She just likes to mention your name."

"You know, she's a remarkable girl. A real natural beauty. You don't see that kind of thing so often, especially around here. Plenty of girls look pretty when they've got themselves up; but she's beautiful all the time. She has a good mind, too. She knows an amazing amount about art history."

"Yes, she majored in art history."

A silence. Miranda stared at the fire, and Will at the ceiling.

"Nothing's happened, you know," he finally said.

"No?"

"No."

"Hm. What's going to happen?"

"Nothing, probably," Will said sourly. "Talk, talk, talk. I don't mind talk, I like it; but within reason. Love has to have form like an other art— It doesn't progress; every time I see her the overture begins all over again. 'Oh, I shouldn't have come, I shouldn't be seeing you; I like you so much, but what would my mother say if she knew?

What would my husband say if he found out? How can I face myself?' "

"Holman doesn't know?"

"Christ, no. He doesn't know anything, outside of his job and the basketball scores. I don't think he's really looked at her for the last two years. He's a typical American husband, a boob."

"I rather like him."

"A solemn ass. He's had a very bad effect on her. This solemn moral self-examination, she's picked it up from him."

"Maybe."

"Absolutely. I can hear it in her voice. These crazy imaginary scruples and guilts. It's not as if she liked him. The really crazy part of it is we haven't done anything at all." Miranda raised her almost invisible eyebrows. "I mean it."

"Just talk, talk, talk?"

"Christ, practically. And eat." He laughed. "She's kind of an expensive girl, you know, she can't drink the coffee in the places around here, and of course the College Inn is out, so we have to drive to Hampton for her to have the twenty-cent coffee in the Hampton Hotel, and coffee cake and turkey sandwiches and vanilla sodas with strawberry ice cream. She loves to eat as much as I love to drink."

Miranda curled up in the chair, wrapping the bathrobe tighter around her. The fire had nearly died down again. "You ought not to go to the hotel in Hamp too often," she said. "Somebody'll see you."

"You're damned right. I wish you'd tell her that."

"Of course, I don't suppose anybody from the college goes there."

"No, but people from town do. She won't listen, just laughs. You know she has an amazing laugh. Crazy. All these moral scruples, but I don't think she gives a damn who sees us together."

"That's admirable, in a way."

"Yeah," Will said, sitting up, "and it could be damned inconvenient. That's what comes of not following the rules." He drank more brandy. "One of these days Holman'll find out what's going on and come after me with a gun: Bang, Bang, Bang! He's just the type." Will clutched his stomach and pantomimed being shot as children do, falling back on the sofa. "And all for absolutely nothing. . . . Christ, I'm drunk. Sorry "

"That's all right."

"It isn't. I'll get on home." Will rose and went toward the hall, Miranda following him.

"Do be careful. Maybe you'd better not drive."

"I'll be all right. Two things I can do in any condition, driving and fucking. Jesus; forgive me. Where's my coat?

"It's here."

"Thanks." Will put on his coat. "And thanks for listening to me. I shouldn't have told all that."

"Oh, no. I like to hear about it."

Will looked at her. "You do, don't you?" he said.

"I'm interested."

They smiled at each other. "Good night," Will said, opening the front door on a rectangle of black winter rain.

"Good night. Come again."

"I will."

Upstairs, Miranda brushed her teeth, looked at the children, and turned out the lights. She felt her way cautiously across the dark bedroom, partly so as not to wake Julian, and partly so as not to trip over anything. The room was always in chaos; the children loved to play there, and when Julian took off his clothes he dropped them wherever he happened to be standing. In the same way he would leave books open face down on the washbasin, wet towels on the hall floor, apple cores or the rind of a sandwich on the arm of his chair. Miranda had long ago given up trying to cure him of this, because when he did make an effort to put things away they immediately became lost, sometimes forever.

She found the bed and put her weight quietly on it.

"Hi," Julian said.

"Hi. You're not asleep."

"Katie's been coughing."

"Oh, Lord! I suppose that means she's getting it again."

"Hey. Your feet are cold."

"I'm sorry. I can't ever seem to get warm."

"There's not enough covers. Let's get the rug."

"It's so dirty."

"It's warm. I'll get it." Julian felt his way out to the hall and dragged the rug back onto the bed. "There."

142

"You're noble."

"Mm."

"You know I was right. Will's been seeing Emmy."

"Really?"

"Really. He takes her to the hotel in Hamp and buys her lunch and she talks about art. He's trying to seduce her, of course, but she won't, she's got moral scruples."

"She won't? That's unusual for him. He must be chagrined. Do you think she'll give in like the others eventually, or will he give up?"

"Emmy's not like the others. I mean, really. I think it's a mistake for him to take up with a faculty wife. Nobody noticed as long as he stuck to his girls from town, but with this he could get into the most awful trouble. Oh, of course I don't think she'll really do anything. She's just flirting."

"She's a good-looking girl," Julian said. "Classic beauty, really. She's built like a Roman statue."

"Her shoulders are too square."

"That's the Roman style."

Miranda turned over in the bed, away from Julian. "Why Roman? Why not Greek?"

"She's more baroque. More breasts and so on. The Greek statues, most of them, have no breasts to speak of, proportionally."

Silence, about three minutes of it.

"What are you thinking?" Miranda asked.

"I was thinking about Keats."

"Keats?"

"Mm. I was wondering whether anything had been done about pre-Christian ritual in him. *Endymion* has some of it, and then the 'Grecian Urn.' "

"Oh." Ordinarily Miranda would have been pleased enough to discuss this, but not tonight. "I was thinking about how we all have colds and it won't be spring for four months and there aren't any eggs for breakfast because I forgot to order them and everybody in town hates us and we'll never get another job and the furnace doesn't work."

"God." Julian laughed unhappily. Miranda began to cry. "Oh, hell." He put his arms round her.

"I'm sorry. I don't mean to be like this." Her sobs subsided, stopped. They lay with their arms round each other, in worn flannel nightgown and pajamas. "It's just that everything's so awful lately most of the time, and I'm afraid it's going to get worse."

"You should have married somebody else," Julian said, stroking her hair down.

"I should not, either."

"You should have married Charlie Robbins."

"I didn't like Charlie Robbins. He was awful. You know he was awful. He had a fat stomach and hands like a troll."

"Your mother liked him."

"Yes, and if I'd married him now I could be the wife of a fat Presbyterian minister troll and my mother would be living happily ever after."

Julian laughed, and kissed Miranda "Mm."

"Mm."

"I love you."

"Yes."

"Let's."

"Yes, let's. I'll get it." Miranda sat up in bed. "Oh hell; heavens."

"Purgatory. What?"

"I forgot to get more jam. Oh, how stupid" She fell back on the bed, beginning to sob.

"Don't start again."

"All right. I'll buy some tomorrow. I wish there were some way of getting it without having to go to the drugstore here. It's so *embarrassing*. The way he looks at me, as if he's counting, and I haven't any idea whether he thinks we use it up too fast or too slow."

"I'll get a supply when I go down to Cambridge in midterms."

"Yes, do. No, don't. I don't know. If you do that, he'll either think we've had a fight, or he'll think we're trying to have another baby, and I can't stop going to the drugstore completely." She gave a laugh which was half a wail. "Oh, small town!"

"You've just got to pay no attention to them"

"I know. I wish I could. I did used to be able not to, when we first came. But now I know them and I know what they're all thinking. It's awful, awful"

"We're leaving."

"Thank heaven.... I hope the children have enough

covers. I put my bathrobe on top of Richard because he's sick, but I didn't do anything about Charles and Katie."

"Mm Let's go to sleep."

Eleven o'clock at night down at the Huts. In the bedroom of Hut (or Veteran's Housing Unit) 3C, Charley and Lucy Green lay awake with a hot-water bottle between them. For the twentieth time, Lucy turned from her right side to her left, with a dim, sad sigh.

"What's the matter, honey? Can't you get to sleep?"

"No," she sighed. "I keep wanting to lie on my stomach, that's the way I've always slept ever since I was a little little girl, but I can't lie on my stomach any more, I always roll off." Lucy was seven months gone in her first pregnancy and had a bad cold.

"Oh, honey."

"Besides, how could anyone sleep with all that going on? Just listen." From Housing Unit 3A, downstairs (the Butlers: History) came the cries of a baby; in Housing Unit 3B next door (the Heaths: Mathematics) Monteverdi was being played on the hi-fi; and from 3D (the Hogans: Physical Education) came the sounds of a male and a female voice arguing. "It's no use. I'm going to take something." She sat up in bed and put on the light, blinking. At twenty-one the youngest faculty wife in Convers, Lucy looked even younger, with her pink-cheeked baby face and tail of yellow hair.

The closet door was stuck shut again; she tugged until it opened with a bang that shook the building. "Look at it, too," she said, coming back in. "Everything's wrong in this apartment, the closet won't open and the bathroom won't close and the icebox won't defrost, and the stove."

"We won't have to live here much longer. It's only for the first year."

"If we get into college housing. Not everybody does. Look at the Butlers, they've been here two years, and so have the Moynahans." She turned out the light.

"Oh, honey."

"I'm sorry. I know I'm being awful, honey. It's just that I have this cold and anyhow I'm upset lately." To comfort herself, Lucy began to rub her husband's back

"Everybody goes through the Huts."

"Mm. I know. No, they don't though. Look at the

Turners." Charles and Lucy looked at the Turners often. "Emmy didn't have to live in the Huts. It's not fair they should have so much money, is it fair, Charley?"

"In a way no, in a way yes," Charley said. He had been Lucy's freshman English teacher and, both by habit and inclination, never treated her questions as rhetorical. "It's the free enterprise system, honey. If a man works hard and is successful, one of the things he can buy, if he wants, is an easier life for his children."

"I suppose that's fair," she said doubtfully.

"It's not only this system, it's the same everywhere, even in Russia. It's one of the strongest incentives in the world. If I had a lot of money, I know I'd want to spend some of it on my children." Charley patted the convex surface covered in pink flannel which was all that he possessed at the moment.

"Charley," Lucy murmured fondly. "Yes, you're right. I would too. I'd want very much to think that we had enough so that our child would never have to live in the Huts. You're so intelligent."

"Of course, on an abstract moral scale, it's not fair that Holman and Emmy have more than we do."

"I don't mind Holman's having it," Lucy said "It's her. She's so affected about it."

"Why, Emmy's not affected. She's one of the most natural women I ever met."

"She is too affected. You just like her because she's pretty. She's nice to you, but she patronizes me. The other day when she and her little boy were here visiting Flo Butler I showed her my new maternity dress and she said: 'You mean you really made it yourself, with those scalloped edges and everything, I think that's frightfully clever! Eoh, I wish I could sew like that." Lucy imitated Emmy's accent as stage English. "Only she didn't think it was clever; she really didn't like it at all."

"Oh, honey. That's just the way she talks. She probably does wish she could make her own clothes the way you do."

"No she doesn't. She thinks it's shabby to have to make your own clothes, like a little sempstress or something, instead of buying them in New York. Her storm coat comes from Saks Fifth Avenue, I saw the label; it probably cost about a hundred dollars. It's not right to spend money that way."

146

"You're a little Midwestern puritan." Charley said, stroking his wife's face. "Strictly speaking, it's worse that Holman should have money, when nobody in his family ever worked for it."

"I like Holman," Lucy said. "He's not sarcastic the way so many of them are here. No matter what he had, he wouldn't make you feel it. You know, Tuesday, when it was so cold, he passed Liz Moynahan walking back from the market with Biddy and her groceries in the stroller, and he stopped and gave her a lift home even though he hardly knows her, and she said he was so friendly. You don't like him," she added, as Charley failed to remark on the thoughtfulness and generosity of this act.

"I like him all right," Charley said. "It's just that I can't help realizing that we're competitors. We came here together, and he has the edge on me."

"I don't see why. He still hasn't finished his thesis and he's the same age as you."

"That's not his fault, he was in the service. Besides, they like him here. He's the Convers type."

"Why aren't you the Convers type?"

"I didn't say I wasn't. I might be, actually. It's hard to tell about oneself. The main trouble with me is I look too young. If I were bigger or heavier it wouldn't show so much. I wish I had thought to grow a mustache before I came, that would be some help."

"A mustache?" Lucy said doubtfully, and in the dark she stroked the area between her husband's turned-up nose and his determined mouth. She thought him perfect as he was; his combination of boyish appearance and mature, thoughtful manner gave her a pleasure which was renewed every time she caught sight of their combined reflection in a mirror.

"I might try it this summer," Charley said. "If it didn't look right, I could shave it off."

"What kind of a mustache?"

"Oh, medium-sized. The danger is, it might grow in red. That would be worse than nothing."

"Your hair is a little bit reddish anyway. It would look silly, brown hair and a red mustache." Lucy laughed; Charley did not join in, and he did not promise not to try to grow a mustache. "You shouldn't worry, honey. You're so intelligent, I'm sure they can see that, and you already have your Ph.D. and Holman doesn't."

"Yes, but when he does get his Ph.D. it will be from Princeton, and mine is from Wisconsin."

"What's wrong with Wisconsin? I thought you thought the Department was one of the best ones in the whole country."

"Intellectually it is. Better than Princeton, actually But that's not the only thing that counts, not around here. There's prestige and tradition and that kind of thing."

"I think Madison is the most beautiful city in the world. I wish we were back there now. People are friendly and sincere in Madison, there isn't all this affectedness and sarcasm and competition."

"Oh, Lucy—" Charley interrupted; she went right on.

"It snows when it ought to in the winter and it rains when it ought to. Look at it here tonight, this horrible raining in the middle of January."

"It's the January thaw."

"I don't care what it is, it's horrible. The window frames are all leaking and there's a big leak in the Heaths' kitchen, right over the stove."

"At least it's not in our kitchen."

Lucy broke into tears. "That's what I mean," she said. "That's just the sort of sarcastic way they all talk around here. You never would have said a thing like that about anybody back home unless you just hated them. You know Bill Heath is your best friend in Convers, but you talk like you were happy he and Mary Lou have a big leak of rain pouring into their kitchen," she concluded, sobbing and blowing her nose.

"Oh, honey. I was just trying to make a joke."

"I'm sorry, honey. I know you were. I don't know what's the matter with me lately. I'm all nerves."

"I know what's the matter with you."

"Mm. Well. Maybe."

"Of course it is. Your endocrine balance is all upset."

"I suppose you're right." Lucy yawned. "Mm. Good night." For the last time she turned from her left to her right side.

"Good night."

Toward midnight it turned colder. The wind began to blow from the north and west, freezing the fine drizzle of rain into snow, and then breaking up the overcast. At two-thirty, when Emmy got up to put another blanket over Freddy and close the window, she saw stars between the shreds of cloud. Back in bed, she lay awake a long while. The wind was blowing stronger all the time, shaking the window sash in its frame, forcing its way in. With each blast the curtains billowed up and the shade trembled and rattled. In the morning, waking from a night of bad dreams and good resolutions, she found a drift of snow inside all along the sill.

"We can't go on like this any more," Emmy said all in a rush, as she opened the door of her station wagon to Will at a snowy crossroads two miles out of town.

"He's found out." His hand on the door, Will froze.

"No, no, but—"

"Thank Christ." His breath smoked up the window as he stooped to get in; it was bitter cold out this morning, only fifteen above zero, though the sun was brilliant. Emmy moved along the seat so that he could drive. Lately they had been leaving Will's car and taking the station wagon, which was more comfortable and better insulated.

"Jesus, you had me scared," he said, turning to her. His face was red with the wind and cold, the collar of his coat turned up high.

"Really. I've thought it all over."

"Ah." He turned on the ignition. "Hungry?"

"A bit."

"English muffins?"

"I mean it, Will. This can't go on like this."

"No English muffins."

"I didn't say that." She giggled.

"Since it's the last time, hm?" He drove up onto the road and started south toward the Hampton Hotel.

"I want to talk to you utterly seriously."

"All right. Talk to me utterly seriously."

"Not like this. Not driving." Suddenly, Emmy was ready to cry; Will saw it.

"All right. Shall we go to the Tree? Or shall we go to the Duck Marsh?" Of these two places in which they had formed the habit of parking, the Tree was the more scenic, but the Duck Marsh was the nearer and the more secluded.

"The Duck Marsh," Emmy said

In spite of its springs, the station wagon jolted and shook on the rough track across the marsh, and the sharp claws of bushes scratched against its side. On warmer days the marsh was wet and muddy, but today these patches of water were stiff with ice.

"Tell me," Will said, pulling on the brake.

"It just simply can't go on, that's all," Emmy said. "It's too much."

"All right."

"It's different for you, you're not living two different lives that don't match, but for me it's absolutely impossible. It's schizophrenic. I'm one person when I'm here and then I drive back to Freddy, and Holman, and I have to turn into someone else completely immediately. I don't even know who I am any more." She laughed nervously, her eyes large.

"It depends who you want to be, I suppose," he said.

"I don't know, I don't know! It's just so uncomfortable. I'm so upset!"

"I'm sorry you feel uncomfortable wth me," Will said, disingenuously.

"No, no, I'm not uncomfortable with you! That's simply the whole trouble, when I'm with you I feel too comfortable, I forget about everything else and it seems perfectly fine, and then I get back home and I think, was that really Emmy Stockwell this morning doing those things with a man in a car behind a barn up in New England somewhere in the middle of nowhere, was that really she? Why if you told me so I wouldn't believe it, and if my mother heard someone say it she'd think they were simply inventing vulgar tales."

"I thought we had an agreement not to mention your mother."

"You're angry."

"No."

"No, you're furious. Oh, don't be cross! Why shouldn't I mention my mother if it occurs to me? After all, she's my mother."

"Emmy. I'm interested in what you think, not in what your mother might think. I want very, very much to know what you feel about me, but I don't give a good damn what your mother would feel. I'm not in love with your mother."

Emmy caught her breath; this was the nearest Will had ever come to making her a declaration. Actually, it was not by chance that he had neglected to do so. He had had

150

for many years a rigid private code in these matters; it was a point of honor with him not to fling phrases about indiscriminately. He distinguished three stages of sexual affection: "liking," "loving," and "being in love with"; only his wife and two other girls, now far away and long ago, had ever made category three.

Emmy smiled at Will; she felt a little better. "I'm so glad you understand. It's awful enough all the things I've already done, and they're going to be in my life for ever and ever and I'll never be able to get rid of them."

" 'If all time is always present, all time is irredeemable.' "

"What's that?"

"*Little Gidding.* Left over from my Anglo-Thomistic phase."

"Did you have an Anglo-Thomistic phase?"

"Oh, yes. Doesn't everyone? In college. I'm sure I was insufferable; I read Saint John of the Cross and wrote an atonal Mass."

"I guess I had mine in boarding school. We all did, you know. It was the thing at St. Kit's. We were all frightfully pi. We prayed, and all that. We used to search our souls for secret sins so that we could confess them in chapel Sunday nights. In public, you know."

"Every Sunday?"

"No, every evening. But Sunday was the big day, because we were encouraged to tell things we hadn't dared to come out with during the week. So of course if you stood up and told them it was more dramatic, and the penalties weren't any worse."

Will laughed, astonished "And what did you confess to?"

"Oh, I never had anything much. I was really a very good girl. I used to say I had wrathful thoughts toward others, or I talked after lights out The worst time was when I had to confess that I had worn silk embroidered underwear under my uniform. Don't laugh, it was awful."

"Jesus. What an inquisition. Were you encouraged to tell on your friends too?"

"Of course not. Well, you could, if you wanted to, but it wasn't D. Decent A girl in my house told on her roommate for smoking the year I came, and got her expelled, and they put her in towel possy for a whole term."

"In what?"

"Towel possy. It was, well, sort of like being sent to Conventry, only worse. If you'd done something really despicable, the other girls would go at night and wrap a wet towel around the handle of your door, and then when you saw it the next day you knew Then for as long as it lasted everybody wouldn't speak to you or hear you or see you and they would simply pretend that you weren't there."

"Jesus Christ. How did your parents ever happen to send you to a place like that?"

"St. Catherine's isn't a *place*," Emmy said. "It's one of the three best girls' schools in the East. Absolutely, it is. People like the Fords and the Rockefellers send their daughters there. It's tremendously expensive and hard to get into."

"And once you get in, you're very, very loyal."

Emmy frowned, and disregarded the tone of this. "I think St. Kit's was a good school. Basically, I do. Of course some of the rules were ridiculously old-fashioned, I certainly admit that. But I'm glad I went to it."

"How long were you there?"

"Five years. I *was* miserable my first year. But we all were. We got to like it."

"Maybe that would have happened anywhere. As Shaw says: 'Get what you like, or you'll learn to like what you get.' "

Emmy laughed. "That's nice."

"Yes. It was my motto once." He looked at his watch.

"You have a wonderful memory for quotations."

"Actually, not. I remember the sense, but I always get the words slightly wrong. There was a girl in Massachusetts I once knew that I used to drive completely crazy that way. She couldn't believe I wouldn't learn if only she corrected me enough times."

"She sounds like a frightfully pedantic and prissy girl."

"Pedantic, maybe. I'd hardly say she was prissy," Will smiled, but not at Emmy. "Well," he said sitting forward. Emmy tensed up, expecting that he was going to try to kiss her. Instead, he put one hand on the ignition key and the other on the steering wheel.

"I like being with you," he said, turning on the motor. "I'm really sorry it's over."

"Oh, don't say that. I hope we'll still see each other. As friends."

Will made a face. "No doubt we'll have to meet socially once in a while," he said. "Considering how small Convers is."

"Oh, don't be angry," Emmy said, in a nervously coy voice.

"I'm not angry," Will said angrily.

"Oh, dear. Aren't we going to have any English muffins?" Against her will, she giggled hysterically.

"I thought we'd better be getting back."

"But it's only ten, practically. What'll I do all the rest of the morning?"

"That's your problem," Will said, shifting into DRIVE.

"Oh, you are angry!" Emmy cried.

"All right, I'm angry!" Will said. "What do you expect me to be?" He revved up the engine.

"Don't be angry!" Emmy shouted over it, directing rather than pleading. "Don't go. Let's stay here and talk." Will took his foot off the clutch; the car started to move. Equally determined, Emmy reached over and turned off the ignition key. They exchanged a stubborn look as the motor died; then Emmy's mouth began to tremble. She had the hideous feeling that she was going to burst out sobbing, but before this could happen Will reached over and kissed her, first lightly, then harder.

"Oh, Emmy," he said.

"Mmm."

"Silly name, Emmy. Like those silly TV awards ... I suppose you have TV."

"Yes," she murmured, leaning her head against his, "but we can't use it much up here. The reception is so bad. . . . It's the mountains. We can hardly get anything at all, only one channel, and that's usually so dim nobody but Freddy can bear to watch it."

"Emily is better. Maybe I'll call you Emily. If you don't mind."

"Of course not." They exchanged a kiss. "I don't know why everyone still calls me Emmy, it's just a baby name. But I've never been called Emily, except when I was being scolded. Even now, when anyone says 'Emily' I'm frightened, because I think it means something serious."

"I mean something serious."

Emmy felt herself sinking under his look, and fought it. "Would you like me to call you William?" she asked.

"Ugh. Never. My father's name is William. Was. You

153

see, I think he's still alive. And don't call me Bill, either. Rosemary ran that into the ground. 'My husband, Bill,' she was always saying. She thought Will was affected, or unconventional, or too Southern, or something, and if she just said 'Bill' enough times I would change. Domestic magic. It's always a sign when people begin to call each other by a special name. I really ought not to start calling you Emily. Someone else might know the signs."

And I ought to tell him not to, she thought.

Will began to kiss her quickly and softly. Her hair, her forehead, her eyes. She responded in the same style, then broke off to ask: "Do you think I'm bad?"

Will sighed. "If you only knew how much that subject doesn't interest me," he said.

Gathering Emmy back to him, he began where he had left off beside her nose and moved topographically down across her face, her neck. Cold outside, it grew hot in the car. Will continued along the shoulder, over the collar-bone, pushing her shirt apart, heading for the hill of her left breast. But as he reached the summit she pulled away with a jerk. "No!" she said. "Really, Will. That's all over."

He stopped instantly, sat back, and began staring out of the window again, his hands on the wheel, but he did not start the engine, or speak. Some time passed.

"What are you thinking about, Will?" she finally said.

"Christ knows," he replied, not moving. "What are you thinking about Emily?"

"I don't know."

"I do. You're thinking how inconvenient it is that I haven't learned my lesson, after the trouble you've taken to teach it to me. You don't want to stop seeing me, no, what you want is to go on seeing me, pretending to have an affair and being taken out to lunch and tea and cocktails, and doing a little bit of twelve-year-old kissing when you feel like it, but nothing they wouldn't approve of at St. Kit's."

"I thought you liked it too," Emmy said indignantly.

"I don't play games. I'm too old for that. I can't turn it off and on the way you seem to be able to do. I can't do it. What do you think I am, a Teddy bear, first you pick me up and then you put me down, whenever you feel like it?"

In the midst of her agitation, Emmy had the irrelevant thought that Will did look something like a Teddy bear,

154

especially around the hair and eyebrows. "No, of course not," she said.

"Do you want to go? It's up to you. Or shall we stay?"

Emmy hesitated looking out at the snow and dead branches, and then in at Will. I can't give him up, she thought, but of course I must. She opened her mouth to say No, and said: "Yes."

This time, as they kissed, Will brought his whole weight to bear against her, so that, slowly, she slid down along the seat. The background of cold bushes and sky past his head was replaced by one of car roof. She began to breathe in gasps. Well, anyhow, we can't possibly do it now here in the car, was her last, mistaken, coherent thought.

* * *

Allen Ingram to Francis Noyes

February 3

... I am quite recovered, thank you, and you can tell Ginny so; use your chillest amateur dramatics voice, as I don't care to encourage her solicitude. I will not have that kind of woman (very well, any kind) coming the Big Warm Mummy over me: how Tommy and Alf can like it I fail to see. If you must say something, tell her that used as I am to simple wholesome country food and early hours, the luxuries of the city were too much for me. Don't *apologize*. It wasn't my fault that the aquarium got broken, it was Alf's. What's more, I know he has been dying to do it for years (I see right through him, see, with my gimlet-like novelist's eyes) and I am sure he got an immense kick when he saw all Tommy's exotic little orange and yellow and black sperm expiring on the rug. . . .

The new semester has started, and I have a whole new selection of little "creative writers" on my hands—twenty this time. I have actually had to limit enrollment, which gives enormous prestige around here; and, even better, I was able to throw out my three most hopeless applicants. There are plenty of hopeless ones left, though, and I have the dreadful suspicion that my popularity is due to the fact that the course is rumored to be a Snap (one thinks of those paper crackers at children's parties).

I have been to more meetings of Convers' famous

155

freshman course, Humanities C, the one McBear invented and runs. Everyone agrees it's the Basic Firm Foundation of a Convers Education (get that rhyme) and so I thought I ought to turn my screwdriver-like eyes in its direction. The laudable purpose of this course, as I understand it, is to get rid of the entire contents of the incoming freshman mind ("break up his preconceptions and destroy his confidence in what he thinks he knows") and thus, presumably, leave a nice clean sheet for the professors to write on. But it's all done on such a high metaphysical plane that I wonder if it really works. My upperclassmen don't especially seem to have been Born Again—unless after McBear and his apprentices washed out their minds with soap they put back the same old opinions.

Really, does *any* kind of intellectual argument or process have more than the most superficial effects? Sometimes I am tempted to regard this whole enterprise as I imagine the natives regard it: with immense indifference. "They talk a lot up to the College," but real life is going on somewhere else.

I was reminded of this by a singular sight I observed yesterday. I was out for a walk with the Williamses' dog (it's Good for Me, I keep telling myself as my feet freeze, and the animal howls far less for some time afterward). We were up the road back of here, in the woods, and I happened to look downhill through the trees. At the bottom was a couple making love right out in the snow. I couldn't see their faces—they were about a hundred yards off. In spite of the weather, the woman was apparently naked to the waist; and quite brown—I imagine there must still be a good deal of Indian blood hereabouts. Beyond them, sloping down to the river, were the fields which were lush with corn and squash and tobacco when I arrived last fall (and will be again this year). It occurred to me that all of us college people here are like the snow, a cold white layer on top of the hot earth; superficial and, in the long run, probably temporary.

PART TWO

CHAPTER

9

"ICE," HOLMAN SAID. "I WONDER IF WE'RE GOING TO HAVE enough."

"Mm." Emmy, by the kitchen table, was arranging the flowers for their party that night. "What did you say?"

"I was wondering if I ought to go out and get more ice."

"Haven't we enough ice?"

"That's what I wanted to know," he said, quite patiently.

"Oh, I'm sure there's quantities," Emmy replied, without thinking or looking. But as she stood there in her red silk dress, a flower in each hand, he forgave her impracticality. For at happy last his wife was back to normal. She had got a little careless about the housekeeping, maybe (he had remarked in jest the other day that the Fenns' life style, as well as the Fenns, seemed to be invading their house). But in general she seemed to have made a good adjustment to Convers. Her sulks and depressions had disappeared; she no longer bothered him about Hum C, nagged at him to spend more time at home, or complained of the climate. Since they had come back from vacation she had been content, even gay, most of the time.

He looked into the freezing compartment of the refrigerator.

"It doesn't matter; if we need more ice, we can simply open the back door and break a piece off the roof. Don't worry about it, darling, everything's going to go beautifully."

Yes; Holman felt himself that the evening would be a success. Nearly forty people had been invited, and they were serving both punch and mixed drinks. It was a pretty ambitious party for a first-year instructor to give. On the other hand, from a Stockwell point of view it was nothing at all. "Who do you think will get here first?" he asked.

"Golly, I don't know." Not Will, anyhow, Emmy thought, he said he would be late. She filled another bowl at the sink, where red and white flowers were soaking. "The McBanes?"

"No; we told him it was at 8:30." It was the inflexible custom of Mr. McBane to arrive precisely at the designated time for every gathering, professional or social. Over the years, most members of the Convers faculty had adopted the same solution to this problem which Holman and Emmy had hit upon independently: Mr. and Mrs. McBane were invited for a later hour than that suggested to the other guests.

"I wonder if he knows what we did," Holman said. "I suppose even if he doesn't he'll realize it once he gets here."

"If he does, it serves him absolutely right," Emmy said, casually but not unkindly. She was not in the least in awe of McBane; Holman looked at her with admiration. During the first few years of their marriage, still inexperienced, she had followed the social forms in which she had been trained; now she used them. One day she would be the kind of hostess of whom a department chairman, a dean, even a college president might be proud.

"Maybe he'll come first anyway, if he's found us out. He's capable of anything."

"It won't matter. He can talk to the Fenns." She replaced a red carnation with a white one.

"The Fenns? I bet they won't get here till ten."

"Oh, no. Miranda promised she would come early to help with the food."

Holman groaned; evidences of his wife's friendship with the Fenns continued to surprise and irritate him. "I wish you hadn't arranged that," he said.

"Oh, darling, why not?"

Emmy asked ingenuously; yet, he thought, she knew perfectly well. It had been her idea that they should employ Mrs. Rabbage to help at the party and pass things, but he had vetoed it. At this stage it might look pretentious; besides, he had the feeling that Mrs. Rabbage would not like being asked to serve as a maid. Next year, maybe, or the year after, when they gave a party to celebrate his promotion (as this one was in a sense a celebration of his reappointment), they could get one of his students in to help.

"Baby," he said. "Ever since that fire the Fenns think they live in this house, as it is. They eat our food and borrow our clothes and forget to return them. They come and take away the magazines and the newspaper before I've even had a chance to read them. And they always want to be driven somewhere."

"I know. But think what a frightful time they've had. First their house almost burned up and then Julian lost his job, and he hasn't found another one, and they never have any money. And all those children. Some months Miranda absolutely can't even pay her bills."

"She wouldn't be able to pay her bills most of the time no matter how much money she had. Whoever gave her that two hundred dollars made a big mistake; now she really thinks the fairies will always take care of Miranda Fenn. And maybe she's right. That kind of shiftless, picturesque family seems to attract charity. I've seen it before when I was a kid. You never hear of any mysterious philanthropist giving money to people like the Greens, who are just as poor if not poorer. And look what she's done with it. Four pairs of ice skates and a table made of sea shells, so far."

"Yes, that's utterly crazy," Emmy agreed. Once she had seen that Miranda did not intend to pay anything toward the repair of the house, she had imagined that she would purchase some large durable object—such as a washing machine—which might serve as a reminder of the gift for many years. Holman had suggested a secondhand car. "I know. Suppose Julian should get a job in the South, all those ice skates won't be any use. And wherever he goes that silly table will probably break in the moving van."

Holman put glasses on a tray. They still had a wedding dozen of everything, all highly polished. "I saw that man in the Music Department that we asked to the party, today," he remarked. "Bill Thomas."

"Oh?"

"He seems like an intelligent fellow."

"Mm."

"You know, I've seen him around several times, spoken to him, but I never had any idea he was in the Music Department."

"I know what you mean," Emmy said after a pause. "He doesn't look like a musician. He looks just like any-

161

body." In her language, "anybody" did not by any means signify "everybody." It was, so to speak, short for "anybody who might turn up at the Rabbit Hills Country Club."

"I don't think he's really U, though, do you?"

"Oh no. Shabby genteel, maybe. He went to public high school in Tennessee; I think Miranda said." I am carrying this off frightfully well, she said to herself; perhaps I ought not to have remembered where he went to school.

"Hard to tell with Southerners," Holman said. "They have these manners. You have to get to know them better before you can tell."

"Mm." I didn't giggle the slightest bit, Emmy thought. But I mustn't say more. To make sure, she picked up a vase of flowers and carried it out of the room.

Passing the mirror in the hall, she thought: I am pretty tonight. And the house looks pretty; these old New England farmhouses are really charming once they're fixed up. The lamps all lit, the ashtrays placed, the fresh chintz curtains, bowls of flowers, nuts, crackers, cigarettes. How happy I am. I ought to feel guilty, think of poor Holman.

Partly as a result of her St. Kit's training, Emmy felt guilt for the moral act of adultery, not for the physical act. All her intermittent remorse was directed toward her deception of Holman, her inability to love him, her loving someone else. When she was with Will she didn't care, she was drunk, carried away. The worst times were beforehand, when she was in the bathroom with the door locked, making ready, thinking: I could/should stop, I could/should stop this. Afterward was also bad, but not as bad. She still believed in all the rules, but she couldn't seem to feel that they applied to her; she was dizzy with happiness.

More flowers; she brought them in. On the tables, on the mantelpiece, on the bookcases. Then the last, the largest: this one all huge roses. All red and white, and of course it was February 14th. On the piano. Was that too much? Would anyone else notice? Would Will himself see that the whole party was a valentine for him?

"What a dear little house," Mrs. Lumkin exclaimed to Emmy, looking round it. Emmy's smile became stiff; what right had Betsy to patronize her? "And what a charming

162

room this is," Mrs. Lumkin added, pushing open a door that had been left shut.

"Freddy's playroom," Emmy explained. "I'm afraid it isn't very neat." It was, though not as neat as the Lumkins' house. "It was supposed to be the study, but I decided to give it to him. It's so nice to have a room like this when you have a child." I must be turning into a terrible bitch, she thought, to throw it back in her face that way about having children, when Will says she minds so. (He hasn't come yet.) She looked anxiously at Betsy, but Mrs. Lumkin's face still wore the self-satisfied expression with which she had entered the house. To make amends, she said: "You are looking simply wonderful tonight, Betsy." It was true, she did look well—for her.

"Thank you." Betsy accepted the compliment, but did not return it. "I feel wonderful." Smug. Bill Lumkin probably had a raise, or something. (He still hasn't come.)

"Oh, Mrs. Rabbage; you know I couldn't stand Mrs. Rabbage," Miranda said to Flo Butler and Lucy Green. "I'd far rather do the cleaning myself. She was always coming up to me with something perfectly good and saying in this snippy way: 'Shall I throw this out maybe huh?' And she was such a snoop, I know she was going and looking in my drawers, and in the icebox even, to see what we were having for supper, I suppose."

"It's always a nuisance having somebody else in one's house," said Flo. "And then cleaning women never do things really right. That's what I decided last year and so I just started to save up that money and when I had enough I bought one of those new vacuums with all the attachments. It's really a much more sensible solution. Don't you think so?" Flo turned and asked this of Lucy Green, who was sitting next to her. Ever since Lucy had moved in upstairs Flo had tried to take her under her wing, for goodness knows it was hard being so young and far away from home and expecting one's first baby. Miranda also turned to Lucy in order to hear her opinion. But Lucy, who could afford neither a vacuum nor a cleaning woman, obstinately or timidly said nothing.

"And how is the thesis coming along?" McBane asked Holman in a loud, cheerful voice. One might have thought that he was drunk, but it was common knowledge that

163

though he sometimes assumed the manner and privileges of intoxication, he never took anything stronger than cream soda. His favorite brand, which Holman and Emmy had purchased for the occasion, was called Fizz. (The phrase: "You love Fizz, Fizz loves you" had once appeared in a Hum C assignment, followed by: "But what if Fizz doesn't love you? Suppose Fizz hates you? What if it should go off in your face, BOOM!")

"Coming along fine," Holman retorted, looking around to discover the size of their audience. He saw three at least who were certainly listening.

"That's good, that's good," McBane roared. "That's the way!" The audience increased to five. "Lay not up for yourself treasures in colleges, where deans break through and steal, but put your faith in bibliographies." Did Bill Lumkin's back grow stiff as he heard the word "deans"? "Keep up your outside connections, get power. What you can't hurt won't see you." Loud as McBane's voice was, Lumkin still did not turn round. He and McBane had not exchanged a word as yet this evening. The rest of the audience laughed; it was one of McBane's greatest virtues that he had never been known to repeat a witticism—he left that to his inferiors in the Department, confident that they would not let him down. Indeed, within half an hour everyone at the party had heard this new one, with the exception of Kittie McBane, his wife.

Coming out of the kitchen with a plate of decorated crackers, Emmy stopped and looked at her party. It was now at high tide, bright with noise and motion. Quarter to ten. He had said he would be late, but still he hadn't come. All the other guests were here, talking and laughing together; about nothing really, though they pretended to be interested and surprised. She could surprise them if she liked. If she wanted to. Suppose she were to walk into the center of the room, climb on that chair there, and clap her hands for attention as the mistresses used to do at St. Kit's. "Attention, attention everyone! I have an important announcement to make!" Oh, they didn't know, none of them knew, they didn't know anything!

It was simply amazing, the impulse she had to do it. Yes, like sometimes when she was at the theater, or a concert, especially if she were sitting toward the edge of the first balcony, she would think how she might stand up and speak, shout, even throw herself down. They would all stop and look at her; even the musicians in the orchestra, the actors on stage.

Only, falling would hurt. So she always remained in her seat, even if it was in the front row—at the most dropping, as if by chance, torn bits of her program (or the whole program folded into an airplane or a fan) on the dark hair and bald heads of the audience below

The door. Will. He had come.

"You look well," Will said to Miranda. "Is that a new dress?"

"No; but my shoes and stockings are. How do you like them?" Tonight, everything Miranda had on was in various shades of dark yellowish-green; her pale, fine red hair, freshly washed, stood out in all directions above.

"Tremendous. You look as if you were in mourning for a plant."

"You." As she sometimes did, Miranda made the gesture of slapping Will without actually touching him. "But you're against everything."

"I am not. I'm one of the stanchest upholders of society there is."

"Seriously."

"Seriously."

"What society?"

"This one. All I do is just what's expected of me. I play my part. I'm the local failure, no-good artist, seducer of little girls. Why, it's chaps like me that keep society going." As he spoke, Will looked past Miranda's head. She turned, followed his glance, and saw Emmy standing across the room, a pitcher in her hand.

"Beautiful," Will said. "She is, isn't she? See, she knows I'm looking at her, but she won't let on, she won't look over." He laughed.

"She was watching you before," Miranda said.

"I know."

"And before you came, she kept looking toward the front door as if it were enchanted. Will."

"Mm?"

"You must be careful." Miranda lowered her voice. "I don't mean about other people. You mustn't hurt her. I think she's in love with you seriously."

To emphasize her words, Miranda put her glass down

on the bookcase. Will, for the same reason, picked his up and drained it. "I'll tell you something worse than that," he said. "I think I'm in love with her. More likely she'll hurt me." Miranda smiled. "You don't believe me."

"No."

"I mean it. I'll tell you something, a couple of nights ago after I'd seen her I was so happy or something I couldn't sleep. So I got out of bed and went for a walk. I must have done about five miles, up toward Greensbury and back, and when I got out of town I found I was laughing and shouting her name out loud in the middle of nowhere, cold as hell and not even a moon, but I was shouting: 'Emily! Emily!' and running along the road in the dark like a maniac."

When he went into the kitchen to dispose of some empty glasses, Holman found Julian Fenn pouring whisky from one of the bottles they had been keeping in reserve.

"Can I get you something?" he asked.

"Oh, no thanks. I can help myself." Julian looked more peculiar than usual this evening. He was wearing a pale green shirt and a red tie, neither of them very well pressed, and his sticky black hair looked as if it had not been cut for months.

"I see you can," Holman said, half jovially. Apparently the other half did not register, for Julian smiled briefly and turned to the sink, where he helped himself to water and ice.

"I was looking at your *Times*," he remarked, not apologetically, picking Holman's newspaper up again.

Rather than leave Julian alone in the kitchen to appropriate more of his possessions, Holman decided to remain. He used the opportunity to inquire about one of his students who had formerly been Julian's student.

"Oh yes, Dicky Smith," Julian said. "He used to come around a lot last term. He was completely shaken up by the course. Very dim bourgeois background, western New York State or something. He used to bring me short stories he'd written. Maybe he's given that up, though; he hasn't been around lately."

"Yeah. That's because he's started coming to see me instead."

"Oh? With stories?"

"If you want to call them that. God-awful Kafkaesque fantasies."

"With me it was more God-awful Hemingway. I suppose you could say this was a step forward, culturally speaking."

"God," said Holman, who regarded it as a step back. "I try to discourage him, but he keeps coming back."

"What do you think of him as a student? I thought he wasn't bad. I had to give him a B for the term because he didn't finish the final. He could have done better, but he got rattled. He was fun in class, though, very enthusiastic."

"I don't care for him," Holman said. "He may be enthusiastic, but he's not serious. I suspect he's the type that goes into everything with a rush and then abandons it when it begins to get hard. He looks impressionable, but in the long run nothing makes the slightest damn impression on him." Julian's face did not express agreement, and it occurred to Holman that he was of this same type. "I've been giving him C and C+ on his papers. It doesn't seem to me that he deserves any more."

"It's important to him to keep at least a B-minus average, though; otherwise he won't be able to stay here. He's on scholarship, you know."

"Yeah, I know. He tells me about it all the time."

"We mustn't be seen standing together like this," Emmy said to Will for the second time that night. "But don't go. Stay late, stay till the end." She put her hand on Will's arm, took it off, put it back, looking up at him. Her thick eyelashes had been made thicker with black paint, her warm mouth was a little smudged, her color high; she was two-thirds drunk.

"If you think it's all right."

"Oh, yes, after all you came so late. Besides I like having you here, even if I can't talk to you. Besides, I want you to meet Holman."

"I have met Holman."

"But I want you to talk to him."

"Talk to him? What about?"

"Oh, golly, I don't know, about politics or sports or something, whatever men talk about."

"To disarm suspicion, you mean."

"No, no, no. I don't mean that at all. I want you to be

friends. Really, I know you would get on frightfully well."

"Yes, we have something in common already," Will said, leaning back onto the wall, so that Emmy's hand slid off his arm. Her mouth turned up in a smile and then down in a sulk as she understood. "It's not a good idea, Emily. I've been in that sort of friend situation before, and it doesn't work. It's dirty."

"But Holman likes you," Emmy said, not listening. "He really does, he told me today that he thought you were intelligent." Will did not reply. "Besides, you promised you would play the piano for us."

"For you."

"For me, then." They exchanged a look. "After all, I've never heard you play."

"He said Hum S was like Zen," Charley Green said. "He came up after class and said so. But I don't think that's right."

"No," Julian agreed. "Actually, it's just the opposite. McBane plays at being a guru sometimes, with his cryptic utterances. And of course we imitate him. But Zen tries to communicate what can't be said in words. It deals only with the inexpressible. Hum C deals only with the expressible."

"Yes; yes," Charley said, waving his glass. "We won't consider anything but words, anything that can't be put into words. 'Define your terms!' "

"It's eleven-thirty," Lucy Green said, holding up her wrist so that her husband could read the little gold numbers on her watch. Charley paid no attention.

"It's the only way," he continued. "Otherwise we'd all be speaking different languages all the time; well, we are, outside of the course."

"And inside it," Julian said. "You define your terms, very well, then you define the terms of your definition, where are you going to stop?"

"I'm so tired, Charley." Lucy leaned against him, her stomach first.

"But you reach an agreement on the terms," Charley said, supporting his wife vaguely with one arm. "I've found that. Then you can communicate."

"You think you reach an agreement, because you're using the same words. There's still no proof that you're talking about the same things. Your 'communication' takes

168

place between dreams, not between actions. Between dreamers, not actors."

"No; no! I don't agree," Charley said. He waved his hand and his glass around so that a large part of his fourth drink fell onto the rug. Half of the ten or fifteen people who remained at the party did not hear him, but the rest did.

"Charley, I think we ought to go home," Lucy said. "Really."

"Oh, don't go," Emmy said to the Lumkins. "Do stay. Will's going to play the piano for us." Her party was melting fast; all the guests who had children at home, and therefore sitters ticking away like taxi meters all evening, had already left.

"No; we absolutely must," Betsy said, stiffly even for her. Emmy was puzzled for a moment, but then she understood that Betsy was simply jealous that Will should play at any house but hers; she understood everything tonight, everything was so brightly colored, so clear. The Greens were leaving too, and Allen Ingram—she looked at Will to see if he would keep his promise. Yes, for when the door closed he sat down again and picked up his glass.

"Will's promised to play for us," she announced to Holman.

"All right. That's fine," Holman said generously, sitting down himself. He really wanted everyone to go, so that he and Emmy could talk about what a success the party had been, but what was a few minutes more? If they were few, for it was after one. He felt a little tired, and Emmy certainly looked disheveled: her make-up was mostly rubbed off, her hair-do falling apart, her bright dress wrinkled.

"McBane was in great form tonight, wasn't he?" Will said.

"He always is."

They began to talk together, just as Emmy had planned. Emmy looked at them, but did not listen. Will was so frightfully attractive, the way his hand was round his glass, and Holman, of course Holman was absolutely tiresome sometimes but now he was serious and interested and trying to be agreeable, she could tell from the sound of his voice. He was talking and Will was listening and they were getting on very well.

"I used to think I had it figured out who was on McBane's side in the department and who was against him," Holman was saying. "Now I'm beginning to think he keeps moving his side around on purpose so that nobody can stay on it for long. Or off it. Baker made this big protest speech last week in the course meeting, you could see he was all worked up about it and feeling very courageous, and scared too, God knows why, because he has tenure. And McBane turned around and said: 'I agree with you completely, Jay.' "

Discussing McBane, Emmy thought, they were always doing that in Convers, although he was quite boring and unpleasant. He had worse manners than Freddy, and those awful fuzzy tweed suits and poor little Kittie McBane who always looked so vague and dim, what had she ever wanted to marry him for? It couldn't be for lack of other chances, for she must have been quite pretty once.

Holman's jaw lengthened and stiffened in the face that tries to hide a yawn; Will had sunk down among the cushions, his head back.

"But you must play for us now," she announced.

"All right." Will dragged himself up off the sofa, smiling at Emmy; he thought she looked wonderful now, all softened and sleepy, her soft, heavy hair uncoiling onto her neck. He slid onto the bench and tried a few chords to test the piano, an old Hamilton upright. It was off key, but not badly, and mostly in the upper octaves.

"Very successful party, I thought," Holman said to Emmy behind him. "I thought it worked out very well; didn't you?" Will disliked to be interrupted when he was playing; he took his hands off the keys and waited.

"Mm, yes," Emmy agreed.

"The ice just about held out. Go ahead. Play us something," he instructed Will. "I don't know much about music, but I like what I know."

Pig, Will thought. He had the impulse to walk out. However, he moved only a small way down the bench and started to play, instead of what he had planned for Emmy, Purcell's *Trumpet Voluntary*. He parodied the piece, playing it as loudly as possible. It was obviously the perfect choice for Holman Turner, a triumphal march full of pompous certainties.

"You'll wake Freddy," Emmy murmured.

"Shh," Holman ordered; he was listening now. Will

went on as loudly as before, burlesquing the piece more and more shamelessly. Emmy knew something was wrong; she blinked her eyes.

Bang, bang, bang. Will brought the music to a close with a portentous ritardando of massed chords, and turned round.

"Great, fine!" Holman said, getting up. "That was fine! Say, you really can play." He applauded, clapping his cupped hands together with a loud, hollow sound.

"Thank you," Will said.

Holman looked toward Emmy for collaboration, expectantly.

"Yes; thank you, Will," Emmy said finally and rather flatly. "That was nice."

"Oh, that was nice!" Emmy said.

"Mm. . . . It's always best in bed," Will murmured without moving, his voice smothered by her hair.

"Oh, but you. You don't know."

"Mm, but you." Will raised his head and smiled, then began to lift himself up on one elbow.

"Don't go."

"I'm not going anywhere." He reached across her for the glass of bourbon and ice which stood beside the bed. "Want some?"

"No thanks. I'd spill it. I don't want to move."

Will drank and put the glass back. Resting his head on his fists, lying above her, he looked down at Emmy's face, at her heaps of hair tangled across the tangled sheet. They lay diagonally across the bed, with clothes and blankets thrown and blown about in every direction away from them, even to the corners of Emmy's bedroom.

"I mean what I said, you know."

"What did you say?" Emmy asked.

"That I'm in love with you."

"Yes; I guess I'm in love with you, too," Emmy said.

"I thought you might have thought I just said it in the heat of the moment."

"No."

Will lay down again, closing his eyes, his thick fair lashes together. A faint, regular pulse beat in his neck under red, shaved skin, next to Emmy's browner skin. She could see each individual hair growing out of his head, some blonder, some browner in the blocks of sunlight that fell across the bed.

"Don't go. You feel so, I don't know, so beautiful and heavy and warm."

"I can't help it; I'm gone." Will rolled over onto his side.

"Say." Lying flat, Emmy felt around her, then on the floor.

"Mm?"

"I can't find the pillow anywhere ... oh, thank you. Where was it?"

"On the floor."

"But how did it get there?"

"*I* don't know. I wasn't watching it."

"Neither was I." They both laughed.

"It's so nice here. I can't think why we never tried it before," Emmy said, but as she said it she thought why; not so much the danger of discovery, as because it was also Holman's bed. She wiped that thought out.

"Will," she said, "isn't it funny to think that everyone else in town is out working now, and shopping and walking around in the snow and going to school, because it's really ten o'clock in the morning, and here we are here? It's funny, I don't feel any guilt, but I have this strange feeling, I think: No one knows about this but me, so maybe it isn't really happening."

"Or maybe they aren't really happening."

"No." Emmy rolled over onto her side. "There's too many of them for that. But, I mean, well, like Hum C, if you don't express it, does it exist?"

"What do you mean, if you don't express it?"

"Well." She laughed, and rolled farther over, toward him. "Mm. You still feel warm."

"So do you."

A few minutes passed.

"And then I think, what if everyone did know, then would I feel guilty?" Emmy asked.

"You're lucky. I always feel guilty, felt that way ever since I was about six; even when I'm being good. Finally I thought, Christ! I might as well give my conscience something to complain about."

"I can't make up my mind about Hum C," Emmy said presently. "I suppose I don't understand it. For instance this about looking at everything to see what it actually

172

basically is, and listening for the inner voice to find out what you really feel. When I listen to my inner voices they only say things like: 'I think I will call up Will,' or 'Let's give Emmy the largest nicest piece of pie.' "

Will laughed.

"No, it's true. You know, ever since I was first married, for years, I used always to give Holman the best helpings of everything. It was silly, because I'm sure he never noticed, but I used to like to do it. And then last fall I stopped, but still I always tried to be fair and make the plates come out even. But now I can't even seem to do that. Sometimes I try to give him the best on purpose, but then I notice after we've sat down that I've somehow subconsciously given him the worst one, it's burned, or something. So mean. And sometimes my inner voice even says crazy things like: 'Suppose Holman should get a cold, a very bad cold, oh, influenza, pneumonia, and die?' "

"What else can you expect from the subconscious? What did you think it would say? 'Beauty is truth, truth beauty'?"

Emmy laughed, but nervously.

"It won't. No. Or else, if you like, that's all it'll say. At least maybe it's the truth. You love Emily and you hate Holman."

"I don't hate him." She sat up and looked at Will as he lay across the bed, at the skeptical curve of his eyebrows and the strong, freckled curve of his back. From an art history point of view he was constructed, not on the principle of the cube and the sphere like Holman, but all of long heavy rectangles rounded off at the corners. "I don't feel anything at all about him, really. I'm indifferent to him."

Eleven o'clock. Will sat on the piano bench with his drink. Emmy, beside him but facing out, was eating a peanut-butter sandwich. She was barefoot and wearing blue jeans and an old sweater. On top of the piano the big vase of roses left over from the party, overblown, dropped red and white petals as Will played a series of minor discords.

"What's the matter? You're sad," Emmy said.

"I don't know. *Toutes les bêtes sont tristes après.* . . . Physiological, I guess. Loss of vital fluid."

"I'm not sad."

"Ah. You haven't lost anything." He played some notes in the treble, up where the strings were flat.

"Only my virtue."

"Does that still worry you?"

"I don't know. It frightens me, a little. I think how if everyone knew they'd be so angry or despise me, and I'm frightened that maybe you really despise me."

"Emily." Three chords from Bartok, then he broke off. "I'm frightened too, you know. It's always that way at the beginning of a serious love affair, both people are a little afraid of each other. 'Those that have power to hurt—' "

"You're not afraid of me, are you really?"

" 'Say it again,' you mean."

"But I'm all for you. I'm utterly on your side." Emmy used the phrases and inflections of St. Kit's.

"I love the tune of your voice," Will said, playing it on the piano with one finger. " 'I'm all for you. I'm utterly on your side.' "

"But seriously. I am."

"How are you on my side?"

"I'm going to help you. I'm going to be a good influence and encourage you to start composing music again."

Will took his hands abruptly off the keys. "No," he said. "That's the way it always is with women," he added. "They swear they love you, but the truth is they don't love you the way you are, they want you to change and *then* they'll really love you."

"I didn't mean I wanted you to change," Emmy protested. "I simply meant, I only thought you'd be happier yourself if you were writing music."

Will turned and looked at her. "It's not as simple as you think," he said finally, putting his hand on her arm.

"And I do love you," Emmy said. "I love you I love you I love you."

"All right." They kissed.

"Let's go upstairs," Will said.

"But I just made the bed up fresh."

"That was a mistake. Now you'll have to unmake it."

"You mean, seriously?"

"Why not? It's only eleven." He stood up, holding out his hands.

"I don't know." Emmy also stood up. It was Holman's practice to wait at least until the next day after making

174

love, and circumstances had previously led Emmy and Will to follow the same pattern.

"Unless you don't want."

"Oh, no! I do want." Taking a breath, she fell into his arms.

* * *

Allen Ingram to Francis Noyes

February 18

. . . I went to a party last weekend too, so there. It was quite a do for Convers; the entire English Department and representative of several others, all drinking and laughing and carrying on (except for poor Julian Fenn who still has no job and was hiding in the kitchen). Usually they go in more here for stiff little dinner parties.

I suppose I'd have to admit that I went not so much as a guest as an observer, a spy if one likes (and one does like, doesn't one?). Well, it was full of amusing tensions, and jostlings for admiration or power, all quite obvious once one knows the signs. This is a real little miniature universe—by which I don't mean The Universe in miniature. Though some of the more intellectual professors like to think so privately, and the less intellectual to say so publicly, Convers is not a microcosm of the world. The world (and we ought to know it if they don't) is a disorderly, dirty scrap heap. Convers, on the other hand, is a botanical or zoological garden, where each flower has its cage, each beast or bird its metal identification tag. When I first turned up everyone was frightened and nervous of me, but now that I have my label and show signs of staying quietly put, I am just one of the exhibits, along with The Janitor Who Drinks and Bad Oswald McBear.

The latter was greatly in evidence Saturday night, booming out his boorish bon mots, laughing his laugh. The only person who managed to pay him absolutely no attention was his wife Kittie. She just sat quietly all evening in a corner of the sofa, her tiny feet crossed, like a good little gray-haired schoolgirl, letting out little Miaows at the gossip which one or the other faculty wife was continually telling her. Yet she has a sharp look.

The party was given by Holman Turner, the Friend of the Foreign Car (but not of its owner) and his wife Emmy, whom I met there for the first time. She is a big, noisy, good-looking provincial deb. Like all the world, she had read *Sardines* and nothing else of mine, and like all the world she wanted me to "explain the symbolism." Quite hurt when I wouldn't; but she forgave me when I gave her explanation IB—the one about how I promised myself years and years ago never to reveal it, "because in Art and Love, explanations confuse the reality rather than elucidating it, don't you agree?" She was flattered and one could see that she would think this over at length; she is the serious, enthusiastic, Bryn Mawr type of deb. Rather like Cousin Martha—who wouldn't however thank me for the comparison, she'd think Mrs. Turner hopelessly suburban. Very good-looking, though—better luck than Mr. Turner deserves, especially when you realize that she must have brought him a good deal of $$: their liquor was well above the usual Convers standard, glasses from Jensen, etc. He was playing it all very offhandedly gracious, but (or rather therefore) I am positive he comes from absolutely Nowhere. I feel a certain sympathy with Mrs. T—maybe fellow feeling because she and I come from somewhat the same background and we have both de-classed ourselves by getting mixed up with the wrong sort of man? Only she doesn't, I suspect, suspect this yet. She seemed almost hysterically happy. Manic-depressive, per-haps—no doubt it's inherited; bulls and bears, you know—her father, who is a big trustee here, made his pile on Wall Street.

CHAPTER
10

"TELL ME HOW YOU WRITE MUSIC," EMMY SAID LAZILY, leaning against Will as he drove. They had spent the afternoon in a disused field fifteen miles south of Convers, over the mountains. The land was flatter there, the earth softer, the sun warmer on the cold dry leaves, and if they were seen it would be by someone who did not know them.

"You mean how I used to write music."

Emmy did not reply; already she had learned not to be drawn into that sort of discussion.

"Well," he said presently. "Tell me how you make a cake."

"Ohh."

"It's the same thing. Tell me. From the beginning. How you decide to and the whole thing."

"All right." She laughed. "Of course usually, lately, I'm in such a hurry, I simply stop at the market and buy a box of cake mix and follow the directions."

"No. That's Vaughan Williams. Nothing good can come of that. Tell me about some day when you have plenty of time, and you just think, maybe I would like to bake a cake."

"Well then. All right. First I'd have to think what kind of cake. If it was cold, I might want something rich and heavy, with raisins. Or it might be somebody's birthday. A day like today, I think I'd want to make something light, white, very crumbly, with lots of icing."

"Yes."

"So first I would get out *Fanny Farmer*, or the *Settlement Cookbook*, which is especially good for baking, and look over the recipes. I wouldn't follow any of them exactly, but they might give me an idea. And then I have a lot of notes and recipes of my own in a notebook."

Will laughed. "Yes. I had the Stravinsky Cookbook and the Tchaikowsky Cookbook, and I had a notebook too."

177

They were in the mountains now, climbing back toward Convers. Shadows of pines fell across the car.

"Then I decide what ingredients to use, and collect them," Emmy went on. "The flour and the sugar and the eggs and oh, you know."

"The instruments," Will said. "The strings and the brass and the woodwinds."

"Don't tease me." She turned her head to look at him. "I absolutely can't stand to be teased."

"But I'm not teasing. It's the same. Usually you begin with a theme. Maybe there's a chord that seems to go with it, or it might be just a series of chords. Then you have to think what kind of piece it's going into, is it short or long, what's the tempo, all that. And then, or maybe earlier, what instruments are going to play it. A series of notes'll sound different in different instruments or voices. Half the work is done before you even begin to write. I mean cook." Downhill now. The pines began to thin out into bare winter orchards, and then Convers lay below them in its tight valley.

"I hate coming back," Emmy said.

"Yes. Then the orchestration," Will went on. "It's like mixing up the cake. Parts of it are routine. But an amateur cook could ruin it at any point, and a professional knows a series of tricks that will make a big difference— A car's coming. Duck!" He put his hand on Emmy's shoulder and forced her down beside the dashboard as he drove.

"Let me up!" she protested.

"Chuck Walsh," Will said as the car passed. "I thought so. O.K." He allowed Emmy to sit up; her expression was indignant.

"Don't let's ever, ever do that again," she said.

"Do what?"

"Hide. I don't like it."

Will looked at her. "You want Chuck Walsh to see you?"

"Who's Chuck Walsh?"

"The man who just went by," Will said. "He's the Convers police chief."

"A policeman? What difference does it make if he sees us? Golly, I thought it must be Betsy Lumkin or somebody, the absolutely terrified way you were behaving. A *policeman*." Will said nothing. "Please don't ever do that to me again," she said. "It's vulgar. Ugh. Hiding from a policeman, as if I were a criminal."

"But we are criminals."

"We are not."

"Oh yes. Adultery is a crime in this state."

Emmy's face flickered; it was not a word she liked to hear. She had laughed, but she had really not liked it, when Will suggested that if the Convers Dames found out they would probably have their Sewing Club make Emmy a big scarlet letter A.

"Please go away," Will said without looking up, his head bent over the parts of Emmy's electric toaster which were laid out in front of him on her kitchen table.

"Really, darling," Emmy insisted. "You simply must leave those machine things alone and not bother Mr. Thomas, or he won't be able to make our toaster go again."

Freddy Turner did not go away, and he did not leave the machine things alone. He stood stolidly by his in his red corduroy overalls, crowding up against the table as if he had not heard a word that was said.

"Why don't you go outside and play for a while, Freddy?" Will asked.

"He can't go outside today," Emmy said. "He has a cold."

"I have a *cold*. Ahuh, achoo." He sneezed artificially in Will's face.

"It's not really very bad," Emmy explained. "I really don't think he's contagious any longer, but he does have a little sniffle and on a day like this. . . ." No one replied to her.

"Please put that screwdriver down," Will said presently.

"I don't hafta. You're not using it."

"I'm going to be using it." Will held out his hand. Without doubt, Freddy was one of the most unpleasant little boys he had ever met: stubborn, self-centered, and disobedient.

Holding the screwdriver in both plump paws, Freddy returned Will's look with one equally unfriendly.

"Give Mr. Thomas the screwdriver, please, Freddy-honey," Emmy said, effecting the transfer at the same time by the use of superior muscular force. "That's right." As Freddy's face began to shape itself for a scream, but

179

before one could emerge, she opened a drawer and handed him a pair of silver asparagus tongs. "There you are!"

Freddy began to play with the tongs rather sulkily. "Now let's see," Emmy went on. "Coffee or whisky?"

"Could I have coffee with a little whisky in it?"

"Of course you may." Emmy went into the dining room; Will worked on, fitting wires together. Suddenly he felt a severe pain in his right side.

"Yow!" He jumped, spilling parts of the toaster, and turned to face Freddy. "If you do that again, I'll hit you."

"No you won't."

"Oh yes, I will."

Deliberately, he turned his back again. Freddy stood contemplating this back for about ten seconds, the asparagus tongs in his hand. Then he pinched it again, even harder. Without a word or cry, Will turned and punched the four-year-old in the arm, so hard that he staggered.

"Aaow! Aaow!" Rushing at Will, Freddy hit out indiscriminately with both hands and feet, screaming, while Will held him off.

"Freddy; Freddy!" Emmy came running into the kitchen.

"He hit me," both contestants explained.

"Freddy, how could you?" Freddy did not reply; he stood stiff in his mother's arms.

"I don't like you," he said over her shoulder to Will. "I wish you were deaded."

And I wish you were deaded, Will thought. Even better, I wish you had never been born. He returned to the toaster. One of the most inconvenient features of adultery, he thought as he worked, is the amount of scheduling and contriving necessary to arrange things. He and Emmy could not meet on Tuesday or Thursday mornings because he had classes. On Monday and Wednesday mornings he could come out to Emily's house, but not on Fridays, because then the cleaning woman was there. On Fridays, though, Emily could leave Freddy with the cleaning woman; then they had a whole day together, but nowhere to go. It was the worst part of the year: all the leaves off the trees, cold and damp underfoot. For miles in every direction Convers was surrounded by bare, soggy wet hills and farmland, with here and there a suspicious rural village or dirty, decaying industrial town.

During the hours when an ordinary love affair is conducted—that is, in the evenings and on weekends—he and Emily could not meet at all except in public. Moreover, every afternoon and all Saturday, when Holman was conveniently away at work and the house stood warm and empty, Freddy was there, making even conversation almost impossible, demanding, interrupting, crying, making scenes.

Will had tried to be friendly with the little boy at first, but to no purpose. They were natural enemies. Will was cutting Freddy out of times when he would have had Emily all to himself. It was an unfair conflict, for Freddy had all the advantages. He did not have to pretend to like Will and he did not have to play by the rules. He could scream and call names; he could hit, kick, and even bite his opponent.

Will was sure that basically Freddy was aware of what was going on: he "knew" that his mother and Will were having a love affair, even if he were ignorant that any physical process was involved. (They had been very careful, and as far as he knew Freddy had never seen them so much as kiss.) Only Emily refused to recognize this; the idea that Freddy might know that she loved Will shocked her. Morally, though not sexually, she was easily shocked. She was a modern mother, and would never have dreamed of protecting her child from the facts of life or even, which was harder, of death—but she would have liked to shield him for a little while from a knowledge of the unruly passions that accompany them. She wanted Freddy to believe in a world where all authorities are kind and all families are happy. She was very angry when Richard Fenn told Freddy what the pound does with extra cats, and angry at Will when he laughed at her for this.

"Here you are!" With a smile and a flourish, Emily set the steaming cup of coffee in front of Will.

"What's that?" Freddy asked suspiciously.

"Just a cup of coffee for Will, darling."

"I want something to drink too, Mummy. I want something to eat. I want a snack."

"Dreadful vocabulary he picks up from Mrs. Rabbage," Emmy said. "It's too near to your suppertime, baby."

"I want a snack, Mummy. I want a snack! I want a snack!"

"It's too near to supper."

"I want one. Aaow! I want a snack!"

"You can have a cookie, one cookie, and that's all."

"A jam one."

"The jam ones are all gone, Freddy-ducky."

"But I want a jam one! I want a jam one! I want a jam one!"

Will put his head on his hands and sighed openly.

"We haven't got any jam ones, Freddy, we haven't got any in the whole house. Would you like some bread and jam?" Freddy scowled. "You can have some bread and jam if you'll take it away into the study. Will has to leave soon and he has to have it quiet so he can fix our toaster for us. You can watch the television."

"All right," Freddy finally said.

"Lord," Emmy sighed, returning from the study where the television was now going. Will said nothing; he thought that she could have sent Freddy away earlier if she had wanted to.

"How's the toaster? Do you think you'll be able to fix it?"

"It's fixed already."

"Honestly? Oh, that's wonderful. Will, you are so clever." Stooping, she put her arms around his neck. "And the marvelous way you mended the back door last week. You can do absolutely anything."

"Yeah, I'm an all-round second-rater." Will always rejected praise; it made him superstitiously nervous, as if something might hear the lie and revenge itself. Criticism he also rejected, at least from anyone in Convers, thinking or saying something which meant: "Who are you to judge me, you fool (or bastard, or both)?"

"Oh, don't be utterly silly," Emmy said, rubbing her head against his.

"Oh, I can do little piddling jobs. The damned trouble is, I never can finish anything big. It's true. I start some big project, and then, I don't know— Like my wife's porch steps back in Arlington."

Emmy let go of Will's neck and sat down on the kitchen stool. "Mm?"

"They were falling apart when we moved into the house, and she was going to get a carpenter, you know what that would have cost, so I said I'd fix them. I was full of honeymoon enthusiasm then. I went out and got some concrete and tools and built a new foundation. I'd

182

decided to enlarge the porch and make a kind of terrace at one side for us to sit out on, oh it was going to be great, and I poured the concrete and put up the posts and frame and got the lumber. I don't know, something happened, I don't know what. We hadn't begun to fight yet; Rosemary still didn't believe a lady ever raised her voice in anger. I meant to finish it, but I never did, somehow I lost interest. Rosemary was so furious finally she wanted to have it put into the divorce settlement. She complained that the way I'd left it, nobody could get in or out of the house. I suppose that was what I wanted. Could I have a little more bourbon in this?"

"Of course."

"I love you," he said as she set the bottle down beside him.

"Why do you love me?"

"I don't know. You're so beautiful, and you have such good bourbon."

Emily smiled, laying the back of her hand against the back of his.

"I wanted to ask you something," she said. "About Miranda."

"What about Miranda?" Will put his finger between hers.

Emmy hesitated. "You know she is so weird," she said. "I was over there yesterday afternoon and I was upstairs and needed something to wipe Freddy's face, so I called down to her, and she told me to look in her top drawer. It was a complete mess, naturally, simply dreadful. But what really upset me was, do you remember that wax doll she made of Betsy Lumkin? Well there it *still* was, in with her handkerchiefs, with a horrid long hatpin stuck through its stomach." Will laughed. "But that's rather dreadful, don't you think? Vindictive."

"Childish." Will stroked her hand, her wrist.

"Of course, lucky you, you're not superstitious."

"Was that what you wanted to ask me?"

"No," she admitted. "It was something she said about North Greensbury. I was saying what a peculiar isolated little town it was, with the paper factory, and the ice in the river all yellow from the dye, and the people all looking alike in the stores, so ingrown, as if they hadn't left town for generations, you know, what we thought. And she said it wasn't so at all, that some of the people who worked in

183

the Greensbury Mill lived right around here or had relatives around here and really whatever you did in North Greensbury would get back to Convers and everyone would hear about it sooner or later. As if she knew all about the motel and everything. Will. You didn't tell her about us, did you?"

Rather than lie, Will said nothing. They looked at each other for a moment.

"You told Miranda," Emmy said, disentangling her fingers as if from an object.

"Emily. She knew already. She guessed it."

"How could you do that?"

Will thought that she was even more beautiful when she was angry. "She guessed," he repeated.

"Oh, don't quibble."

"It's not as if you'd been doing much to hide it from her," he said agreeably. "She really thought you knew she knew, from some of the things you've said to her."

It was true that in order to have the opportunity to discuss Will frequently with Miranda, Emmy had admitted to having seen him on several occasions, and also to his having made remarks which would indicate that a flirtation, at least, was going on.

"So all this time I've been telling her things she already knew."

Will did not deny it. "Do you mind so much?" he asked gently, stretching out his hand; implying: Are you so ashamed of what you've done?

"I don't know. It's frightfully embarrassing." What I mind most is knowing that you've been talking about me between you, she started to say, but for some reason was afraid to. "I suppose she's told Julian and that Allen Ingram and all their friends and everybody," she said instead.

"No. She hasn't told anyone." Will stood up. His instinct, as well as the clock, told him that it was time to go.

"I don't believe you. . . . Oh, very well, I believe you."

"I haven't lied to you yet," Will said, thinking: Well, I haven't, have I? Looking hurt, he began to wind a long woolly scarf around his neck.

Emmy glanced from him to the clock. "You have to go," she stated. "Right away."

"I know."

"You better go around by Baird Road, so you won't pass him coming home."

"Don't be angry," Will said. "You aren't angry, are you?"

"I don't know."

"Don't be angry. I'll call you tomorrow morning after my first class." Will put one hand into his coat sleeve, the other on Emmy's. "We'll talk then."

"All right." She smiled almost unwillingly.

"I hate to leave now."

"I hate to have you leave." This was not true; actually Emmy was nervous to have Will out of the house before Holman walked into it, and she also wanted to be alone for a time so as to think over the discovery she had just made.

"I thought you told me you never gave away secrets," she added as she walked him to the back door, laughing uneasily. "You said a gentleman never tells tales. Didn't you?"

"I never said I was gentleman." Will opened the door and went out, quickly disappearing into the freezing gray mist.

Emmy's smile faded, but she stood on at the open door, listening to his car drive away, feeling unsettled, unhappy, and soon, cold. At last she could hear nothing except blasts of music and gunplay from the television in the study. She hurried in to turn it off, just as two bad guys collapsed from stomach wounds. Freddy was supposed to watch only children's shows and cartoons. Click; death shrank to the center of the screen and went out.

"Now, that's more than enough television," she said. "Come into the kitchen now and help Mummy fix your supper."

"Okay." Freddy looked up at his mother with the innocent charm which Will had never seen. How quickly children forget, she thought, how soon they forgive us. Of course, she had lived seven times as long as Freddy; in his terms nearly a day had passed since Will hit him.

"That's right," she said as he stirred milk into his soup with a wooden spoon. "That's a good boy."

"I'm a big help for you, Mummy."

"You're a big help, Freddy."

"I help you allatime. I'm a big boy."

"You're getting to be a big boy. Really, big, big boys

185

don't pinch people with asparagus pinchers. You'll have to be good, Freddy, if you want to be a really big boy."

"Okay." Freddy let go of the spoon, which slid down into the pot. "I going to be good," he said looking at her round-eyed, "because you know what going to happen if I do bad things?"

"No, what?"

"God going to come," Freddy said.

Emmy stopped, holding the pot in midair. She had been brought up to believe in a distant and abstract, though benevolent deity, a kind of Good Principle, who interested himself in the creation and preservation of nations and virtues rather than individuals. When he was older, she hoped to pass this concept on to Freddy.

"You know God?" Freddy asked.

"No."

"He has big wings. He's half a man and half a lady. He has big, big wings, Mummy!"

"Who told you that?" With difficulty, Emmy prevented herself from giggling.

"Nobody."

"Did Charles or Richard or Katie Fenn tell you that about God?"

"Nope." But Freddy looked down; the long dark lashes (almost the only feature he had inherited from his mother) lay on his cheeks in a thick concealing fringe. "I just know, cause I saw him. He lives in the cemetery."

"In the cemetery!"

"Yep." Delighted at having his mother's full attention, Freddy gave her a big smile. "An when God gets angry, know what? He makes it rain and rain and rain. Know how?"

"No, how?"

"He squirts in the air with his squirt guns. Squirt, squirt!" Freddy pantomimed this with both hands. "He got many, many, fourteen squirt guns."

Letting herself laugh aloud at last, Emmy took Freddy into her arms; he laughed too, for pleasure. "Oh, Freddy— Freddy, my dear bear," she said, hugging him. "Mmm, I do like you." Partly because she could not kiss Will in front of Freddy, Emmy was inhibited about kissing or petting Freddy in front of Will. So she spent whole afternoons of uncomfortable and unnatural self-restraint.

"And I like you, too, Mummy."

186

Tuesday morning. Emmy climbed the wet outside steps (smelling of ashes and leaves) and the dry inside steps (floorwax, incense) of the Episcopal Parish House, and pushed open the door of the Tuesday Ladies' Exchange (dust, coffee, mothballs). She spent two hours here every week as a volunteer worker: sorting the stock, making entries in the log book, and helping the women who came in to buy or sell second-hand clothes.

Usually the Ladies' Exchange was crowded with workers and customers when she arrived, but today no one was there except Kittie McBane, who sat in her place behind the cash desk knitting (and wearing) something dim, woolly, and blue. Though it was an extremely dark morning she had allowed herself only one light; the rest of the long room was in semi-obscurity. The racks and tables of used clothes were neat and undisturbed, as they had been left on the previous Tuesday evening. Rain and sleet mingled together sluiced against the windows, but it was warm, even stuffy, inside. Mrs. McBane always turned up the heat.

"Good morning!" Emmy said.

"Good morning, Emmy. Not a very good morning, though, is it? I hope you didn't have too much trouble getting in today?"

"Not really," Emmy replied, hanging up her coat in the workers' closet to prevent its being tagged and purchased. "Once I got out of the driveway; the snowplow—" They discussed the local climate and road conditions; Mrs. McBane volunteered the information that the weather was not at all unusual for this time of year and that we (Emmy) mustn't expect real spring for at least two months.

"Shall I put on the light?" Emmy asked.

"I don't know, I expect you might," Mrs. McBane said. "Rebecca's gone to Randall's to get more marking tags, she said she'd be back about ten, and Mrs. Manning's coming in soon I believe. Rebecca said she didn't think there'd be very many customers with this weather." Rebecca Scott, wife of the college and town physician Dr. Scott, was president of the Ladies' Exchange and of many other organizations in Convers; Polly Manning (wife of the Convers Creamery) was a regular morning worker. Mrs. McBane's designation of the former by her given and the latter by her husband's name did not indicate the

187

lesser age or prestige of Mrs. Scott, but rather the reverse.

Not just anybody could become a "volunteer" worker at the Ladies' Exchange; it was a considerable privilege which Mrs. Scott had conferred on Emmy; one which many women in town might forever be denied, no matter how well their husbands did in local academic or business competition. As it was, Emmy was the youngest worker there, and she never felt younger than she did on Tuesdays; she was their pet; their ingenue. She did not mind; she found the Ladies' Exchange comfortable, familiar. The women had a kind of ease of manner which was painfully lacking in most of the academic wives, and after all, it was not the real world, only a game, a little New England town.

"Well! Isn't it frightful out," Polly Manning cried, bouncing in in a clutter of scarves and bits of fur. "Hello, hello there!" She plopped into a chair and with some difficulty, for she was fat, began to take off her fur-edged galoshes. "But, do you know, I do think it's letting up!"

"And where's Mrs. Lumkin?" she asked presently.

"Oh, she's not coming in at all today," Mrs. McBane said. "She's not been feeling too well."

"The flu," Polly Manning announced with some satisfaction. One of Betsy's most irritating qualities was that she was never sick. She believed, and frequently stated at the Ladies' Exchange, that it was unnecessary to be so unless one had a poor constitution.

"Oh no, I don't think so," Kittie McBane said with her air of timid authority. "I imagine it's something else."

"I wonder what," Polly said, lowering her voice so that she could not be heard by the two farmers' wives who had just come in. "She definitely looked to me as if she was coming down with something last week; didn't you think so?"

"She didn't look well," Kittie agreed.

"And she was so cross," Polly went on, opening the log book to record some of her own old clothes—she had a large well-dressed family, and always brought something in. "Really, the way she spoke to that poor little Mrs. Green from the college, the one who wanted us to lay aside the baby things for her, *she* didn't know that we never hold anything for more than a week. I mean, really,

188

it wasn't so much what she said, but there is such a thing as driving customers away by your manner."

"Betsy had a dreadful headache last week, I know," Emmy said in her little-girl Ladies' Exchange voice.

"And the week before. Didn't she?"

"Yes, that's so, she did," Kittie agreed, casting on.

"Moody. Gaining weight, too. Change of life." Polly stage-whispered.

"Oh, I think not." Kittie tittered. "Can I help you, Mrs. Sturak?" This was to one of the customers who had just placed a mound of clothing on the cash desk.

"I didn't believe we'd ever get rid of that hat of Mrs. Baker's," Kittie cried delightedly as the door shut. "I always think, how could any woman bear wearing another woman's hat, because people do remember hats, at least I do. Oh dear, I wish Rebecca would come back, I do so want a cup of tea."

"I'll put the water on now," Emmy said.

It was growing lighter outside, and several more customers came in, some with bags and boxes of old clothes to sell. Polly and Emmy set about pricing them. Just as the kettle began to simmer, Mrs. Scott arrived, shutting the door behind her briskly and simultaneously giving the room a practiced sweeping glance and the workers a cheerful good morning. "Heavens above," she said. "It's boiling in here; how can you stand it?"

Nobody offered an explanation, and with a brisk step she went to the thermostat by the cash desk and turned it down. Kittie McBane gave only the faintest sigh. Every Tuesday for years she and Rebecca had engaged in this conflict over the heat. It had never come out into the open, for Kittie conducted her side of the war in the most discreet and innocent manner imaginable. Presently, when Rebecca was not looking, she would reach over and turn the thermostat up again, a little bit at a time.

"Taking in clothes. Oh, and I see you put the kettle on, that's *good*," Rebecca said to Emmy and Polly. One of her best traits was that she never practiced irony—she gave praise frequently, and with a whole heart. Rebecca was a natural leader and manager; she would have had a highly successful career in big-city business or society. She was kind, practical, and intelligent. Her only fault was that she was inclined to be suspicious without cause (in the Ladies' Exchange she was always looking out for shoplifters and

189

at home for signs of infidelity); her only failing that, though over fifty, she still wore Tyrolean dirndls. She was broad-shouldered and full-breasted, with regular features and a high color; her gray-blond hair was pulled back in a Tyrolean knot, so that she looked like a head waitress in a Swiss restaurant. A pair of horn-rimmed glasses provided the only incongruous note.

"Emmy," she said presently, "I wanted to speak to you about those clothes that Miranda Fenn brought in last week." Emmy looked up. "They just simply won't do. I thought so when I saw them, but I hoped that we could accept a few things at least. I know she would like to have the money, but I went over them and really I couldn't find anything that I thought anyone would want to buy." According to the rules of the Ladies' Exchange, all second-hand clothes had to be clean and in good repair. If they were not, they went into the African Aid box under the stairs, along with all articles not sold or reclaimed within six weeks. "So there they are," Rebecca added, pointing to a large dirty cardboard carton. "I thought you could tell her about it."

Emmy looked at the carton with dismay. She had seen the clothes in it already and could not have agreed more with Mrs. Scott's decision. But the idea of conveying this decision to Miranda, who had already in imagination made at least ten dollars on the transaction, embarrassed her dreadfully.

The kettle began to whistle. Emmy made the tea, and Polly Manning brought out some Manning's Creamery Heavy Cream and sugar from her large bag.

"Ahh!"

"Nice and hot."

"Could you pass the sugar, please?"

Putting back a pile of log books, Rebecca addressed the workers. "I have exciting news about Betsy Lumkin," she said, "and know she won't mind if I tell you, for it's quite definite now." She lowered her voice, and they all leaned nearer. "She is expecting a baby."

"No!" Polly said. "Imagine!"

"That's so nice," Kittie exclaimed, not quite with surprise.

"Oh, how wonderful!" Emmy cried automatically. She put her cup down. It was wonderful, exciting news, of

190

course, but there was something about it too that worried her, something upsetting.

"I never *dreamed*, actually I thought—" Polly was saying.

Yes, it was that lump of candle end up in Miranda's drawer, worked into the shape of a doll, with a hatpin stuck through the stomach. Magic. She got up. It was utterly silly and impossible, of course, a coincidence. Only, as the others were now discreetly whispering, it was really a miracle, at Betsy's age, after she and the Dean had long ago given up hope. Even Dr. Scott had been surprised, Rebecca admitted, with her air of knowing All and distributing it to the faithful in small parcels.

"Can you help me, please, Missus Turner?"

Emmy turned and saw Sallie Hutchins, her former cleaning woman, who had just come into the Ladies' Exchange with four small soiled children, including the one whose birth last October had been the cause of her leaving Emmy's employment after only three weeks.

"I wonder if you could hold the baby for me, Missus Turner, please, just for a sec, while I try this coat onto Margie."

"Of course, Sallie."

Emmy took the heavy bundle of baby, smiling at Sallie and even reaching out to pat the next oldest child with her free hand. Sticky and soiled as they were, she looked kindly on them because they were so obviously the result of carelessness on the part of Sallie and her husband and not of some unnatural outside influence.

Carrying the baby, and listening to its mother's talk about colds and clothes, Emmy followed Sallie Hutchins down the rooms. As they reached the table marked IN-FANTS, the door at the other end opened. Will came in. He saw her, but made no move, turning instead to the other ladies.

"Well, hello there!" Rebecca exclaimed. The visits of men to the Exchange were rare, and always interesting occasions.

"You're early today," Polly said.

Will answered something that Emmy could not catch. He had the kind of voice that does not carry, unlike the Ladies, including Emmy herself. They did not by any means scream or shriek, but their clear precise accents, high- or low-pitched, could be heard across any room;

they spoke as if both the manner and the matter of what they had to say could not help but be of public interest and benefit.

"Oh, my goodness!" Kittie cried. Will said something else, and all three women laughed. Emmy hesitated whether to go over to them. If Will had something important to tell her she would do better to stay here and wait, but if not it merely looked silly.

"Nothing, really," Rebecca said. "A tweed jacket did come in later last Tuesday, but I didn't save it for you; it wasn't nearly big enough in the shoulders."

Will smiled and spoke at length, inaudibly. Provoking, Emmy thought; it was like listening to the wrong end of a telephone call.

"Oh, holy God!" Sally cried. "Now look what you've done, all over Missus Turner's lovely sweater!" She snatched the baby away from Emmy, who was by now holding it at a somewhat awkward angle. "Alvin, you bad, bad boy!" With a crumpled diaper, Sallie dabbed and scrubbed at the splotch of half-digested milk on Emmy's shoulder, loudly apologizing. Meanwhile Emmy could see Will making his way along the racks of men's clothes toward her. Insisting that it was quite all right, that it did not matter in the least, Emmy managed to get away from Sallie. She rounded a corner of a table and met him by BOYS' WEAR.

"Hello," she said.

"Hi, nice to see you, Emily," he returned aloud, and then, lower: "I canceled the class for this afternoon. Half of them are out with the flu anyhow. When can you get away?" Emmy hesitated, feeling cross and nervous for a variety of little reasons.

"Oh can't you get away?" Will stopped smiling.

"I suppose I can. I'd have to take Freddy home and ask Mrs. Rabbage if she would mind watching him. Only, though, the car's supposed to go to the garage this afternoon."

"I have a car. We could drive to Hamp for lunch, if you could make it." This was a bribe, so Will characteristically presented it in a childish, offhand manner, looking aside.

"Well. All right."

"What is it, something's the matter with you today,"

Will said, stroking Emmy's hair as she leaned half against him and half against the drive shaft of his car.

"No." She shook her head, and pulled at her tweed skirt, trying to bring it back round into position. "It's not."

"But it is. I know. And just now, your heart wasn't in it."

Emmy met his look for a second, and looked down. "It was, really. But like this out in this car; and when everything's so cold and wet and ugly: here it is actually the end of March, and it might as well be January." They were parked behind a tool shed in back of a fundamentalist church northwest of Hampton, in among rotting firewood and half-frozen mud. Lacking the station wagon, Will and Emmy had first sensibly decided not to make love that day; then they had tried to force the doors of the tool shed and of the church; then tramped about in the woods looking for a dry spot among the dead, wet leaves and stones and melting ice. Finally they had been reduced to the MG, in which it was not, as Will had once said, impossible for two persons of more than average size to have sexual relations—only very difficult and uncomfortable. "And oh, Freddy was so cross today when I said I was going out and so was Mrs. Rabbage, she had been counting on my taking him with me so she could do the floors." She shifted against him restlessly. "And the Ladies' Exchange is so utterly, sometimes; well, you must know what it is. . . . Actually, I didn't know you ever went to the Ladies' Exchange."

Will laughed. "Oh, all the time. How else could I be so well dressed on my salary? Why, right now— These slacks, for instance, they came in last month from Hal Humphrey, the track coach. They're still in good shape, he just got too fat for them." Emmy sat up, away from Coach Humphrey's slacks. "And my sweater, I got that last year from a rich student who had to sell out to pay his poker debts. Oh, I get nothing but the best."

"And your jacket?" Emmy was laughing lightly, but not happily.

"You don't *mind*." He looked at her. "They've been cleaned, of course. They're only clothes." Emmy looked at the surfaces of wool against which she had so often rubbed her face, her naked breasts. "And the jacket?" she repeated. "You didn't get it from Brooks Brothers?"

"Silly, how would I afford a hand-tailored tweed jacket from Brooks Brothers? No, it belonged to a Professor Whittier who used to be in the History Department." Suppressing his impulse to suppress the whole truth, Will added: "He died last spring. I had to have it altered some. Jesus, you don't really mind, do you?"

"I don't know. I'm surprised. One takes it for granted that people's clothes actually belong to them." Will made a face at this. "Of course, I suppose it's silly of me."

"Of course it is," he said.

"It's superstition too, I suppose. I'm dreadfully superstitious, you know. I'm as bad as Miranda about things like omens and—Oh!" For the first time in some while she faced round and really looked at Will. "Do you know what I heard this morning at the Ladies' Exchange, the most amazing thing? The Lumkins are going to have a baby!"

"Really," he said.

"Yes! Isn't it absolutely amazing; after all this time. Well, but you know, when I heard I was so upset, and I thought almost immediately, suppose Miranda's sticking that hatpin into the wax doll of Betsy made her get pregnant somehow. All these years she hasn't managed to have any children and now, suddenly—I mean, one feels someone must be responsible for a thing like that."

Will laughed. "Someone usually is," he said.

"I mean, someone besides Bill Lumkin."

Will made no reply, only a face, and nodded. Emmy giggled. "But, of course, that's not what you actually think, is it?" She giggled again. "It would be funny. I'm sure it's not so, though, Betsy's too unattractive. I can't imagine anyone's wanting to make love to her if they didn't have to," she added with the cruelty of beauty.

"Oh, come on. She's a good-looking woman."

"Oh, Will, she is not. And she's forty, at least." Emmy really did not care for the idea that there might be other love affairs besides hers going on in the vicinity of Convers. "Simply because of us, you think—"

She stopped. A fantastic suspicion had just entered her mind, or had it been there all along? She examined it in a silence which Will did not break. "You wouldn't," she finally said.

"Wouldn't what?" Will took out a large white linen handkerchief (from the Ladies' Exchange) and wiped his nose. He still had the damp, disagreeable cold which he

194

had caught the previous week from someone, most likely Freddy Turner.

"Wouldn't have an affair with Betsy Lumkin yourself." Will did not reply. "I mean really—if you could actually say that you thought she was good-looking! Really, how should I know? All those times this winter you went over to her house to play the piano for her, and to dinner there—"

"For the love of Christ, Emily," Will said after a pause. "You are in a fantastic state today. What is it?" What's the matter?" He stroked her hair.

"I don't know. Nothing's the matter! And don't ask me if I'm going to have my period, the way Holman always does."

"I wasn't going to. I only thought you might be getting my cold."

"No. I don't think so, at least. How is your cold?"

"So-so."

"I'm sorry." Emmy subsided; she put her head down on the shoulder of his coat and looked out the window. The hood of the MG was streaked with dirty red reflections of dead branches, dead sky.

"We've got to get back, love," Will said softly. "It's four-thirty."

"I know."

He started the car. "Maybe you *are* coming down with something."

"No." She nestled into the sheepskin collar of his coat, and they drove the four miles into Hampton in silence, along narrow country roads wet with melting ice. Will drove with his left hand, holding hers in the other. But as they turned toward Convers onto the highway, where there was more traffic, she sat up away from him and let go.

"I love you," Will said.

"I love you. I honestly do, you know."

"I know." He smiled at her. "Whoops." The car had curved out toward the center of the road; a truck swerved to the right to avoid them, and passed with a loud blast of its horn. "You see how much."

"And it isn't true, about Betsy," she murmured. "I know it isn't true; I only want you to say it."

"Oh, Emily— Suppose it were, would it make such a terrible difference?"

"I don't know. It wouldn't, I suppose. But I'm glad you didn't. . . . You didn't, did you? I know I'm silly. I'm a very silly girl. But tell me."

"Tell you what?"

"Promise me you never made love to Betsy Lumkin."

Will did not reply. He had turned off the highway now onto a road which wound up south of Convers College toward the garage which Holman and Emmy patronized. Bare cornfields, broken cornstacks, sloped up from it on both sides. The sky was heavy, white-gray.

"Well?"

"Do you really want to hear?"

"Of course I really want to hear."

"All right. . . . I did, then." Emmy made a noise. "But it was nothing, it meant nothing, Emily."

"And it's yours, that baby?"

"Christ, I don't know. It was a long while ago, months, it was before we—"

"But of course it's yours. How can you not care?"

Will shrugged. "I don't, that's all. . . . It meant nothing to either of us, Emily, it was just an incident."

"But that makes it worse, even! How could you? How could you do a thing like that? Oh, it's disgusting!"

Will groaned. "That's the way," he said. "Women are always at you to tell them the truth; please dear, I want nothing but the complete truth; and then when you do they spring on you like a tiger. If you only knew how little it meant, Emily."

"Oh, stop driving!"

Angrily, but obediently, Will stepped on the brakes; the car stopped abruptly. Emmy opened the door, jumped out, and began running away up the road. Will looked at her and then climbed over, shut the door which she had left hanging open, climbed back, stepped on the gas, and drove after her.

"Emily," he said, coming up alongside, craning his head out the window.

"Leave me alone." She strode on ahead of the car. "Don't speak to me."

"Emily; please."

Emmy did not even look at him this time, but walked on, directly through a puddle, splashing up freckles of mud all over the backs of her bare legs. She paid no attention to this either. They were now only a quarter of a mile from town and less than that from the garage. Lord Jesus grant us nobody comes along here just now, Will thought, and looked nervously at a farmhouse to his left. It was still full daylight.

"Get back into the car, you silly fool, before someone sees us," he said, driving up parallel to Emmy.

"I will not." She kept on walking steadily; he followed her in little spurts of speed, feeling at an absurd disadvantage because, sitting in the car, he was so low down.

"Emily, for Christ's sake. What do you want me to do?"

"I want you to go away!" she shrieked, turning. "Get out! Get away from me!" She stood back to the edge of the road, making shooing motions with her hands.

"All right!" Will shouted back. "If that's what you want!" He jammed his foot down on the gas so that the car leaped ahead. In a moment he was climbing the hill, in another at its crest. Very rapidly, Emmy shrank into a red spot in the rearview mirror; then, as he rounded the curve into town, she disappeared entirely.

* * *

Allen Ingram to Francis Noyes

April 1

In reply to yours of the 22nd: no, No, NO! I hadn't *the slightest* intention of suggesting that you were a social climber or parasite of the H. Turner type. Can't you see how ridiculous and shamming it is for both of us that I should have to make this disclaimer at all? "If you ever have the slightest need for that sum," etc. etc! What can I say? How excruciating it is not to be face to face with you. Dear Francis, don't you realize that I am planning to retire to the Riviera in my old age on the sale of the *smallest* of the paintings you did for me that summer? I shall keep the others to inspire—or to enrich—my grand-nephews beyond their wildest dreams. So let's consider the matter closed forever.

Nothing, but absolutely nothing, has happened here. Poor Julian Fenn still hasn't found a job, and shows it—misfortune is always so unbecoming—holes in his gloves and his eyes great bruised holes; his wife looks like

197

a Pre-Raphaelite watercolor that's been left out in the rain.

I have a cold, am red-nosed and hideous. But it's all for the best: vanity and fear of Complications keep me "home" where I am writing hard. I've actually got up to the big blood-and-tears scene, which is full of problems. How I wish you were around to talk to. The idea of confiding in anyone here is unthinkable; in desperation I've begun talking to the dog. "Beowulf," I say, "don't you think *J* would react hysterically to the discovery that *D* was missing?" If he's awake, he whines agreeably—the perfect critic—and thumps his tail on the floor beside the stove. I've let him in from the back pantry, where he was still howling day and night—and no wonder, I finally realized; there's no heat in there at all. Here in the kitchen he is amazingly well behaved (it's the only room in this ten-room house fit for man or beast in the current weather).

I still haven't heard from the Williamses what to do with the animal. No one has heard from them. Of course, these New England types always go completely wild when they get to the sunny southern shores where there is no influenza. Sunken in the fleshpots of Rome (why on earth *fleshpots*—it sounds like those fur saucers), they've quite forgotten their faithful old retainer, not to mention their faithful old tenant. One understands their not wanting to let the smallest thought of this frozen valley darken their sunny days and moony nights: "Take me, Harold!" Mrs. Williams cries from the balcony of the *pension*, at this very moment, struggling out of a nightgown from Hastings Dry Goods and Sundries—but I digress. If *we* go abroad next winter I know I shall bore you considerably by recalling What It Must Be Like Back in Convers Now; but the Williamses' escape is too pathetically brief for this. A few months in London, a few in Rome, and back to prison for six more years.

Truly, this place is death. Think of us all shut up in this narrow little valley, the interminable iron months of the northern winter, the cold, the mud, the ice, the illness, the isolation. By now everyone is sick or half insane or both. Will spring ever come? (there's not a sign of it yet) and if so, what extravagances of release will it produce?

CHAPTER

11

"COULD YOU PASS MR. TURNER'S SUGAR IN THIS DIRECTION, Mr. Green?" Julian said to Charley. The three junior members of the English Department were having afternoon coffee in the small, cold, stuffy room in Gibson House which had been allotted to this use.

"Gladly." Charley passed the sugar, of which very little remained.

"With Mr. Turner's permission," Julian said.

"Go on, use it all, don't consult Mr. Turner," Holman said with heavy irony. As he often did at coffee time, he looked about at his surroundings with disgust. This was not, of course, the only place on campus where one could drink coffee. He and the other instructors were quite free to go to the Faculty Club, where there were roaring fires and deep carpets and leather chairs. But it was a long walk across campus to the Faculty Club on a wet day, and appearing there had some of the aspects of a public performance. One had to feel strong enough to face the courteous, curious hospitality of the senior faculty members and their scrutiny of one's tie and opinions. Holman went there once a week on the average; Charley went less often, and Julian, since Christmas, not at all. Much nearer by, just up the hill, was a large warm Coffee Shop attached to the student dining hall. Unfortunately, going there was discouraged by the administration; Bill Lumkin thought that the students ought to have some pleasant gathering place free from faculty surveillance.

"There was another communication from Dr. Flory of Bowdoin today," Julian revealed, pouring a stream of Holman's sugar into his instant coffee. The others waited. "He has raised his offer by five hundred."

"Well," Holman said. "'We see that reluctance pays off.'"

"In cash, we see," Charley said.

Julian stirred his coffee and said no more. "Then you're

going to accept?" Charley asked. He was always the first to abandon the elaborate, impersonal mode of discourse they usually affected, always the one who found it least congenial.

"The idea of northern Maine still doesn't attract," Julian said. "I understand they don't heat that state very well. I have a strong feeling the Fenns might all be dead of pneumonia after the first winter."

Charley and Holman gave him identical glances. Both thought that he was crazy to hold out for the chance of a better job at this late date. He had already turned down offers from Tufts College ("a dying animal") and a big city university in Cincinnati ("I detest urban concentrations"). He had received notice to vacate his house, and on June 30, when his appointment at Convers terminated, he would be out on the street with a wife and three children with no visible means of support. His nonchalance in this situation was either wicked or insane (Holman inclined to the former view, Charley to the latter).

"Dr. Flory will be disappointed," Holman said. "It sounds as if he were anxious to add Mr. Fenn to his staff."

"He did say something of the sort," Julian admitted, casually but not modestly.

"Did he indeed?" Charley asked, fishing for a look at Dr. Flory's letter. Half competitors, half allies, the three instructors watched for the smallest signs of each other's professional success or failure, yet were unable to take wholehearted pleasure in either event. When, for example, one of them had an article rejected by a scholarly journal, the others might feel a thrill of competitive relief; but the realization that the scholarly article of a Convers English instructor could be rejected soon cast them into nervous gloom. Julian's dismissal had had this same effect on Charley and Holman, although they congratulated themselves that they would never be guilty of his particular kind of careless irresponsibility.

"Mm." Julian only nodded, and did not offer to show anyone the letter from Bowdoin; he had a strong natural streak of secrecy.

"It seems too bad to disappoint him," Charley said, the nearest he would come to offering Julian advice.

"After all," Holman added, "Mr. Fenn need not stay there forever. He might regard it as a springboard."

"It would be a three-year appointment," Julian let on.

"Ah." Holman and Charley again gave identical glances, but this time to the floor. Both their appointments at Convers had been renewed for next year, but McBane had suggested that the future was still uncertain. Charley was not pleased by this: he thought that he should have received at least a definite two-year contract. It was insulting—hadn't he proved himself sufficiently yet? Did They—which might mean either the administration or McBane—still think he might do something wrong? Surely there should have been some recognition of the fact that he already had his Ph.D. and Turner did not. Holman had exactly the same feelings about his reappointment, except that he thought there should have been some recognition that he was a popular and successful teacher, while Green was not.

"Why not string Dr. Flory along?" he said. "Maybe Mr. Fenn could arrange to go to Europe when it gets cold and have his salary sent to him there. To Dublin, of course."

"That's a gra-and idea," Charley said, stage Irish.

"Inspired," Julian agreed.

"He could continue teaching his courses by mail," Holman added. "Correspondence courses."

"Holy Mary, it's the answer to his problem from heaven," Charley elaborated the joke. "Never any need to be on time to classes at all. Why! he wouldn't have to leave the house, except to chase the birds and bars. Only the correcting of a few papers. Or maybe he wouldn't even have to do that, maybe he could work by telepathy."

"No, achone," Julian returned. "I'm afraid that's beyond me. That's more in Mr. Green's line; Charley Green, the Mind-Reading Machine."

Another hearty laugh all round. Charley, of course, joined in; it was part of the game to do so when one was mocked, to show that you approved the ritual release of aggression. It was the less painful since what was attacked was not one's real self, but a puppet. All their coffee-room personalities bore some relation to reality: they were caricatures of what in each of the instructors was least like the Convers ideal, or type, as they saw it. Julian played and was mocked as the bohemian foreigner, the lazy, crazy Irishman; noisy doubts were cast upon his

American citizenship, his possible police record, whether he ever actually read his students' papers, etc. Holman appeared as the illiterate ex-Marine from the city slums, proponent of tough methods and corporal punishment for freshmen. Charley, as a rule, was the hayseed enthusiast, the naïve believer. He was ridiculed for his faith in human nature and in the hidden talent of certain earnest students. Since his child had been born a few weeks ago, he had also taken on the character of the ridiculously devoted family man. These diversely grotesque puppets had one thing in common: they were all creatures of instinct, of primitive emotional impulse. So they appeared as especially alien to Convers, which was assumed to stand for order, reason, and upper-class New England Protestantism. Of course the puppet Holman, the puppet Julian, and the puppet Charley could not be friends, having nothing in common. But their owners had much: since, outside of the coffee-room, they were all engaged in trying to conceal (and thus perhaps finally to do away with) these elements in themselves, they were allies, and even fellow conspirators.

"Incidentally," Holman said, "there was a strange object in my mailbox today." He held up a blue memo. "I wondered whether anyone else had received one." It was a rhetorical question: the boxes of the Languages and Literature Division had been symmetrically decorated with blue that afternoon. He put the memo down on the table.

NOTICE REGARDING STENOGRAPHIC SERVICES

In order to equalize the over-all work load of the Division of Business Operations and to if possible decrease budgetary expenditure or at least hold it to a minimum, the following rules for stenographic services have been instituted effective as of 27 April.

1. All requests for routine typing and duplication of classroom materials should be sent to the Central Stenographic Office together with a pink order slip stating the name of the faculty member requesting the order, the Department concerned, and the number of copies desired. A minimum of 24 hours should be allowed for the return of all materials of five pages or less, except that materials received after 3 P.M. each day may be held over to the second day following if work load necessitates.

2. All requests for emergency stenographic services and for the typing or duplication of materials of six pages or more shall be made through the Business Office.

WWL

"Superb," Julian said. "C-minus. Jargon, repetition, inclarity—"

"And look at that split infinitive."

"It's the lack of an object that I particularly like," Julian continued. "Think what McBane would make of 'all requests' as an object."

"What it means, I suppose," Charley said, "is 'don't ask Dorrie to type any papers for you any more, Mr. Green, or mimeo your assignments, send them over to College Hall, and it'll take at least a day and a half.' "

"God."

The front door slammed, letting in a wave of cold, wet air. Voices were raised in the English Department office where Miss Cowie and her assistant, Dorrie Hutchins, worked.

"Mr. Lumkin attempted something like this previously," Julian said; "about three years ago. It didn't go into effect for Gibson House, though; Mr. McBane was somehow able to prevent that. Of course, most of the other departments already send everything to Central Stenographic."

"Perhaps we can hope that it will be prevented again," Holman said. Julian shrugged his shoulders. A minute of gloomy silence passed.

"Hello." Will put his head in the door.

"Hi."

"Hi there!"

"Come on in." The three instructors spoke less loudly and more naturally, dropping their habitual tone and game. They were glad to see Will: each thought of him as a real friend, or potential friend.

Will came in. "Cold in here," he remarked.

"You're telling us."

"Have some dehydrated coffee."

"No thanks."

"How've you been?"

"Oh, terrible." Will grinned. "I've still got the flu. I ought to be home in bed." Instead he unfolded a metal

203

chair and sat down, sliding into his usual semihorizontal position. "What's new?"

"Not much. Big message for us all from Bill Lumkin today," Holman said, pointing to the blue memo.

"Yeah; Dorrie and Miss Cowie showed it to me."

For some reason, those women tell him everything, Holman thought; and it's probably the same thing all over the campus. He said: "What I don't get is what Dorrie's going to do all day if we start sending our stuff to Central Steno."

"Dorrie? She's moving over there too," Will said.

"God damn."

"But we can't get along without Dorrie," Charley objected. "With nothing but Miss Cow." Dorrie Hutchins was twenty years old, a member of one of the oldest and worst Convers families. Most of the Hutchins girls got into trouble and had to leave school before they reached the age of consent, but Dorrie perhaps because she looked so much like a blond guinea pig, had managed to complete the commercial course. She was a moderately fast and accurate typist, and immensely obliging to everyone. In this she differed from Miss Cowie, who was obliging only to Professor McBane and, to a lesser extent, to Professors Knight and Baker. Miss Cowie was elderly to an unrevealed extent; she should have been retired years ago, but instead she stayed on, functioning more and more slowly like an old typewriter. For the last thirty years she had been referred to behind her back, and occasionally by mistake to her face, as Miss Cow.

"Couldn't we do something?" Charley said, "couldn't Dorrie protest or something?"

"But Dorrie wants to go," Will said. "She's dying to be up in College Hall with the other girls. It's not much fun for her here, shut up in that office all day with Miss C."

"She has us," Holman said half-jocularly. Early in the year the instructors had formed the habit of treating Dorrie with exaggerated courtesy ("Darling Dorrie, light of my life, could I possibly persuade you to type this up before the mail goes?"). She had responded first with blank stares and giggles, later only with giggles, but she continued obliging—she would stay on until six to run off a stencil if necessary, even come in on Saturdays. Gratefully, they brought her candy for Christmas and Valentine's Day, in the most vulgarly elaborate boxes they could find, and continued to imitate the gestures of courtly love to the music of her mimeograph machine.

"Are they going to move her soon?"

"She said next week."

"God."

"It will be impossible with Dorrie gone," Julian declared.

"Miss Cow won't do a damned thing for us," said Charley, of whom this was particularly true.

"Not only us," Holman said. "The whole course'll fall apart if nobody can get anything mimeographed without waiting two days. It would be the end of Hum C as we know it." He thought a moment, and said: "We'll have to persuade Dorrie she wants to stay."

"Candy and flowers," Julian said.

"Work on her feelings," Charley suggested. "How can she betray us this way?" He got up to turn on the hot plate and reheat the water for coffee: "I should think McBane could explain the situation to Lumkin," he said.

"Explain!" Holman laughed. "Damn all ever gets settled that way. It's all power politics up at College Hall. Frankly, isn't that so?" He turned to Will.

Will shrugged his shoulders, and said: "Who knows?"

"I heard McBane was slipping," Charley said unexpectedly. "Jack Butler was saying the longer President King stays away from the college the worse it is for his cronies in the old guard."

"I don't believe it. McBane gets what he wants," Julian said with what Holman thought a childish bitterness. If he ever lost a job, he would be damned before he'd show that he cared; that way was the pit. Holman firmly believed that if you let the world see your weakness it would trample you. People who said: "I'm no good at skiing" fell with their legs and skiis broken beneath them; germs fed on people who gave up and went to bed with their colds. Weakness was also infectious. He felt a revulsion from Julian.

"Well, four o'clock," he said, pushing back his chair; it scraped on the cold floor. "Got to finish up my papers and get on home."

"That's right, got to stick to the old schedule," Charley said.

"Yep." Holman got up slowly. Actually he was not at all anxious to go home. In the last couple of weeks Emmy had turned moody and difficult again, even more so than in the fall. Her cooking and her appearance had deteriorated, there was dust on the floor and on his suits, and a perpetual ring around the tub. When he arrived home in the evening the house felt cold, and Emmy usually met him with some complaint: Freddy had acted up, the telephone was out of order, when was he going to fix the screen on the bathroom window? She would cry suddenly, for the least of reasons: if she spilt the milk, for instance. Strangest of all, she didn't want to start trying for another baby. He hoped to God she was not coming down with a neurosis. Women. Men had more restraint, were more dependable—maybe not types like Fenn and Green, but men like himself, McBane, Will Thomas.

"See you," he said to the others, and to Will: "Come around again, why don't you? Or drop out to the house this weekend, we'd both like that. Emmy was asking if I'd seen you just the other day. Why don't you come for—" But he broke off, thinking that it was hardly safe to ask anyone to dinner the way she had been burning things. "How about Sunday afternoon, for a drink?"

"I wish I could," Will said, "but I've got to start practicing this weekend, or that concert will be even more of a fiasco than it's going to be."

"You're giving a concert? When?"

"Next Tuesday. Don't look at me, it wasn't my idea. Oska fixed it up." Will grinned. "He's putting me up for a promotion, and he thinks this'll help."

"There's posters for it all over the place," Charley said. "Haven't you seen them?"

Holman had not seen the posters for Will's concert, or rather he had not read them past the word CONCERT, which always aroused his automatic disinterest. But Emmy had. To her inflamed imagination, the whole of Convers was papered with these posters, on which the awful words WILLIAM THOMAS glared out in huge letters. The first time she had seen one, coming down from the washroom in the library, it had been with the shock of a hallucination. There on the stairs, one foot out, she felt about to fall. She clutched at the rail and turned her head nervously from side to side, closing and opening her eyes to see if this would wipe out the image. It remained. As she went about the town and the college during the days that followed, it was as if her obsession had taken material form everywhere.

After Will left her on the road outside of Convers, Emmy had been more miserable than since her first year at boarding school. In the beginning she was sure that he would call up to apologize, to beg, to explain, or best of all believably deny what he had done. Certainly he didn't expect that she should call him. She looked often at the spiteful telephone, sometimes picked it up; once she got as far as saying his number, but at the first ring she hurried the receiver down again. It was his place to call, not hers. As the days succeeded each other and he did not do so, she became more and more furious. How could Emily Stockwell Turner have let herself become involved with a man like that, a liar, a sneak, a complete cad. "You are a complete cad," she imagined saying to him when he should call. She planned many telephone conversations, her absolutely crushing remarks, even more crushing silences; scenes to be played if they should meet in the grocery, in the library, at someone's house. Etc., etc. Sometimes she forgave him eventually, more often not. Pride, anger, desire, and despair chased each other monotonously around in her head; she burst out sobbing if she so much as burned her hand on the stove, she knew the meaninglessness of solitary experiences, games played in private ("If I don't eat any dessert tonight, he'll call me tomorrow"), unwritten and unsent letters; she thought each thought a hundred times.

By chance, or design (whose design?) she had not seen Will since the quarrel. Driving around Convers, she saw his car parked here and there at the usual times—as adulterers must, they knew each other's schedules by heart—but never Will, and she had too much pride to lie in wait. She was ashamed when she caught herself driving slowly past his house. To make up she would hurry home and start some complicated domestic project, like a lemon meringue pie or teaching Freddy to write his name, lose interest, and finish it, if at all, in a botch of exasperation.

But she was not often home. A kind of unsatisfactory restlessness kept her running about, calling on this or that acquaintance or shop in town. She also formed the bad habit of driving around the country to all the places she and Will had used to go. The winter had broken for good now; it was not cold out, but wet, wet, the sky heavy, the

207

ditches running, the bare trees heavy with tears. With her windshield wipers pushing the water back monotonously, rhythmically, she drove miles over back roads around Convers and Hampton, circling sometimes toward and sometimes away from The Tree, The Deserted Graveyard, and The Church of the Faithful (monotonous ironies were composed upon this name). There was always the half-conscious idea that he might be there too; that there might be a big scene, sometimes of denunciation, sometimes of reconciliation, of all forgiven and explained.

He never was there. Alone in the car, she would turn off the engine and cry uncontrollably, while the rain flowed unrestrained down the windshield.

She had fantasies of suicide; of Will's face when he heard that her body had been found on a certain back road. . . . But when would it be found, and how would she look by then; and even more to the point, how would she have done it? . . . And what would her family say? No doubt about it, there was something vulgar about being discovered in a car in a state of disintegration. . . . Stories in newspapers, and such an embarrassment for Freddy when he grew up; and who would look after Freddy until he grew up?

This afternoon, because it was Tuesday and Mrs. Rabbage was looking after Freddy, Emmy had been pursuing her bad habit. It was late when she turned the station wagon back toward Convers, about four-thirty; the day's rain had stopped, and the sun, emerging at last, made a brilliant streak low on the horizon across the soaking fields. Pretty; but it only made her angry; she knew now that it was a cheat, a trick of the climate. It would rain again tomorrow, it would not be better in any way.

She felt even worse when, passing Miranda's house, she saw Will's MG parked in the driveway, again, for the second time that week. Of course she was not jealous of Miranda; she remembered too well the pity or humor with which Will always spoke of her appearance. But it made her furious that he should be there, furious that he should be carrying on with his social life just as before, when she was so hysterical, so desperate. Of course she hadn't stopped seeing people completely, but it was her job to go where she and Holman were asked and to take Freddy to play with his friends, it wasn't as if she enjoyed it. She hadn't been to the Fenns, though. Ever since she had found out that Miranda knew of her affair she had begun to avoid her; and now that the affair was over she had too much pride to go there. But Will didn't care, there he was sitting around in Miranda's kitchen getting drunk just as before, telling her all about it, no doubt (his version); probably he didn't feel anything much, he didn't care, probably he had practically forgotten about her.

"You might as well tell me all about it," Miranda said.

Slumped on his spine in a dining-room chair, his hand attached to a glass half full of whisky, Will said nothing. As Miranda continued to look at him, however, he at length turned his head away.

"Come on. You know you will tell me eventually." Miranda asserted this more confidently than she felt, for it was three weeks now since Will had broken up with Emmy, and he had managed to tell her nothing but that bare fact. At first, since he seemed so miserable, she had been tactfully silent, but now her curiosity had become too much to bear. I must know, I must know everything, she kept thinking. It was time now: the house was quiet, the children had gone visiting, supper was in the oven. "What was it?" she said.

"She found out something," Will said after a pause.

"Ah." Miranda wiped her hands on her faded-red apron. "Which something?"

Will hesitated. "Avis Walsh," he finally said.

"The girl in the bank."

"Yes," Will lied; actually Emmy had never heard of Avis Walsh.

"But that's all over, isn't it?"

"Oh, absolutely." (The loud, relieved emphasis with which one tells, for a change, the absolute truth.) "You know that's been over for months, even before I met Emily. But she didn't see it that way."

Miranda tried to imagine how she would feel if she learned that Julian had had an affair with Avis Walsh. Surprised, mostly: incredulous. But cross, certainly. "Well," she said, leaning on the back of a chair. "It's a pity she had to find out. . . . She must mind it's being someone who works up in town, of course." Will did not reply; he frowned, and looked out of the window, so she hastened to explain away this accusation of snobbery. "I mean, I suppose she's embarrassed that every time she goes to the bank, there is Avis; I can see that."

No answer. I'm talking too much, she decided. As quietly as possible, she walked around the chair and sat down in it, trying to project the kind of attentive silence that encourages confidences.

"She takes everything hard," Will said at last. "You must have noticed it, under that ladylike manner; Christ, violently. Not that that isn't great sometimes. But that day she just went wild, when she found out." He proceeded to tell how Emmy had jumped out of his car and left him on the road. "She didn't look back once, just walked away, she didn't care, just like that she deserted me," he concluded.

"Mm," Miranda said.

"Since then, not a sign, not a telephone call, not a word from her for three damned weeks."

"She's probably waiting for you to call her."

"You don't know Emily. She's waiting for me to call, all right, so she can hang up on me. . . . I thought I'd get over it. Jesus! you know I usually get over these things, but it hurts as much as ever. I'm really beat up."

"Mm." Will did have a physically bruised appearance; his nose and eyes were red and slightly swollen from his cold or from drinking, his collar and tie crumpled, the skin of his face scarred with the dried blood and stubble of shaving wounds. It all gave him a dissolute, suspense-movie look which Miranda rather liked; she could not bear prissy, sissy, little-boy men. People should look as if they had lived, even suffered.

"Christ, I was so happy with Emily! On top of the world, on top of them all. I admit there's always some euphoria at the beginning of every affair, but this was different. I even felt as if I might start working again, I had some ideas. Well, that's over, I'm going to the dogs now, I admit it. The dogs: Cerberus. The Hound of the Baskervilles."

Miranda laughed, not only at the joke, but because it was so good to have him talking freely to her again.

"That damned concert next week. I haven't practiced."

She laughed again. "Not true."

"Not seriously. To play decently, I'd have to have practiced at least two hours a day for the last six months. . . . The trouble is, I'm a lazy bastard and I always will be. I just can't be bothered. Oh, I'll give them what they want; I won't make any mistakes or shame Oska. I've warmed the pieces up some, but it's all mechanical."

"I don't believe you."

"It's true." Will dragged himself out of his chair and over to the Fenns' piano, a shabby old upright. He put his glass down on the music rack beside *John Thompson's Piano Course for Children* and played a series of chords. The effect was indeed mechanical—it was positively metallic, due to the sheets of tinfoil which Miranda had attached to the piano strings to make the instrument sound like a harpsichord and also to reduce the noise of Charles's lessons. Tin, tin, bing. Will began on a piece by Schoenberg.

"Oh, don't practice that dreadful stuff now! Play some real music."

Will broke off and gave Miranda the first smile of his visit. "All right. To please you." He began Haydn's Andante and Variations.

As the notes met and echoed each other, Will's face took on what was for him a rare expression: one of ordinary concentration. Usually he was like an actor, a man before a mirror, moving his handsome features around into conscious images of interest, disinterest, pleasure, displeasure, irony, surprise, or resignation. Miranda most often saw this real face when Will played the piano, and even then only when he played for her alone, or for her and the children.

He trusts me, she thought. It's because he knows that I care for him quite disinterestedly. I like him, love him, whatever one wants to say, but I'm not asking for anything, not trying to use him the way the rest of them are, to give concerts or entertain at parties or teach harmony or make love to me.

A faint frown went with this last denial: the truth was that Miranda did use Will to make love to her. In the tales she made up when she could not sleep he alternated the role of romantic lover with a boy she had known in college and a red-haired man who had once talked to her about ghosts on the train between Boston and New York. But Will, like the others, would never know of the part he played, which physically in truth was a very innocent one. Nor would he, probably, have recognized himself in the

211

exotic settings and costumes in which Miranda placed him. Miranda's fantasies seldom took place in the contemporary world. At the moment she was reading Balzac, and they were laid in nineteenth-century Paris; earlier she had favored, among other backgrounds, the Trojan Wars and a witches' Sabbath in Scotland during the reign of James I.

But that was a game. The real life of romantic love, after its early flights, is nasty, brutish, and short, or so Miranda had found it; it deals in false images and false expectations. Marriage is kinder, but it also lives on lies, little tame ones—one makes the best of the bargain. Only friendship is completely real. Because he dropped all his disguises in front of her she (and nobody else) really knew Will Thomas. And knowledge was power, the only form of power worth having. The other kinds were gross, material—and because material, ephemeral: sooner or later, like all matter, they would rot and decay. Will would belong to her forever, never to Emmy and the other girls he lay next to between dirty sheets, giving them what they wanted, pretending to be some imaginary lover they had invented. She didn't blame him, she didn't blame them; not even that.

Between the third and fourth variations, Will looked up. "By the way, you won't tell Emily I told you about Avis and all that," he said.

"Of course not."

He began to play again. Leaning her head on her arm, Miranda looked past him now, out the window. The sodden sky was splitting apart from the sodden earth, and through the trees a long bright streak of light widened. How happy I am, she thought. Drops of leftover rain shone light and dark on the glass.

"I love Haydn," she said when Will had finished. "He always makes me feel so much better."

"Were you feeling so much worse?"

"Oh, I don't know. Some."

"And I didn't even ask. I'm a pig."

"No."

"Coming over here and running off at the mouth, probably boring you to hell." Will glanced at her.

"No, really."

"I have a compulsion to confess, I suppose. I can't help myself."

"If you do, I suppose I have a compulsion to listen to

you." She smiled, wanting to show how much she meant it. Instead of smiling back, however, Will gave her a look that she had never seen before. He swung round on the piano bench, his eyes wide and pale.

"Miranda."

Miranda felt as if her stomach had dropped down through the floor. Still staring at her, Will stood up. She stood too, but looked nervously away, at a corner of the wall. There was a bat-shaped mark on the paper there where Katie, in a tantrum, had thrown a plate of scrambled eggs. Will put his hand on her arm.

"No," she heard herself say, taking a step back. He paid no attention. "Really, no." With some effort, she pulled away and backed round the dining-room table. Will followed a few steps and then stopped. They stood looking at each other across the varnished surface, golden oak in the descending sun, on which each crumb cast a long shadow.

"Twelve o'clock," Will said, though it was about five. "All your mice have turned into coachmen." She laughed nervously. "Miranda— Listen, Miranda." He came after her round the table.

"My name isn't Miranda," she said rapidly. "It's Mary Ann."

"Mary Ann?" Will stopped.

"Yes, I changed it, when I went away to college. Don't tell anyone."

Will stared at her for a moment and then began to laugh. "Well Mary Ann, or Miranda—" He laughed some more, but did not move toward her.

"I'm sorry." Miranda held onto the back of a chair; her stomach had not yet returned from the cellar.

"Why won't you?" He leaned against the table— disturbed, perhaps, but less so than she. "Who knows, maybe you really don't like me. You disapprove of me, at bottom," he suggested.

"No, I don't. You know I don't."

"Maybe you're against adultery on principle. Moral."

"I'm not."

"Only in practice? You're the reverse of Emily, she has everything against adultery in principle." He laughed bitterly, a bit theatrically. "I know it's not because of Julian," he added. In truth, Miranda had rehearsed Julian's faults to Will too often to deny this. "You're not still in love with him."

"I like him," she protested.

"Oh, Christ. I like him too."

I like him better than I love you, was the odd statement that came into her head, but she did not voice it. "No, then, besides," she began, talking rapidly and nervously, "you know it would be completely against your rules, and really it's a good rule, you know. I mean, don't you have an important rule about never have affairs with your friends' wives and your wives' friends, if you had wives, I mean a wife?"

Will replied nothing. He looked hurt and angry.

"I'm sorry," Miranda repeated. "I always thought I probably would, you know," she added suddenly. "If you ever asked me."

"But you won't."

"No." Assuming or trying to assume the tone in which she and Will had so often discussed the motives of others, she said: "I don't know why not; I suppose partly because it would all be so complicated, with Julian and the children and everything. And then I think I'm afraid something bad would happen if I, we—" Rather than choose a verb, she broke off. "Like I might fall in love with you or something terrible like that."

"Would that be so terrible?" Will gave Miranda his seducer's look; dishonest, she thought. He even took a step toward her around the table.

"Yes— Love makes trouble, it only makes trouble," she went on, trying to remember the arguments she had just a few moments ago thought.

"But it's pleasant. I don't think you know how pleasant it is," he said.

"And you could show me?" she said, trying for sarcasm.

"I think I could."

"No thanks. But it's because I like you! I'd rather be your friend for ten years than your mistress for ten weeks. . . . And when you look at it, that seems to be the choice."

"Thanks." Now Will really looked angry. He straightened up and moved toward the door.

"Will." She followed him into the hall; they had never quarreled before.

"Thrown over by everyone," he said. "First Emily, now you. Even Avis is through with me." He looked round for his coat.

"Don't go. Stay."

"What for?"

Miranda could not answer. Will walked around the hall aimlessly.

"Well, see you, Mary Ann," he said, pulling open the front door, which he never used—almost no one did. The sun had just set: the yard was a waste of mud, trampled new grass, and wet cinders. Before she could think of anything to say, he was gone.

* * *

Allen Ingram to Francis Noyes

April 22

Suddenly, SPRING! The whole landscape is giddy, the gutters running, the roads cracked and tilted, the yards as soft underfoot as quicksand. Bushes called forsythia are in bloom at every door—long branches of skimpy little yellow flowers—so that the houses look like old queens that've got themselves a new peroxide job. Beowulf is a mad puppy again, chasing his muddy tail round the driveway, bounding up against the car when I arrive—I've trained him not to bound on me, but the poor Renault, which can't scream "Down!" is a mass of muddy paw marks and canine kisses.

Puppy love—and he's not the only one. Couples courting all over town and campus. Even I am not neglected. Late this afternoon, when I got back to the house, I found this creepy little student from my writing class named George Wedge sitting on my doorstep with two of his gay pals. Obviously it was intended as a delightful surprise for me. I was supposed to fling my arms around them and invite them to dinner, maybe even to spend the night. Instead I was just incredibly polite, thanked them very sweetly for coming, and gave them some really unspeakable sherry the Williamses had left me. Ignored all their innuendoes and asked them to tell me about their home towns and where they had gone to school. They went away in a complete fury after about an hour.

No, since I seem to hear you asking, I didn't find any of them attractive. There is one I do feel rather sorry for, a sad little 6½-foot freshman named Dicky Smith, the most completely lost soul. He Wants To Be A Writer—don't we

215

all? He was in Julian Fenn's class last term and persecuted him for months with original short stories—hung around the house so much that they began calling him Fido. Now he's trying poesy, and has apparently been taken up by the sinister element among the undergraduates, which is a miserable minority here. Big brown eyes, black string ties, spots, and a stammer. Poor boy, I don't even think he's really queer, whatever Wedge may have persuaded him into (or vice versa). He just hasn't matured sexually yet—is still polymorphous perverse. In a year or two he'll probably find himself a nice normal little spotted bitch.

He left a great bundle of dog-eared mss. for me to "look at." I took a peek after supper—it turned out to be almost pure Vachel Sandburg. Magnificent cultural lag, literary and every other kind of innocence. Touching in a way, but stupefying. How does anyone in this world manage to reach 18 without having any, anything happen to him At All? So many of these Convers boys are like Mr. Smith, absolutely untouched. When I think what I went through at sixteen, at fifteen—or even, or most of all, at thirteen, with Mother's second divorce and that episode at Newport the day of the boat race which, although (or because) I was in the main a spectator, certainly marked me for life.

CHAPTER

12

ELEVEN A.M. THOUGH HOLMAN HAD ATTEMPTED TO SHUT it out, the sun leaked into the bedroom through every crack, slicing the room up into dark sections separated by bright yellow angles of light in a way which he had never seen before for the good reason that he had never before been in bed at this hour in the morning. If he could have avoided it he would not have been there now. For five days he had refused to admit that he was sick—gone on dragging himself up and out and about and back and forth. But today, when he raised his head from the pillow, everything wheeled about; he was too dizzy to stand alone. Supporting himself on the furniture, he staggered into the bathroom and took his temperature. It rose up hot and red to 103.2, and he announced his defeat.

Disgusting. To have made it (not without efforts of endurance, not—he admitted—without self-satisfaction) through the entire winter, not missing a day of classes, and then to succumb on a day like this, when it was nearly as hot outdoors as in. . . . He turned in bed, trying to sleep. Even flat on his back he was dizzy, couldn't breathe, his mouth was rough and dry, his head ached. The room tilted about; motes squirmed in the sun when his eyes were open, and when he shut them his whole body seemed to pivot dizzily backward and down infinite gulfs. He felt weak, ridiculous, angry.

Beneath him, downstairs, a series of little noises announced the movements of Mrs. Rabbage from room to room: the dry scrape of the broom, the suck of the vacuum, the squeak-squeak of a cloth on glass. Identifying these noises kept him from sleep, and when they stopped for a few moments the house was so quiet that he could hear water dripping in the sink at the other end of the hall (when was he going to fix that?), the faint electric hum of the clock across the room, his own pulse. Then the idea of Mrs. Rabbage standing absolutely still in the center of one of the rooms downstairs, doing for some reason absolutely nothing, persisted irritatingly, in itself keeping him awake, until the sounds began again.

Determined to sleep off his flu and the day, he heaped Emmy's pillow into a barricade between his head and the light, and shut his eyes. Moments passed. He heard Mrs. Rabbage, with brush and dustpan, working her way up the stairs. Thump, knock, brush, step. With a sigh, Holman opened his eyes: Mrs. Rabbage's head and torso rose above the level of the hall floor; she looked at him.

"Hi," he said.

"Hiya. I *thought* you were awake." She climbed the remaining stairs. "Here's your mail. Looks like you got a card from your Ma."

"Thanks," Holman said; letters and bills, together with yesterday's *Times*, fell in a heavy heap on the bed.

"Say, you look real bad. You really got the flu this time, huh." She grinned at him.

"Guess so."

"Missus Turner said for me to fix you some lunch. What could you fancy? There's some cold meat for sandwiches, or I could open up a can of soup."

"I don't care, Mrs. R. Anything. Nothing." Holman groaned, turning on his side.

"Got to keep up your strength," Mrs. Rabbage regarded him, resting the dustpan on her hip. "Feed a cold and starve a fever," she said meditatively.

"Take your choice, Mrs. R., I've got both."

"O.K. You want me to leave this room go for today, or you want me to clean it?"

"I don't know." Holman raised himself on his elbow. "What'd my wife tell you?"

"She didn't say. Most times I do it Tuesdays. It could use it. Only I don't want to trouble you, is all."

"No, go ahead."

"O.K." Mrs. Rabbage dragged the beetle-like form of the vacuum in by its neck. "Got to put up the shades, OK? so's I can see what I'm doing," she said, "put them down afterwards."

"OK." Holman lay down again; Mrs. Rabbage put up the shades, snap, snap. Sun flooded the room blindly; her broad bony figure moved across it.

"That's quite a racket you've got riding around in the mail truck," he remarked. "Isn't there something in the postal regulations about unauthorized personnel? Or is the mailman sweet on you?"

"Haw!" She laughed loudly with pleasure. "Naw. Ed Walsh, he's my cousin."

"Yeah? Lot of cousins you've got."

"Yep; it's a fact. People around here are mostly related." Untrue, Holman thought; he and Emmy were not related to anyone except Freddy, and neither were the majority of the faculty or the twelve hundred students. It depended, of course, on one's definition of the word "people."

"My husband, though, he was a foreigner. Rabbage. You don't hear that name around here. Came from Rhode Island." Half listening, Holman half shut his eyes as she swung into her monologue. ". . . aggravated bronchitis, and complications they were afraid of . . . then he was laid off from the garage, so he got the idea from some place to move down to Florida, it was more healthy there was his idea. You're loony, I told him, healthy, it isn't healthy all that heat it weakens the resistances maybe you don't feel it at the time but what do you think is going to happen the first time you put your foot outside of Florida?" Disease, trouble, change, death. But these were the realities of life. And not only what Mrs. Rabbage said, but the way she said it, was without pretense, unlike the conversation of his colleagues. Though her accent was harsh, he found it restful, even soporific. "Pigheads some people are, didn't listen to his boss or the doctor either. . . ." She said it *eether*; Holman had said *eether* too for the first twenty-five years of his life, but sometime during the last five he had started saying *eyether*. Drifting off between sentences, he was almost asleep; he refocused his attention when he realized that she had begun talking about Dean Lumkin.

" . . . traded in his Pontiac got him one of those new Valiants, sky-blue white-wall tires luggage rack, kind of sporty for a man his age Ed was saying, well he got to celebrate someways I said, since his wife's expecting after all these years. Take a look at him next time you get a chance I told Ed he looks like he just won the Hamp County bowling championship, you can't blame him it drags a man's pride down when he can't make kids. Who would have thought it Betty Walsh was saying it wouldn't surprise me if he had a little help from somewheres, it

219

don't seem likely but you never know. Just got to wait and
see and you mostly can't tell even then though sometimes
like with Annie Hutchins' third that was born when Ed
was in the Service bald to start with of course but when
he got about a year he came out all over red hair and that
Cowie asthma kind of like a steam radiator the same as
all the Cowies mostly have. Well cat's away too much, the
mouse'll play. . . ." Giving up all pretense at dusting, Mrs.
Rabbage leaned against the dresser, rigidly, as a broom
leans; Holman began to drift off again. " . . . wouldn't take
a hint, but it's always that way the husband is the last to
know, even what with Bob Cowie dropping over to the
house to do a little carpentering the whole time. The same
way as some people keep dropping in here. I always think
it's doing a kindness to drop a hint here and there before
it's too late but you'd be surprised how slow most of them
are to catch on, they don't see a thing. . . . Even the smart
ones like you, the educated ones. . . ."

Frowning, Holman opened his eyes fully and looked at
Mrs. Rabbage, trying to see her expression, but she had
turned away and presented only her sharp profile. "Well,
gotta get on with it," she said. Gathering up the cleaning
things, she left the room, pulling the vacuum behind her.
Its electric cord, like a long black tail, was the last to
leave.

Holman had hardly time to give himself up to uneasy
speculation before noises below announced the arrival of
Emmy. Leaving the motor of her car running (something
he had often asked her not to do) she dashed up the stairs
and into his room.

"Darling, how are you?" she said without interest, in a
voice which hurt his ears.

"All right."

"Oh, good; darling, I'm going to pick up Freddy now
and take him over to Flo's for lunch, and stay for a
while."

"Flo's?"

"Flo Butler, you know, darling," Emmy said, opening
drawers, "to play with Davy Butler, so you won't be
bothered. I'll be back before Mrs. Rabbage leaves. It's so
stuffy in here; wouldn't you like me to open the window?"

"No."

"How do you feel, darling?" She began rapidly to
change her clothes.

220

"All right," Holman repeated.

"How is your fever?" Emmy dropped her skirt, stockings, and shoes in a heap and left them there. She had become very sloppy of late, most unlike herself. Also, he realized as she pulled on a pair of slacks, she had put on about five unnecessary pounds.

"Still a hundred and three."

"Oh, that's awful. You absolutely must go to bed with a fever like that."

"I am in bed."

"Would you like me to call the doctor for you? ... I could call him now," she added from within a sweater, "and if he wanted to prescribe something for you I could pick it up in town. Would you like me to do that?"

"No."

"I'll be going by the college," she went on, leaning over the dressing table and rapidly applying fresh red lipstick to a grimace in the glass. "Would you like me to bring you any work from the office? Or if you don't feel up to working" (powder) "I could try to find something for you to read at the library—"

"Just leave me alone!"

"All right! I will!"

Holman closed his eyes so as not to see Emmy's angry face. She said no more, and presently he heard her go downstairs, the door bang shut, the car moving.

He lay in bed and admitted that he had been a little unreasonable. He disliked being babied by his wife, indeed he hated and avoided showing her any weakness, mental or physical. Even after five years, she was still one of the many Them, one of the enemy in front of whom efforts must be made, pretense kept up. When he felt low he would far rather see Mrs. Rabbage.

But God damn it, the way Emmy had dashed in and out, gushing all over him with inane suggestions and hardly looking at him. The truth was that though he resented both her solicitude and her disinterest, at times like this she managed to combine the worst features of both.

All right. Had Mrs. Rabbage meant what he thought? Or was it all a by-product of flu, of a "fevered imagination"? His wife certainly had been acting peculiar for weeks, most unlike herself, distracted and abstraught. Abstraught? He was feverish, no doubt of it. But she had been distracted for weeks, letting things fall apart. And he didn't ask much, God knows, only that the house should run smoothly, that reasonable meals should appear reasonably on time. She had nothing else to do: no job responsibilities, only one child, help twice a week. . . . He had had to remind her again yesterday about keeping up his supply of clean shirts; it only meant remembering to stop at the laundry, but Emmy blew up like the Fourth of July. She jumped so high, she touched the sky, yi, yi. What did he think she was, his laundrymaid? she said, and left the room before he could answer. His head hurt.

He hadn't followed her, he hadn't said that his mother had washed and ironed his shirts for twenty years and taught school too, he had done his best to overlook it. Women went through these emotional periods, in his experience, and in his experience the best way to deal with them was to get out of their way. Maybe he had been getting out of the way too much, and Emmy. . . . But it was unlikely; impossible.

Holman had never seen, and could not even imagine, a woman he would have preferred to his wife. Young, rich, beautiful, good-natured, well born, well educated—when he had first observed that she liked him he could hardly believe his luck. It had been a fluke that he had met her at all, of course. If he had not happened to be walking along Fifth Avenue that afternoon of Thanksgiving vacation, looking through glass at things he could not afford sprinkled with artificial snow, on the second visit to New York of his life, he would not have run into Douglas Richards; and if Doug Richards had not been a little bit drunk already he would not have asked Holman to come along with him to a cocktail party, because he did not know Holman very well, and at that stage, during his first term in Princeton graduate school, Holman was definitely not the kind of thing for Doug's kind of cocktail party.

But there he was, in the apartment on East 65th Street, and he had hardly been there five minutes before he was introduced to Emmy. It would not be too much to say that he loved her on first sight. He loved even her faults. He did not care that she was not a belle in that set. The childish, clumsy, innocent look had attracted him; sitting exactly in the center of a brocaded chair, she was like one of those good, plump, well-cared-for little girls who are photographed for *Vogue* in velvet dresses with white col-

lars and white gloves, ready for dancing school. He was so
damned tired of all the girls he had known: the over-
dressed semivièrges at college who had seen everything
at eighteen, the opinionated daughters of dentists and
accountants; arty girls with sticky eye make-up, party girls
with sticky mouths. Emmy's obvious inexperience, even
ignorance, of the ways of the world was all to the good.
She was intelligent, ready to learn, and he could form her
mind. In these matters, like many men, he preferred the
damp clay to the Ming vase.

He had not been disappointed. Emmy today was, in the
main, perfect; and a great deal of what she was was due to
him. It was impossible that such a girl should be physically
unfaithful.

"Wouldn't take a hint." It was very unlikely, at least.

"You'd be surprised how slow most of them are to
catch on, even the educated ones like *you*." God damn it
to hell. Emmy had been pretty damned lukewarm toward
him sexually too, just lately. He hadn't felt up to much
himself with this flu, but. The last time they did it she had
not been only lukewarm, but downright chilly. Downright
icy. Cold as death. Downright.

> John Brown's baby lies a mould'ring in the grave;
> Down went McGinty to the bottom of the sea;
> She's my Annie and I'm her Joe;
> Listen to my tale of woe:
>
> WHOA!
>
> Any ice today, lady?
> NO!

Icy sea, I see. My mind is all unhinged tonight, Holman
thought, or I mean this morning, as against his will he
found himself embarked on a new-critical analysis of these
lines. Disgusted, he broke off and began the usually salu-
tary exercise of composing in his head the next Hum C
assignment. But fragments of nonsense kept breaking in,
and the sentences he composed, steady one moment, drifted off into hyperbole the next. The midterm exam, which
he had just finished correcting, was as clear in his mind as
a map, but now it seemed all to refer to him.

This is an Optical Illusion. What do you do to see these
lines not only as lines but as an Optical Illusion? What

223

other kinds of Illusions have you come across in your experience?

She's my Annie and I'm her Joe.

The more he thought about it, the more possible it seemed. At the same time he did not believe it at all.

"The individual creates his own universe by naming the things that he sees." What is meant by this statement? Give some examples from your own experience.

"Dropping over to the house the whole time"?

The standard Hum C phrases expanded into ambiguous meanings. It was no use. He gave himself up to brooding.

Emmy was not going to Will's concert. She had decided not to even think about it; in fact, to stop thinking about Will entirely. Some people can forgive; some must wait to forget, he had once said; nobody can do both. And she could do neither. My life is ruined, she said to herself frequently with an unhappy giggle. It was an old joke, a cliché: "betrayed by a cad"—but that made it worse, not better. Her only consolation was that nobody knew about it. But she must stop behaving this way, or they would begin to suspect. Instead of mooning about, she must keep busy and occupy herself with good works. So she had spent the morning doing errands, which was good for the house, and the afternoon with Freddy at Flo's, which was good for Freddy. She was determined to be active, and as far as possible cheerful.

It wasn't easy to keep it up. When she came home at noon, for instance, and found Holman lying in her (well, their) bed, sick, sloppy, heavy, unshaven; the air stale, the sheets dragging on the floor, a wave of disgust and misery rolled over her. She thought how nothing was left of her affair with Will except the revulsion from her husband which she had stupidly and wickedly encouraged herself to feel for three months. And when she tried to choke it down and be nice to Holman, to do something for him, he was rude and unpleasant; absolutely impossible.

But Will was worse than impossible. Two days ago she had resolved to stay away from all the places he might be and go instead to Hampton to shop. It had worked at first. She was less nervous, less hysterical there, not on edge for the sight of his car, his name to be mentioned, the phone to ring, etc. She felt better than she had for weeks: not well, but as if she might one day be well. She enjoyed shopping: she bought a sprinkler for the hose, half a dozen linen dish towels, a copy of *Vogue*.

At the end of the afternoon she was in a bakery waiting for her last purchase to be wrapped. It was raining again, a fine spray against the plate glass behind the cardboard wedding cakes. Suddenly, coming up the street, she saw Will. It was really he. He had on a raincoat, but was bareheaded, his face wet; and holding, really clinging disgustingly onto his arm, was a blonde girl in a pink plastic cape. A cheap, ordinary girl, with spike heels and a bad permanent. They walked past her, laughing and talking. Emmy's nails tore holes in a paper bag; bad dreams that night, and the next, and the next.

Naturally she was not going to the concert. But after eating her supper alone (Holman was still sick, lying in the dark upstairs), what should she do? There was no one in the house to talk to, nothing to read. She decided to go to the library for a book.

She went upstairs. "Are you awake?" she said to Holman.

"Dhh." The room smelled stale, of flu.

"I'm going out to the library."

"Dhh."

He turned over, away from her. Emmy went downstairs, took her coat, and opened the door.

All day it had been getting warmer, and now the night was like summer, dark and still. She heard frogs in the gully below the house, a car pass on the road, water running. Coming out of the drive she turned away from Convers and the library and drove rapidly south. Five minutes later she stopped the car behind a barn at the edge of the Duck Marsh where all her miserable troubles had begun. She had not been there for a long time, even before the quarrel, for the field above the marsh was noisy now in the daytime with men and machines plowing and planting. But in the dark it was absolutely deserted, absolutely safe.

Emmy got out of the station wagon and stood beside it. A dim blue of light hung in the air over Convers; otherwise it was heavily dark. Everywhere in the valley was safe for lovers now: the trees growing in kindly to hide them, the grass in the fields rising, the air warm, the river melted and full. She put her head against the cold metal of the car, prepared to cry. But it was so monotonous to cry again, so meaningless, so useless. Choking it down, she climbed back in. Eight twenty-five. The auditorium would be lit up, the doors open, the audience crowding in. She didn't want to go to the library, she might as well go home.

Emmy stepped on the gas. The engine started, the gears meshed, but the vehicle did not move. After several more trials, she got out and found that her rear wheels were half a foot deep in mud and sand.

The next half hour was hysterical. Emmy laughed at first; later she swore, finally using words that (coming from her) would have shocked Holman and made her mother positively ill. What was she to do? There was no house very much nearer than her own. If she could not get the car out of the mud she would have to walk home in the dark, about two miles, and telephone to the garage. And what on earth would she tell Holman that she had been doing there?

She must get out by herself. So she ran back and forth in the headlights looking for sticks and branches to put under the wheel, getting in, trying to start the car, getting out again. Several times she stepped off the road into the marsh, ankle deep. Finally, afraid of using up the battery, she turned off the lights and stood in the silent darkness. She put her head against the door and burst out crying, not with the soupy ease with which she had cried for Will, but noisily and breathily, like an indignant child. How did I ever get here, she thought, how did this ever happen to me?

If only she had something large and flat and dry to put under the wheel. But everything within reach was damp and soft, damp grass and mud, branches full of sap; and there was nothing in the car but a couple of roadmaps which she had already used. Struck with an idea, she took off her raincoat, and with the help of a stick wedged it in around the wheel, right in the mud, but thank heaven it was too dark to see what that did to it. On the other side she put more sticks and branches.

She got in, started the engine, shifted, and let out the

226

brake. The wheel spun, then caught. Almost before Emmy knew it she was up out of the mud. She put the car in reverse and backed out of the marsh.

As she drove past her house, Emmy sighed with relief, and even laughed. She felt almost dizzy. The danger was over: nobody would ever know. And if nobody knew, it was as if it had never happened, wasn't it? After all, in Hum C terms, an experience or emotion which could not be communicated to anyone was meaningless. It was a rule that Emmy, brought up in a society where every significant action from christening to funeral—and many insignificant ones—was publicly announced and recorded, could easily understand. She ought to feel better because of this, but she felt worse; it was as if big sections of her life were being crossed out and thrown away.

"No, no, it did happen," she said aloud. "I remember it." But memory alone is weak: now, for instance, though hours seemed to have been used up, it was barely nine o'clock. Emmy drove on, into town. She parked by the common, and walked straight up the path to the college auditorium. The doors of the building were closed, but yellow light poured into the trees from the arched windows above. Emmy could hear the piano going faintly. She pushed open the door. Applause broke out while she was crossing the empty lobby; it went on rising and falling as she climbed the stairs to the balcony. When it ceased, she went in.

The balcony was narrow and steep, and only sparsely occupied. Standing at the back, Emmy could see almost the whole auditorium, up to the empty stage. She felt out of breath, and sat down suddenly at the end of a row. Below people were talking, turning, getting up, going into the aisles. Everyone she knew in Convers seemed to be there: the Fenns, the Lumkins, the Butlers, the Greens. . . . They all passed out without looking up except for Allen Ingram. Gazing vaguely around in the way he had, he caught sight of her and smiled, but stared more than smiled. Suddenly Emmy felt dreadfully exposed. What was she doing alone up there, in her old clothes and covered with mud? Yes, her feet and ankles were caked with it, her skirt streaked and still damp, and of course she had no coat. She opened her compact, keeping it concealed inside her bag (a lady does not look at her face in public). She had a smear of dirt across her forehead, no lipstick, and her hair was a bird's nest. But she could not leave now, when everyone would see her; more, she would not.

The lights blinked, the audience returned to their places, everything in an orderly manner. Emmy waited sitting stiffly. Suddenly Will walked out onto the stage, much larger and nearer than she had expected. He was wearing a dark suit and looked serious. Emmy had the feeling that he and she were alone in the auditorium, that he could not help but see her. She felt dizzy, as though the balcony were about to tip up yet more steeply and precipitate her onto the stage; she clutched the back of the seat ahead and held her breath.

Will either did not see her or did not care. The audience applauded, he sat down, the boy who was going to turn pages for him moved near. He began to play. Emmy's first thought was that she had at last gone out of her mind from the unhappiness and strain of the past four weeks, for it was as if Will took hold of the piano and shook it so that its teeth rattled together. Strange noises, not music, burst across the auditorium, jangles and xylophone-like discords interspersed with uneven bits of complete silence. Then, gradually, it came over her that he was playing a modern composition. Looking down into the auditorium, she realized that the rest of the audience was confused as well as she. Heads turned; there was whispering.

A student three seats away offered Emmy his program. She took it automatically, smiled automatically, and read:

INTERMISSION
Sonata in C major (1956) . . . . . . .Louis Fuchs
Opus 78 in F # major. . . .Ludwig van Beethoven

The deafening sounds continued, even increased. She was surprised, looking at the piano, to see that it remained fixed to the floor. Just when the noise seemed piled up to fall in a louder wreck than any before, it slipped sideways into an almost classical minuet full of oriental tones. Continuing to play, Will looked over his shoulder suddenly at the audience, and it occurred to Emmy that it was all a deliberately contrived joke. She was even more certain of this a few minutes later, when the notes of the second theme began to crowd closer together on each repetition, grew rapidly louder, and turned into a crashing discord. A few minutes in the original manner, but not so loud,

228

succeeded, then the minuet again, the noises, the minuet—all increasing in tempo and pitch and turning round each other, until the piece ended in what could only be described as brilliant confusion. Will took his hands off the piano and gave the audience another look, almost as if daring them not to applaud. They did not dare, except for Emmy.

And now, to make up, he gives them some ice cream for dessert, she thought, as he began the Beethoven. Knowing it, she stopped listening consciously and instead watched him play. She noticed the deliberate, even sneaky approach of his hands to the keyboard at the beginning of a section, and the contrasting way in which he snatched them off as though they had been burned at the end of one.

He played as if he were making love, with his whole body; not like a child, with only the fingers. Before he struck it, each chord rose up his back into his shoulders, then down. The single notes he sounded deliberately too, as if choosing them, with a delicacy and strength of touch she had thought only she had felt. She was struck by a feeling of unreasonable but real jealousy of the grand piano. With its artificial ebony gloss, its toothpaste smile, its Junoesque curves, it was like some vulgar corseted actress. When she heard the music again, the romantic throb, it was too much; she should not have come.

Tears, embarrassingly hot and prickly, rose to her eyes. She stood up, hurried up the steps, and out the balcony door. Then, almost running, she rushed downstairs, across the hall, and out into the spring night.

At home, Emmy turned out the lights and crept upstairs quietly to avoid waking Holman; she had a brief feeling of disgust at the idea of getting into bed with him and the flu, but she was really too exhausted to care. She began to pull off her clothes in the dark.

"Emmy."

She jumped, startled. "You're awake!"

"You're back late."

"Mm." She was too tired to invent an excuse. "How are you feeling?"

"It's ten-thirty."

"Mm."

"The library closes at nine."

"I went to Will Thomas' concert," Emmy said, fatigued by this meaningless cross-questioning.

"Really?"

"Of course, really."

A silence fell. Emmy put on her nightgown and sat down on her edge of the bed.

"Emmy."

"Mm-hm." She yawned meaningly and lay down. The sheets were moist and creased, and it felt as if Holman had put on at least two superfluous blankets. Annoyed, she sat up again and pushed them aside into a heap between her and her husband.

"I want to ask you something."

"All right."

"I wanted to ask you, are you mixed up in something? . . . Are you mixed up with some other man, for example?"

" 'Mixed up'?" Emmy replied stiffly. Holman made a face in the dark, thinking that what he heard in her voice was scorn of his vulgar colloquialism.

"All right: Are you having an affair?"

"Darling!" Her conventional epithet was never less of an endearment. "No, I'm not. Of course I'm not! What do you mean?" Her voice did not sound calm, but she was surprised at how positive it sounded. Of course she was telling the exact factual truth.

"The way you've been acting lately," Holman said, and his tone became a shade apologetic. Emmy said nothing. "Letting everything, well, letting everything go to hell in the house, the meals and the laundry and, hell. You know what I mean."

"I suppose so," Emmy said. Her voice seemed to come from some cold and distant place. "You mean you're still angry at me for not having remembered to bring your shirts home from the laundry on time and so you accuse me of having an affair."

"No, I—"

"I suppose in your mind it's practically the same thing." It was characteristic of Emmy's family, perhaps even of Emmy's class, to act on the principle that the best defense is an offense. Although she was worn out and shaken up, Emmy did this automatically. "I suppose you think a wife is nothing but a, a, an ironing board." She burst easily into the tears that she had repressed twice already that evening.

230

"I do not." Holman had been trained in another theory of defense. "You know I don't think that," he went on, ignoring her sobs. "It's because I care about you that I naturally— Oh, Emmy, for God's sake!"

"Oh, you care, you care about me, all you care about is my b-body!" Now that she had really started crying, Emmy could not stop. "If I'm unhappy the absolutely first thing you think of, n-naturally—"

"There. There there." Rather heavily (partly because he was lying in bed, and partly because he was not in the habit of expressing sympathy or tenderness) Holman put his arm around Emmy's shoulders. "It is natural, baby. . . . Men are different from women, darling. We're all materialists; we're all obsessed by the physical facts." Emmy sobbed less.

"Women care more about emotions," he went on. "Why, I remember you once told me you wouldn't mind so much if I had sexual relations with some other girl as long as I didn't fall in love with her."

"Yes," Emmy said. "Of course I wouldn't. . . . And you think that's stupid, I suppose."

"I don't at all. I like you to feel that way," said Holman, who as a matter of fact had been unfaithful to Emmy on two and a half occasions since his marriage. But two and a half is not very many in five or six years, he said to himself, and it had always been with sordid companions and in sordid circumstances, such that it was almost impossible Emmy should ever hear of it. The idea of love did not enter into these occasions at all.

"But wouldn't you care too, wouldn't you be angry if I were in love with somebody else?"

"No," Holman said after consideration. "I would be hurt, I suppose, but I'd certainly prefer you to tell me about it. I could stand anything as long as I didn't have to know that you'd been to bed with another man. If it was only that you were infatuated—"

"Yes." At this point, Emmy had opened her mouth to tell Holman half of the truth. She was prevented by two things; one, his use of the unflattering word *infatuated;* and two; the circumstance that as he spoke Holman removed a Kleenex from the box and blew his nose with a loud, wet, trumpeting sound. Emmy had been brought up to believe that no decent adult did more than wipe his nose in front of others. When she had a cold, which was

231

seldom, she went into the bathroom and shut the door before blowing her nose like that. Several times during the early colds of their marriage she had spoken of this to Holman, but though he was usually very willing to learn small rules of behavior from her, he had dismissed this one as applying only to females.

"Is that it?" he asked. "Have you got a crush on someone?"

"No." It went against Emmy's nature to lie; she crossed her fingers, saying to herself: It's not a *crush*. "It's just that, I don't know, this whole place. Convers. I thought I was going to like it so much when we first came, but I don't. It's so dreadfully small and dull, nothing ever happens; and the people are so utterly provincial. I wish we could leave."

"There," Holman said vaguely.

"Don't you think so? Don't you wish we could leave?"

"No," Holman said. "I like it here. . . . You like it too," he added. "Why, just a few weeks ago you were telling me how much you liked it." He laughed, as if at the inconsistency of women.

Emmy felt disinclined to enter into an argument on this point. "Maybe I did," she said.

"You did." He laughed and patted her shoulder.

"Let's go to sleep, darling, I'm simply dead."

"All right."

She turned onto her back, sighed once, and began to drift off. Several minutes passed.

"Emmy. Did you really go to that concert?"

"What?"

"Did you really go to that concert?"

"Yes, darling."

"I only asked because you already said you weren't going to go, because you couldn't stand a whole evening of piano music. I'm glad you went; it would have been rude to Will for us not to be there. I hope you told him I was sick."

"Mm."

"Actually, I feel better now. I think maybe I'll get up tomorrow."

"Let's go to sleep, darling."

Five minutes passed.

"It must have been a very short concert," Holman said. "To be over so soon after ten."

"Mm."

"If you didn't go to it, I wish you'd tell me. You don't have to lie to me, baby."

"I did go to it."

Two minutes passed.

"What did Will play at the concert?" Holman asked suddenly. Emmy sat up in bed.

"Don't let's go on this way," she said. "I did go to the concert, I did go to the concert, I did go to it! Why are you acting so peculiarly?"

"I'm not acting peculiarly," said Holman, who preferred not to admit that he had been made suspicious by Mrs. Rabbage.

"Well then, why don't you believe me?"

"I believe you," Holman said dubiously.

* * *

Allen Ingram to Francis Noyes

May 7

You can stop gnashing your teeth now and clawing at the empty mailbox. All will be explained and, I trust, forgiven.

The reason I did not write to you was account of Beowulf got himself hit by a car. Be calm: he survived. To make a short story long, one sweet spring day nigh onto noon Bard Ingram was perched upon his porch perusing of papers. Beowulf below, gamboling on the green. Cometh by on the byway, about 30 mph, station wagon containing Mrs. Holman Turner. Beowulf rusheth, barketh, chaseth. One minute later, cometh by on the byway, about 50 mph, Volkswagen containing Mr. Holman Turner. Beowulf rusheth, barketh. Collision. B and VW both knocked sideways, dented. B yelping. Bard, yelping, bounds from porch, Turner, or as we are now calling him, Grendel's Father, stops sulkily, emerges from engine. Angry words are winged. Spectacle of two adult males attempting to introduce large, yelping, bleeding dog into back seat of small Volkswagen. Attempt fails. Spectacle of Volkswagen proceeding to veterinarian with Bard Ingram holding Beowulf on his lap.

A real scene: how you would have enjoyed it! But I was, frankly, too furious to do so. I felt a pure, Early Middle English hate for Turner, and it didn't go away when the

233

vet said B was probably going to recover. After all, it's seldom in this world that one has the opportunity to be really righteously angry—so often one's rage, or the expression of it, is hobbled by guilt or some other extenuating circumstance. No doubt there are such circumstances here too, but I don't want to know them. I refuse to concern myself with why Grendel's Father was chasing his mate up a back road in his VW; I don't ask myself why she turned up at a concert last week all alone with mud on her face. At least, not more than twice a day.

Naturally, the local population has been vitally interested in this local event. I've experienced a tremendous upsurge of popularity, and dine out on my firsthand account (Next week—no doubt—Turner Tells His Side of the Story). Even at the Lumkins, where I thought I had quite used up my credit, as I never return invitations. It's lax of me, I know, but I can't fancy myself in the role either of host or hostess. This was not at all a bad dinner, though served with a lot of tiresome ceremonial silver, etc. They have a biggish house right on campus, all varnish and chintz—a model of airy speciousness. Did I tell you that Betsy L. is now pregnant? She wears quite unnecessarily huge maternity clothes. I suppose as a kind of good-luck charm. Billy the Boy Dean had on a paternal air, along with what you might call paternity clothes— solemn socks and a vest, instead of his usual College Shoppe outfit. He has put on weight—solidified, perhaps, by his (rather belated) physical efficacy. I understand that he has also been effective in the professional area of late, and has won several little long-standing battles. Sometimes one sees this place as a feudal survival: each department head a petty baron, supported by a gang of untrustworthy vassals, squabbling over the ownership of serfs, engaged in endless skirmishing with his peers, and more or less disloyal to King King.

Anyhow, the atmosphere in the Lumkin mead-hall was cloyingly cheery. I'm afraid I couldn't join in properly; I was obsessed with the image of Beowulf howling in his nasty little wire dungeon at the vet's, and I never have understood the conventional enthusiasm for the reproduction of the species. The addition of yet another formless, mindless homunculus to this cluttered world seems hardly a matter for rejoicing.

The only shadow cast on the Lumkins' joy all evening

was a piece of news about Julian Fenn: he has got a very good job at Princeton. Head-shaking. Definitely an unwise movement on the part of Princeton (one sees the whole town shifting about uneasily on the map). Of course we all hoped that Julian had learned his lesson* and would not repeat his unfortunate behaviors, but really, was it to be expected? Etc. I was tempted to contradict them, but what would have been the point? After all, it's hard enough to swallow a friend's good fortune, let alone an enemy's. Even Fenn's well-wishers are a bit aback-taken by the event—they never wished him quite *that* well.

*The metaphors of their trade. They all do this constantly— very amusing—I keep meaning to start a collection.

CHAPTER

13

"EMMY! HOW NICE TO SEE YOU!" MIRANDA CRIED, HER ENthusiasm heightened by a shade of irony. When one has too many misfortunes, one's acquaintances avoid the house, she thought, as if they thought bad luck catching; perhaps it is. Now that Julian had a new job, and a good one, everyone in Convers was calling them and calling on them.

"May I come in?"

"Of course." Miranda stood back. "I'm spring cleaning. Everything's chaos, but then it always is."

"You're looking frightfully well," Emmy said, following her into the kitchen. It was true, though Miranda was dressed in a collection of what looked like cleaning rags.

A month since she came to visit me, maybe more, Miranda thought. "Do have some coffee," she said. "I've got to put the wash in, but I'll be right back."

Left alone, Emmy sat at the kitchen table and stared at her reflection in the toaster: chrome greenish, distorted above a tweed suit which was too hot for the day.

"Hi." It was Richard Fenn, in pajamas.

"Hello," she said wearily.

"I have the chicken's pox."

This was obvious. "Shouldn't you be in bed?"

"Charles has the chicken's pox too, but I have more spots than Charles. Show you."

"Yes, you certainly have spots."

Richard went on removing his pajamas. "Don't do that, Richard," Charles said, appearing. "It's not polite to take off your clothes in front of ladies that aren't your relations."

"I have to, to show her my spots. There. Don't I look like a savage leopard?"

"Richard, put on your pajamas! Go back to bed. Charles, go back to bed," Miranda said.

"Aw."

"Go back to bed!"

"Aw right. I'm *going*."

Miranda sat down and began conversations on the topics of Julian's job, housing in northern New Jersey, chicken pox, spring cleaning, and the accident to the Williamses' dog Beowulf. It was her impression that Emmy responded to all of these subjects with only a thin show of interest, that she seemed depressed. To cheer her up, Miranda related several comic incidents of her husband's and children's behavior, ending with the story of how Katie had come home from Sunday school praying: "Our Father who art in heaven, hallooed be Thy name; Thy Kingdom come; give us this day our daily trespasses." Emmy began to laugh, gasped hysterically, and then broke out crying.

"Emmy. What is it?"

"N-nothing." Emmy could not stop. "Everything."

"What's wrong? Tell me."

"Oh, uh, it's Holman. He's being. So absolutely impossible. I don't know what's the. Matter with him," Emmy said interspersed with sobs. "He's always in a state, complaining about absolutely everything, the meals. And the laundry and Freddy and he's got this idea that. He keeps asking where am I going and what I did there. And he's got the idea that I'm having an affair with somebody."

"Ah." The two women looked at each other, and Emmy giggled noisily; her eyes were huge, wet, red-rimmed.

"Of course it's not true, you know," she said.

She knows I know, Miranda thought. "Who does he think you're having an affair with?" she asked.

"He doesn't know. Anybody. Everybody. He's just madly suspicious. Really, it's *too* much!" She spoke nervously, in an incongruous exaggeration of her social manner. "He even follows me around. He was following me the day he ran into Allen Ingram's dog, you know. . . . No, it's too utterly much. And when I tell him I've been somewhere, he doesn't believe me. We keep going through this awful thing about whether I really went to Will's concert that night. I suppose it's frightfully funny, really."

"But you didn't go to Will's concert," Miranda said.

"I did too go. I sat in the balcony. I didn't go down for intermission," Emmy said in the deadened voice of a witness at a retrial. "I came late; and then I couldn't bear it, so I left early."

237

"Ah."

"You believe me, don't you?"

"Yes, I believe you." He was wrong, she still cares about him, Miranda thought.

"I'm sorry, it's just that I'm beginning to expect not to be trusted." She began to tell Miranda all that Holman had put her through during the past week: his suspicions of her movements, his reiterated cross-questioning, his detective investigations among their friends ("I know you didn't go to the concert, because Will didn't see you there. I asked him today.... Charley Green didn't see you there either, and neither did Bill and Betsy Lumkin. . . . You expect me to believe that you would go to Will's concert and then leave without speaking to anybody, without congratulating him? God damn it, Emmy.")

"He sounds bewitched," Miranda said. "Or possessed, more likely. It's all so unlike him."

"He is possessed." Emmy laughed, partly hysterical, but partly with relief at having someone to talk to. "Do you know one night in the middle of the night he got me out of bed to swear on the big Bible that I wasn't deceiving him? Only we couldn't find it; we were both running back and forth all over the house in our night clothes and it wasn't anywhere. Finally I remembered that I had lent it to you months ago when Julian was writing some article. And then, if you can imagine it, Holman thought I had done it on purpose. I offered to swear on something else, anything he liked: his complete Shakespeare, or my yearbook from St. Kit's, but he said they wouldn't do." She collapsed into wild giggles, and Miranda did not try to prevent herself from joining in.

"But he'll get over it, surely," she gasped at last, "when he sees that you're not . . ."

"But when? He's already gone on like this for a week, and he simply seems to be getting worse."

"Really," Miranda said slowly, testing the ground; "you might just as well be guilty. I mean, one might as well be hanged for a sheep. . . ." Emmy laughed, but did not reply.

A feeling of power came over Miranda; she held her breath. She was long used to (and encouraged) her children's coming to her with their quarrels and questions to settle; her friends and relatives, too—sometimes in person, sometimes by mail—occasionally laid small sections of

238

their lives at her feet. She listened, she interpreted—re-arranging the bits and pieces they brought in. Advising them what to think and do, and then looking on while her words were made flesh, was her deepest pleasure. A chance like this—I could make it up between them, she thought. Everything could be as before: Will seeing Emmy and coming afterward to talk it over with her. (During the last few weeks, Will had been at the Fenns' only twice, and both his visits had been full of sodden silences.) I could keep them apart, too, by saying—or just by saying nothing. Holman is so suspicious, it might be positively dangerous for it to start again. Only Will was so unhappy. Julian had a wonderful new job in a warmer climate and Charles was the best reader in his class and Allen Ingram was going to Europe and the Butlers were moving into a house with apple trees. Will ought not to go on dragging around believing that Emmy had thrown him over, looking so bad. Emmy didn't look very well either. It was unlike her, too, to be silent for so long.

"Will misses you very much," she said abruptly.

"I doubt it."

"He does."

"I'm sure he can find someone to console him."

Miranda interpreted this as a question. "He hasn't," she said. Emmy said nothing; she could not bring herself to relate the example of Will's consolability that she had seen in Hampton.

"I know he's very unhappy," Miranda went on. "He wants to see you, but he's afraid to call you up; he thinks you wouldn't speak to him. He's miserable."

Emmy was not miserable to hear this, yet it set her nerves on edge to hear Miranda speak so intimately, edging her way into Emmy's life. She moved her chair back some. "You know what we quarreled about, I expect," she said after a pause.

"Yes," Miranda replied. "That is, I know some of it," she added, hoping to hear Emmy's version. "Really not much." Her hopes were disappointed; Emmy just sat, staring at the sink. "You take these things too seriously," Miranda said. "After all, it's all in the past. It doesn't mean anything to him now, why should it mean anything to you?"

Now Emmy did look at her, and with a sort of horror. Miranda did not suspect the whole truth, but it did occur

239

to her that Will might have been lying when he said that
he had stopped seeing Avis Walsh long before he met
Emmy. Perhaps he had been stupid enough to have seen
Avis more recently.

"I'm not trying to excuse him," she said hastily. "Heaven knows, I'm sure Will has done some impossible things.
And I'm sure he knows it. Only it hurts him to think that
you would refuse to speak to him completely. More
coffee?"

"I haven't refused to speak to him," Emmy said.

It was warm under the trees; the sun slipped down from
branch to branch onto a floor of dry leaves and pine
needles which had been accumulating there since the forest began to grow. Thin green grass grew in the clearings,
and adder's-tongues with their leopard-spotted leaves. A
few feet downhill to Emmy's right were some wild pink
orchids of the kind called "lady's-slippers." Emmy's shoes
lay near them, under a heap composed of all her and
Will's clothes.

Will's eyes were closed. He was breathing slowly making a noise not quite a snore and not quite a purr—or, if
so, like the deep purr of a lion or some other big cat. He
looked something like a lion as he lay there asleep on the
side of the mountain, brown and tawny on a pile of brown
and tawny last year's leaves, with his mouth curved in a
slight smile, and the shadows of this year's leaves flickering over everything like camouflage.

She yawned, and he opened his eyes.

"What were you thinking?"

"Nothing. I was asleep. What were you thinking?"

"Oh, about your concert. Are you really, absolutely
certain you didn't see me there?"

"Absolutely." Will stretched, turned on his side, and put
his arm lightly across her.

"You looked straight at me."

"I was playing."

"You know, you play very well; everyone said so. The
Beethoven especially. Paul Knight said you had an excellent technique and unusually something phrasing. The Bakers thought so too."

Will made a popping sound with his mouth. "Amateur
experts," he said. "Visitors from another world. They
don't hear a thing. Bubbles. They all have a big bubble

over their heads. They think they're space men. 'I too can have an opinion,' they think."

Emmy laughed.

"They're crazy. I hardly did a passable job on the Beethoven. I couldn't play the last movement anywhere near as fast as it should go. . . . Lou's thing, on the other hand: that wasn't bad."

"You chose that piece on purpose, to confuse them," Emmy said. "Didn't you?" Lazily, she rubbed her hand across his head, brushing off bits of dry leaf. Will smiled, but said nothing. "Who's Lou? Is he a friend of yours?"

"Mm. He's a composer. . . . I suppose you might say he's my artistic conscience. When I'm working I write and tell him about it."

"I'd like to meet him."

"You wouldn't like him."

"Why not?"

"He's not your type. He's a little fat man who lives in Southern California and wears loud sport shirts."

A pause. Will followed the outline of Emmy idly with his finger. "I'll tell you something," he said abruptly. "I've started working again."

"Oh, that's wonderful! When did you start?"

"Before we had the fight. I think it might have been your influence. Miranda says I was under a bad spell, and something broke it—I didn't tell you because I was afraid it wouldn't last." He lay back on the dead leaves. "Then I stopped, after the fight. The funny thing was, I started again just before the concert."

"Golly, I'm so glad," Emmy said, turning over onto her stomach. She propped her face in her hands to look at Will. "I hope it *was* me. What are you composing?"

"A serenade for flute and piano; but I've finished that. I sent it off to Lou yesterday. It's short, only about six minutes. Now I'm starting something longer; what I want to do is—"

"Will you play it to me?" Emmy interrupted. "I mean, on the piano."

"Of course. I'll even dedicate it to you, if you like."

"You will?" She opened her eyes, black-silk-fringed. "I've never had anything dedicated to me."

"Got to start sometime." Will sat up; then he leaned over and kissed Emmy's brown shoulder; first gently, then harder. "You taste of salt." He put out his tongue and licked a circle round the mark of his kiss. "Almost all the way down," he said a moment later.

"Mmm."

"Here, turn over. . . . Oh, look at you." From her breasts to her knees Emmy was covered with a pattern of the leaves she had been lying on. "Christ, you are beautiful, Emily," he said, not looking at her face. He began to kiss her again.

"Yes, yes. Do." She turned toward him.

In many ways, Emmy was strangely unshockable for a "nice" girl. She had come to Will completely ignorant of most of the variations on love. Not only had she never heard that certain games were low and dirty, she had never heard of them at all, and so she had no opinion about them until they turned out to be rather fun. The girls at St. Kit's who had used to talk about sex were in a clique which was bad at both games and lessons and was looked down upon completely by Emmy's clique. Marriage with Holman had left her nearly as innocent as before; his idea of love-making with one's wife was that of a brief and energetic routine which seldom varied, and in which little attempt was made to arouse or please the other party.

"Ahh," she said finally, when she could speak. "I love you."

"I love you," Will said at the same moment; they began to laugh delightedly.

"I was waiting to tell you that," she said, still laughing.

"Yes. That's one of the disadvantages of this way, that you can't speak. Not that you always want to conduct a conversation; but you can't even shout or say when it's especially good. And I like to talk while I'm making love. I expect you've noticed. When I can't I feel like the deaf-and-dumb."

Holman never says anything in bed, Emmy thought, and was silent, looking down the mountain into a web of branches and twigs and needles. She felt guilty, not of her love-making with Will, but of her relations with her husband. On the other hand, Will had not been innocent either. "I saw you once, in Hampton," she said suddenly. "About three weeks ago."

"Really? I didn't see you. . . . And you didn't speak to me," he added reproachfully.

"I was in a shop, and you walked by on the street."

242

Emmy sat up to watch his face. "It was raining, and you were with a blonde girl in a plastic raincoat that I never saw before."

"Emily. You've seen her a hundred times."

"I have not."

"And you've spoken to her." He looked up to see if Emmy were joking. "That was Sheila May, from the Hampton Hotel." Emmy still looked blank. "Jesus, she waited on us almost every time we were there."

"Oh, the waitress! I didn't recognize her. What were you ever doing with her?"

"I was walking her home. You know I used to go over to the hotel a lot all that time after we broke up. Christ knows what for, revisiting the scenes of former happiness I suppose. It was as good a place as any to get drunk. I hoped you might come in some time, but you never did."

It was the one place Emmy had never thought of looking for him. "Walk into the bar of a hotel alone? How could I do that?"

"It wouldn't be St. Kit's," Will said resignedly.

"Heavens, no." Emmy laughed. Then she said: "I used to drive out by The Tree and sit there in the car. And all the other places."

"Oh, Emily." Will put up his arms and pulled her down beside him. "If I'd only known," he said, his voice moving against her face. They kissed.

"You know," she said, "when I saw you I was so utterly furious, I thought, here I am still absolutely miserable and he's already starting some thing new with some cheap girl."

"I wasn't even thinking of it. Sheila's already married."

"That hasn't stopped you in the past."

"I mean." He laughed, but went on. "She's happily married. She really loves her husband; she's putting him through accounting school." Emmy felt rebuked. A dingy feeling passed across her like a damp wind. "You know you don't have to be jealous of Sheila," he said, misreading her face at a distance of two inches. "She was completely on your side. She thought I had behaved abominably."

Emmy sat up. "You mean you told her the whole story, that waitress?"

"No; Jesus, of course not. But hell, anyone could figure it out, my coming in alone that way to drink, looking like death warmed over. She asked me where my friend was;

243

and so I said we'd had a fight. She said it was probably my fault and anyhow it was my job to go around and make it up with you. So don't be jealous of her."

"Hm," Emmy said after a pause.

"Hm what?"

"Hm I'm not jealous of her."

"Good." He pulled her down to him again, and she let herself slip, filing away the resolve never to enter the Hampton Hotel bar again as long as she lived.

"You know whom I am jealous of," she murmured presently.

"No."

"Betsy Lumkin."

"Oh, Emily." He sighed, and rubbed his nose against hers, but she would not let it go.

"I'm awfully sorry for her, too."

"Sorry? What for?"

"Why, because you left her." Emmy moved off of Will, the better to see him.

"Believe me, it was mutual," he said.

Emmy did not believe him. "Didn't she want to marry you? After all, you're the father of her child."

"Marry me! Not Betsy. What would she want to do that for? She's the wife of the Dean of Convers College; pretty soon she'll be the wife of the President of Convers College. She wouldn't want to leave all that and turn herself into the wife of a second-rate musician six years younger than she is. Christ, what would her friends think? Might as well marry the gardener."

"But wasn't she in love with you?"

"I don't know. Maybe she thought she was at the time. Some women have to fool themselves that way. . . . She wanted something and I obliged her, that's all."

"How awfully helpful of you." Emmy was unused to employing sarcasm, and this came out as a kind of squashed scream.

"Well, hell. I did get some fun out of it too," he said, beginning to be annoyed.

Emmy said nothing; to hide her face, she turned over, away from him.

"Emily?" He sat up. "I'm sorry. Let's forget it."

"And did you think you were in love with her?" Emmy said into the ground, in a stupid voice with lumps in it.

"No. And I never said I was either. You know that's

one of my principles. Emily." He began to stroke down her shoulder and arm in a calming way, as one strokes a horse.

"Did she say she loved you?"

"Well. Maybe once or twice. You know, there are moments when one gets carried away."

"And you didn't say: 'I love you' back?" She turned and looked at him, too serious to push out of her face the heavy strands of hair that had fallen across it. Will shook his head. "Do you think she minded?"

"I don't know." He laughed impatiently.

"I would." She sat up. "I'd mind frightfully; frightfully."

"Oh, Emily. I love you."

"Say it again." She lay back, laughing softly.

"I love you. I love you." Laughing too, he moved nearer. "I love you. See how much I love you?"

"Oh, Will. We haven't time." Emmy raised her head; out past the mountain the sun was halfway down the sky, falling in a net of twigs and leaves. "Oh, how nice—lovely."

One evening after supper Will sat at the piano, playing with chords. He was through work for the day and feeling good. That morning he had had a letter from Lou Fuchs expressing a favorable opinion of his composition for flute and piano. Lou had written that with Will's permission he would show the score to certain persons of musical significance in Southern California and try to arrange for its performance at a concert during the following winter, or what passes for winter in those parts. "Why don't you get the hell out of that hell-hole and come out yourself?" Lou had also said: a well meant suggestion, though not a very practical one. It was a warm spring evening, not quite night. Will would have liked to call up Emmy, but this was also not practical.

There was a loud knock on the door, repeated impatiently while he was crossing the room to answer it. He opened the door. There in the hall stood Holman Turner, with the light behind him and his face dark.

Christ, he's found out, was Will's first thought; his first impulse was to shut the door again.

"I thought it was about time I came to see you,"

Holman said in a somewhat strained voice. "Are you busy?"

"No, no," replied Will, looking to see if his guest were carrying a weapon. PROF SHOOTS (STABS, BASHES?) WIFE'S BOY FRIEND.

Holman appeared to be unarmed. "Come on in," Will heard himself say. Holman came in. I am a couple of inches taller, but we are about evenly matched as to weight, Will decided, measuring him in the dim light.

"Convenient place you have here."

"Thank you." Convenient for what? Maybe he only suspects. He's come to test me. "Like a drink?" he said as casually as he could manage.

"Thanks, I could use one."

But look how he is staring at me. In that part of the long attic room which constituted his kitchen, Will opened a drawer and took out the bread knife. "Bourbon?" he asked. The bread knife was not very sharp. Also, it was awkwardly obvious. His Boy Scout knife would have been better, but he had lent it to Henry Oska, a Boy Scout.

"Anything."

One doesn't murder a man from whom one has just accepted a drink, surely. Will replaced the knife. But he felt some reluctance to turn his back to Holman, and kept looking round while he put in the ice and water.

"Jack Daniels, hm?" Holman observed.

"Why not?" On the other hand, Holman might consider it the Somerset Maugham kind of thing to do, to have a drink with your rival before you killed him. He opened the drawer again.

"Cheers," he said, handing Holman his glass and placing the bread knife nearby on the coffee table, together with a loaf of bread which had unfortunately already been sliced by the bakery. They drank in silence. Well, go ahead, you don't expect me to bring up the subject, do you? Will thought.

"Nice place you have," Holman said again. Will realized that he was slightly drunk.

"Thank you."

"I always wanted a place like this, live alone, lot of things you can do in a place like this." Very slowly, Holman began to take something large and heavy and metallic out of his pocket. Drunk, he would be more likely to shoot on impulse, though maybe not as accurate. Will

246

leaned forward and put his hand on the hilt of the bread knife.

"Yeah; you can accomplish a lot when you have a place like this and no responsibilities," Holman said. He took out of his pocket a large heavy cigarette lighter. "Smoke?"

"No thanks." Will sat back and audibly let out his breath. Then, to explain this noise, he said: "Maybe. I managed to do nothing in this room but fuck around" (he stopped for a second on hearing the metaphor) "for three years."

"Yeah, but when you've got something definite to do. . . . My thesis." Holman pronounced this noun with an awkward loudness. "It was OK all year when I was just going along making notes, but now I've got to start writing. And damned if I can." He looked at Will for some response to this confession, perhaps for the surprise and disapproval he felt himself; then, apparently satisfied, he looked away. He said: "When I try to work in the office I've got that ass Charley Green breathing down my neck and when I go home there's my wife and the kid climbing all over me, nagging at me, would I please play cowboys and fix the bathroom faucet and decide about who we should invite to dinner. You don't know how lucky you are."

"I was married for two years," Will said. "Three, technically." In spite of himself, he felt sympathy, even warmth. He had to remind himself that the tiresome wife of whom Holman spoke was the same person as his beautiful mistress. Holman was an enemy who would possibly try to kill him if he knew the truth. The very least he could do was to stop him from going on this way. As a gentleman.

"It's getting me down," Holman said. "I can't sleep, and I know I'm not teaching worth a damn any more."

But apparently I am not a gentleman. Not even an honest boor who doesn't know the rules. I am what Emily once called me to herself, a cad. He drained his drink. "More whisky?"

"Thanks. I really appreciate this. You're a decent fellow, Thomas." Though Holman said this with coffee-room irony, it was obvious that he meant it.

"Not at all. Just a coward who can't face life." Will put down his glass. He ordinarily had a strong head, but due

247

to the tension of the visit or some other reason he was beginning to feel fuzzy.

"Don't say that. Sure, society wants everybody to get married, raise a family. They're right, of course. Categorical imperative. Civilization has to continue, keep up the species. But just for that reason there's a lot of courage in your position."

"Yes," Will said. "I've sometimes thought that, but you're the first person ever said it to me. Other times I tell myself, even if you're not a coward you're a parasite, living in other people's houses, eating other people's dinner, sl—" (he caught himself) "playing with other people's children." It struck him that he was making these self-accusations in order to avoid others. Also it was as if he said to Holman: See what a louse I am? If you go on trusting me it's your own god-damned fault.

"Oh, come on." Holman, as many others had been before him was reassured, even touched, by this frank self-exposure; and, as many others had, he began at once to explain to Will that he was not as bad as he had said. Will thought: This is the result of a trick, a technique of deception which I habitually practice. At the same time he could not prevent himself from being stupidly pleased at Holman's good opinion.

"You overestimate me," he said at intervals. Holman denied this, and went on to express, slowly and not too clearly, some general ideas about character. Will, sitting listening, had the sensation of intensely rapid mental activity that he had got years ago from smoking pot, or as it was then called, tea: as if his mind could run up the walls and out the window and all round the house inventing long statements between two of Holman's words. At the same time, he found it harder and harder to speak.

"Why does a man get married, what for?" Holman asked.

"Christ knows. Falls in love," Will suggested, bringing the words out with difficulty.

"Aw, no." Holman waved this possibility away with his hand. "What I mean is why he gets married at a particular time, like now and not then. I'll tell you. A man wants something that's his own property. He gets tired of screwing around. You know the old story about the Scotchman and the whore."

Speechless, Will shook his head.

"Tell it to you." Holman related the story; it reminded him of several others, less relevant but of the same type; so he related them too, one after the other. Though Will did not greatly care for this form of literature, he laughed loudly at the end of each example, so loudly at the last that he had to lie back on the bed. Christ, I am getting positively boiled, he thought. He sat up and pushed the bottle of whisky away. Get him out of here.

"Thanks, pal." Holman slopped whisky into his glass. "Reminds me of a guy was in my fraternity. Tommy Gould. He was a great guy. . . . Pig night."

"Pig night?"

"Yeah. It was a kind of a custom we had once a year. Big party. Drinks. Everybody brought in the easiest lays they could find, see. Kind of a competition. God, what a collection. All dressed up, cheap jewelry and those fake fur coats. Pigs. But turn out the lights and you couldn't see them. . . . Girls like that will do anything. They enjoy it, actually. Well, come on, you must know."

Will did not respond, though it was obviously his turn. Holman was waiting: his smile, half ready, was broken by a hiccup but replaced at once. Christ, what if he goes and gets sick on me, Will thought. That would be the end. Rousing himself, he looked at his watch. "Jesus, it's eleven o'clock," he announced, lying slightly.

"That late?"

"Got to get up for an early class," Will said firmly, rising.

"Yeah. Don't want to keep you up." Holman rose and went toward the door, which Will opened for him. "Good talking to you," he said, with his hand on the knob. "God, I've been in a state last few weeks. Not just the thesis. Something somebody said to me I got the idea my wife was cheating on me."

"Emily?" Will put into this word all the astonishment he could summon.

"Uh huh. I've been suspecting everybody. You ever go through that kind of thing?" Holman did not wait for a reply. "My colleagues, Charley, Joe Baker, my students, the mailman, everybody. I even thought of you." Will swallowed. "Sorry, but I did for a moment. Crazy. Everybody knows about your chick in the bank." Holman was the kind of person whom gossip always reaches at least six months late, if at all.

"You are crazy," Will said.

"No, I'm not." Holman swayed, holding onto the open door, toward Will. "Admit I'm not the kind of man makes a profession of understanding women" (he said this with some pride). "But I know. There's something going on. And I'll tell you who I think it is."

"Whom."

"Whom." If Will was drunk enough to correct him, Holman was drunk enough to accept it. "It's that bastard Julian Fenn, that's whom. I should have seen it from the beginning. With his bird walks." He swayed back again with the door, so far that it slammed shut.

Will looked at the wooden surface for a moment; then it opened, and Holman's head appeared again.

"Goonight," Holman said. "Thanks a lot."

"Listen, take it easy driving home," Will said, holding the door open. "You could crash up the condition you're in." At the same time he had a clear picture of Holman crashed up, his Volkswagen squashed against a tree. It would solve all his problems. Like an accordion. And create twice as many more.

"Don't worry. I'm going walk around a little first," Holman said. "Goonight."

"Goodnight."

Holman slammed the door again, and could be heard descending the stairs. Will turned back to his room. "Christ!" he said. He walked across the room and sat down on the bed.

"Christ," he repeated. "Christ. Jesus. Holy Bloody Mary." He picked up the telephone from the floor and dialed Emmy's number.

* * *

Allen Ingram to Francis Noyes

May 17

So Ginny and Tommy really intend to get married! I doubted your words when I read them, but I see today that she (or he) has actually put it into the *Times* so that he (or she—and after all, which *is* which?) can't escape. Seasonal hysteria. No doubt each thinks that the other will be a means of salvation for him. As with most couples, they are like two people jumping out of an airplane clasped together, each believing the other to be a parachute.

Spring fever marches on here too: the latest excitement is the student campaign against the new Religion Building. The trouble began last week when the plans were released. The student paper printed an editorial complaining about them and asking why the job hadn't been given to a good modern architect instead of to a firm in which one of the trustees is a partner. What had been designed, of course, was a brick cake iced with white shutters and columns and gables in the best Traditional Colonial Split-Level Ranch-Style. (The alternative would presumably be one of those dreary factories with Mondrian façade and a steeple made of stainless-steel tableware. As Betsy Lumkin says: "Modern public buildings do look so cheap"; she means, I suppose, that they ought to look expensive.)

The boys took up the cause enthusiastically—they always like to get excited about something at this time of year. Religion and sex are the favorites: they get together and have riots against compulsory chapel, or no-girls-indoors rules. One evening after supper they put on a parade, about a hundred of them, with signboards reading: "DOWN WITH HOWARD JOHNSON'S"—the name by which the student paper has been referring to the proposed building. They all brought their wastebaskets; they marched round President King's house, round the library, and dumped the wastebaskets out into the excavation. I am desolated to report that I missed the whole thing. By the time I got there next day there was nothing to be seen but a couple of workmen patiently shoveling out the debris. However, I hear from George Wedge that an even bigger demonstration is planned for Memorial Day, when a collection of dignitaries will be here for the cornerstone-laying, and I am determined to be on hand. I doubt that anything will really happen—it never does here (though how one wishes it would.)

Beowulf is back from the vet's. His nerves are obviously still in a state: he trembles at the sound of a car, and tries to climb onto my lap to hide; a pretty picture, since he weighs 50 or 60 lbs. Physically, however, he is recovered.

The vet's bill was promptly, and very properly, paid by Grendel's Father. Incidentally, I hear that he and Grendel's Mother aren't getting on too well of late. Apparently this is All Over Town (like a kind of red dye). I heard it

251

solemnly regretted by Frau Professor Oska (music dep't) and Frau Professor Baker; I heard it genteelly hissed by the English Department's secretary; I even heard it from my neighbor Mrs. Hutchins, who heard it from her sister-in-law in the grocery who heard it from her aunt who cleans house for the Turners, if you follow me. This college may be run by men and for men—the town is run by women for women. And not the slightest event can occur here (or not occur) without its being noticed. Out in the world a scandal spreads quickly and is gone, expanding in fading rings like waves from a stone tossed into a river, washed away down to sea. In this pond—this puddle—the ripples reach shore and bounce back, interlacing, till the whole surface becomes a net of lines.

CHAPTER
14

"Ahh," Emmy said as Will left her. She lay back on the steep, overgrown river bank full in the sun, naked among crushed green leaves and weeds. "Oh, I'm so wet."

"Here." Will passed a handful of leaves over his shoulder.

"Thank you. Golly. It didn't break, did it?"

"No. That's all you." Just lately, Holman had formed the habit of spying on Emmy's diaphragm. She dared not take it out of the bathroom cupboard too often, and she had no spare.

"Why 'Trojans'?" she asked, picking up a small box.

"Who knows?" If anyone was embarrassed, it was Will.

"They lost the war, after all." She dropped the box, yawning. Will pushed it under a bush with his foot, so as not to litter the scenery.

"Lost causes are more exciting sexually," he said, lying down beside her. "Look at the Civil War—or the French Revolution. Women like to do it plumb in the shadow of doom, it makes them feel good. I've never met one who didn't like my being a lost cause myself."

"You're not. Not any more."

"I keep forgetting." Will laughed. "And then," he went on, "Paris had the most beautiful woman in the world. Maybe it's a kind of implied compliment to your girl to buy them. I always have. There's not much choice. The other brand is called Rameses: that's for men who want to pretend to be Egyptian mummies. Pyramids, and slaves, and immortality and all that."

Emmy laughed, and then fell silent. "It's so nice here," she said presently. "Not just here, everywhere. It's as if all outdoors was our lovely big house, and we could make love in all the rooms. I'm so happy, so happy. Aren't you?" Will did not reply. "What's the matter?"

"Oh, nothing."

"No, something." It was very quiet, very warm. Insects

253

buzzed, and a yard below their feet the river poured by behind a screen of bushes.

"I suppose I was thinking of Holman. That whatever we do, no matter how far we go, sooner or later you go back and go to bed with him."

"Not very often."

"Often enough."

"I haven't now since—" She stopped to count.

"And he lies there, next to you, every night, all night long."

Emmy was silent. She shut her eyes, her mind.

"How is Holman, by the way?"

"Oh, the same. Not too bad, actually. I think he's really been better since he talked to you."

"Thanks." Will yawned, and pulled her back toward him.

"You have little white lines at the corners of your eyes," Emmy said, lifting her head. "I can count them: one, two, three."

"Age and decay."

"I don't think it's that. You're not old."

"Thirty-three. Past my prime."

"You don't look thirty-three," she said loyally.

"You don't look twenty-eight. Of course that's only to be expected; you didn't do anything to age you for twenty-eight years. It's odder in my case. I expect one day I'll wake up and it'll all show at once, like Dorian Grey. Then everyone will know." He stroked her face, kissed her, and then drew back. "You look sad," he said. "You look as if you were going to cry."

"You said that before. Do you want me to cry?"

"I don't know. I suppose so, yes. To make it up to me."

"Make what up?"

"I don't know."

"The Fenns' house? But I don't want to move into the Fenns' house," Lucy Green protested. "It's so big, and dark, and horrible and gloomy."

"But, Lucy—"

"I'm positive it would be a bad influence on Petey to live in a house like that."

"But Lucy—"

"Wouldn't it, Petey?" Lucy put her pink, plump arms

round the pink, plump baby on her lap; he responded with a wet, joyful coo.

"I suppose we could stay here, if we asked them to let us stay here. Everyone would think we were crazy, though."

"I don't want to stay here. Why can't we have some place like that place the Butlers are moving to, with the garden? Coo."

"Coo!"

"We weren't assigned there."

"And a nice lawn to put the baby out on. Couldn't you just ask them?"

"Coo, coo!"

"I think that would be a very bad mistake. You know they don't like people making any kind of trouble about college housing."

"Do we really have to live in college housing? Couldn't we find something else?"

"How could we afford it? Be reasonable, darling. The Fenns' house is only seventy-five dollars a month, including heat. We couldn't find anything outside for that price."

"The Turners did."

"The Turners are paying at least two hundred."

"It's not fair," Lucy wailed, so loudly that Petey began to cry. "Shh, lovey. Shh."

"They have their troubles too," Charley said.

"That'sa baby. I know. But they bring them on themselves. She certainly does, at least. Walking out and leaving him in front of everyone like that at Dean Lumkin's party, and refusing to go to the Wilbur reading with him. Shh. Coo."

"Maybe he refused to go to the Wilbur reading with her." Lucy made a face of disbelief. "All we know is that they're having some trouble, we don't know anything about why."

"I can guess."

"Well, I'll bet Holman isn't the easiest person in the world to live with either," Charley said. "He's been very unpleasant around the office lately. Restless. Rude even. Definitely rude."

"Whatever you say, I'll never believe it isn't all her fault, whatever it is. Cooey!"

"Something absolutely dreadful has happened," Emmy said, opening her kitchen door to Will. "I have poison ivy."

He began to laugh.

"What's so funny about that?"

"*I* have poison ivy."

"Oh, golly."

"Let's see."

Emmy lifted up her dress. She was wearing nothing underneath, and she was covered with scarlet rash.

"It was that day by the river. Christ. A regular social disease. Wait till you see me."

"What if everyone notices that we've both got it?"

"We must avoid public appearances." He moved closer and kissed her.

"Mm."

"I'm glad you have it. I was thinking I'd have to leave you alone for at least a week for your own good."

"I wouldn't have liked that."

"No."

"Freddy's not here," Will suggested hopefully a minute later.

"He is, though. He's outside playing, but he might come in at any moment."

Will groaned.

Freddy's behavior was growing worse and worse; even Emmy had to admit it. His stubborn independence had turned bad: he was becoming unreasonable and destructive. When Will came he went apart and broke things. Then he refused to say that he was sorry; sometimes, standing in the midst of the smash, he denied that he had done it, so violently that Emmy found herself looking around for some other, invisible destroyer. This could not go on much longer; she could not bear it. Will must stop coming to the house, which meant that she must stop seeing him every day, something she could not bear.

"I don't see him," Will said, letting the curtain fall back over the kitchen window.

"He's probably around the other side of the house. No! Come into the other room. Tell me how you are. How is the new piece coming?"

Will laughed ruefully, but he followed Emmy. "All right," he said. "And I've started something else. I'm finishing it, rather." He sat down on the piano bench.

"See, about four years ago, when I first came up here, I was still brooding over Rosemary and trying to write music. I started to set a poem by Louis Simpson. Goes like this:

> I fear the headless man
> Whose military scars
> Proclaim his merit.
> And yet I fear a woman
> More than the ghost of Mars,
> A wounded spirit.
>
> That look, all kindness lost,
> Cold hands, as cold as stone,
> A wanton gesture—
> "What do you want, old ghost?
> How long must I atone?"
> So I addressed her.
>
> "Did you not call?" she said,
> "Goodbye, then! For I go
> Where I am wanted."
> Till dawn I tossed in bed
> Wishing that I could know
> Who else she haunted.

"I went at it like a mad dog. I was all worked up over my own stuff, emotional, and that's not a good sign. When I'd finished the first two stanzas Lou Fuchs came to Boston and I couldn't wait to rush down and show it to him. He didn't like it. He said anyway it wasn't my wife I was haunted by, it was my mother."

"How mean," Emmy said. "And beside the point."

"Oh no. He was right. I looked at the thing again, and Christ, I'd even scored it for my mother's voice. She had a very narrow range; and what I'd done, I'd written it all in the first octave above middle C, all in here." He struck the interval. "But it wasn't only that. The second part of the stanza was all wrong. It wasn't until yesterday that I saw what it was. It used to go—" He played a collection of notes. "Well, now it's all changed, it goes—" He played a collection of notes.

Beside him, Emmy sat forward eagerly. "Yes!" she said.

257

Will looked at her face and saw that she had heard nothing.

"Oh, Emily."

"Now play me the whole thing."

"It's not finished yet." Will reached to kiss her. She turned her head, and the kiss slid onto her cheek.

"But you said it's nearly finished. Please." She insisted rather than implored. On a perverse impulse, Will turned back to the piano. He played the first two stanzas of the song and then without a break a stanza of "Oh! Susanna" in F-minor. Then he stopped and looked at Emmy.

"Oh, that's beautiful."

"Thank you." He took hold of her strongly. "Now."

"Now, we mustn't. Freddy. It's not right."

"He can't see through walls," Will said, not letting go.

"No. He might come in." Once already Freddy had caught Will and Emmy embracing, coming into the kitchen suddenly when he was supposed to be looking at television. He had never made any remark about this incident and neither had his mother and perhaps he had not noticed.

Emmy kissed Will hard but briefly, and turned away. "Please. It's too dangerous." Will pulled her back. "Don't you hear me?"

"I hear you," Will said, "but my body doesn't. It doesn't understand words like 'right' and 'dangerous.' It says: 'I want, I want.' "

Professor J. M. Lane (English Department, Princeton University) to Holman Turner

May 26

... and plan to leave immediately after examinations for Wellfleet, where we shall be spending the summer.

In clearing my files preparatory to departure, I was surprised to observe that I had not yet received from you the first portion of your Johnson ms., which I believe was originally promised for *April*.

I mention this, not because I have any doubts concerning your seriousness of purpose or your ability to complete the Ph.D. thesis, but because experience has taught me how fatally easy it is for the weeks alloted to this task to expand into months, and the months into years. I am most anxious that you should not become one of those unfortunate "thesis cripples" who are the despair of every University department.

I shall say no more of this matter. Incidentally, did you happen to see J. R. Leed's article on Johnson in the recent ELH? He raises the, I think, exceedingly relevant question. . . .

"I have news," Will said. "I heard from Lou today." He held back a branch for Emmy to go from the pasture into woods. The air was still, cloudy, warm, and heavy as if rain were coming on. "There." Behind the branches, they kissed.

"You have news," Emmy said.

"Yes. It's all settled. He's got me a fellowship at the Institute for the whole year, starting in July. Here's the letter."

Emmy sat down to read it, Will watching her. "So you'll be leaving. For good?"

"I hope so. Let's talk about it later." Will took the letter away from her. "Here." He pulled off his T-shirt and put it down for Emmy to lie on.

For once, neither of them spoke as they made love. Emmy pulled Will to her with all her strength, as if she could keep him from crossing the continent that way, and he responded. When he lay down on her for the last time they were both sopping wet from head to foot; wet ends of Emmy's hair stuck to her face and neck like black seaweed.

"That was—" Will said.

"Yes."

They breathed; Emmy wiped hair off her face.

"It's summer now," she said, looking up. The trees had grown in heavy and dark green. It was hot and extremely quiet. "Don't go," she added, as he shifted his elbow.

"I'm not going." He turned onto his side, pulling Emmy with him. "Going to rain." They lay there.

Suddenly there was a trampling, rustling noise. Will and Emmy looked up, at the same time struggling to disengage themselves from each other. About ten feet away the head of a Jersey cow appeared through the bushes.

"Christ!" Will laughed.

"Go away!" Emmy said. "Shoo!"

The cow ate leaves, looking at the two naked people with large cow eyes.

"Do you think there's anybody with her?"

"Not at this time of day," Emmy said. "Shoo!"

Will got to his knees and looked out through the bushes. "No, nobody around. She's a spy. Holman sent her." Emmy laughed. "Shoo! What do you do to get rid of cows?"

"Hit them across the nose with a stick, I think," Emmy said.

"You do it."

"I couldn't."

"Shoo! Come on, now. Go home!" The cow turned and moved off.

"How did you ever manage that?" Emmy said.

"I have a way with women." They leaned against each other, both still laughing.

"I simply can't bear to think of your going all the way to California," Emmy said finally, in the tone of one continuing an unimportant joke.

"Come with me, then," he answered in the same manner. They looked at each other for a second, wondering if he meant it, and then both looked away.

"It's starting to rain," Will said. There was a noise like fine sand falling through the leaves. "Not hard. We won't get wet here."

"I'd like to get wet." Emmy stood up and took a few steps out from under the tree. "There. Oh, it feels marvelous!" Will followed her.

"Yes."

"So cool. I wish it would rain harder."

It did not.

"Look at you," he said. "Christ, you're so beautiful."

"Look at you. No. I want to talk, to ask you—" When are you going, why are you going, where are you going?— she could not phrase it.

"Ask me."

"Can I have a strawberry soda?"

"All right." Will laughed. "I think we have time." Both checked this by reading the wrist watches which were all they wore. "If we go now."

They resumed their sticky clothes under the tree.

"Watch the branches," Will said. "Wait. . . . Spies everywhere," he added in a different voice, holding her back.

260

Emmy looked out through the damp leaves. Below, across the overgrowing, sloping pasture, another car was parked at the edge of the dirt road beside Emmy's green station wagon, like a beetle next to a cucumber; a Volkswagen. As they watched, its door opened and Holman Turner got out, about one inch high.

"Oh, God."

The Holman one inch high was carrying a black stick. He waved it in the air and it turned into an umbrella. Holding this above his head, he climbed the stile into the meadow.

"What'll we do?" Emmy whispered, as if her voice, could carry that far.

"You go on down. He knows you're here, because of the car. Tell him you just went for a walk."

"Yes; I'll say I came to pick flowers, or something."

"I'll go off in the other direction."

"How will you get home?"

"Walk."

"But it's miles!"

"Doesn't matter. Maybe I can hitch a ride. Go on before he comes this way. I'll call you tomorrow morning."

Below, Holman was growing larger as he walked across the meadow by the cow path, looking down to avoid cowpies. Emmy climbed through the bushes and started sideways downhill, pulling black-eyed Susan as she went, affecting not to have noticed him. The rain still fell faintly. When at last Holman looked up and saw her, she gave him a big ingenuous wave and quickened her pace; she met him just inside the corner of the field with her arms full of bright damp flowers.

"Mrs. Turner isn't here again today," Polly Manning said to Rebecca Scott, halfway between a statement and a question. She spoke in a normally loud voice, for the Ladies' Exchange was closed to customers this week.

"No; she said she had too many errands to do." Rebecca went on snapping red markdown tags onto a row of rubbers. "Again."

"That's the third time in a row, isn't it?"

"What makes it so *difficult*," Rebecca said, "is her not letting me know earlier. If she would only let me know I could easily arrange for someone to take her place, but she always waits until the last minute."

261

"Yes and with the sale coming up. . . . Seven eights are fifty-six."

"Well, something is going on, I am positive of that. You see, that red coat never went out. I knew it wouldn't. Betsy always prices her own things too high."

"My Maggie saw them again driving past our house the day before yesterday," Polly said. "Each in his own car again, first Mr. Turner and then Mrs. Turner this time, not five minutes apart. I think I'll put the water on, shall I?"

"Yes, do."

"There. Do you really think something is going on? I can't believe it of Emmy."

"Oh, not her. Him."

"But she's the one that May met up the dirt road back of her barn last month."

"Well, he's been seen walking around town very late at night at least three times."

"Dear. . . . Who do you think it is?"

Rebecca declined to say, perhaps because she had a reputation to keep up as a local seer.

"Perhaps he's just Troubled," Polly said charitably. "Twelve, and nine is. . . . Oh! That Hutchins girl, you know, the one who works in his office at the college. He gave her a big box of chocolates for Christmas; Emmy told us so herself. Do you think? Six nines are forty-five."

"Fifty-four. Nothing would surprise me."

"I am hopeless; fifty-four. . . . Really, that's dreadful, if it's true. And she's not even pretty. Men have such dreadful taste. . . . Oh, here's Betsy! How are you, Betsy?"

"How are you? Just fine! I thought I'd come along over and help you get ready for the sale."

"Oh, sit down," Rebecca said. "The water's just about to boil. You know you mustn't feel you have to come in to work any longer, unless you really want to."

"Oh, no; I like to get out." Betsy settled herself into a folding chair among bulging waves of maternity dress. "Tell me all the news," she said.

"Let's see. Well, poor Carolyn Hastings is officially engaged to that dreadful Cowie boy."

"Tsk."

"And Professor Higginson had another attack, and as you might expect he's refused to go to the hospital again."

262

"I heard about that from Bill. Tsk. He said, who would look after his animals."

"That's ridiculous of course," Rebecca said. "I could easily find someone for him. I told John to tell him so, but he said— Oh, and Mrs. Turner isn't coming in again to-day."

"Again? Really." Unnoticed, the water began to boil for tea.

"Dorrie Hutchins," Betsy said presently. "Isn't she the girl who runs the duplicating machine? Because you remember at our cocktail party before the poetry reading, when Emmy arrived first, and Holman was so late, he said he had been over in his office waiting for something to be run off on the machine." There was a pause.

"But when Emmy asked him where he had been," Rebecca said, slowly and ominously, "he told *her* he had been out driving in the country." The kettle began to bubble loudly and rocked about on the electric hot plate, but no one attended to it.

"Oh, lord," Polly said, "and it was just then that she left the party! She simply walked out on him." The three women looked at one another.

"Now I remember something," Betsy said. "You know, a while ago Bill wanted to get all those girls transferred up to College Hall into a typing pool. And Dorrie Hutchins was the one who petitioned to stay on in the departmental office."

"No!"

"No!"

"Yes."

"But that's dreadful," Polly said. The noise behind her rose to a shriek. "It's— Oh, heavens, the tea!" She jumped up and pulled the empty, hissing kettle off the hot coils. "It's all boiled away!"

"Sit here on the wall," Will said. "It's not too wet."

"I don't mind if it is." She climbed up beside him. It had been stormy all week; spring storms, sudden, green with rain. The grass in the fields was soaked, the trees dripping, the sky heavily bright. Emmy's feet were wet, her legs wet, her skirt wet to the knees.

"So beautiful," she said, looking down the view.

"Yes." Will looked at her.

"I wonder why it is everyone doesn't come outdoors to

make love? It's so much nicer. But they never do, they stay shut up in their houses."

"It's because they're married."

"But you'd think— I mean, if they're married, who could stop them?"

"They stop themselves. That's what marriage is. They feel the invisible bars."

"They don't really like each other," Emmy said.

"Maybe. . . . I wonder, if we were married would we go indoors? I don't think so. Not right away, anyhow. Look, here it comes again." Will pointed down the slope. Smoky clouds were rising toward them over the trees. "Shall we run for it?"

"I don't care. No."

"We're going to get wet, then. Come under here anyhow."

They got off the wall and sat under the tree, a small maple. The rain came up the field and beat on its leaves, then through them.

"Let's do it," Will said.

"Yes. Let's put our clothes under my raincoat, then they'll stay dry."

"Oh, good idea." The tree was soaked now; sheets of rain began to pour off the branches. "Wow! Doesn't this remind you of when you were little and it was hot enough to take off all your clothes and play in the sprinkler?"

"We were never allowed to take off our clothes and play in the sprinklers."

"Poor little rich girl."

Water streamed down them vertically as they kissed, and then horizontally as they lay down wet in the long wet grass.

"Christ, I love you."

"I love you."

The rain began to slack off; by the time they had finished only the tree dripped. Emmy sat up, laughing.

"Are you cold?" Will asked.

"No. It's warm, really."

"That was fun."

"Yes." She leaned against him for a moment. "I like it at the end when you get bigger and bigger and I can feel myself slowly exploding and nothing can be done about it."

"Mm." Will stroked her hair, wiping the water down.

264

"Mm. Well." She began to get up.

"Don't let's go yet."

"All right."

"Rainwater." He licked it off her arm. "I wonder how long it's been since I drank rainwater. . . . Lie down."

"Golly."

"You like that. . . . Ah. You're so open, so soft now. Let me in."

"We haven't much time."

"Just a little quick one. Just a little rondo to finish off with." He began to laugh. "You know I once had an affair with a girl who always wanted to do it to music. She liked Mozart especially, something with three movements. And cool jazz. . . . Oh, lovely. I don't know whether I can come again so soon, though. . . . Just a short visit, Mrs. Turner, I won't stay long—"

Emmy's body grew stiff; her arms dropped from around Will. "Don't call me Mrs. Turner," she said. "I hate it when you do that."

"Change your name, then," Will said, not stopping.

"What shall I change it to?"

"Oh." He did pause now, as if to consider. "Well, you might change it back to Stockwell, for a start."

"But—"

"Shh. We'll talk about it later. . . . Christ, how wonderfully slippery. Do you know, I think I can after all."

In a patch of sunlight, Julian and Will came out into a clearing on Mount Baird, the nearest of the large hills to the east of Convers. The sky was torn up, part blue and part gray, and a hard wind moved patches of light and shadow rapidly across the valley.

"There it is," Julian said, looking down at Convers College. "See the administration building? If I had a .300 H. and H. Magnum I could just about put a shell through the window of Lumkin's office." He and Will had been discussing the uses of firearms, with examples from their war and peace experiences. Now, like a child playing army, he bent and squinted at the target. "Bang!"

"Why not drop a bomb while you're at it and smash up the whole place?"

"Oh no. Too messy. Bad for the elms."

"One wants to make a mess sometimes. A thousand-pounder; that would about do for the college."

"Look, I want to talk to you about something," Julian said with an air of embarrassment unusual for him. Will turned. "I hear your friend Holman thinks I'm sleeping with his wife."

"Who told you that?"

"Miranda."

"He's been suspecting everyone," Will said. "For weeks."

"But lately he seems to have settled on me."

Will did not deny it.

"He cuts me when we meet," Julian complained. "And he makes threatening gestures. I don't want to interfere in your life. But what am I supposed to do when he comes sneaking up behind me some night with a knife?"

"Oh, Holman wouldn't do that."

"No. I suppose a sawed-off shotgun would be more his speed." Julian laughed, but he continued to look at Will, waiting.

"Well, tell him he's wrong. Tell him it's me, if you have to. He's going to have to know sooner or later. As a matter of fact—" He stopped. Julian said nothing. He did not like to know the personal secrets of his friends any more than he liked them to know his. "As a matter of fact, she's going to leave him after school ends."

"Oh, yes?" Julian took a step away.

"Oh, yes. She's going to take Freddy and go back to her parents in New Jersey. That'll look better."

"Mh," Julian murmured vaguely. "Well, congratulations or something."

"Thank you. Actually I think it will be best if she tells him herself. That's what we were planning. After I've left. We don't want to make waves."

"Emmy's going to leave Holman," Julian repeated, to fix the situation in his mind. "Is she going to divorce him?"

"Christ, I don't know. I suppose so, if he'll let her. I can't see him going to Nevada to be the injured party. I only wish to God she could divorce Freddy."

Clouds crossed overhead; Julian shaded his eyes and stared up into them. "A hawk!" he said. "Over there, look!"

Will looked; he saw a spot moving. "I'm afraid of marriage," he continued. "I suppose I want it, but I don't like to be subject to any more laws than I can help. It's

266

bad enough having to drive under sixty and pay taxes. They're at you all the time."

"If you pay any attention to them."

"How can you not?"

Holman finished typing up the new set of examination questions, took the sheet of paper out of the machine, folded it, put it into his brief case, and locked his brief case. There. Now let them think they had sneaked a look at the exam ahead of time. Who was Them? He did not know, but they existed. Someone had been in his office that afternoon while he was at the library, opened his drawers, and moved papers about. Even in Convers they would try that kind of thing.

He had been naïve to think that because this was basically a just universe it would contain few or no unjust men. On the contrary, they were boring away everywhere under the surface. Wherever he looked now he saw fraud, falsehood, sloth, and corruption. Federal, state, college and natural laws were perverted: students plagiarizing their term papers, short-changing in the stores, cars running red lights, bad strawberries at the bottom of the box; homosexuality, tax evasion; and adultery. Virtue went unrewarded, vice unpunished. People got away with things.

Though it was now only four o'clock, Holman set out for home, leaving Charley Green in possession of the office. (Suppose it had been Charley who had moved his papers; but why?) He had recently begun coming home at irregular times during the day, hoping to catch his wife (or hoping not to catch his wife) with whoever she was (or was not) seeing behind his back. So far he had completely failed at this (or succeeded), and if it went on much longer, Holman said to himself, I shall go completely cuckoo.

All his suspicions had seemed to gather together when he found, one afternoon last week, the prints of strange rubbers or galoshes in the mud by his door. They were definitely not his. His rubbers were larger and marked in wavy lines, whereas these were waffle-patterned. His first act was to preserve the best-defined print by covering it with a dead branch and leaves. That evening he craftily obtained from Emmy the statement that no tradesmen or other men had visited the house that day, and the next morning at college he devoted to the observation of feet.

It was not difficult, for most of his colleagues and almost all the undergraduates were no longer wearing rubbers. The black galoshes of Julian Fenn stood out glaringly.

Luck (luck?) was on his side, for when Julian went to his office after lunch he removed his galoshes and threw them by the hall register to dry. It was easy for Holman, on his way out, to pick them up, first one and then, rapidly returning, the other, for while the theft of two galoshes, if discovered, might just pass as absentmindedness among professors, the theft of one would suggest madness. From the point of view of credibility he should have sat down on the bench in the hall and absent-mindedly put Julian's galoshes on, but in order to do this he would have had to take off his own shoes. It was not until he got into his car that he noted the waffle pattern on the soles.

He drove directly home in a state of near-hysteria and confronted Emmy with the galoshes. "I suppose you won't try to deny that Julian Fenn was here yesterday," he said.

Emmy did deny it.

"You are making a mistake," he said. They went outside, followed by Freddy, and Holman got down to compare the clue with the evidence.

"They don't match," Emmy said, and it was apparent to Holman even in his then state that Julian's galoshes were too small and the pattern on them too large.

"I think those tracks were probably made by Mrs. Rabbage," Emmy suggested, and began giggling uncontrollably. Freddy, for some reason of his own, joined in. Perhaps he thought it funny to see his father squatting on the lawn holding galoshes.

In any case, Holman's discomfiture was such that it was not until late that night that it occurred to him that the fact that the prints had not been made by Julian's galoshes did not prove that Julian had not been in his house, or indeed anything at all.

So often had he rehearsed finding someone with Emmy that it was with a sense of *déjà vu* that Holman observed, as he came in view of the house, a car leaving the driveway and turning south: a dirty, noisy 1952 Chevvy. From this he deduced instantly that some dirty, noisy, disreputable person had been visiting his wife. He thought first of pursuing the car, but changed his mind and turned into the driveway. He felt quite calm, but as he walked across the grass he could hear his heart beating.

Emmy was seated at the kitchen table cutting up vegetables. She wore no make-up and her face had a smudged look.

"Someone was here. I saw him leaving," Holman said ominously.

"Yes, Dicky Smith. He brought you a paper to read."

"Smith. I would never have thought of Smith. No; I did think of him, but I didn't believe you were capable of that kind of thing."

"What on earth are you talking about?" Emmy said.

"You know what I'm talking about. I'm talking about you and Smith."

"You mean you think I'm having an affair with Dicky Smith," Emmy said. "That little boy, with those spots." She gave a great sigh of exasperation and ran her hands into her hair. If not innocence, it was a wonderful imitation of it. Holman's stare wavered.

"I don't know," he said.

"I thought you thought he was a homosexual."

"He runs with queers. That doesn't prove anything. Nothing proves anything!"

"Darling, really. Freddy will hear you."

"Why don't you tell me?" Holman reduced his voice to a whispering shout. "Tell me you're not mixed up with Smith. Tell me you're not mixed up with anybody. Tell me something. Maybe I'll believe you."

Emmy got up and shut the kitchen door. She turned and stood with her back to it. "All right!" she said. "I was going to wait until after school was over but it's absolutely too much. All right, there is someone."

"Ah." Holman let out a long, angry breath of air, which felt as if he had been holding it for several weeks. "Who is it?"

"I can't tell you."

"I thought so." He heard in his voice the intonations, almost gratified, of "I told you so." He felt very little as yet; he was observing his own reactions clinically. "Who is it, is it Smith?"

"No, of course not. Really!"

"Is it Julian Fenn? It's Fenn, isn't it?"

"No."

"Or maybe it's Bill Lumkin. You've known him for a long time, haven't you?"

"No, no, no."

Holman clutched hold of something, which happened to be the rubber dish drainer. "All right," he said. "Who is it?"

"I can't tell you now. I promised not to. It wouldn't be fair."

"Oh, fair." Holman looked at Emmy, her smudged, rosy face half averted. Now he began to feel hot and cold, as if he were coming down with something. "Fair!" He struck on the counter with his fists, but since he still had hold of the dish dryer, which contained dishes, this produced not heavy thuds but a loud rattle. Forks and cups and knives fell out and slid across the sink and floor. "You 'promised,' " he said. "How serious is this?"

"I don't know." Emmy sat down behind the kitchen table. "Oh, Holman, you must see that we absolutely can't go on this horrible way like this! The way it's been. You don't love me, you practically hate me." Holman said nothing. The emotions he felt at the moment were more like bewildered hatred than anything else: he wanted to crush nameless hordes. "Well," she went on. "Anyhow, I think we ought to separate for a little while, so we can think things over."

Holman continued to stare at her, and suddenly the answer occurred to him: Emmy was lying. She was not really having an affair, she was only pretending to be having one. "I don't believe you," he said. "I don't think you're having an affair at all. You just want to get back at me. Isn't that it?" Of course. To punish me for having accused her.

"No."

"And you expect me to believe you now? When you admit that you've been lying to me since at least April?"

"I wasn't lying then."

Holman considered this. "You mean you weren't having an affair then, but now you are?"

"Yes."

"I don't believe you," Holman said, but he almost did. His mind was wavering like a battery gauge. Suppose Emmy had gone out and perversely started something with somebody, anybody, *after* he had begun accusing her? Even because he had begun accusing her? No, that was crazy. Asserting that something was true was not the same thing as knowing it, or causing it. But then what about what Mrs. Rabbage had said, and all that wandering

270

around in the woods Emmy had been doing, and— "Who else knows about this?"

"No one. Except Miranda."

"Miranda." That meant that at least it wasn't Julian Fenn she was mixed up with. Or else that it was. If she was mixed up with anybody. "If you're really having an affair," he said, "why can't you tell me who it is?"

Emmy was silent, apparently unable to answer this objection. Holman felt a little better. "All right," he said. "Tell me this. How did it start?"

"We just," she said. "Well, we just went out for a ride in the car and it simply happened."

Holman laughed. "Really, you'll have to invent a better story than that."

"We did. Not the first time. It wasn't until almost the end of January."

"January? I thought you said it hadn't started in April."

"Well. It started in January, but we had a fight and broke up and then it started again," she said.

"Now, come on, baby. Why don't you admit you're making this up? I know you're angry, and I realize maybe I've been unreasonable lately."

"I'm not making it up," Emmy said stubbornly.

Holman looked at her. He felt angry and confused. Or maybe Emmy was confused. Maybe she was going crazy, and imagined she was mixed up with someone because he had said it so often. Or maybe she really was mixed up with someone, and then maybe he was responsible. He had a strong wish to leave the house and return to his office where things were organized logically and remained where he put them.

"And so I'm going to take Freddy and go back to Rabbit Hills, for a while anyway."

"You can't do that."

"I can too. Why not?"

"God. Well, for one thing, the way it will look. Everyone will say you've left me, if you suddenly pull Freddy out of school and leave Convers."

"All right, I'll wait until his school is over. It's only a week and a half. That's what I was going to do anyway."

Holman looked at Emmy. She didn't look insane. Suppose she *was* doing it with someone, letting someone into her. "You bitch," he said. "You stupid bitch." His voice sounded funny to him, like a tape recording, as he used

271

these words which he had never uttered to any woman before, let alone Emmy. Nevertheless, the situation seemed to call for them.

Emmy made no response whatsoever. She did not even look at him. Maybe he had not said that, only thought it. Maybe he was going crazy. "Why don't you tell me who it is?" he asked, in an imitation of his normal voice. "Why can't you—"

"Please don't," Emmy said. "Please, please, please don't!" Her whisper rose into a shriek. Putting her head down among the carrots and celery, she began to sob. Her face quickly became wet and distorted, he observed. But all of her was distorted.

"I don't understand," he said. "You couldn't. How could you? How *you* could. . . . Is it Smith? I don't believe you. . . . Oh, hello there, Freddy."

* * *

Allen Ingram to Francis Noyes

May 31

Well, I have got my wish. Something *has* "happened," and I would have done better to have asked for a pudding to stick to the end of my nose. Two students are in the infirmary with cuts and bruises and one with a broken leg and second-degree burns, and all three on the verge of being expelled. It was the riot, of course. But let me attempt to collect myself and begin in the middle.

Imagine evening: about 8:30. Only dusk at this time of year, but slowly darkening. The south quadrangle is packed with students: two hundred? Three hundred? Maybe half of them are official members of the parade, with signs ("28 FLAVORS" is a nice one) and wastebaskets as before and lighted torches. The rest are just there for the show, but they are helping by shouting and pushing. Thickest jam is next to the building site. Noisy, disorderly activity there as wastebaskets are brought up and dumped out. The excavation is two weeks deeper now.

I am standing on the steps of the administration building with Holman Turner and a couple of other faculty members who have also come out of their offices to watch. Vague discussion among us: Ought we to do something? We do nothing. Soon some of the boys have the clever idea of throwing other and larger things into the pits. Stakes and string from the construction. Wastebaskets. There they go! Bricks. Lordy, a wheelbarrow. It is growing darker; we glimpse these things intermittently by torchlight. Suddenly Bill Lumkin appears behind us. (Has he been watching?) "Break it up!" he shouts. "Come on, break it up! You. Heath, Turner, Mr. Ingram," (even in the midst of crisis my rank is recognized, I am glad to say) "would you get on down there and help break it up?"

Feeling cross and ridiculous, but not daring to disobey, I follow the others down into the crowd. "Go on home, why don't you?" I hear myself saying once or twice to students I happen to know. They smile nervously at me and take a few steps off into the dusk. Thick as it is, the crowd manages to melt or turn away from me as I go—a curious phenomenon—so that I never come face to face with anyone. In a surprisingly short time I arrive beside a construction shack at the lip of the excavation. It is a deep rectangular pit, partly filled with the debris of a school year: newspapers, bluebooks, textbooks, comic books, *Playboy* and *Mad* magazine (and I see one *Atlantic*), cigarette packages, worn-out T-shirts and sweat shirts, bath mats, paper bags, and cracker boxes. There are also some noncombustibles such as beer cans, coke bottles, and shoes. Bricks, boards, wheelbarrow, as mentioned before.

A few feet from me, a loud noise and confusion is going on; Turner is arguing with two students who carry torches. Then a scream: ten, twenty, fifty screams; one of the students has fallen, or been pushed by Turner, into the excavation (I suppose it was inevitable). His torch, inevitably, falls onto the rubbish, and in a second it is alight. Instant bedlam: people shriek, push, fall down, and are trampled on. I am shoved against the wall of the shack, immobilized in a crush of bodies. The student in the hole is burning, is screaming, is being drawn up and extinguished by the coats of other students.

Next, surprisingly soon, the sound of sirens. Fire engines, policemen, and official cars begin arriving, summoned by those anonymous beings who seem always to have their hand on the phone waiting for a crisis. "Get their identification cards!" Bill Lumkin suddenly shouts to me. The excavation is blazing like a barbecue pit, and it is bright enough to see the students' faces, but all the students are

273

melting and running away. Embarrassed, I get only a few names before the quad is empty. Now, standing by the site of the religion building are only officials and faculty members; lying on the ground are two trampled-upon students, and, a little to one side, the student who was in the hole, his clothes blackened, his mouth an open hole. I recognize him: it is Fido, Dicky Smith.

THE FENNS' LIVING ROOM LOOKED AS IF A HURRICANE HAD hit it. Boxes and books and dishes and papers lay in heaps on the floor and tables—the cupboards all were open, the drawers of the desk had been pulled out, and the curtains dragged down off the windows. Miranda and Julian had started to pack. At the same time they were finishing up the odds and ends of their food and liquor, since there was no point in saving opened boxes and bottles which might break on the way to Princeton. Will sat on the sofa; he was helping them.

"Look what I found, Julian," Miranda said. "Those olives stuffed with almonds. I thought I'd lost them months ago, but they were under the potato bin all the time. Would you like some?"

"No thanks."

"I'll have a few," Will said. "Maybe food'll cheer me up."

"Cheer you up? Why should you need cheering up?" Julian asked. "You're leaving Convers, you've got a fellowship, and you're engaged to a good-looking girl."

"I feel guilty," Will said, eating. "Guilty of everything."

"Oh, come off it." Julian poured out the dregs of a bottle of cherry brandy.

"But I am guilty. If it weren't for me, none of that mess would have happened. I ought to be in the infirmary with burns and my leg broken. Instead I'm leaving town in what for me is practically a blaze of glory. . . . That poor kid Smith."

"It's Fate," Miranda said. "It's just his Fate to be the scapegoat."

"For my sins? That's not very fair; why I'd be willing to bet he's a virgin."

"Will believes in fair and unfair," Julian said. "He's not really an enemy of society. He wants his crimes to be noticed; and if he suffers enough for them then he can feel perfectly happy and virtuous. That wouldn't work at all for me. The worse things get for me the guiltier I feel, whereas if they go well I don't feel guilty at all, no matter what I've done. But you really want to be punished for all your crimes."

"Christ, not that," Will protested.

"Or rewarded for them," Miranda suggested.

"That's more like it." They laughed.

"I really love her," Will said some time later from the sofa, apropos of nothing. "I think I can go on loving her. I really believe we'll get on. She wants to go to California. We might drive out; she's never seen anything of the country. She's toured all over Europe, but she's never been west of New Jersey."

"But getting married," Miranda remarked. She sat back on the floor, among the books that she was packing into dusty cartons. Julian had disappeared. "It's not like a vacation, you know; it's more like moving in with relatives."

"You don't want me to do it, do you?" Will said suddenly. "Why not?"

"No, that's not so." Frightened by the accusation, Miranda instinctively replied with a lie, then recovered herself and qualified it. "It's true, I never meant— expected it to go this far. I guess I overdid that spell," she said, smiling, but Will did not smile. She had noticed that he had recently lost interest in the witchcraft game, or joke, as if he wanted to take his own responsibility. "I want you to do whatever you really want to do," she therefore went on. This was not true either, she remembered. Did he remember? He continued to regard her. "I was wondering though if Emmy realizes what it'll be like, living with you." This sounded spiteful; she hastily particularized it. "I mean, if she thinks she's just going on a guided tour of the West." What was the matter with her today?

"No; I told her. I told her I wasn't going to use the grant just to bum around with. I said I'd have to shut myself up and try to work and when it didn't go I would be plain hell to have around. And Christ knows it's no picnic trying to write music. There's no public: even if I do better than I dare hope I'll never make any money, and most people who hear my stuff will be convinced I am insane."

"But you want to do it," Miranda said doubtfully.

"But it's the only thing that exists. Everything else is just performance, pleasing people or fooling them, fucking around, excuse me. But that's all it is. You do your job, you love or you hate, you get a little charge or a big charge. But it doesn't last; you have to start all over again the next day."

"Maybe you don't want to be married," Miranda said, cramming potholders and dish towels in between the books.

"I do, though. I'm coming round to it. I had a letter from Lou that really convinced me. I wrote him that I was having an affair with a beautiful girl who had hair a yard long and eight thousand a year and wanted to marry me. The only trouble was, I told him, she didn't know a thing about music. He wrote back. Here." Will took out a letter and read from it. "You are crazy. What are you holding out for? She's rich, she's beautiful, she loves you, and you want her to be musical too? In the first place, the girl you're looking for doesn't exist. Also second, you should thank God she's not musical, so she should let your work alone."

"Eight thousand a year? You mean Emmy has an income of eight thousand dollars a year all her own?" Will nodded. "From what?"

"I don't know. Stocks and bonds. I suppose eventually it comes from somebody being cheated somewhere."

"Good heavens, eight thousand. But you could live on that! Why, you'd never have to get a job again. You could go somewhere and just write music. You could go to Europe to live. Italy, France, anywhere."

"We've been thinking of it."

"Anywhere in the world. . . . But that's good, isn't it?"

"I don't know. Living on a woman, like a kid. I don't know if I could do it again. I suppose I could do it if I was really working. And if I wasn't, well, I guess I could always find a job somewhere. . . . Money is strange. It gives you a kind of free will I'm not used to. But I want to be used to it. When you have enough money to be able to choose your own life, everyone else looks like the slave of necessity."

"Eight thousand," Miranda repeated.

"Yes." He laughed. "When I first found out, I wished it was a little less. But it's amazing how quickly you can get used to the idea of having money. Yesterday when we were talking about where we should go after my fellowship is up, I found myself wishing that it was a little more."

Emmy was also packing. She packed with tissue paper, as she had been taught, in suitcases from Mark Cross: E.K.S. from college, and the matched set of E.S.T., smooth red calf. She was leaving Convers, leaving her husband! (Definitely lucky, she wouldn't have to have her monogram changed.) Suddenly, all Holman's opposition had collapsed; he had apparently decided that she had made the whole thing up and was simply being flighty, and had taken a tolerantly mature attitude toward her. She tried to receive it with mature tolerance. Soon the whispering behind her back would stop; she would be living in a new state, in a new house, with new furniture; she would have nothing around her that could remind her of cold, incomprehensible Convers College or of Holman Turner, that cold, selfish, opinionated academic booby who had never really loved her.

Whereas Will. . . . Being married to Will. It would be like arriving at the seaside for vacation, like Easthampton, all hedges of roses and sea breeze after the long hot train ride. Of course there would be some tiresomeness on the way, some local stops, arrangements to be made. Arrangements for getting a divorce, for instance.

The back door slammed below. Holman had returned. His footsteps walked into the dining room and then into the playroom. "Daddy!" she heard Freddy shout. It was worrying that lately Freddy had become frightfully enthusiastic about his father. The conversation she would soon have to have with him was something she did not like to think about at all, and the fact that it would have to be in a nursery-school simple vocabulary ("We aren't going to live with Daddy any more . . .") made it even worse. Freddy would need time to adjust to Will, and Will just as much, if not more, time to adjust to Freddy.

Holman walked into the front room. He walked into the front hall. Then he walked back through these rooms to the kitchen.

"Emmy?" he called.

"I'm upstairs."

"Could you come down, please? I have something I want to tell you."

"All right." With rather bad grace (but why start anything now, on her last day here?) Emmy put down a pile of sweaters and went.

Holman was standing about in the kitchen.

"Listen, Emmy," he said. "I had an interview with McBane just now." Emmy's insides contracted, but they relaxed at his next words. "I'm in trouble with the administration, it seems." She waited. "About what happened at the riot. That stupid little pansy bastard Smith is saying I deliberately pushed him into that hole."

"But you didn't, did you? You were simply trying to break it up, like Bill asked you to."

"That's true. Of course he just wants to make trouble. They've decided to expel him along with two other leaders of the riot, and he wants to make as big a stink as he can."

"But surely, Mr. McBane doesn't think you—" Her anxiety passed, Emmy began putting dishes away into the cupboard.

"I don't know. When I talked to Bill about it I thought there wouldn't be any trouble. I even got the impression he was glad of the opportunity to get rid of those three queers. But McBane seems to be down on me about the whole thing." Holman looked for Emmy's reaction or comment, but she offered none. At last he was telling her what went on at school, but it was too late, she thought. "He kind of stood up for Smith. He said he was opposed to the new religion building himself; which is completely irrelevant, and he was opposed to the new religion." Emmy finished the plates and began on the silverware. "And he made threats, kind of."

"Threats, really?"

"Oh, nothing specific. You know the way he mumbles on. He said: 'I'm an old man. I don't want to see this campus or this department desecrated until after I'm gone.' 'An old man,' " Holman repeated with ironic emphasis. "He's not much over fifty."

"Oh, he can't be. He looks at least ten years older than that. Even fifteen. He must be about sixty-five."

"Fifty-one. I looked it up in the Library of Congress catalogue. It's an act, that's all. He wants people to think he's old. When he really is sixty-five, he'll look eighty, and when he's eighty he'll have the whole place at his feet admiring the vigor he shows as a man of ninety-five."

Emmy could not help laughing. "Don't worry," she said. "He may want to scare you, but I'm sure he'll come around. After all, you're in the right."

"I don't know. I said something kind of stupid." Holman looked at Emmy's expression and, reassured, went on. "I'll tell you. He said that Wedge and to some extent Fogelson, the two other leaders, you know—he could believe that they wanted to cause trouble. But not Smith. He said he thought Smith's basic intentions were good." Emmy sat down, listening. "Then I put my feet in my mouth. I thought it was all right, so I laughed and said something like: 'How can we know that? In Hum C terms, we can only take account of words and actions, not of intentions.' Casual, chummy, all professors together. I should have known McBane doesn't want anybody trying to be his chum."

"But that's true, what you said."

"Maybe. It was a mistake, though. He turned on me and said: 'Holman Turner! In you I see the kind of Doppelgänger I have created with this course.'"

"Well, really." It irritated Emmy that anyone but she should call Holman names.

"I suppose what it is, he likes Smith and he doesn't want him to be expelled. I should have seen that. He told me to think it over and let him know. The trouble was, I couldn't believe anybody could like Smith that much, and I couldn't believe McBane could like anybody that much."

"He wanted you to say something that would get Smith out of trouble," Emmy said.

"I suppose you're right."

"Even to lie. I know I am," she went on triumphantly. "To say it was all your fault."

"I'm not going to do that. Not for damn sure."

"Of course not."

"Emmy?"

"Yes?"

"I want to ask you something." Holman made his request as if he were asking Please pass the butter. "Would you put off going to New Jersey for a while, until this clears up?" Emmy hesitated, surprised to find that her first impulse was to agree.

"Well, golly." Of course, from Holman's point of view she was only leaving town to "think things over." And after all she had no particular wish to go to New Jersey; Will wouldn't be leaving Convers for another four days. "All right. I will. I want to find out what happens anyway."

"You're a good sport," he said awkwardly. "Emmy. You realize what this means. We possibly won't be able to stay in Convers permanently." He misread her silence, and added, "I'm sorry; I know how much this place means to you."

"Means to me? I hate it!" Emmy said. "I never saw anything so cold, narrow, provincial, limited! Of course it's pretty, and there are some nice people here, but— Well, what Allen Ingram says about it is perfectly true, it's a survival from the worst parts of the past. You're the one who likes it."

"I don't know," Holman said. "No. I'm in favor of the principle of Convers, but the personalities—McBane. He doesn't like me. I think he would like to fire me, if he could."

"Oh, he couldn't! He couldn't do that. Look at all the extra work you've done for him. And the students like you; two fraternities asking you to be their advisor. And I know Bill Lumkin thinks you're good."

"It's nice to have some moral support." Holman laughed, and Emmy regarded him almost with affection. The trouble with her and Holman was that they had ever got married at all; as a husband he was impossible. They should have just remained friends.

Will and Emmy stood on the platform of the Old Greensbury railroad station saying goodbye, but neither one was leaving. No trains had departed from (or arrived in) Old Greensbury for eight years. The station was boarded up and the boards had been defaced with the names of teen-age gangs and teen-age lovers who had quarreled or married, reformed or been arrested by the police, some time ago. Coarse grass grew along the track, and the signal arm was rusted at All Clear.

They had not visited the railroad station before, since it was too exposed; but finally the scrub oaks (always the last tree to leaf) had grown in between the station and the highway, making a strip of woods only a few yards wide

281

but so thick that they had been able to observe the cars passing while they made love among the trees, and yet remain unobserved.

"Jesus, I'll miss you," Will said, leaning on the ticket counter below the boarded window. "I've got used to seeing you every day. I'm spoiled."

"Yes," Emmy said sleepily, leaning on Will. "Me too."

"Saturday," Will said. "Five days. But it should be fun meeting in New York. . . . I'll call you, let's see; what did we say, Thursday night? About seven. Will you be in by then?"

"I don't know. You know, darling, Holman asked me to stay on again until the end of the week. He says he still needs my moral support."

"Christ." Will laughed. "What did you tell him this time?"

"I said I would."

Will's expression changed, as Emmy had thought it might. A tiresome discussion began, the more tiresome because most of the lines had been spoken a few days ago in a discussion of the same topic.

"He knows you're leaving him," Will said at length. "He might as well start getting used to it Thursday as Saturday." Emmy said nothing. "Or doesn't he know it?"

"He doesn't want to know it," she said. "I've tried to tell him, but he absolutely doesn't believe me. And, well, I thought, why not let it go? It's only for a few days."

"So he still thinks you made the whole thing up. Do you want him to think that?"

"No, of course I don't." Emmy put her hands on Will's and looked into his face; he looked back, but he responded to her hands about as much as if they had been mittens.

"Then tell him."

Emmy gave a big sigh. "I can't. Not now. Look," she added quickly, "couldn't you stay on too?"

"Oh, Emily. You know I couldn't. I have to be in New York on Wednesday." Emmy knew he could, if he wanted to. It was only a matter of changing an appointment with some musicians. She said nothing, stubbornly. Will said: "Why don't you leave Thursday, the way you planned?"

"I can't. I promised."

"I don't like it. It makes me feel as if I didn't exist." He laughed. "All right. Then when will you come down? Saturday or Sunday?"

"I'm not sure."

"How do you mean you're not sure?"

"Holman's in such a state," Emmy said. "I couldn't leave him while he's this way, it wouldn't be fair. It would be absolutely hateful, and I don't hate him now." She looked at Will. "You don't understand about marriage," she said fondly.

Will made no reply. It was true, she thought. She was used to being married, but he had forgotten how, or had never known. He would have to learn, or relearn. He had unmarried habits: solitariness, secretiveness. And infidelity.

He had not really, technically, been unfaithful to her, but things kept turning up. For instance, it had come out the other day, almost by accident, that he had made love to Sheila, the waitress at the Hampton Hotel bar. "But you said there was nothing with Sheila!" Emmy had exclaimed. Will shook his head. "I didn't say that." "But you let me think so." "Emily," he had said. "You mustn't do this. What does it matter? We'd had a fight, I hadn't seen you for weeks. I thought it was over for good. I was depressed, and Sheila felt sorry for me. It didn't mean anything." "It didn't mean anything, nothing means anything!" she had raged. "That's not true; and you know it," Will had replied, pulling her down into a long kiss.

And then about Betsy too, one sunny afternoon in a field when they were so happy, joking about being married, about children. "We ought to have a fine one," she had said. "Intelligent *and* beautiful. Easily." "I'll do what I can," Will said. "You never know." "But with a record like yours," she said, laughing, "100 per cent success—" "How do you mean?" he said. "Well, golly, with Betsy Lumkin." "That was an accident." "Oh, an accident." Emmy was still laughing—even the idea of Betsy had stopped bothering her. "If you want to know," Will said, "she was sure she couldn't conceive, so we never took any precautions." "Never?" Emmy said after a pause; "I thought you said it only happened once." She looked at Will. "Oh, Emily," he said. "For the love of Christ!"

Emmy had sworn to herself and to Will later on that same day never to bring up the names Sheila or Betsy again. Now, on the platform of the railroad station, she broke her oath; realized it, and apologized. "I'm sorry. Golly, I'm sorry, darling."

"That's all right," Will said, putting his arms round her. "There." He held Emmy against him.

"I'll never mention them again. I absolutely promise. Mm. But, Will, promise me something."

"Sure," he whispered into her ear.

"Promise you'll never really be unfaithful to me."

Silence.

"Emmy raised her head. "You won't promise?" she said incredulously.

"I can't, Emily. Listen." He held onto her. "Right now I feel as if I'd never want to touch another woman. But how the hell can I promise what I'll feel for the next ten years? You want me to lie to you? You could change, I could change, I could meet somebody—"

Emmy pulled away. "Don't you have any principles?" she asked. She went on smiling, although Will's speech had made her deeply nervous.

"No. I guess I don't," he said cheerfully. "Not that kind of principles. I love you, though."

For once, Emmy did not reply automatically that she loved Will. "I promised Holman that I'd never be unfaithful to him," she said. "When we were married."

"By the authority vested in the State of New Jersey," Will said. "So you see." He stroked the side of her face with his hand. "Emily," he went on. "You've got to realize that that's all over. You don't owe him anything now."

"No, that's not true," Emmy said. "I think there are some obligations, as long as I'm still actually married to him." She sat down on the edge of the platform and described to Will, quite seriously, a plan she had formed to continue giving Holman a little money after they were separated, until the divorce was final and perhaps longer, at least until he was making enough to live decently on.

"Alimony, you mean," Will said, with a short laugh on one note.

"Well, yes." Emmy giggled. She was quite capable of seeing the ridiculous side of her own behavior.

"How much were you thinking of giving him?"

"Oh, not very much. Not much at all. Maybe a hundred dollars a month."

Will slid off the platform beside Emmy and stood on the track, facing her. "A hundred a month," he said. "Twelve hundred a year. Is that what you think you're worth to Holman? Let's see, you said you used to do it with him about once a week, so let's say fifty times a year. Twenty-four dollars a time. That's pretty cheap for a girl like you. Why not fifty? Why not a hundred?" Emmy now laughed angrily. He really hates Holman, he really wants it all for himself, went through her head. Will continued: "Why not? In New York, with the right connections, I bet you could get at least a hundred a trick. And cheap at the price. . . . At any rate, you owe Holman at least five thousand a year."

"I do not," Emmy said. "Five thousand dollars a year is a lot of money." She laughed, but crossly. Money was going to be a problem. For instance, Will seemed to assume that after his fellowship ran out they would go abroad to live while he wrote music, not just for a few months, but for a year, or even years. His idea was, if you had money, why not spend it? True in a way, and she didn't mind supporting Will; lots of artists had patrons, and it was really a privilege to be the patron of a famous artist. It could be an utterly marvelous life, traveling to exotic places, meeting fascinating musicians and people, being important in the creation of wonderful music. But what Will didn't realize was that eight thousand a year wasn't really enough to live on. He had very vague ideas and behavior about money. She had been disturbed to learn that he habitually did not pay his bills until he was dunned, and because he laughed when she protested that this was unfair to the tradesmen ("Unfair to the New England Telephone and Telegraph Company!").

"Oh, I agree with you." Will laughed softly now. "I respect money. I don't underestimate it. Sometimes I even think it's got the kind of supernatural power you think it has."

"Not supernatural, just natural," Emmy said.

"No. Supernatural. Like that two hundred dollars that you gave the Fenns last winter. You thought you would buy me from them with that two hundred dollars." Emmy looked up abruptly. "But it's like all magic," he went on. "The spell doesn't work unless the victim knows it's been cast."

Emmy discarded several denials of all this. She refused to let Will see that his teasing hurt; she said instead, in a tone of light sarcasm. "And who was the victim?"

"Why, Miran— No. I suppose I was."

"It wasn't that," Emmy said suddenly, after a minute.

"It was because it was my fault that Julian lost his job."
Will raised his eyebrows. "Because you remember you told
me about Richard's starting the fire and not to tell anybody but I told Holman, he promised not to tell but I
think he must have told Bill Lumkin because somebody
did," she said very fast, not looking up. Will said nothing.
"I wasn't sure of it at first," she went on, "but the more
Holman got to dislike Julian the more certain I was,
because you know people always hate anyone they've done
a meanness to. I think that might be partly why he
thought it was Julian that I was . . ."

"Hm," Will said. "Did he admit it? Holman."

"I didn't ask him. I didn't want to; it made me, I don't
know, I couldn't really look at him after I knew he'd done
that. I sort of put him in towel possy." Emmy laughed
briefly.

There was a silence. "No," Will said finally. "It wasn't
Holman." In contrast to Emmy, he spoke very slowly. "I
don't think he had anything to do with it. It was Betsy
who told Bill Lumkin."

"Betsy? But how did she know?"

"I told her." Emmy looked at Will. "I didn't think she
would—" His voice faded off. "It probably would have
happened anyway," he resumed. "Julian would have quarreled with them anyhow, or he would have done something
else they could pick on, or they would have got him some
way. I keep telling myself."

"But Julian is your best friend," Emmy said.

"I could have not told you," Will said. "Only I want us
to start out honest."

"Ye-es. But why did you tell Betsy? When?"

"But why did you tell Holman? When?"

Emmy remembered that it had been in bed. She shut
her mouth and said nothing. When she looked up, she saw
that Will had moved. He stood a little way off along the
track, balancing on the rail like a child, frowning.

"You're upset too," she said.

"Some. Yes."

"And Holman's upset; it's so difficult! And Freddy, you
know he's all mixed up. I keep telling him we're leaving
for New Jersey and then we don't leave, and he's been
awful; I simply can't decide anything!"

"Decide? I thought you had decided," he said distantly.

"I mean, about whether to leave on Saturday. It's so

simply dreadful lately, but one can't blame him. It's all so awful, changing everything."

"Maybe you don't want to change," Will said. "Maybe you like it this way. You like having both of us—all of us, Freddy too—hanging around, in a state, fighting over you, waiting for you to make up your mind."

"I don't. I do not!" Emmy was indignant. "How can you say that?"

"It's easy," Will said. He crossed to the other rail. "I've enjoyed that kind of situation myself."

"I don't enjoy it. Oh, how can you stand there like that, as if you were completely out of it all? How can you be so provoking? Why don't you say something?"

Will walked toward and past Emmy along the far rail. "I'm not going to fight," he said. "You know I want you. . . . I'll call you in New Jersey Saturday evening. No, Sunday evening. If you're not there, it's off."

"Off? What's off?"

"Everything."

* * *

Allen Ingram to Francis Noyes

June 12

It's almost over. The last lecture has been lectured, the last Creative Writings destructively read, and only a hateful heap of 129 bluebooks stands between me and you. Then, free of Convers! But alas, not scot-free; at the last minute, a Moral Choice was set down in my path.

The riot, of course. I had congratulated myself on the way in which I had conducted my post-riot interview with Dean Lumkin (Billy to us). When he asked for the names of students I had taken on that confused occasion, I produced, with bland ingenuousness, two pseudonyms and one illegible scribble. Half the student body was there, and I saw no reason why some of them should be penalized for not having run away from us professors fast enough.

I congratulated myself too soon. Yesterday I received a note from Mr. Richard Smith imploring me to visit him in the college infirmary. It is a dreadful place: a damp little cement building stuck down on the side of a hill in a quarantined corner of the campus. Inside, damp walls, dark halls, a smell. Old, old magazines, coarse sheets, pale stained linoleum. Poor Fido was a sight: his leg in plaster and most of the rest of him in bandages. He was alone in the ward, the sole charge of an angry nurse; staying on until the doctor decides that he is well enough to travel, although he has officially been expelled for being one of the leaders of the riot. (The others were nasty little George Wedge and a friend of his whom I am glad to say I have never met.)

It was all a mistake, Mr. Smith hysterically protested. "Mr. Turner said I hit him! I didn't hit him, he hit me, he pushed me, didn't he Mr. Ingram? You saw it, Mr. Ingram, didn't you?"

"I don't know," I heard myself reply, thinking madly through a silence. And then, the best I could do was merely to repeat that I simply did not know, could not swear to what had occurred. He believed me at once. After all, to lie convincingly, elegantly, usefully, is the writer's art. Yes, usefully too; I feel that Mr. Smith will be far happier away from Convers. He is a born enthusiast; I can see him being whole-heartedly butch in some state university, or bohemian in some city college—he is already a natural beat poet—any place which is free of the local smooth, priggish skepticism.

Suppose I had said that I saw Turner push Smith (and I am not even sure that I did see it). Imagine the trouble and confusion, the messy, tiresome interviews. The nasty possibility of being suspected of partiality. (As Bobby R. said in another context: "Just because I'm a Jew and all of my best friends are Jews, why must people assume that all Jews are my best friends?") Then there is no guarantee that my testimony would prevent Smith's explusion. Or/ and—one never knows—they might take it into their little minds to do something to Mr. Turner. And Turner is *made* for Convers, no question of it: it would be against the natural order to part them. I had the impulse to destroy Turner, all right, or rather to maim him, as he did Boewulf, but I stamped it down the way one stamps down the impulse to run over disagreeable pedestrians who cross in front of one's car, reminding oneself that they would be hung round one's neck for the rest of one's life. I dislike doing him what he would consider a favor, but console myself that it is the kind of favor he deserves. Besides, it is not in the natural order for me to be an actor here.

All for the best, but I must admit I was in rather a state

at the time. It wasn't until tonight, really, that I was able to see how relatively unimportant the whole thing was. In spite of your cautionary letters and my own good intentions, living in a small town had subtly affected my mind, and I had begun to Think Small. I admit it, so you can cease your admonitions.

16

EMMY WAS PACKING AGAIN. HER SUITCASES WERE OPEN ON the bed, and the bed was piled with clothing, but she could not decide what to put in. She wanted to take everything, so that she would not have to return to Convers ever again; and she wanted to throw everything away and walk out of the house free and clear. Free and clear! But when she arrived at Rabbit Hills without any suitcases her mother, and Walter whose job it was to carry the suitcases in from the car, and Helen whose job it was to unpack them, would think it most peculiar and inexplicable. They would think it more peculiar still if she were to arrive with piles of suitcases and trunks, but less inexplicable. Such an amount of luggage would be the same as a public announcement that she had left her husband, and Emmy wanted to make this announcement privately, in her own good time, whenever that was.

The truth was, no time would be good for such news. It was utterly impossible that it should be well received. Previously it had not occurred to Emmy to wonder what her parents would say. She did not have to wonder now; she knew. Dads had not liked Holman in the beginning, but now he was used to him. He was accustomed to the idea that his daughter was Mrs. Holman Turner, and he disliked altering his ideas. When he heard that Will had been married before and had not made a go of it, he would consider him a bad risk, like a corporation which had once already been liquidated, and he would look upon him with suspicion and scorn, as a lazy bum who probably wanted to marry his daughter for her money. He would advise Emmy to return to her husband and house at once.

As for Mummy, she had always liked Holman. She would certainly take his side. Emmy could hear her now telling Emmy not to be childish. Will was a musician, which was as bad as a painter and probably worse than a writer; or else he was a music teacher, which in some ways was even worse. Mummy would be more difficult than Dads. Emmy had expressed something of this fear to Will, who had made light of it. He thought that he would be able to charm Mrs. Stockwell, to "get round her," as he put it. Emmy was not so sure. Mummy would not forget that Will was a divorced man, and that if Emmy married him she would be a divorced woman. Everts (Mummy's family) never got divorced, and Stockwells, whatever their neighbors and business associates might do, seemed not to get divorced either. Like their connection with Convers College, it was one of the symptoms of their moral superiority, their kinship with higher things.

Her mother had a cousin, one Poor Phyllis Lord, who had left her husband and made an unfortunate remarriage. She had married a man no one had ever heard of who lived in Rhode Island. Emmy had not seen her since she was a little girl. When the Stockwell children's weddings took place, an announcement was sent to cousin Phyllis, instead of an invitation. As Emmy's mother said, she had dropped out of sight. The phrase suggested that Mrs. Stockwell did not usually glance below a certain height—and correctly. She did have the air of one looking round at or above eye level, her firm chin slightly raised. Or was this just her way of hiding a second, less firm chin? When Emmy divorced Holman and married Will would she drop (or be dropped) out of sight? Would she become "poor" or "unfortunate" (another favorite word of her parents, who were above all those upon whom fortune smiled)?

Perhaps her brothers would not be so bad. After all, both of them had come back from Convers boasting to each other and their friends of wild pranks, drunkenness, and even sexual exploits. Not only did these things apparently not cancel out the spiritual gain which resulted from attending the college, they seemed somehow to be necessary to it. Emmy reflected that she also could claim to have sown her wild oats at Convers. But Clark and Bobby would distrust Will. Bobby would not think he was a good guy, and Clark would not consider him a reliable or decent person.

"If they don't like it, let them not like it," Will had said. "We don't have to see them." But Emmy did not want to stop seeing her family; she felt that to do so would be very unnatural.

"Anything else you want me to do today?" Mrs. Rabbage said, putting her head into the room. "I run out of moth-killer for the back closet like I told you so I left that, packing, what a job."

Emmy looked at Mrs. Rabbage, whom she would probably never see again, from her rusted hair under the pink bandana to her long feet in Ladies' Exchange men's shoes. Many other things had changed, but Mrs. Rabbage looked the same as she had last November, and Emmy did not like her any better, although she had often described her as a simply marvelous cleaning woman, a real find. "No thanks, Mrs. Rabbage," she said.

"But I always say, it mostly turns out either you take too much or you don't take enough, some is one way and some is the other way." It was no use. Whatever Emmy had arranged for her to do, Mrs. Rabbage always managed to finish it or abandon it in time for a conversation, or monologue, before her cousin came by to pick her up in his mail truck.

"I expect you're absolutely right," Emmy said, falsely and vaguely cheery, her manner to strangers or when distracted.

"Well off to the big city," Mrs. Rabbage continued. "Park the kid with his grandma and have yourself a time huh, each to his own taste." Mrs. Rabbage, as she had remarked several times, had seen New York once and once was enough for her thank you. She wouldn't live there if you paid her to and she also didn't think it was a nice place for a visit. She said so again now. "My sister's husband Ray Hutchins, him that had the shingles I was telling you about, he was down to New York City year before last, he wanted to see something so he went on one of them sightseer tours and got his wallet robbed. Seventy-four dollars, never got it back of course, and all his personal papers was thrown on the floor of the bus in the dirt. I never saw a place so dirty, filthy, but there's some that doesn't notice that, they like the bright lights and the noise and make whoopee and throw your money away."

She is insolent, Emmy thought. And she thinks she knows something.

"No thank you I said when my husband asked me if I
292

wanted to go down there with him for our brass anniversary—brass is right! Like my Ma always said don't do anything for fun you don't like, Myra, so we went to Buzzards Bay instead and it rained the whole time you can't win sometimes."

Emmy put three pairs of shoes into a shoe bag. Then she took two of them out. "I guess not," she said.

"Well," Mrs. Rabbage said. "So I better be getting on. You want me to come in next Tuesday same as usual, and I'll take Fridays off till you get back like we said."

"That'll be fine," Emmy said, getting her purse from the drawer.

Mrs. Rabbage took ten of Emmy's dollars and went away and Emmy went on packing. When she got to New Jersey, she thought, there would certainly be scenes, perhaps dreadful scenes. They might last for days, and she would need something to wear during them, she mightn't have a chance to get to the shops. Freddy had to have clothes too. A clean cotton dress, petticoat, shoes, sweaters; the weather was unsettled, and it would be simply dumb not to take this; and this—she moved things about from the bed to the floor in a confused way. But no, now that was too much again! It was all too much; tears of confusion (fatigue, exasperation, guilt?) began to run down Emmy's face; she half fell onto the bed among piles of silk and wool and cotton and shut her eyes. Will, she thought, and made a conscious effort to remember his appearance and words the way one tries, on waking, to keep hold of an important dream. It was not the first time in their four-days' separation that she had made this attempt.

There was something else to consider: Holman could not help but see what she had packed, and if she took nothing or everything he would know at once, and so would Mrs. Rabbage as soon as she came to clean and then so would everyone.

She didn't want to cause an explosion in Convers. Well, that wasn't true, she did want to, in a way. But she would give it up for Holman's sake. He had to stay on here, and it would be frightfully important to him that there should be no noise, no scandal. He could say now that she was visiting her parents, and then that they had agreed to a temporary separation. And then later he could let it quietly get about that there had been a divorce, and maybe later

293

still, much later if at all, that she had remarried. That was how he would like it, that was what he would care about—much more than he would care about losing her. If it weren't for the scandal and inconvenience he would probably be just as glad to get rid of her.

"Hi," Holman said.

"Oh, hello."

"Freddy's still at the birthday party?"

"Yes; Flo's bringing him home."

"You're packing." He took a few steps into the room. During the last few days Holman and Emmy had made many remarks of this meaningless sort to each other. They exchanged information which was already apparent, like well-bred strangers who have been forced to extreme circumstances to share a taxi and, rather than remain silent, comment that it is raining heavily.

"How is your back?" Holman had recently developed pain in this area.

"OK, thanks. The same."

"It's so damp out again today."

"It is." Holman sat down on the bed among the empty suitcases. "You don't have to do this, you know, Emmy," he said. "You could think things over here. I wouldn't bother you."

Emmy moved a pile of slips. "I know, but it's simply the idea of it," she said, not looking up. "It's simply going to be easier if we're in two different places." She looked up now, but not exactly at Holman. "I mean, I think it's an awfully good idea for couples to separate sometimes anyhow, don't you?"

"No," Holman said. "I think it's a terrible idea."

"Well, I still think we ought to try it," Emmy said after a considerable pause. "After all, you might find out you were much happier without me and Freddy. It might turn out that you didn't miss us at all."

"That's impossible," Holman said shortly.

"Why is it impossible?"

"Because it is." His voice was growing angry. "You're my wife, and Freddy is my son. I don't have to experiment to find out whether I still love you when you're out of town, or any childish kind of game like that. I already know that I'll always love you, worse luck."

"Always?" Emmy asked, in a tone of assumed flippancy.

"How can you promise that? What about when I'm old, and fat, and ugly?"

"What difference does that make?" Holman asked. Emmy stood looking at him with a puzzled expression.

"You don't love me," she said. "You don't love me because I'm Emily Stockwell Turner. You just think you love me because I'm your wife."

"Emily Stockwell Turner is my wife," Holman said in the voice of one talking to a stubborn child. He stood up. "Ow."

"Your back?"

"Yeah."

"Poor back. I think it must be psychosomatic. It's actually your thesis or the riot or something."

"Or something," Holman said, walking to the window.

"You're not still worrying about that riot, are you?"

"Yes."

"But I thought that was all settled. You know it's all settled, you told me so. And you did the right thing. Why should you be upset?"

"It's not what I did," Holman said stiffly. "It's what I felt. Or what I didn't do, if you like."

"I don't understand. Tell me."

There was a silence.

"All right," Holman finally said. He turned round, looking out through the small colonial window panes into the damp light, and spoke with his back to Emmy.

"McBane was right," he said. "He guessed or something. That even if I didn't consciously try to shove Smith into the excavation, I wanted it to happen. I was hurt and I wanted somebody else to get hurt." He spoke to the window, in a peculiar voice. "I saw when he was falling, and I just stood there. I heard him scream, and I stood there; I stood there and watched him burn. And I liked it. It was some other students who got him out. I didn't help; I couldn't have helped. I think if we had been alone I might have stood and watched him burn to death." Holman stopped himself shaking and looked round at Emmy, who was saying nothing. "Guilty," he said finally.

"Is that all?"

"All? Isn't that enough?"

"But that's nothing."

"It was unforgivable."

295

"I forgive you." Emmy smiled at Holman—almost laughed.

"That makes no difference."

"What do you want? Do you want Dicky Smith to forgive you? You feel guilty because he's been expelled, you mean. But you know, darling, that might have happened anyhow. . . . And you could make it up to him, you know. We could pay for his medical expenses, whatever it's going to cost," she went on, coming over to Holman and putting her hand on his back affectionately. "That might actually be a good idea, and it needn't imply—"

"You don't understand," Holman said, still not moving. "I don't care what Smith thinks of me. I don't give a damn about him. It's what I have to think of myself. I'm supposed to be a teacher here, not one of those goons that get a charge out of watching accidents. . . . McBane knows. That's why he was like that. That's what his course is about, in a way. That every man is alone and responsible for making up his own moral universe."

"Yes." Emmy understood this. It was what her parents believed, what was taught at St. Kit's: the categorical imperative of the aristocracy. Behave so that your every action could be the basis of a social law. Like, women should leave their husbands? Like they should break their vows and quarrel with their families and get divorced and go off with men who betrayed their best friends and hated Freddy? But, she had a flash thought, I don't have to marry him. I belong to myself. I haven't decided yet, and nobody can make me.

She focused her eyes again and saw Holman. He was still standing by the window, his arms braced against the sides of the frame, as if he were holding up the house. He looked sad, solid, and serious, waiting for her to speak. He looked all right.

"Golly, I think you're too hard on yourself," she rushed on, without thinking further. A voice from St. Kit's sounded in her head, and she added: "You're harder on yourself than God would be."

"I don't think so."

"I do," Emmy said definitely, more sure of this than she had been of anything for weeks. "Come on now, darling, forgive yourself. After all, it's over. Try. Do try."

Holman laughed at her earnestness, but he did laugh, a thing he had not done for some days. "All right," he said.

296

He turned round and faced into the room. "Why do you care so much?" he asked.

Taken aback, Emmy dropped her hand from her husband's shoulder and stood off. "I don't know—I suppose I—I suppose I think," she said slowly, "that if you can't forgive yourself, how will you ever forgive me?"

The moving van was pulled up to the Fenns' house and the moving men were eating lunch on the back porch. Inside, on the floor of the dining room, Will, Miranda, and the children were finishing sandwiches which Will had brought from the town drugstore off paper plates left over from a Halloween party. The children were drinking orange soda, Will and Miranda beer. Julian had just gone to return some rediscovered books to the library.

"I'm finished, Mommy," Charles said.

"Me too, Mommy."

"All right. You can get down, I mean up, and go play. Now listen, all of you. Go outside. Don't come into the house again, and don't go near the moving men. I don't want them to pack you into their truck. Okay?"

"Okay, Mommy." Giggling, they rushed out.

Miranda and Will looked at each other.

"Did you see her?" Miranda said.

"Briefly. It's no good. I should never have come back. I should have got the message when she didn't come to New York. She wants to stay with him. She says he needs her more than I do. He's been in some trouble over that business of the student riot; McBane had him on the carpet, and he was afraid he was going to lose his job."

"Holman? He hasn't lost his job, has he?"

"Oh, no. It was a false alarm. But it seems he's still all worked up about it. She's afraid that if she left him now it would just be too much, he might have a nervous breakdown or something. She wants me to wait."

"Wait until when?"

"Yeah. That's exactly it. She said she simply didn't know."

"Hm."

"I think it's an excuse. Letting me down gently. Or else it isn't. She says it isn't. Who knows? And then a lot of other things came out. She's afraid I wouldn't be faithful to her, and her family would carry on, and Freddy, and I don't know what. I don't know. Jesus, I feel bitter."

297

"I'm sorry."

"I don't know. Maybe if I really wanted her I would hang around waiting for the word." He shrugged. "Or maybe I provoked her to do this. I kept telling her things she didn't want to hear. Maybe it would have happened sooner or later. But I still think we could have had a fine year together, or two years. Or more, who knows? I said that, and it shocked her. She's a pretty conventional girl in some ways. She said she wouldn't think of getting married if she didn't believe it was going to last forever. *Holman* told her he would always love her. Well, maybe that's what he believes. The kind of love he's been giving her, maybe he can promise to keep that up. If that's what she wants—4½ per cent compounded quarterly for life. The really crazy thing is, she says she still loves me. She says she loves us both now." Will laughed unpleasantly. "She was upset, too; she cried. I don't get it. She loves me, but she went ahead and betrayed me. Everyone betrays me."

"I haven't betrayed you."

"Yes, you have. You told Julian about Holman's suspecting him. That was a surprise. I used to think you kept all my secrets."

"Well; after all, I didn't want Holman to walk up suddenly to Julian and shoot him, or something," Miranda finally said.

"Yes. You'd rather he walked up and shot me. You see, when it comes to a showdown, women stick to their husbands, apparently."

Miranda found nothing to say. She looked round the empty room. "If Holman's not going to lose his job, though, and he doesn't know about you and Emmy—or does he?" she asked a minute later.

"Oh, no. She's convinced him, or he's convinced himself, that she never had an affair with anybody. She had a crush on me, but she was only pretending that something was going on."

"Well, then, I don't see why he should be so upset."

"He's upset because he's convinced that he killed Dicky Smith. And Emily says she has to stay with him because it was her fault he got into such a jealous rage, so really she killed Dicky Smith."

"But Dicky isn't dead. Julian says he's nearly recovered enough to go home."

"Yeah, well, its the principle of the thing."

"Everyone wants to be guilty," Miranda said. "I don't understand it. Why, when it first happened you were claiming it was all your fault." She laughed.

"When really, of course, it was all yours."

"Mine!"

"Certainly. You introduced me to Emily, you told me she was unhappy with her husband, you suggested that we might have an affair, and you encouraged her to fall in love with me. Christ knows why. You even cast spells. And when we had a fight you made it up between us. You wanted it to start, and it started. Then you thought you would like it to stop, and by Jesus, it stopped." Miranda laughed nervously. "So you see, after all, it was your fault."

"My fault! I like that!"

Will stopped laughing and looked at her. "I think you do," he said.

Miranda was silent, drawing the dirty paper plates printed with cute pictures of witches to her and piling them together. "I'll tell you what it is," she said. "We all want to be guilty, because guilt is power. It's the proof that one's magic works."

The moving men were beginning to tramp through the house again. Miranda gathered up the remains of lunch. Followed by Will, she went into the empty kitchen and put them into a carton of rubbish. Meanwhile beds and chairs and bookcases moved down the stairs and out the front door. All the kitchen furniture had gone; the bare walls showed the scorched map of last winter's fire. Miranda took a broom and began to sweep up the debris that collects under iceboxes.

"Leaving here," she said. "Free and clear. There's only one thing that still worries my mind. You know that two hundred dollars Professor Higginson sent us anonymously? Well, Princeton gave Julian a great big travel allowance, so I took part of it and went to pay him back. I went to his house three times but there was nothing home but animals. And today I found out that he's in the hospital over in Hamp, and they don't expect him to live."

"Don't worry about it," Will said. "He would have wanted you to keep it." He looked at the clean place on the wall where the kitchen clock had been. "What time is it?"

"I don't know. About two, maybe?"

"I'd better leave, if I'm going to be back in New York tonight. Unless there's anything I can do for you."

"No. Thank you." She walked him to the door.

"I've got your new address," Will said. "And I'll send you mine as soon as I know it."

"Sad."

"I know." He shrugged. "But we'll see each other again."

"In a better world," Miranda completed.

"Or a worser." He laughed. "We won't meet in hell though, too bad. I'll be up in the second circle with the lustful, and you'll be down at the bottom of the pit, among the evil counselors."

As the afternoon wore on, people continued to arrive: Mrs. Lumkin, Charley and Lucy Green to measure for their furniture, friends and neighbors saying goodbye. The movers cleared the house, and Miranda followed them from room to room, sweeping up behind. She was upstairs in one of the bedrooms when Emmy and Kittie McBane, arriving at the same time by different doors, met in the hall.

"I'm so glad I ran into you!" Kittie said. "I did want so much to see you again before you left. But now of course you're not leaving, are you?" She directed at Emmy a dim, mild stare, as of someone who knows everything or nothing.

"Well, not right away," Emmy said. "We may go to New Jersey for a while after graduation."

"I'm so glad. You've been such a help at the Exchange this year. I did hope you would be able to stay on. You make such a good tea, you know."

"Oh, thank you."

"Amy Priest, the girl who was with us last year; she was a nice girl too, but she made the tea *so* weak. . . . Such a lot of turnover," Kittie continued. "It always seems to be that way. Poor Mr. Fenn having to leave. And it wasn't for very much of anything either, was it? But all these young men are so violent nowadays. I keep reading about them in the magazines. Angry young men. But of course that is in England, isn't it?"

"I guess it started there," Emmy said.

"But it spreads, doesn't it? I'm afraid you're right. Such a pity. Oswald always particularly liked Mr. Fenn. He was quite surprised and disappointed when President King wouldn't let him stay." Emmy remained tongue-tied. "Mr. Thomas is leaving today too, a little bird told me," Kittie added. "It's the best thing for everyone, don't you think?"

"Oh. Yes," Emmy said distractedly. She saw these horrible little birds, a horde of them, swarming over the valley, with fat bodies and little sharp beaks like Mrs. McBane.

"I've often wanted to speak to you about that," Kittie continued, "but I didn't quite know how to put it. I wanted to tell you to be more careful. But it's so difficult to know how to put that sort of thing, isn't it?"

"Yes." To her disgust, Emmy blushed.

"But you see, I needn't have. It's all turned out for the best. And really, I think everybody's going to forget about it quite, quite soon. They always do, if one doesn't remind them, and never admits to anything." Miranda was descending the stairs; Kittie's voice fell lower and lower. "I'm so glad," she said, "because now I'm sure you'll be in Convers for a long, long time."

Emmy stayed on briefly after Mrs. McBane had said goodbye to Miranda and gone, but only to exchange summer addresses and other superficialities. "Will was over here just before you came," Miranda remarked in a hinting way, but Emmy ignored the hint.

"I guess we'd better be going," she said. "I wonder where Freddy can have got to? I left him outside."

They came out onto the front porch, which was stacked with dirty cartons and Miranda's peculiar bedroom furniture. Below, on the lawn, Freddy, the three Fenn children, and some others whom Emmy did not know were running wildly about. They dashed, stopped, staggered, shrieked, and whirled in circles.

"What on earth are they doing?" Emmy asked.

"I think they're playing blind-man's buff."

The children ran back and forth. Laughing and screaming, they bumped against each other, bounced apart, waved their arms, and fell down singly or in couples on the grass.

"Freddy!" she called. He did not hear.

Something was wrong with the game, though. "But they're all blindfolded!" Emmy objected.

"Yes," Miranda said. "They like it better that way."

* * *

Allen Ingram to Francis Noyes

June 16

It is full summer here now: hot, heavy, and still. I am quite alone at last; for this morning I took Beowulf over to the vet's to be boarded until the Williamses return next month. I *finally* heard from them on this matter. Their first suggestion was that I should keep Beowulf for the summer, since we "seemed to be getting on so well." In fact, they offered to *give* him to me. Do you know, when the letter came, I actually considered it? Images flocked to my mind of you and I, for example, arriving on the pier at Southampton, and Beowulf trotting down the gangplank after us with the liquor basket in his mouth. (He is part St. Bernard, I sometimes think.) But it would be a bit *déjà vu*, when Truman and his friend Freckles have already gone round the world with Butch and Buster.

Still, taking him over to Hamp to the kennel, I felt a beastly betrayer. He adores to go for rides, and one can't *explain* to animals. As I left him I experienced a sort of dumb yearning in the small intestine, such as, I suppose, mothers feel for their dumber infants. It was, thank God, momentary.

I felt a bit better immediately when, on the way out, I ran into Emmy Turner doing the same thing to her cat. She was most sympathetic, and said that if I were to take Beowulf abroad with me he might be so much trouble— hotels refusing us, waiters bitten, friends fleeing in dismay, etc.—that I would get to simply detest him. I'm sure she's right. Then, after all, as she pointed out, if I find later on that I want a dog I can always buy one. She is an agreeable girl: cheerful and good-looking—but dreadfully big, quite towering over little Allen in her high heels. (The very large are different from you and me.) It was an agreeable thought, too, that I had acted (or not acted) so as not to disturb that cheerful composure.

. . . Later. I have finished the bluebooks. The novel is FINISHED, this year of economy and discipline is over. Delicious to be leaving this close, dreary little valley for the real world. I am packing now as if for the trip back out of a bad dream. Freedom! (For what?)

Vital Contemporary Fiction

From Avon New Leader in Paperbacks!

D. Keith Mano
HORN N272 95¢

Kurt Vonnegut, Jr.
PLAYER PIANO YN235 95¢
MOTHER NIGHT VS27 75¢

Elie Wiesel
NIGHT YN243 95¢
DAWN YW175 $1.25
THE GATES OF THE FOREST NS19 95¢
THE TOWN BEYOND
THE WALL NS42 95¢

Muriel Spark
ROBINSON YW167 $1.25
MEMENTO MORI VS14 75¢

James Purdy
THE NEPHEW SS12 60¢
MALCOLM VS6 75¢
CABOT WRIGHT BEGINS V2136 75¢